P9-CEX-474

THE KILLING HOUSE

GAYLE RIVERS

CHARTER BOOKS, NEW YORK

The quotations at the head of each chapter are taken either from *The Tragical History of Doctor Faustus* by Christopher Marlowe or from *The Revenger's Tragedy* by Cyril Tourneur.

This Charter book contains the complete
text of the original hardcover edition.
It has been completely reset in a typeface
designed for easy reading, and was printed
from new film.

THE KILLING HOUSE

A Charter Book/published by arrangement with
the author

PRINTING HISTORY
G. P. Putnam's Sons edition/February 1988
Charter edition/January 1989

ISBN: 1-55773-131-4

Charter Books are published by The Berkley Publishing Group,
200 Madison Avenue, New York, New York 10016.
The name "CHARTER" and the "C" logo are trademarks
belonging to Charter Communications, Inc.

PRINTED IN THE UNITED STATES OF AMERICA

10 9 8 7 6 5 4 3 2 1

THE KILLING HOUSE

Captain Tim Bell fought terrorism with firepower. Then the elite of the British military unit SAS forced him into early retirement . . . they should have killed him. Because now Bell has gone over to the other side . . .

"Will send chills through you as you contemplate the ease with which the actions told here could take place . . ."
—*Ocala Star-Banner*

"Keyed to the realities—or horrors—of modern-day life."
—*The News* (Evansville, IN)

AND PRAISE FOR GAYLE RIVERS'

THE SPECIALIST

"Reads like a high-class thriller!"

—*Booklist*

"Sensational . . . frank . . . a revelation and a shock . . . You may be tempted while reading the book to think of it as a powerful thriller novel . . . Read *The Specialist*—and shudder!"

—*John Barkham Reviews*

Books by Gayle Rivers

THE FIVE FINGERS (with James Hudson)
THE SPECIALIST
THE WAR AGAINST THE TERRORISTS: HOW TO WIN IT
THE KILLING HOUSE

THE KILLING HOUSE

A PETTY CASE OF PALTRY LEGACIES.

▌1▐

"YOU'RE A RUTHLESS bastard, Tim," said Colonel Robert McAlister, "and we'll have to fire you. Have another Scotch."

Tim Bell, captain in the SAS Regiment, wearing his only presentable suit, looked around the bar of the Athenaeum, as his colonel went off to get the drinks. It was not his kind of place—the green leather armchairs, the murky oil paintings, the white marble statue of Psyche simpering in one corner. Nor were the members his kind of people— the senior civil servants, the well-known scientists, faded politicians, a bishop with his entourage, all of them men stepping softly down the corridors of power.

The colonel came back with the drinks. Bell said, "What do you mean, boss—fired?"

"What I say. You're out, Tim."

"Just like that?"

"Just like that. Look, the Home Office wants you out, the Ministry of Defense wants you out. You're a menace. No one's shedding tears over those two IRA buggers but you shot them in cold blood—and in front of witnesses. No, don't give me that crap about 'shot while trying to escape.' "

"You should have seen what they'd done to Charlie Barnes."

"Yeah, I know about that blowtorch business. And I know he was your mate. But we wanted them alive—and you knew it. They'd have sung a loud song once we got down to interrogating them. And you walked in like John Wayne, bang, bang—and now the shit's hit the fan."

"So I'm to be sacrificed, Bobby?"

The colonel looked at him for a moment and then said, "That's right, Captain Bell."

So we're getting all formal now, Bell thought. It'll be name, rank, and number next. "But, sir, what if I demand a court of inquiry or a court-martial?"

"Demand away. You won't get it. And if by any chance you did manage to force the issue—which you won't—the court-martial would be held in camera."

"It's that tough?"

"Of course it is. Wake up, Bell. Being in the SAS doesn't give you a license to go around killing unarmed civilians. Count yourself bloody lucky. There was a big move behind the scenes to have you charged with murder and made to stand trial. That's the way the Home Office wanted to play it. It was touch and go that the Ministry of Defense and the Northern Ireland office didn't want a scandal right now. That saved your neck."

"Cut the hypocrisy, Colonel. We both know it's happened before. Maybe the others were the *real* officer class, gentlemen and all that. They didn't get slung out on their necks."

"You can think what you like, Bell. The fact is you're a double murderer. It's been a hell of a job to keep this under wraps. It's been buttoned down—tighter than a duck's arse. Just as well. Already *The Observer*'s been ferreting around and if the Opposition got hold of the facts . . ."

"What's to stop me going to a newspaper myself?"

"A D Restricted Notice went out to the press yesterday. The Special Branch has all the main offices under surveillance. If you're seen approaching any newspaper office or spotted talking to a journalist, your feet won't hit the ground. We could hold you under close arrest for six months, don't forget. You're an orphan, there's no family around to stir things up. You've done your time, Bell—what is it now?—eighteen years or something. You should know you can't buck the Army—certainly not the Regiment. You know the rules. The integrity of the Regiment at all costs."

"So what's the deal, *sir?*"

"This. In my inside pocket, I have an envelope. It contains two thousand pounds in tenners and fivers, used notes. It's out of special funds, there's no record. We're not allowed to be seen doing business in this club, so when you go, I'll come outside with you and hand it over. And that'll be that."

"No volleys over the grave, sir?"

"No ceremony. You have already put in your official request to retire from the Army in order to take up civilian employment and have been granted an honorable discharge."

"I have?"

"Oh, yes, Bell. I signed the papers before I left Hereford this morning by chopper. Which reminds me. You will *not* be welcome at Hereford, nor at the Duke of York's. You're out. The Regiment doesn't want to know a thing about you from here on."

"That's just great," Bell said. "I'm a boy soldier, then a squaddie in the HLI, then at nineteen I pass the selection tests for the SAS. You're right, I've given it eighteen years, just on half my life. No one in the Regiment's seen more service than me—no, not even you, sir. The Laos border, Oman, the Falklands, Ulster—I've done my stuff there. And how does it end? 'Here's a lousy couple of grand, get lost, don't come back.' You're a merciless bastard, *sir-r.*"

"That's better than a murdering bastard, Bell. Let me talk to you straight. I've seen just one or two in the Regiment who've gone like you. Great soldiers, great leaders. At first, they don't like killing but, under orders, if they have to, they'll do it—fast and clean. Then, after a while, they begin to enjoy it. It gives a guy a real sense of power to know he can snuff out a life—just like that. They get kill-happy. *You've* got kill-happy."

"That's not true."

"It is—and you know it. You had everything going for you. You made sergeant—and that's probably the best rank in the Regiment. The bloody thing's run by the NCOs! And then you were commissioned in the Falklands campaign—and there were numerous jollies in between— and ended up a captain. And that Military Cross you won down there should have been a notch higher. It would have been if they hadn't already given two posthumous VCs to the Special Forces."

Bell said, fighting for restraint, "You pinned the gongs on me, sir, gongs I didn't need. Being part of the Regiment was enough—and you know it."

Ignoring Bell's outburst, the colonel went on, "I don't know just what happened but somehow since then you've changed. If I were a psychiatrist, I'd say you've become a psychopath. You got too close to the enemy, lost sight of the big picture. And we don't want you in or anywhere near the Regiment."

Bell said slowly, bitterly, "So I've just been bloody used."

"Grow up, Bell. In this outfit, we're all used. The big difference is, I've got somewhere to go when I'm all used up."

"Yeah, that damn great estate in Scotland. Easy for some is what I think. Where have I got to go to? After you pay me off like a mercenary?"

The colonel grinned but there was no mirth in it. "Mercenary is right. Why don't you try your luck in Nicaragua?

They could use guys like you down there.'' He glanced at his wristwatch. ''Well, we'd better get it over with. I have a guest for lunch in ten minutes.''

They threaded their way among the green leather armchairs and the side tables, across the marble hall of the Athenaeum and out under the Doric columns above the steps. The colonel slid a thick envelope out from an inner pocket and without a word handed it over to Bell. It was unsealed; Bell riffled the notes with a thumb. There seemed enough there. The Regiment was hardly likely to gyp him over a tenner or two. He stuffed the envelope into a pocket and held out his hand. ''Wish me luck, boss.''

Colonel McAlister ignored the hand. Turning on his heel and moving lightly through the swing doors, he said, ''Take care.''

And up yours too, Bell thought. Okay, he knew now he'd been a fool. Shooting those two IRA guys in front of the rest of the Pagoda team had been crazy. He could easily have waited till he alone was guarding them before the SIB arrived, ordered them to have a pee, and then let them have it. He had to go and lose his temper and do it on the spot. But he'd seen Charlie's balls and thighs after those two sods had gone to work with their blowtorch . . . a quick bullet each was too good for them.

And now the Scottish mafia in the Regiment had gone to work. As he walked slowly toward the Duke of York's Steps, he wondered if all that guff about the Home Office and the MOD wanting him out was not a bloody fairy story. Funny thing about the SAS. Officer or plain soldier, they were all good and they were all hard; you didn't survive if you weren't. And when they bled, it was all the same color. But when you got to upper-level promotion, who was going to command the Squadron at Hereford, who was going to be his second in command, the system changed gear. If you just happened to be the eldest son of a Scottish baronet, promotion floated your way. If you were the son of a Newcastle miner who'd died in a pit fall when you were two, whose mother had gone on the game and then run away, so that you were brought up by an uncle and aunt in Glasgow, enlisted as a boy soldier at sixteen, transferred to the Highland Light Infantry at eighteen and had passed the severe selection course of the SAS a year later, you were not really "officer material." Not "senior officer," anyway. After all, the Regiment itself had been founded in World War II by a Scottish gentleman and Guards officer.

Bell walked past the equestrian statue and down the white steps. The nursery rhyme came back to him. So what had the "grand old Duke of York" done to warrant a statue? He'd taken his ten thousand men, marched them up to the top of the hill, then he marched them down again. Bit bloody stupid. But if you were a duke, you got away with it. They shot that other guy around the same time, Admiral Somebody, to encourage the others. But he didn't have a title.

Bell turned right at the foot of the steps and walked along the Mall toward the Palace. A troop of the Household Cavalry—the Blues, he noticed from the color of their plumes—came clattering toward him, cuirasses and helmets gleaming in the pale winter sun, plumes tossing and polished metal jingling as they cantered past. He stood still for a moment in admiration. The power, the precision, the great traditions of the British Army. And then he thought, they're just a bunch of fucking tin soldiers. One expert with a light machine gun would do them in a couple of bursts—before they had a chance to draw those long ceremonial swords.

He walked back to his room in Earl's Court, turning over the prospects in his mind. He had a few pounds in a savings account and that plus the two thousand "bribe" would keep him going for a month or two. Perhaps the colonel had been right in that gibe about Nicaragua. What use was an SAS man in his mid-thirties—an *ex*-SAS man— except to fight? He had no trade, no qualifications, no experience of anything except the Forces.

Back in the dingy room, he poured himself a large neat Scotch and drank it in a swallow. He sipped the next one and then aimlessly began to pack his grip. He just had to get out, though God knew where. He picked up his SAS beret, looked at it for a moment and then flung it across the room in a sudden burst of rage. It skidded across the cluttered desk and knocked over a framed photograph, which Bell picked up and gazed at. It was of a one-time girlfriend, Angela. God, they'd had their moments! He could still remember that convulsive climactic shudder she used to give and the unearthly keening noise from her open mouth. And she'd married a friend of his in the U.S. Special Forces, Bob Yardley, though he knew she'd have married him if he'd been the marrying kind. She had talked about it enough—more than enough. The thought of matrimony had made him back away, fast.

Bob Yardley—now that was a thought. If there was anyone in the U.S. Special Forces he liked and respected, it was Bob. A big guy, must be over six feet and over two hundred pounds in weight—but all of it bone and muscle. Solid—the kind of guy you'd like to have alongside if things got rough. A bit of a hero, too, if what he'd heard on the Hereford grapevine was true. And it usually was. There was talk that Bob had taken a snatch team into Lebanon and lifted one of the American hostages—and secretly been given a medal for it. Bob Yardley, he knew, was now building up counter-terrorist teams at Fort Bragg— he'd know which way up the dice landed.

He and Bob had always got along well together. They were what the Army would call "a pair of muckers." Yardley had been on assignment a few times at Hereford and he had done one or two stints at Bragg and Bad Tolz in Germany when Yardley was there. You get to know a man pretty well when you're sweating up a Welsh moun- tain or lying out at night in a bivvy under the icy rain. Why not try his luck by going over to the States and looking up Bob? That business with Angela was long gone and, anyway, Bob hadn't been on the scene when they'd had their fling. Through his counter-terrorist contacts, Bob would have a list of the civilian hotshots who needed security and surveillance, the way ex-SAS men here in England joined outfits like KMS to look after visiting sheikhs and other VIPs. Fat chance he'd have of staying in England and joining something like KMS now that the fucking Regiment had given him the boot.

His anger boiled up again. He poured another slug of Scotch and noticed, almost as if it was happening to someone else, that his knuckles showed white where he squeezed the glass as though to crush it. Given the boot—more like tossed away like an old boot. That arrogant Colonel McAlister—"We're not allowed to be seen doing business in the club"—so let's go outside onto the steps and I'll pay you off like a lousy cabdriver! The shit. It was all very well for him. When he retired from the Regiment, he had that big estate—must be nearly half the Highlands—to go back to. He wouldn't be out on his ear with a miserable two grand for the rest of his life. Christ, he thought, I'll show you, you stuck-up bastard, you and all those other so-called gentlemen. If I can't fix a legit job through Yardley, the other side could use a man like me. If England's out from now on, America is where the action is.

He started to tidy the drab room, picked up the SAS beret and put the photo back on the desk. With a pair of nail scissors, he began gently to unpick the cloth badge from the beret, the pair of wings supporting the Roman short sword. That was it. He'd kill two birds with one stone, fly to Fort Bragg in the States and look up his old friends, the Yardleys. And if that didn't work, there was always the bar outside the camp where they recruited mercenaries for Nicaragua. He slipped the badge into his upper pocket.

BY NATURE PHLEGMATIC, SLOW TO WRATH, AND PRONE
TO LECHERY.

|2|

BELL PARKED THE rented car outside the motel office and
went in to book himself a room. Memories of the place
came flooding back; it was just the same—nothing ever
changed in Fayetteville. It was the motel all the visiting
Services men used and he had been there several times
when on assignment to the Special Forces at Fort Bragg,
just a few miles down the road. And there, beyond the
swimming pool, as an annex to the motel, was the famous
bar. He'd like to have a dollar for every beer and glass of
Scotch he'd swallowed there. What was the name of the
manageress—an Englishwoman married to an American
soldier? It began with a B. Barbara? Billie? No, Betty, that
was it. He hoped she was still there.

He checked his bag in the motel room, changed his
shirt, and strolled over to the bar with its red silk swinging
doors. It all came back to him. Just inside the swinging doors
was that same old partition. If you went one way, you
came to the area with tables and chairs, ironwork table
lamps, with waitresses in gingham check aprons serving

the tables. And beyond the table area there were booths for the more discreet visitors. On the other side of the partition, you found yourself approaching the bar with its mock-leather black cover and barstools raised on a step.

It took a second or two for Bell's eyes to get accustomed to the typical darkness. Not for the first time, he thought there must be a Puritan streak in American drinkers, if they had to hide their shame in the dark. He threaded his way past the tables and along to the far end of the bar, where he perched on the stool furthest from the swinging doors. Now he could see anyone entering the bar from behind the partition long before they could check him out.

He ordered a beer—it could be a long morning and he needed to keep alert—and asked the barman if Betty was around. "Tell her an old friend from England wants to say hello." Business was slack in this prelunch session and there were only three other drinkers, one pair and the other on his own, down the whole twenty-five feet and more of the bar's length.

A few moments later, the manageress appeared through a curtain at the far end of the bar. She hadn't changed in the couple of years since he'd been attached to Fort Bragg. Dark-haired, lively, well made up and with the same trace of a Midland English accent when she spoke. "Why, it's Timmy from good old Hereford, England! I'd know you anywhere, luv, but I'm blowed if I can remember your last name."

"It's Bell," he said, smiling, as he leaned over the bar to shake her hand.

"Of course, Tim Bell. You were—let me see—a lieutenant last time round?"

"Captain now."

"My, my—you'll be a general next! What brings you over here? No, let me guess—it wouldn't be to see a certain blond lady who looks like an angel and sounds like one, too?"

"Oh, you mean Angela," he said. "Angela *Yardley*. She's married to a good friend of mine these days. What was between us is long gone."

"Don't you believe it," she said. "I see a lot of Angela— she's pretty lonely cooped up on that base with Bob away for spells. She's still carrying the old torch, luv, you gotta believe it."

"I hope that's not awkward," he said. "I wanted to look Bob up while I'm here. They get along all right, don't they? I haven't seen either of them since the marriage but Bob was in love with her right enough then."

"And still is. Don't get me wrong. Angela's a great girl and she's made Bob a good wife. And he's a helluva nice guy himself. But you just being here could stir things up."

"Oh, shit," he said. "Excuse me. There's another reason. Are they still looking for trained soldiers for a bit of action down south?"

"No need to be coy," she said. "If you mean Nicaragua, you bet. See that guy at the far end of the bar, looks a bit like a young Kojak? He's always here, looking out for the right guys. No, he's not the recruiting officer, that's a sergeant at Bragg. This one just gets the word back to his boss if a likely recruit turns up. Go over and buy him a drink. He'll have the hots for you. But what's a guy like you—a captain in the SAS—hiring out for?"

"Easy," he said. "I had a rough time in Northern Ireland, so they gave me six months' leave. I can make some big bucks down there in Nicaragua—and I could do with hard cash. Besides, we hear tell they've got some interesting new small arms from East Germany. It would help the Regiment if I came back with some practical experience."

"As long as you do come back. Do you mind if I give Angela a call and tell her you're here?"

"Not a bit. I want to see her and Bob, anyway."

"Where are you staying, Timmy?"

"Right next door—at the motel."

She leaned over the counter, kissed him lightly on the cheek, and then disappeared behind the curtain. Bell swallowed the rest of his beer and moved down the bar to the stool next to the shaven-headed, thick-necked man who sat hunched over his elbows, gazing morosely into space.

"What'll you have?" Bell asked.

"Are you some fag trying to pick me up?"

"Do I look like a fag?"

"You sound like an Englishman—and all Englishmen sound like fags to me."

Bell's hand moved like a striking snake. Between forefinger and thumb, he grabbed the man's little finger, doubled it forward, and began pressing hard, then harder. The soldier gave an involuntary yelp and then straightened up as Bell applied the pressure. The veins bulged on the man's neck as he fought against the temptation to scream out loud.

Bell said softly in his ear. "I could break your little finger right now, couldn't I?"

The soldier nodded.

"And I could break every other finger if I wanted to, couldn't I?"

He nodded again.

"And I could break every other bone in your big fat ugly body, if I had a mind to. You call me a fag, you cocksucker! You're the fag round here, aren't you? Now you're going to say after me, slowly and clearly, 'I am a dirty bumboy.' Got it? 'I am a dirty bumboy.' "

"You fuck off," said the soldier through clenched teeth. "O-o-oh."

"Goodness me," Bell said, "I think I've broken your little finger. Careless of me. Still, I can make it go on hurting if you don't say after me, 'I'm a dirty bumboy.' " He applied more pressure.

"I'm a dirty bumboy"—the words came out with a rush of air.

Bell released his grip. "I don't buy drinks for bumboys

like you. Now you go off and tell your sergeant that I'll be here for another hour. If he wants a real recruit, he'd better hustle his ass over here. Got it?''

The man nodded. He had his broken left little finger cupped gently in his right hand.

"Do that first," Bell added. "You hear me. Then you can get your finger treated. And then you can stick it right up your dirty ass for all I care.''

Half an hour went by while Bell slowly sipped another beer. For some reason he couldn't define, he felt he was in enemy territory. Betty had greeted him cordially enough and the other drinkers in the place took little notice of him but still the feeling persisted. He would feel more at ease once he'd signed up and was on his way down to Nicaragua.

He was just about to order another drink—a Scotch this time—when three men walked around the partition at the end of the room and approached the counter. One came on in front, the other two a pace in the rear, like bodyguards. Bell was perched on his barstool; the three men stood at the bar alongside him, with their leader nearest. Two of them were complete strangers but he recognized the man closest to him—and in the same split second the man recognized him. He was Sergeant Drucker, late of the Fifth Special Forces Group. Their paths had crossed a few times over the years—and they hated each other's guts.

Drucker was your typical long-service U.S. Army sergeant, close-cropped hair, nose flattened and bent through a hundred fights, thick neck, big shoulders. Not a man to be tangled with in a dark alley. Not a word was spoken while he ordered a beer and then leaned on the bar, clasping the glass with the thick fingers of both hands. Then he did an exaggerated double-take and said with a sneer, "Why, it's Sergeant Bell!"

"*Captain* Bell to you, Sergeant."

"Christ, the British Army must have sunk if they made you an officer. How come?"

"I learned to read and write. Pity you're too dumb to try."

"So you want to have a go against those spics, *Captain Bell*?"

"That was the idea, *Sergeant* Drucker. But when I remember how our SAS team had to pull your mob out of the shit on the Laos border in '71 and how you fucked up in Iran with Delta, I'm not too sure. Charlie Beckwith deserved a better lot than you. The only safe place for you is the U.S. Army where they go to any lengths to avoid fighting."

Even in the halflight of the room, he could see that Drucker's neck had gone red and looked swollen. Why did I have to stumble into this prick, of all people? he thought. But guard your tongue, Tim my boy, he said to himself. No need to tangle with this big goon.

Drucker said slowly, "I don't think you're wanted, Captain Bell. We don't need English *officers* down there in Nico. I suppose you'd like to take your batman along and change for dinner every night. I need soldiers, not fucking pimps."

"Drucker, you wouldn't know a real soldier if he tapped you on the shoulder. God, when I think of the way you were when we first met—up there on the Laos border. Run out of rations, run out of ammo, wandering around the jungle like a bunch of Girl Scouts! Boy, were you glad to see us. There were tears in your eyes, Drucker, baby. For saving your lousy life. I remember it well. You'd have kissed my ass if I'd let you!"

Without warning, Sergeant Drucker swung his left arm in a back-knuckle blow at Bell's head. He had started to duck, so it caught him above the eyes and tilted him backward. Drucker kicked the stool away from under him and Bell went crashing, skidding under a table and knocking it sideways. If he comes in now, I'm done, Bell thought, but Drucker stood back, squared up with his fists, and grunted, "Come on, you bastard, stand up and fight. I'll tear you apart."

Betty came out from behind the curtain, having heard the crash, and said plaintively, "Hey, you guys, break it up. If you want a fight, go on outside. Don't ruin my furniture. Come on—forget it, or else I'll have to go call the MPs."

They ignored her. Bell stayed down on the floor, half under the collapsed table. He understood Drucker's mentality precisely. Drucker was a fine soldier, provided you pointed him in the right direction first. He would always do it by the book, by numbers. And he was a macho American, who'd seen too many John Wayne movies in his youth. If the situation had been reversed and Drucker had been lying on the floor, he would have half brained him with the stool, not pranced around like a bare-knuckle fighter.

"Get up, you yellow bastard," Drucker shouted. "One punch and you've had enough? Make a fight of it, you fag."

Still, Bell stayed down. He wanted Drucker to get a shade overconfident, to come toward him and narrow the gap between them. And Drucker, mouthing insults, did just that. He stood less than six feet away, gloating, with fists raised.

Bell came off the floor like stretched rubber snapping back. His right foot lashed at Drucker's crotch. Drucker instinctively bent his knees and swiveled his left leg in front of the right, to take the blow on his upper left thigh. But that had the effect of lowering his head. Bell went straight in and jammed his right elbow into Drucker's solar plexus. He grunted and his face automatically jerked down. Then Bell smashed down on his nose, the many-times-broken nose, with the knuckles of the same right hand. Drucker's nose, broken yet again, spurted blood. He grabbed Bell by the lapels and gave him a head-butt.

Bell managed to tuck his chin in fast and took the

jarring blow on the hairline above his forehead. At speed, he swung his arms up above his head and jabbed his elbows down onto Drucker's forearms, breaking his hold on his lapels. He saw in a flash that his opponent had lifted his head back for another butt—and Bell struck first with his own head, catching Drucker flush on his mangled nose. Half stunned with the pain and the force of the blow, Drucker slid toward the floor, smashing a table and knocking over a couple of chairs as he went.

Unnoticed by the two fighters, Drucker's comrades had edged their way behind Bell—and now each of them grabbed an arm. He knew that he could not tackle three street fighters at once, particularly when two of them were fresh and untouched. So for the moment he relaxed, awaiting the next move. It was not long coming. Shaking his head and muttering, the blood-stained Drucker came up off the floor, grabbed a stool, and swung hard at Bell. As he did so, the other two stepped aside. Bell just had time to swing and lift his tensed left shoulder to catch the blow. Even so, it jarred right down his side with numbing force.

The sergeant came straight in, swinging a kick at Bell, who had gone down on one knee with the force of the blow. Bell grabbed his boot, twisted, and shoved. Drucker, off balance, went skeetering back until yet again he crashed into another table and smashed a chair as he fell.

Without pausing, Bell turned on one of the two soldiers who had held him. He swung a double kick, one to the base of the man's neck as he turned to run and the other high on the diaphragm, driving the breath out of his lungs. Choking and gasping, the man rolled on the floor. His mate slid away toward the partition and out of the bar.

Bell turned back to the sergeant, who had groggily risen to his knees. Almost tenderly, Bell put his hands under his armpits and helped to lift him to his feet. The sergeant stood there swaying—but just in balance. Then Bell hit him in the face—fast, one-two—with straight arm blows like pistons. Drucker's head lolled, exposing his corded throat. And Bell raised his right hand, edge on like an axe blade for the killing blow above the Adam's apple.

"Hold it!" a voice from behind him rapped out. "Hold it right there."

Bell paused, his hand frozen in midair. He looked around. Sergeant Drucker teetered slowly and then collapsed on the floor of the bar. Bell recognized the commanding figure standing behind him. It was Major Bob Yardley. "Hi," he said, "where did you spring from, Bob?"

Yardley came over, grabbed him by the elbow, and hustled him up to the bar counter. Betty had appeared again from behind her curtain. "Get him a large Scotch, would you please, Betty?" he said. "On my account. And don't worry about all this damage"—he waved an arm at the smashed tables, the broken chairs, the gouts of Drucker's blood staining the carpeted floor—"you just tell me what it costs to replace it and I'll settle out of special funds. Let's keep it quiet and unofficial, you hear me?"

Betty smiled. "You're a decent guy, Bob. None of this 'put in an official complaint on a 1098 or something and then wait three months while they doze off at a court of inquiry.' No, sir. Glad I called Angela just now to tell her Tim's in town."

Yardley nodded, lips tight in a straight line. "Don't say a thing right now," he said to Bell. "You just climb into that Scotch. You've done enough damage for one day, so just freeze right there. Shoulder all right?"

"It'll be a bit stiff but nothing to worry about. You should have seen the other guy."

"I did," he answered grimly. "If he's not back on parade in a week, ten days, there'll be trouble, questions asked."

"He will be. It's only his nose that's damaged—and his pride."

The soldier Bell had felled with the double kick had by now climbed gingerly back onto his feet. His breath was rasping in great gulps but he was more or less recovered.

Yardley turned to him and said sharply, "You know me, soldier? I'm Major Yardley, U.S. Rangers, attached to Delta Force at Bragg. Brawling and fighting in public—that's a court-martial offense. I could put you down for a long stretch in the stockade if I wanted. But this time out, you've got lucky. I'll ignore it. I don't want it to get all round Bragg that one medium-sized Englishman beat three Special Forces men in a fight. And one of them a sergeant instructor. So pick up that thing"—he pointed contemptuously at Drucker, who was trying to drag himself up off the floor hand over hand with the help of a stool—"and get him back to camp right away. Take him to the medical center and tell 'em Major Yardley sent you. Got it? Yardley. And if they ask any questions, tell 'em *I* said he wasn't looking where he was going and walked into the back of a reversing truck. Does your addled brain take in that much?"

The soldier stood to attention. He looked straight ahead and grunted, "Sir."

"Right, get along." Betty was hovering behind the bar counter. "Betty, could you rustle us up a couple of sandwiches, please? I'd like a quiet talk with my old pal from Hereford. Oh, and get some of your staff to tidy the place up. It looks like a bomb went off in here. Don't worry—there's not going to be a court of inquiry, so we don't need to leave the evidence in place."

He turned back to Bell, who was back on his barstool, delicately stirring the lumps of ice in his drink with a little finger. Bell said, "You're a cool bastard, Bob."

"What d'you mean? You been looking at my paybook again?"

They both smiled at the tired old Army joke. Bell went on, "You asked about my shoulder. That means you must have seen that goon hit me with the stool. And that was about halfway through the fight, not right at the end."

"So all right. It was too good to stop halfway. Mind you, I'd have done the same for you, if you'd been on the receiving end. But what's gotten into you, Tim? Are you

going round looking for action? When I was assigned to
the SAS, it was always drummed into us that we had to
keep a low profile all the time. If a fight broke out in a
pub, we were to stay clear. Pay up and get out—never get
involved. You don't have to prove anything, Tim. There
was a time when you'd have kept your cool and walked
away from a fucking ape like Drucker.''

"He started it.''

"But you must have said something that started him.
Even a baboon like Drucker doesn't suddenly swing a
punch at an innocent bystander. And what was that Betty
said about seeing you mangling some guy's hand at the
bar?'' He saw the surprised look on Bell's face and added,
"Yes, I was back in quarters when Betty called Angela—
and I had a few words with her myself. Why else d'you
think I got here so fast? It wasn't that I'm jerking off to
see you in such a hurry, you shit.''

He took a deep swallow from the glass of beer the
barman had slid in front of him. He glanced at his wristwatch. "Holy Christ! I'm due to make a HALO jump with
some of my guys in under an hour. I've gotta move fast.
Hey, that's a thought. You've got adrenaline to burn.
Come along and jump with us. We're going to do some
high-level testing today—twenty-five thousand feet. You
ever jumped from that height before?''

Bell nodded. "A few times.''

"Well, come along. You've got nothing on this afternoon, have you? Okay, so let's find out if Hereford is as
smart as Bragg when it comes to falling out of an aircraft
at height.''

As they moved away from the counter, Bell said, "Will
we get the chance of a quiet chat? Afterward, I mean.
Couple of things I'd like to discuss with you.''

"Oh, sure. I have to work latish tonight—off to Washington at sparrow-fart, as you might say, tomorrow—but
why don't we have a drink here around nine tonight? I

could bring Angela along—unless what you want to talk about is top secret?''

"Lord, no. It'd be nice to see Angela again. How's she keeping?''

"Great—just great.''

Yardley drove Bell to Fort Bragg, turned left, and presented his credentials to the sentry on the Delta stockade. Then he drove on to a long, low bunker-type building, where Bell was issued with standard kit, combat boots, combat fatigues, and helmet. The jump suit went on over the lot. He noticed that the twenty other men on Yardley's team were struggling into backpacks—bergens—as well. He gestured to Yardley, as much as to say, 'Me, too?' but the leader shook his head. Just as well. It had been a good few months since Bell had done any "high-altitude low opening" jumps, especially from an oxygen-thin height like twenty-five thousand feet. The less weight and equipment he had to worry about, the better.

When everyone was kitted out, Yardley gave the order to move into a neighboring room, which had a platform and a blackboard on the wall. He motioned to Bell to stay at the back; Bell realized that he had made no effort to introduce him to the string. Just as well, he thought. Bob could be taking a bit of a risk in bringing a limey into an official trial jump.

Yardley went up onto the platform and waited for the string to sit down. Then he said, "Right, men, listen hard 'cause I'm not going to say all this twice. We're going to carry out a HALO jump from an altitude of twenty-five thousand feet. Sergeant Forman here is the jumpmaster and he'll be giving you a detailed weather briefing when we're airborne. All I need say on that score for now is it's gusting up to twenty-five miles an hour at ground level over the DZ—and that means extra-special care. So listen good. We'll be using the Raeford DZ today, you all know the approaches.

"You've all done your qualifying jumps on standard chutes and you've all done high-altitude low opening details. But today we're going to use GQ ramair chutes. The GQ is the Cadillac of chutes—with practice you ought to be able to land on a dime! But it calls for greater care and attention. That's why I want you all to take in what I'm saying.

"First, we'll be using the rear exit today—not the side exits. There's no great difference but there could be that much more turbulence going out of the back. So be ready for it. And I want no crossovers once you've embarked. You'll have your number in the string and your place—just stick to it. You get me?

"Once you're in free fall, stay separated. I want no Fancy Dan stuff. This is a tactical jump, remember. Your task is to land on the cross at the DZ, that's all I'm asking.

"Now, all of you who've never jumped with a GQ ramair, get this right into your heads. Once you open up, you have to *fly* it right down to the ground. All the way—and watch your speed. And don't try any clever stalls when you're almost touching down. With a thoroughbred like the GQ, you'd go into a sudden twist—and end up with a broken leg. Maybe two. Turn late, run half a dozen steps when you touch down and then kill the lift of the chute. Got that?

"I'll repeat the main points. You go out the rear exit, keep well apart on the free fall, no funny stuff, and when you open up, fly the chute with the guiding toggles onto the DZ. Land, run forward a few steps, then kill your lift. Temperatures are low up there, so watch the ice buildup. I don't want any frostbite. That's it—and happy landings. Any questions?"

There were none, and he ordered the string to number off—one through twenty—and in that order they marched out of the building and clambered onto a five-ton truck that ran them the short drive to Simmons Army Airfield. There, a lumbering Hercules C130 awaited them. The men's para-

chute kits were laid out in two parallel lines stretching
toward the aircraft. By numbers, each man walked forward, struggled into his parachute harness, and checked
every strap in turn, making sure that the split pins that held
the ripcord wire in place were not bent or twisted but
would pull clean when the moment came. Then the man
behind him doublechecked his harness—and so on down
the line to the end, which was occupied by Bell and
Yardley.

Bell saw that, as usual, on top of the emergency chute
were the dials of the altimeter and the small pressure gauge
for those using the new automatic chute-opening device.
As they would be jumping from such a great height—only
a few thousand feet below the height of Mount Everest—he
was glad to see that oxygen packs and goggles were
lovingly checked by the men.

Kitted up, the string marched up to the aircraft in pairs
and took up their places. Bell and Yardley were to be the
last pair out, numbers twenty-one and twenty-two. Bell
had calculated that it would take the C130 about twenty
minutes to reach the jumping height, so he tried to relax,
working his left shoulder gently to keep off any stiffness.
He had lost count of the number of times he had jumped
from an aircraft, mostly in training but several times in
action. Nevertheless, the tightening in the gut and the
tingle of excitement were always present on the ascent.

The jumpmaster's voice came over the broadcast system
in the droning aircraft. "Right, now, listen good," it
crackled. "You've all heard the major give out the orders.
This is once more for luck. First, mainfeed oxygen check.
Right glove off, all of you. Okay, okay, left glove if
you're a southpaw. Some of you guys wouldn't know
which hand to wipe your ass with! Now make sure your
altimeter is set at ISO—standard atmospheric pressure to
the beginners, 29.92 Hg. How often do I have to tell you?
We will get a QFE ground pressure reading at the DZ at
the top of climb. Now, you're going to open up before

you're down to two thousand feet above ground—and the ground beneath us, let me tell you for the hundredth time, is 600 feet above sea level. So for Chrissake, make sure you've set the cursor at 2,600. Got it? I'll say it nice and slow—2,600. We don't want to have to use a shovel to send you home to your loved ones. Right, check mainpack oxygen. Make sure it's flowing. You babies ain't supposed to fall asleep on the way down.

"Here's the latest wind computation, hot off my intercom. Update. The top winds up here are blowing at sixty miles an hour, gusting over the DZ at fifteen to twenty-five miles an hour. That's a mean wind average of twenty miles an hour, for those who can't count. The jump starts fourteen miles upwind of the DZ and it's a four-minute drop. Bearing is 210 degrees. Got that? It's 210.

"And last of all. You pull at three-five. Memorize it—3,500 feet. That's a nice safety margin for the ones that're better at pulling their cocks than a ripcord! That's the lot. Now, go onto self-oxygen and watch for the green."

It was the usual patter. Bell had heard it a hundred times before. He knew—and so did everyone else aboard—that beneath the swagger and the insults, the jumpmaster looked on them as his chicks and he wanted each and every one of them to land softly without a feather disturbed.

Yardley, sitting alongside, nudged him and said, "This is old stuff to you, pure routine. Me too. Like to have a little fun?"

"Like what?"

"A game of chicken. You were acting tough back there at the bar. Now let's see how tough you really are."

"I don't get you," Bell said, although he had a shrewd idea of what was coming.

"Just this. We jump, free fall down to six—maybe five—thousand feet, link up hand to hand, and then see who pulls first. We've both gotta pull at two thousand feet—or else there'll be two large dents in the landing area! What d'you say?''

"Suits me," Bell said.

"Okay. The rest of the team will go out the usual way, falling starfish, but you and me—we'll dive out headfirst and go for max descent to 15,000 feet. You with me?"

Bell nodded. If you want to play games, he thought, right, let's play games. He reckoned Yardley must be a pretty slick parachutist—but so was he. They'd see who would be the chicken.

The Hercules was in position upwind of the DZ and the warning light was flashing inside the aircraft. Conversation was overpowered by the roar created as the rear ramp lowered, revealing a widening precipice. Bell could feel the adrenaline rising, cocooned inside the sound of his own breathing in the mask.

Two by two, the string of twenty moved to the rear ramp. They fell away into space. They were heavily kitted up with backpacks as well as their two chutes, so no fancy footwork was allowed before they jumped. Bell and Yardley, more lightly laden, were free to indulge.

"Let's go!" Yardley yelled, and, side by side, they ran the last few steps and dived out headfirst into the thin, cold air. Bell had adjusted his goggles and tightened his oxygen mask while waiting for the string to jump but now his goggles misted up as he plunged headlong into the icy, turbulent atmosphere from the warmth of the Hercules. Careful to move both hands in unison—to move only one would invite a corkscrewing spin—he wiped the glass rings with his leather mittens.

It was like diving into a wind tunnel. The vortices spewing from the four turbo propellers of the Hercules buffeted and flung him around as he fell away. He saw that Yardley, some twenty feet left, was being tossed about in the plane's slipstream, like a spider being flushed away into a gutter by the force of a water jet.

Every trained parachutist knew that in a free fall the

terminal velocity was 120 miles an hour. And that was a fall of something over ten thousand feet each minute. He glanced at the altimeter needle on top of his emergency chute and through eyes blurred with the misting of the goggles saw it steadily coursing round the diameter, marking off the descent by hundreds and thousands of feet. When you are dropping at the rate of 176 feet *a second*, there's no time for indecision or error. He could see from the altimeter that they were already down to seventeen thousand feet. That intense cold and almost slipperiness of the thin air at twenty-five thousand was gone. The air around him now felt thicker, nearly tangible. Instinctively, he checked his oxygen meter.

He felt a light tap on the back of his helmet and sensed a dark body sliding over the top of him. It was Yardley making a pass in the old parachuting game. He angled his body in turn and swept diagonally down and across the starfish shape of Yardley, tapping his helmet as he went. Then Yardley did a couple of back rolls and, not to be outdone, Bell did three.

They were down to 5,500 feet, with the brown earth of Fort Bragg rushing always nearer. Automatically, the highly trained pair turned toward each other. Yardley, as the "holder," held out his hands, palms forward and fingers wide stretched. Bell, as the "threader," threaded his fingers between Yardley's and gripped tight. So they fell suspended together, eyes behind the goggles a few inches apart. Bell could see a strange look in Yardley's eyes—or was he being fanciful? It wasn't exactly anger; it was almost a kind of gloating awareness. He tried to make his own eyes impassive.

And down they fell, linked as one. He could see the altimeter needle at four, three-five, then three. Less than twenty seconds from eternity. Yardley's fingers were rigid, unmoving. Christ, Bell began to think, this is a bloody silly game—and then, impulsively, his right hand jerked free and tore at the ripcord. The jerk flung him clear of Yardley, who fell away beneath him, still in free fall.

The main parachute half opened, then candled in a long sausagelike roll. It hardly checked his descent. Bell pulled the ripcord of the emergency chute. It spurted open and then snagged in the tangle of the main chute. There was nothing between Bell and the ground but two thousand feet of empty air.

Except that Yardley, as Bell went down, scissored his legs around his body and pulled his own ripcord, and together they plummeted down. The last two thousand feet, supported by Yardley's main chute alone, allowed just enough time for him to set up a wide pendulous arc to retard their rate of descent. As Bell's feet touched the ground, he ran a few steps forward to keep the momentum; Yardley broke free from the leg grip and yanked hard down on his control lines, stalling the ramair chute and killing its flight. They were so experienced that they made it look like a normal landing—but they both knew it had been touch and go.

Bell, having broken the momentum with a practiced roll onto the hard turf, gathered himself to his feet, let himself out of the tangled chutes and slowly removed the goggles and oxygen mask. Yardley was doing the same. They stood there in silence for a moment or two, looking at each other.

Bell said, "You saved my life."

Yardley said acidly, "You fucked my wife. I should have let you go in hard, you shit."

"Hey, that was a long time ago. And she was nobody's wife then. What's come over you? I was the chicken, not you. And you *did* save my life, for Chrissake."

"Forget it." Yardley turned away and began to gather up his chute. Several members of the string came running over and one said, "Jeez, that looked spectacular, boss! You trying a new stunt or was it accidental?"

Yardley said in a crisp voice, "Gather round, all of

you.'' He motioned to Bell to stay well in the background.
''That didn't happen, you understand? You never saw a
thing, any of you. We went up for a nice HALO jump and
it all went well. Right, that's it for this afternoon. Sergeant, do a full debrief, then have the men hand in their
equipment and repack the chutes. The rest of the day's
their own.''

He turned to Bell and said, ''Sorry, I shouldn't have
talked out of turn just now. Bit on edge.''

''Aren't we all? That was too damn close for comfort. I
can't say I'm over-impressed with the standard of parachute-
packing here at Bragg!''

Yardley was grim-faced. ''You can say that again. I'll
spend the next hour or two getting to the bottom of this.
Someone's hide will be nailed to the wall before today's
out. We had another Roman candle last week. Luckily,
like this time, the guy got away with it, but one of these
days . . . Look, why don't you go back to your motel—
I'll dig up some transport for you—and take it easy while
I'm sorting this lot out? Then we'll meet for that drink at
nine. Okay?''

''Fine with me—but will you be able to make it? After
this?''

''Sure, why not? We've a lot of catching up to do.''

You said it, thought Bell.

TO SLAY MINE ENEMIES, AND TO AID MY FRIENDS, AND
ALWAYS BE OBEDIENT TO MY WILL.

131

BELL ARRIVED TEN minutes early at the bar. He had relaxed
under a long hot shower on returning to the motel and had
noticed with professional objectivity that a dark blue bruise
had formed on his upper left arm, where Drucker had
slugged him with the stool. It was nothing to worry about;
he had exercised the arm for twenty minutes in the way the
SAS taught and knew there was nothing broken. You
should have seen the other guy, he thought.

He ordered a Scotch and looked around the place. There
was no evidence left of the lunchtime fracas and the big
room was half empty, with a few hardened drinkers prop-
ping up the bar and several parties occupying the booths at
the back. And no sign of anyone who might be a friend of
Drucker. Just as well—he'd had enough activity for one
day.

Sharp on nine o'clock, the swinging doors parted and
Angela came around the partition—alone. He waved and
she walked straight over to him.

"Tim! It's great to see you." She hugged him impulsively and then stood back, arms at full stretch lightly holding his shoulders. "Here—let me get a good look at you. Still the same old Tim, I guess." She leaned forward and kissed him, first on one cheek and then on the other.

"You look great, Angie. You really do. Marriage agrees with you, I can see." And she did look good, he reckoned. He guessed she had altered her hair style. It now seemed more flowing, more—more feminine, perhaps. Memories prickled deep in his gut.

"Where's Bob?" he asked.

"You might well ask! He came in late, like a bear with a sore head, and said he was going to cancel the date. Just like that. I said the hell with it, you hadn't come all this way to be left high and dry at the last minute. He'd had a rough time with his CO—something about a parachute failing in a jump this afternoon. Anyway, he quieted down after a bit, said he'd take a shower and change and then come along. I wasn't going to keep you hanging around, so I came in my own car. He can walk for all I care! Say, there's nothing wrong between you and Bob, is there?"

"Not that I know. He was quite okay this afternoon."

"Oh, I'm glad. You and he are old friends. I wouldn't like to think you'd fallen out. Hey, what does a girl have to do to get a drink around here?"

"Hell, I'm sorry, Angie. Your usual?"

"You're bluffing, Tim! You don't remember."

"Try me." Bell turned to the barman. "A vodka for the lady, just a splash of tonic—and no ice."

"So you do remember. That's nice," she said. He saw that she was blushing.

They moved over to one of the tables and sat down. They clinked glasses, drank, and then she said, "It's been three years and three months—almost to the day. What have you been up to, Tim?"

"Oh, a bit of this—and a bit of that."

"You men! You're all the same. Keeping those great big secrets to yourselves. Bob never tells me a damn thing.

I sit in that married quarter until the walls start closing in and when he comes home, I ask him what he's been doing and he gives me some guff about 'don't you worry your pretty head.' I'm a big girl now. I can keep a secret—if anyone'd give me the chance.''

Bell said, ''Relax, Angie. It's all pretty boring. I'm sure Bob'd tell you if he could. Me, I'm taking a break. I've got a spell of leave due and I thought I'd come over and look up a few old friends. Besides, I haven't all that long to go in the Regiment and Bob might put me onto one or two useful contacts.''

''You mean you might be over here for quite a while?''

''Could be. Who knows?''

''That'd be lovely! We might see quite a bit of you.''

He looked her in the eyes. After a couple of seconds, she looked away. ''Would that be wise?'' he said quietly. ''Last time I saw you in Hereford, you didn't want to know me. And I don't blame you. We had our moments, God knows, but that was then—and this is now. You're Bob's wife.''

''But that doesn't put me in purdah. You and I can still be friends.'' She reached across the table and grasped his hand.

Just then, Yardley came round the partition and saw them together, even in the dim light of the bar. He walked over and said, ''You taking Tim's pulse?''

Oh, Christ, Bell thought. Great moment to walk in. Now he'll get all suspicious—with no cause. Well, if that's the way he wants to play it, two can play. He disengaged his hand slowly and deliberately, stood up and said, ''Well, hi, Bob. Good to see you. Let me get you a drink.''

Yardley said, ''I'll buy my own drink, thanks. A Scotch and water,'' he addressed the barman, who was polishing glasses a few feet away.

''Hey, what the hell's all this?'' Bell asked. ''I thought

we were going to have a nice quiet evening over a few drinks.''

Yardley said, "So did I—until three hours ago. I had a chewing out from my CO for breaking military regulations by taking a *civilian* up on a Delta Force parachute jump this afternoon. Yeah, you heard me—a civilian. News travels fast, Tim. Word came through to the stockade this afternoon, right when we were airborne, that you'd been cashiered from the SAS. Kicked out, in plain English. You might have told me.''

Bell said, "It's a long story—"

Yardley interrupted, "Yeah, but it's a short ending. I just don't want to know the miserable details. Something about two IRA suspects being shot while under arrest. I wouldn't have thought it of you, Tim.''

"There's another side to the story—"

"There always is. But I don't want to hear it. Now or ever. If Hereford says you're out—in disgrace—Delta Force doesn't want to know you. We can't afford to know you. Pity you screwed up that ape Drucker this morning. I hear they're still looking for mercenaries for Nicaragua—but you won't be the flavor of the month right now.'' He stood up, drained his drink, and threw a note onto the bar. "You coming, sweetheart?''

He threaded his way between the tables and strode toward the partition and the swinging doors. Angela looked reluctant, doubtful, but then rose and said in an urgent whisper to Bell, "I'd better go. I don't understand all this. Call me tomorrow morning—Bob's away in Washington all day. You know Betty here? She has my number. See you.'' Bell watched her walk toward the partition. She turned and blew him a kiss before she followed Yardley, who had disappeared.

Bell ordered two more drinks. The first he emptied in one long swallow. If Colonel McAlister had walked into the bar that moment, he would have killed him—slowly. That toffee-nosed sod! Not content with slamming the door in England, he'd made damn sure that the word would reach the cousins fast. Bell didn't really blame Bob Yardley, though he might have kissed him goodbye with more grace. Bob was a professional, he knew that if someone was in the shit, you had to walk wide of him. Shit sticks to the sole of your shoe like nothing else—and a career soldier had to keep his boots clean. But now all bets were off. If Angie was still interested—and he sensed she was—that might be the open back door. Well, tomorrow would prove it, one way or the other. And, by Christ, McAlister and the rest of the mob were going to regret the day they slung him out.

Next morning, he waited until he was sure Yardley would have left for his Washington briefing. He dialed the number Betty had given him. Angela answered on the second ring; it was as if, he felt, she had been sitting by the telephone, waiting for the call.

"Hi, Angie, it's me—Tim."

"Oh, I'm so glad you called. What on earth was all that about last night?"

"Didn't Bob tell you?"

"Not really. He got all mysterious—official secrets and all that. I told him not to treat me like a child and we ended up in a bit of a row."

"Sorry to hear it. It's all my fault. I'll tell you what happened—nothing secret about it. A couple of IRA suspects—suspects, they were real hard-nosed killers—were shot while attempting to escape. I was in charge of the SAS team, so I got the blame. Fair enough. It was my responsibility. They didn't have to make a hanging case of it, though. There was no proper court of inquiry. They fired me—just like that."

"Gosh, I *am* sorry. Why didn't you tell that to Bob last night?"

"Didn't get much chance, did I? Talking of Bob, is he still there?"

"No, he left for Washington hours ago. Knowing him, he won't be back this side of nine o'clock."

"Well, would you like a spot of lunch today? After that fuss last night, I owe you one."

Angela said, "Is that all? I thought you might like to see *me* again as well."

"Goes without saying. Would you like to have lunch?"

"Tim, I'd love it. Will you come over here or shall I drive around to the motel?"

"Neither," he said. "I wouldn't want to put you to more trouble after last night. Besides, although we're old friends, I'm not sure it's wise for the major's wife to be seen in public with some stranger. Not when people know he's off the base."

"Oh, phooey," she said. "You always were one for weighing everything up. But okay, if you're ashamed of being seen in public with me . . ."

"You know it's not that."

"Sure, I was just teasing. You've got a car, haven't you? Right, if you go north on 87, about ten miles up the road you come to Spout Springs. Keep on 87—Route 24 breaks off at that point—and in another two or three miles you come to a little place called Pine View. It's just one street, you're through it before you know you've come to it. Well, just north of Pine View, there's a roadhouse set back in the trees—on your right as you're going north. I can't remember the name but there's a big sign out front with the horns of a buffalo or something on top. You can't miss it."

"You ought to have been in the Army, Angie. You'd have made sergeant at least. That's very clear."

"It's living with Army louts that gives me the knack. So what's the drill, as you would say?"

He glanced at his wristwatch. "Let's see, it's nearly ten-thirty. What do you say we meet there around noon? That'll give us time for a little drinkie before we try one of their steaks."

"It's a date," she said. "See you at twelve."

This was all proving too easy, he thought, as he drove up
Route 87. God, women took some understanding. He
knew he had treated Angela badly. She may or may not
have had a man before she met him—he never asked and
she never volunteered—but he doubted it. She was the
daughter of a country vicar with a parish a few miles
outside Hereford and he had met her at a social function in
the town. She soon found out that he was something to do
with the SAS and from then on he had become her knight
in shining armor. They had met just after he had returned
from the Falklands campaign and she had seen him once in
Service dress with the purple and white ribbon of the
Military Cross above the breast pocket. When she discovered from one of his friends that it was a medal for
gallantry in the field, she flung herself at him. It had been
like trying to stop a flood with your bare hands.

She might have been a prim and proper vicar's daughter
with her clothes on but in bed she had proved a cross
between a tigress and a boa constrictor. There was a spell
in the summer when he was unable to go swimming in a
pair of trunks because of the deep-scored scratches on his
shoulders and back. And she was insatiable, always grabbing at him the moment they were alone. He preferred
women with a bit more poise, more reserve—so that winning them was a real victory.

Once, after a specially frantic bout, he was lying back
half asleep in the rumpled bed with her arm around him
and her warm breath not an inch from his ear. She murmured something about her mother continually asking when
they were going to get engaged. It was all he could do
with a concentrated effort to stop his whole body going
rigid. That had been the beginning of the end in their
relationship. From seeing her almost every day, he managed to cut it down to three times a week, always pleading
pressure of duties with the Squadron.

He also made sure that they appeared in public more often at social functions and made a point of introducing her to his various unattached friends, including Bob Yardley, then a captain in the U.S. Rangers attached to Hereford for a three-month training course. Boy, had marriage changed old Bob! In those days—what was it, three, four years ago?—he had been a carefree fun guy, always there with a joke and a laugh.

Even so, after a few more weeks, Angela challenged him directly one night. It was after another bout of love-making and he lay there, feeling that he had been run over by a slow but thorough steamroller. It was funny, he thought, looking back now: vertical, Angie had been a shy, almost diffident girl; horizontal, the inhibitions just poured away.

"Tim," she had said, "we can't go on like this indefinitely."

He chose to misunderstand her. "You bet. Another go like that and I'll just float up to the ceiling."

"That's not what I meant, and you know it. Stop fooling for just a minute, will you? We've been lovers now for—it'll be exactly five months next Wednesday—and everybody round here thinks of us as a couple. Why, the other day, a friend of Daddy's, another vicar with a parish outside Shrewsbury, came to tea—luckily, I wasn't there—and asked Mummy whether my husband was going to stay on in the Army. Mummy was *terribly* embarrassed!"

"Poor Mummy," he murmured.

"Will you *please* stop playing the fool! This is serious. You're over thirty and I'll be twenty-four next birthday. You're wonderful in bed—but making love's not getting us anywhere. So let's be serious for a moment. Tell me straight, Tim—do you want to marry me, or don't you?"

Her hand was between his legs, cupping him gently. He lifted it away with his free hand and sat up. He said quietly, "Angie, have I ever, ever said anything to you about marriage?"

She shook her head.

"And did I ever make that an excuse to get you into bed?"

Again she shook her head.

"Well, I've tried to play this straight all along, so let's keep on that track." He followed at once with a lie. "I'm sure you'd make a marvelous wife but, don't you see?—I'm not looking for a wife. In my job, a wife's liable to turn into a widow anytime. And I'm not the marrying kind. Sorry—but that's it."

She burst into tears and he put a clumsy arm around her shoulders to stop her shaking. "So all this's been for nothing?" she sobbed.

"It's been wonderful for me but if it's marriage you're after, this is where I get off the bus."

"Damn you, Tim," she moaned. "Oh, damn you, damn you."

She curled up like a little girl and seemed to put a thumb in her mouth. He slipped out from under the tangled sheets and began to dress. Neither said a word, even when he tenderly patted her shoulder as he left.

A week later, when he was strolling down the main street in Hereford, he saw that she was coming toward him from the opposite direction. He was about to say "Hi, Angie" when she swept straight past, head flung back. Three months later, her engagement to Captain Robert Yardley of the U.S. Army was announced in *The Times* and *The Daily Telegraph*.

He found the roadhouse beyond Pine View with no difficulty and parked his rented car on one side of the graveled forecourt. He was nearly ten minutes early but when he entered the oak-paneled room and went over to the bar, Angela was already there. "Tim!" she said as she stood up, "it's great to see you again!" She stood up against him and kissed him full on the mouth.

"Hey, steady," he said. "We met again only last night, remember?"

"Okay, be literal if you want to. Here, let me look at you. Still the same old Tim Bell. A real creep!"

"And I love you too," he said. He wondered whether she had been drinking hard already that morning. "Here, let's have a drink. What'll it be?"

"I'm way ahead of you," she said. "I've already had one—and there's yours, just the way you like it, right there in front of you."

"Thoughtful lady. Here, good luck."

After the third round of drinks, they moved into the dining room, which was half empty, and Bell asked for a corner table. There, they went on gossiping about the past and mutual friends over the inevitable underdone steak and green salad and a bottle of California burgundy. Angela's knee was pressed against the lower part of his thigh and with the tip of her shoe she was tracing small circles above his ankle bone. The sensation was not unpleasant.

She suddenly burst out with, "Oh, Tim, maybe I was a bloody fool to let you go."

He thought to himself, Who says I'd've wanted to keep you on? Aloud, he said, "Look what you've got—a nice home, a good husband, plenty of money. What more do you want?"

"Excitement, fun. Oh, Bob's the salt of the earth, they don't come better. But he's not exciting—at least to me. He's worth two of you, Tim, any day, but when I heard from Betty you were in town, I got that old feeling right in here. I'm fond of Bob but he doesn't rouse me, not the way you can by just looking at me. And when he gets onto his secret military stuff . . .

"Come on," she pressed on, gripping the top of his thigh under the tablecloth, "let's drive back to the fort— now. I want you in bed so badly it hurts."

He called for the check and then said, "Terrific. Look, you drive on ahead—it won't look too good if we both turn up in different cars at the same time—and get things organized. I'll settle up here. Hey—and don't break the record driving back. When I make love, I prefer the woman to be all in one piece.''

She stuck out her tongue at him, ran her fingertips softly down his jawline and then was gone toward the exit. There, she turned and blew him a kiss before disappearing through the swinging doors.

As he drove steadily back down Route 87, he was thinking that so far it had gone as well as he had hoped. He just had to get inside Yardley's bungalow to run through his secret files. If taking Angela to bed was the only way to achieve this, so be it. He realized he felt no compunction at the thought of betraying an old friend who had saved his life only yesterday. A man should look after his own. If he couldn't keep a woman tamed, then it was really his fault if she ran wild.

He drove up to the main gates at Fort Bragg and showed his pass from the day before. He was waved through and made for the Special Forces stockade. There were a few women strolling about, one or two with young children, and several off-duty soldiers busy doing nothing, but most people were indoors on this late February afternoon, which was cold and raw for the balmy South. He parked the car seventy-five yards from Angela's place and walked the last part.

She must have driven like the wind and she must have been looking out for him as he walked up the short path to the front door. He had stretched out one hand toward the doorbell but, before he could press it, the door had swung open. Angela, barefoot and wearing only a light robe, pulled him through the opening and slammed the door behind him. Then she was all over him, grabbing, probing, moaning broken phrases as she gripped the lobe of his left ear in her teeth.

''Gently,'' he said, trying to disentangle himself, ''gently. Leave a bit for the main course.''

Hand in hand, she pulled him toward the bedroom. The covers were drawn back on the double bed—her and Bob's bed. She dropped the thin robe on the floor, then lay naked on the bed watching Bell's every move as he undressed. And when he went straight into her, he thought it was like making love to a mincing machine. She tugged and pulled at him and tried to envelop him with her legs and arms, all the time gasping and giving little high-pitched screams, as though in agony. He hoped the house was soundproofed or that the neighbors were away for the day.

After she had exhausted herself, they lay for a while in each other's slippery-sweaty arms. He felt her breathing going back to normal and her pulse beat decelerating. Gently, he pulled himself clear. "I don't know about you, but I could use a drink," he said, "a very large Scotch. If we're going to do this again—I hope—my stamina needs building up!"

"I don't want one right now," she said. "You get one yourself, darling. You know where the drinks are kept, and there's fresh ice in the fridge—top compartment. Oh, Tim," she went on, "that was gorgeous. God, it took me back a few years!"

He smiled, and then on an impulse walked back to the rumpled bed, leaned over and kissed her lightly on the mouth. She grabbed him and held him tight for a moment, then let him go. "Here," she said, "you've just borrowed Bob's bed, and his wife, so why don't you borrow his bathrobe—there, hanging behind the door? Don't want you catching your death of cold right now."

He slipped on the short bathrobe and, as he padded on bare feet toward the living room and the drinks cabinet, for the first time he felt bad. Somehow, wearing the other man's bathrobe felt like the ultimate betrayal. There were intimate smells around the collar and neck—of shaving cream and bath talc and hair fixative. A bed was just a bed; you put on clean sheets and clean pillow slips and the past was obliterated. And Angela had been his woman before she became Bob's. But there was something wrong and unclean in borrowing the husband's bathrobe, he felt.

In the living room, he made unnecessary noises in clinking the bottles, just in case Angela was listening through the open bedroom door. Then he gazed quickly around the room. He knew these married quarters from visits on previous tours of duty; they ran to a large living room, a main bedroom with a bathroom alongside, and a kitchenette. There was no separate room for Bob to use as a study, so if he kept his papers in his quarters—most senior officers did, whether they were supposed to or not—the documents had to be right here.

Bell padded over to the desk under the window. He tried the top righthand drawer; it was locked. He tried the other drawers swiftly, one after the other. They were all locked. Christ! Now he really had to enlist Angie's help.

On cue, her voice came faintly from the bedroom. "Have you fainted or something? I thought you were going to get yourself a large Scotch, not distill it!"

He poured a large slug of Scotch into the nearest glass. "Coming," he shouted. "Going ten rounds with you slows a man up."

"Pig," she said, as he walked barefoot back into the bedroom.

"By the way," he said, "I don't want to sound anxious—but what if Bob were to walk in suddenly? You feel such a fool, prancing around naked when an irate husband is trying to knock your block off."

"My hero," she said, "always thinking of his own skin. Relax, Tim sweetie, Bob won't be back till late tonight, if then. Sometimes, these briefing sessions run on into the next day. And he's a real Southern gentleman, which is more than I could say about you. If his plans are ever changed, he always calls me. So drink up and come back to bed."

They made love again—slower and more prolonged than the first frantic time. As Bell straddled her, plunging

methodically, he looked down at her flushed face, eyes
screwed shut, mouth opening and closing convulsively,
giving little gasps and moans as though in exquisite agony.
He had read in a book somewhere that love was only the
rubbing together of two different sets of membranes. That's
all it was, he thought. Angela might feel she was passion-
ately in love with him—but how long would love remain if
he couldn't get it up and keep going like a marathon
runner?

He must have dozed off afterward, because the room
was dark when he came alert. He felt Angela slip out of
bed and pull on her own robe, which she found lying
crumpled on the floor where she had flung it two hours
before. He heard her tiptoe off to the bathroom, the click
of the door shutting and a few moments later the muted
sound of flushing. At once, he put on the bedside lamp
and began to dress hurriedly. No more of another man's
bathrobe for him.

She came back into the bedroom. "Darling, what's the
rush? How about a nice cup of tea the way Mother makes
it? None of those little teabags suspended in lukewarm
water!"

"Great idea," he said. "I could use a cup of tea." He
went on dressing.

"So the afternoon performance's definitely over?"

"God, woman, what more do you want? You've put me
through the wringer twice. I'm not a boy anymore, you
know." He went over and patted her rump affectionately.

"So when do I get to see you again?" she asked.

"Steady, I'm still here. How about that cup of tea? And
shouldn't you put a few clothes on? What if one of the
neighbors called?"

"The neighbors don't call. They're friendly enough to
my face when Bob's around but behind my back they
reckon I'm a stuck-up English bitch! That's another reason
why I can't stand it here. It's so lonely. Bob's away a lot,

and there's nothing for me to do but watch every quiz program on the box. I'm bored out of my skull.''

He held her hand for a moment, then disengaged. Tea, maybe, but not too much sympathy.

She had her back to him, as she stood by the stove, boiling the water and heating the teapot. ''What's going to become of us, Tim?'' she said softly.

''What do you mean?''

''You know damn well what I mean! *Us*, darling. You and me. Or were you thinking of disappearing again as suddenly as you turned up?''

This was getting serious. But he sensed it gave him the opening he desperately needed. Aloud, he said, ''Of course I'm not going to disappear. Not now I've found you again.'' To his own ears, it sounded too corny for words, but as she turned and brought the full teapot over to the kitchen table, he saw her eyes were shining.

''Darling.'' She bent over his chair and kissed him on the mouth.

''Angie,'' he said, ''will you help me?''

''Of course, I will. Is it money? I've got some saved out of the housekeeping.''

''I love you.'' he said, ''you're wonderful. No, it's not money. Nothing like that. I've enough to get by for a while but I'd like to stay on in the States—do I have to say why?—and I'm going to need a job.''

''But how can I help?''

''Simple. If Bob hadn't walked off in a huff last night, I was going to ask him. No, not for a job, just for some information. You see, there are a lot of VIPs over here who need protection. Superior bodyguards, basically. When guys retire from the Special Forces, they get recommended to various big shots—politicians, leading senators, big businessmen, that crowd—who could be at risk from terrorists. I wouldn't know where the hell to start looking but Bob must have a list of the likely contacts as long as your arm. And I'd lay a bet there's a copy right here in these quarters. All I need is a quick look. Once I know who needs a strong-arm man, I can get straight through and cut out the red tape.''

The excuse sounded pretty thin to him but Angela, that lovable fool, took it right in.

"Bob has a load of stuff in that desk,'' she said. ''I haven't the vaguest idea what's there but you're welcome to look. He locks the drawers and keeps the key on his keyring—but there's a spare key in his bathroom cabinet. Here, I'll get it for you.'' She was gone for under a minute and came back with the key in her hand. Bell stood up, kissed her, emptied his teacup, and walked over to the door.

"How long will you be?'' she asked.

"Half an hour at the most, maybe a lot less. Depends how soon I hit the right file.''

"While you're looking, I'll go and have a shower—and dress, I suppose. Unless you'd . . .''

"Darling, you're insatiable,'' he said. "I'll have to take a rain check.''

"Weakling,'' she said—but left him with a smile.

He went into the living room and over to the desk. The key opened every drawer, as Angela had hinted. This was amateur night, he thought. One key for the whole desk, and the spare kept in the bathroom cabinet. Served Bob bloody right if his secrets were used against him. The top two drawers on the right side of the desk were full of paraphernalia, personal letters, old invitations to Service functions, last year's diary. He riffled through them but there was nothing there to interest him. The bottom deeper drawer yielded results. It contained half a dozen buff-colored folders, each with a neatly typed label on the front. He picked out a couple and glanced inside. This was it—the real stuff.

He lifted all the folders out of the bottom drawer and placed them on the dining-room table. There was a scribbling pad on the desk and he tore off half a dozen sheets for taking notes. He was too old a hand to use the pad itself, for he knew that the indentations on the page beneath can easily be picked out without even having to use ultraviolet rays.

As he moved back to the table, his eye lit on a clutter of framed photographs on the mantelpiece above the fireplace. There was one of Angela, laughing, with her head thrown back. Hell, she was certainly a looker. A couple were of military groups and yet another was of an elderly man and woman. There was a strong resemblance to Bob, particularly in the man; they must be his parents. But the picture that caught his attention was of Bob Yardley in full Service dress standing to attention while the president of the United States pinned a medal on his chest. The background looked like the White House garden.

On a hunch, Bell went back to the desk and looked more carefully through the top two drawers. At the back of the lower one, he found a medal on its ribbon; it had obviously been tossed into the drawer. He picked it up and looked at it carefully. The Congressional Medal of Honor— the highest award for valor the U.S.A. could bestow. So Bob really was a hero. That snatch raid in Lebanon must have been a hairy one. And typical of the man just to chuck the medal into the back of a drawer. Most men would have had it framed and displayed under neon lights for all to see and wonder at. His respect for Yardley rose even higher.

He got down to studying the files. There was a bulky one on likely Hispanic terrorists in Southern California. As Bell already knew through his own contacts, the Spanish government had cracked down hard on the Basque ETA separatists, several of whom had fled to Mexico. They had formed cells across the border with disaffected Hispanics around San Diego, forming a part of the Marxist bridge under construction in Central America. Interesting—but nothing in it for him.

He also dismissed a new Black Power and FALN Puerto Rican organization in Chicago—they wouldn't want whitey interfering in their affairs. The same went for various Arab legations to the United Nations, which were suspected of infiltrating terrorists from North Africa. He smiled when running through the next file, a slim one, which consisted of copy letters between the Israeli embassy, the NYPD, the National Security Council, and the head of the CIA. A number of prominent Jews were due to hold a celebration dinner in the restaurant at the top of the World Trade Center in New York on May fifteenth to mark the fortieth anniversary of the founding of the state of Israel. The Israeli ambassador was to be present, as well as a few distinguished Israelis. The ambassador had ruffled everyone else's feathers by firmly refusing to let the NYPD or anyone else local provide the security. He had insisted that trained Mossad men be brought in from Israel for the task, even though at least ninety of the hundred guests would be American Jews. Bell could spot the frustrated anger concealed in the stiffly worded letters of protest from the Yank officials but the ambassador wasn't going to budge an inch. Good luck to him.

There were two files that really interested him. One dealt with the Anglo-Saxon Brethren, a neofascist bunch of gun freaks centered in Idaho. There was a note attached, hinting that a very rich man named Holliday, who had big oil and lumber concessions, was suspected of being the moneybags behind them, but there was no evidence to prove it. A State Department memo, clipped to the papers, pointed out that Holliday was a very liberal contributor to Republican funds. In other words, don't bug him, Bell thought. He made a note of the unlisted telephone numbers.

The other file dealt with the opposite political camp. An even richer man named Eugene Minter—the file called him one of the three wealthiest men in the U.S.A.—had been serving as a career diplomat but some years earlier had abruptly left the Foreign Service just when he might have been in line for an embassy. He had started a college, Minter College, in the Arizona desert but the professorial staff and the curriculum were not the usual products of the humanities. There was a radical Palestinian with known PLO contacts, a black teacher who had been active in the African National Congress and any number of bearded weirdos who were apparently pouring out hard left propaganda to the impressionable young. There was an orange tab on the file. Bell knew that a red tab would mean round-the-clock close surveillance with experienced FBI personnel and all electronic devices including phone tapping and audio bugs. Orange was a step down—a matter of "just watch it in case." All the same, he sensed that this could be his first target.

The last file dealt with individuals. Most of the names meant nothing to him but as he flipped through the file— hell, Angie must be taking the longest bath since Cleopatra— his eye was caught by one he knew. Ex-sergeant Philip Brown, an EOD demolitions expert, served in Vietnam, transferred to the Green Berets, attachments to 22 Squadron SAS, Hereford, then sergeant instructor at Fort Bragg, then transferred out with a disability pension. He'd met Phil Brown, "Fingers," they used to call him, because he was so quick and neat at setting up the deadliest of booby-traps, up on the Laotian border in '71. Warped sense of humor the guy had had. Once he'd taken a violent dislike to a pompous senior officer when they'd been back in civilization in Saigon. The officer was very particular that none of the rank and file used his private lavatory. That bastard Brown had set a booby trap under the lavatory seat—a minute one, or they'd have had to scrape the officer's ass off the walls. But it gave him a nasty surprise when he sat down, and no one had given old Brown away.

According to the memo on the file, when he was an instructor at Bragg, Fingers had been experimenting with a phosphorous grenade that went off prematurely, burning him right down one side of his face and damaging his left eye. His hands were undamaged but the plastic surgery on his face hadn't taken and he must have looked a dreadful sight. The findings of the court of inquiry were that he should be quietly discharged with full pension rights. They wanted clean-looking guys in the Special Forces, not burned-out wrecks. So there was another good man sent packing without a band to march him off parade. And after all he'd done in 'Nam and elsewhere. The note went on to say that he'd been rechristened ''Flamer'' Brown by his unit and he was now living in a derelict dump on the Lower East Side of New York. He was suspected of working for the hard drug chiefs, helping to booby-trap their private caches. Bell wrote down the address on his sheet of paper. An explosives expert like Flamer, disillusioned and vengeful, might come in handy.

Angela came into the room. He was relieved to see she was fully dressed, in a sweater and skirt. He couldn't face another session in bed right now.

''Still at it?'' she said. ''Haven't you found what you want?''

''You bet,'' he said. ''Lord, am I grateful to you. I've got some very promising pointers to follow up from this lot, thanks entirely to you. Better not tell Bob, by the way. Guess I'm not his flavor of the month right now.''

''As if I would. Here, let me help you put 'em away.''

''No, it's all right. I know exactly where they go in the drawer. You know, I could use another Scotch. Or will Bob notice the level in the bottle's gone down?''

''No, he's not that sort, thank God,'' she said. ''He's got his faults but there's nothing petty about Bob.''

He put the files away and locked all the drawers while she was pouring him the Scotch and adding some ice. She brought the glass over to him, took his other hand, and pulled him gently over to the sofa by the fireplace. Then she said, ''You know, you changed the subject just now. Before I went for my bath.''

''Which subject?''

"Us, silly. I asked you—what's going to happen to us?"

"I don't get you."

"Oh, come on, Tim, you're not that stupid. I've got to know. Was that just a one-night—a one-afternoon stand and it's 'Thank you, ma'am,' old Tim's on his way? That leaves me feeling pretty dirty. Or is there a future? One way or the other, you must tell me."

He was tempted to say, you asked for it and by God you got it, but swiftly realized he might need an ally. And right in the enemy camp. He said slowly, "Of course there's a future for us. A bright one. But first, I must find a good job. My cash'll run out in a few weeks, and you couldn't afford to keep yourself, let alone me. And I'm not the type that wants to be kept. So the job comes first—it has to. Once I'm fixed up—it shouldn't take long—I'll give you a call and we can arrange to meet and talk things over. Can you manage to get away from Bragg for a day or two?"

"I'll think of something."

"Good. You see, we can't just rush off like babes in the wood. Bob is not going to take this quietly, if he finds out you could have a divorce on your hands."

"Did you say divorce?" she asked softly.

He nodded.

"My God, I don't want to think about it. I don't want to hurt Bob, but you make me feel reckless and hungry." She held his gaze, searching his face for truth.

"The hunger is mutual." He instinctively felt he must not hesitate. "You lit a fire in me a long time ago and it never went out."

"So you really are serious? This time you really do want me in your life?"

"Looks like it," he said.

"Oh, darling!" She put her arms around him and hugged him. "I think you mean it. What's happened to old 'love 'em and leave 'em' Tim Bell?"

"Got hooked at last, I suppose," he said. "But look—

not a word to Bob just yet. I've got a lot of sorting out to do. So have you."

"But what if Bob senses something! I mean, he is my husband."

"If you mean demand your sexual delights, darling, that's your problem. Bromide in his coffee, that'll do it."

"Be serious. But you're right—it's my problem. I'll work something out."

He drained the mug of tea and rose to his feet in one springy movement. "I'd better be going. There's a lot to do before my plane leaves in the morning."

"Must you?"

He made a grimace and shrugged. "Sorry, my love, but I must. Still, it's only a week or so before I give you that call."

"Don't go out of your way," she said. "After all, it might cost you a buck or two."

He aimed a mock punch in her direction and then took her in his arms, kissing her full on the mouth. He held her at arm's length and gazed at her face, the way he had seen Paul Newman do it in a movie. "Be good," he said.

"And you be careful."

IT WILL BE TWELVE O'CLOCK AT NIGHT; THAT TWELVE

. . . .

IT IS THE JUDAS OF THE HOURS, WHEREIN
HONEST SALVATION IS BETRAYED TO SIN

▌4▌

NEXT DAY HE went underground. He took a flight to Washington under his own name, paying cash for the ticket. He took a taxi into Washington from the airport, paid the man off, and went into various banks, changing travelers' checks. Then he took another taxi out to Dulles International Airport and bought a multistop ticket for cash, but not in the name of Bell. The money was running away fast, he noted. What with his payoff from the SAS and the other money he had managed to scratch together, he had left England—was it only three days ago?—with around three thousand dollars. Already a thousand had disappeared. The first gamble just had to come up.

He flew to Denver, Colorado, then took a feeder aircraft to Colorado Springs. He stayed the night at an airport motel and early next morning took a flight to Salt Lake City. Then back south to Albuquerque, where he rented a car under a phony name, paying a cash deposit. Then he drove west across the desert toward Flagstaff, Arizona. It would be over two hundred miles and the nights drew in early in February, so after driving for three hours he pulled up at a trucking town named Holbrook, best known perhaps for its display of Indian artifacts.

He had a set of Exxon touring maps and that night after a hamburger and a beer he spent an hour poring over the maps in his motel room. The old Army saying came back—time spent in reconnaissance is seldom wasted. He saw that if he stayed on Route 40 and drove on through Flagstaff for another forty miles he would come to the junction with Route 89 at Ash Fork. Turn south on 89 and thirty-five miles away lay Chino Valley. That would be the obvious way to take, so he decided to go south from Flagstaff to Sedona and follow the twisty road through Clarkdale and Jerome to Prescott. From the map it appeared to be the largest town between Phoenix and Flagstaff—and under fifteen miles from Chino Valley.

Having made up his mind, he decided on an early night. But he was sharply aware that his highly trained body was beginning to go soft. For the last few days, he had done nothing except loll around in different aircraft, eating plastic food from plastic trays and drinking too much. Oh, there had been the fight with Sergeant Drucker—he could see in the bathroom mirror of his motel room that there was still a dark bruise on his left upper arm where the stool had hit him—and the HALO parachute drop, but neither was enough to keep a man in real condition.

So he stripped down to his underpants and lay on his back on the floor with his ankles resting on the side of the bed. He put his arms back and on his fingertips raised his shoulders off the floor. The idea was to bring the arms up in a full circle, clap hands and then get the fingertips back on the floor before the unsupported back and shoulders crashed down on the floor. It put the biggest strain on thigh and stomach muscles but soon every part of the body from the toes upward felt as though it had been ground on the rack.

After the first twenty nonstop, he lost his concentration

and slumped to the floor, panting and sweating. He cursed himself for a weak shit and, teeth clenched, tried again. This time, he went over fifty and then had to pause for breath. The sweat was rolling off his chest and shoulders and he felt as though an iron bar had been inserted in his gut. His stomach muscles were quivering with the effort.

A few minutes' rest and he drove himself again. This time, he got up to eighty-three before collapsing in a huddle on the floor. It was not good; at his peak he could do the exercise well over a hundred times nonstop. But it was not bad; the muscles had not altogether lost their tone. Three or four days of the same exercise morning and night would find him back over the hundred mark. Pleased with himself, he took a long cold shower and went to bed, where he slept like a baby.

The next afternoon, he made a late start and drove in a leisurely way into Flagstaff, which seemed to be just a collection of shopping malls and filling stations. He stopped for another hamburger and a coffee before taking the side road down to Sedona through the pine forests. And he was glad he had done so. Bell was a fighter of vast experience and there was no poetry in his soul. To him, trees and open spaces and lush meadows were not things of beauty or joys forever. His keen eye would be looking to see where the dead ground was, which were the best arcs of fire, what line of approach to take from here to that grassy knoll.

Even so, as he drove slowly down the twisting, jinking road into Sedona with the winter sun setting across the valley, he caught his breath briefly at the sheer beauty of it all. Away to the east of the valley were the most grand and grotesque sandstone shapes, carved out by millions of years of wind and rain and the freezing and melting of innumerable droplets of water. Some looked like fairy castles, others like gnarled fingers reaching out, yet others like a cock's crest or the ridged back of an angry iguana.

And the setting sun caught the red of the sandstone and turned it blood red. Even Bell felt there was something awe-inspiring in the sight, as he drove around the corner into the main—and just about only—street in Sedona. That night, he treated himself to a real steak and half a bottle of good red wine. The challenge was still all ahead of him but somehow he felt in a buoyant mood. If it didn't work, fuck it. There was always Nicaragua to fall back on—and several interesting situations developing in and around Africa. Smoke goes up, leaves fall down, there are always wars and rumors of wars for the fighting soldier. That night, he managed to get up to 107 fling-ups and felt ready for any physical effort.

Next morning, when he got up, he combed his hair down across his forehead and in a junkshop off the main street of Sedona bought a pair of old-fashioned gold-rimmed spectacles with virtually plain glass lenses. Glancing at himself in a mirror, he reckoned that he might pass as a mature student if spotted in the environs of Minter, particularly if he were carrying a few books under one arm. The junkshop also had a display of secondhand books and he bought a few of the more scholarly looking ones.

It was time to drive to Prescott and on to Minter College. The road wound to and fro up the side of the pine-clad mountain, through Clarkdale and on up to Jerome. When the local copper mines had been busy, Jerome must have been a boom town with garish hotels and saloons. But the copper lode had been exhausted, the miners drifted away, and Jerome was now a ghost town with its cobbled streets, potholes, and the dejected air of an elderly person waiting at a bus stop for the last bus, which had already gone. It was almost a relief to wind on down the mountainside to the plains and Prescott. He booked himself into a motel on the north side of town and then, donning his disguise—the changed hairstyle and the old-fashioned spectacles—drove on up Route 89 toward Chino Valley. A side road led the mile or two up to the campus and he parked the rented car in a communal parking lot, picked up his secondhand books and tucked them under one arm, and began to walk with apparent purpose around the campus.

Some years before, he had attended a military conference at a college in Cambridge, England, and he at once saw what Eugene Minter had taken as his model. There were large expanses of lawn, surprisingly green and smooth considering the desert climate, surrounded by low gray stone buildings. It looked to his inexpert eye like Portland stone specially imported from England. But when you've got a few billion dollars to fling around, what are a few hundred tons of stone shipped five thousand miles? He saw that Virginia creepers and even ivy had been trained along some of the buildings. Less than twenty years ago, this had been open scrubland; the only moving thing on it would have been the occasional ball of tumbleweed rolling aimlessly along on the wind. And now it was thronged with students, laughing and chattering as they moved from one lecture hall to another.

He walked quite quickly, with apparent purpose, around the campus. He knew from experience of undercover operations that people often take you for granted if you seem to have the right and a reason to be in that spot at that time. It is the aimless stroller, the person who keeps stopping and staring at something, who arouses suspicion. He passed the lecture halls, the laboratories, and the halls of residence before coming to the playing fields, set away behind the buildings. All the time he was making mental notes. A high wall with an archway formed the main entrance to Minter College and a lower wall extended on either side, forming a half circle and encompassing the main college buildings. But the two wings of the wall came to an end when the playing field area was reached. A wire link fence took over and completed the circle away at the back of the games fields.

Forming a rough figure eight but with a gap of perhaps

two or three hundred yards from the far side of the campus was Eugene Minter's estate. Bell decided that it would be too risky to inspect the perimeter fence in daylight. He would wait for the cover of darkness. So, satisfied with what he had taken in on the first inspection, he strode back to the parking lot and drove quickly back to Prescott.

He stopped off at a shopping mall and went first to a hunting and sporting goods store, where he bought a Rambo knife and a camouflage suit made of denim, a pair of lace-up boots with rubber soles, and a pair of thick socks. Next door, at a dry goods store, he bought a pair of wire cutters. Each time, he paid cash. He blessed his fore-thought at having brought with him from England one of the latest Pilkington image-intensifying nightscopes, which he had "liberated" from Army stores. He had guessed that, whatever he did on arriving in the States, night operations could be involved. And before leaving Yardley's married quarters that afternoon, he had slipped a half-used tube of camouflage grease into his pocket. It had been lying in a welter of old pencils, ballpoint pens, and china-graphs on Yardley's desk. It would be useful for darkening his face and hands when he did his night reconnaissance.

He locked all the items in the trunk of the car and drove the short distance back to his motel. He guessed that approaching Minter formally by telephone for an interview held out no hope at all. But at least he could make Minter aware of his presence in the neighborhood, arouse his curiosity perhaps, before the confrontation—because there was going to be one.

First he put in a call to the college switchboard. "Can you put me through to Mr. Eugene Minter, please?"

"Mr. Minter does not reside in college."

"Then would you give me his private number?"

"I am not authorized to disclose his number to outside callers."

This jerk makes like a professor, Bell thought, just

because he's on a college switchboard. He put the receiver down.

Then he dialed Minter's private ex-directory number, which he had taken from Yardley's files. The telephone at the other end rang for about twenty seconds before a voice—which sounded like a superior servant's voice, the butler perhaps—said gravely, "Mr. Minter's residence."

"Is he there?"

"Yes, but he's not to be— Who *is* that speaking?"

"A man he needs to meet."

"I'm sorry, sir, Mr. Minter does not speak to strangers." The butler rang off.

Bell waited for two minutes. At least he had established that Minter was at home. He dialed the private number again. This time, the butler answered after the first ring.

Bell said, "I want to speak to Mr. Minter."

"Oh, it's you again," said the voice. "I don't know how you managed to get hold of this number but let me tell you, Mr. Minter does not speak to all and sundry."

"He's going to speak to me, and soon enough," Bell said. "You just tell him that. Got it?" And he rang off before the butler could beat him to it.

That night, he went on his reconnaissance. He drove up through Chino Valley and parked his car under a clump of evergreen trees off the road. He had brought just the nightscope, the wire cutters and the tube of camouflage grease, plus a heap of tissues from the motel bathroom to wipe off the grease afterward. Without risking putting on the courtesy light in the car, he covered the backs of his hands, his wrists, his neck and face, even his eyelids, with the grease, using deft, experienced strokes. God knows how often, he thought, I've done this before. When he had emptied the pockets of his good suit before changing, he had come across the SAS felt cap badge in the top lefthand pocket and on an impulse had brought it with him. It was nestling in the equivalent pocket of his denim blouse.

There was a thin moon that would soon be setting behind the range of hills away to his left, but there was a time when he had been known as "Cat's Eyes" in the Twenty-two Squadron. With his own extraordinary night vision and the occasional help of the nightscope, there was little difference to him between daylight and dark. The evening was chill and he set off at a fast lope across the fields toward the Minter redoubt. He had the pair of wire cutters stuck in his belt in case of strong and high fences but the fields were open. Every now and then, he halted and lay flat on his stomach, peering ahead to discover what undulations in the ground lay in front and to catch his first glimpse of Minter's outer perimeter fence. After moving briskly but silently for something over ten minutes, he saw the fence.

Just then, floodlights suddenly came on at the four corners, each of them shining down its own side of the rough square. They remained on for fifteen seconds, he judged from the sweep hand of his luminous dial, and then went out simultaneously. He lay absolutely still in a small hollow, looking at the luminous dial of his watch face, which he was cupping in his right hand so that not even a speck of light would be seen. Exactly five minutes went by and the lights came on again, stayed on for the fifteen seconds and went out. Again, he remained still, gazing at the watch face. This time, four minutes elapsed before the lights came on. The next time it was three minutes and so on. After the one-minute interval, the frequency switched back to five minutes, then four minutes, and way back down to one minute, and then back again and back again. Bell stayed without moving for an hour, during which time four sequences of the lights took place. Stupid rich sod, that Minter, he thought; goes to some fancy-dan electronics expert, probably some whiz kid from the college, and gets a nice program you could set your watch by. No surprises for the would-be burglar, no erratic time scheme to keep him off balance. Some people asked to be turned over.

Silently, he rose to a crouch and walked slowly around the perimeter fence. He kept all of two hundred yards away as he went but, even so, he kept an eye on his watch and dropped to the ground each time just before the floodlights came on. He reckoned that the outer fence—when the floodlights came on, he could see there was an inner fence as well—was about two thousand meters in length. He remembered his field studies—multiply by seven and divide by twenty-two to get the diameter. He did some mental arithmetic and calculated that the diameter would be a shade over six hundred meters. Which made the distance from the outer fence to the house itself around three hundred meters. The next time there was a five-minute interval coming up, he slid over to the fence, making sure first that there were no trip wires extending from it, and minutely inspected the outer fence, then the lower inner fence and the area beyond. He slipped back into the darkness beyond the floodlights before they came on but, as soon as they were extinguished, he was back for the four-minute spell. Through the nightscope, he inspected the eastern side of the large house in the center of the grounds. Once he was satisfied that there was no more to be gleaned from inspecting the eastern side, he moved around to the north and followed the same procedure and then, finally, the west side. As there was no great distance between the perimeter fence on the south side and the fence around the college playing fields, he decided it would be too risky to inspect that side, not least because the main gateway into the Minter estate was sited there. There was a small building alongside it, inside the wire—a kind of keeper's lodge, he thought—and there was bound to be someone there all the time. He had gained enough information for one night, and now that bottle of duty-free Scotch back at the motel beckoned. He slid away into the enveloping night.

He wiped the camouflage grease off his hands, face, and neck before driving back to Prescott, but once inside the motel he took a long, hot shower, poured himself three fingers of Scotch, and lying back on the bed and sipping the Scotch, made a mental summary of what he had discovered. The lighting system was a doddle—a crying shame to have spent good money on a stupid toy. No problem there. The outer fence was more serious. It was three meters high and had an electric wire threaded through the top links. The rubber sheath of the wire was the wrong diameter for an electrocuting charge. Anyway, Minter would not risk animals blundering into it or students out on a lark being fried by a high-voltage charge. No, it was an alarm system that must be wired through to the house.

The inner fence, which was sited five meters inside the outer one, was on similar lines but lower in height. Without being able to measure it accurately, he estimated that it was four to five meters high. It too was wired up but again the workman had been either lazy or stupid and had run the wire along the top of the fence. In places, Bell had noticed that it hung in loops between one support and the next.

He had studied the ground level on either side of both fences with the utmost care, using his own keen night sight and the scope when necessary. It was as well, because just inside the inner fence he had noticed that the ground was a lighter shade—indeed, that a belt, some six feet wide, of that lighter shade ran around the whole inside length of the inner fence. A pressure pad! That was quite smart, Bell thought, draining his Scotch and pouring himself another. Even if you got over or through both of the wired-up fences without killing yourself or raising the alarm, how did you fly in the air across that pressure pad without touching it? And if you did touch it, the warning bells would ring loud and clear back in the house. An idea came to him and his lips twitched in a mirthless grin.

Now for the house itself. It had appeared to be in total

darkness but that could be due to shades and thick cur-
tains. It was a sizeable house, built mainly on two floors
with a turret making a third story on each corner. It
recalled to Bell the kind of Georgian country mansion,
standing in its own park, that he had occasionally visited
when being lunched or dined by one of the richer officers
in the Regiment. There were clumps of trees in the grounds
of the Minter estate but none close to the house that would
provide hidden access to an intruder. But there had been a
series of low buildings alongside the main one—kennels,
he guessed, because he had heard faintly the low-pitched
yelping and growling that spelled out Doberman pinschers.
And hungry ones at that. He had picked out two of them
from the alternating noises, and he hoped to Christ he had
gotten that one right. The house itself would of course be
wired up against intruders, but there were usually ways to
get around that. Some years before, the SAS had been
called on secretly to test the British prison security system.
Wormwood Scrubs, Dartmoor, the top security jail at
Parkhurst—the order had been, "Go and break in and then
get out again without the warders knowing." They had
done it. And he had been on one of the successful teams.

On the whole, he thought that Minter had protected
himself pretty well. The various systems combined would
be a match for a good professional burglar: eight marks out
of ten, perhaps. But they were not going to keep him out.

The next afternoon, he went back to the same shopping
mall. He was taking a certain risk that his face would be
remembered, but tonight's the night, he thought. If it
doesn't work out tonight, I'll be out of Arizona like shit
off a shovel. So the risk was small enough. At the dry
goods store, he bought a three-foot length of wire with two
dog clips, a glass cutter, and a roll of strong plastic tape.
At the small supermarket, he bought a large piece of fresh
fish. Behind the mall, he stole a sack from a pile lying in a
corner. Finally, he called in at the sporting goods store.

There he bought a stout fishing rod. As the storekeeper, a little man with pink cheeks and wire-rimmed spectacles dipping on his snub nose, was wrapping it up, Bell leaned across the counter and said casually, "How do I go about getting some personal protection? Know what I mean?"

The man's eyes gleamed, "You mean you want a handgun, sir?"

"That's about the shape of it. You have some mighty unfriendly citizens here in Arizona. Why, on the way up here, I was buzzed by a bunch of Hell's Angels. You know, guys with beards and headbands, riding those crazy bikes with high handlebars."

"I know them. Scum, real scum. The state police should lock 'em all up and throw away the key. I take it you're from out of state, sir?"

"Sure am."

"That's too bad. You have to show a state driving license before I can sell you a handgun. I'd like to help, honest, but the sheriff here is as strict as hell. Spends all his time watching honest traders when he ought to be out chasing those Hell's Angels off the highways."

"That's a real shame," Bell said. "I'd have paid good money for a Browning nine millimeter."

"I can see you know a thing or two about guns, sir." The little man leaned forward confidentially across the counter and lowered his voice, although there was no one else in the store. "Reckon I could help you. You know Flagstaff—just a piece up the road? There's a permanent gun fair on the east side of town, on the highway to Holbrook, on some open ground just beyond the big Exxon gas station, on the left as you're leaving Flagstaff. The guy who runs it's a friend of mine. Big fat guy, name of Richards. You go see him. Tell him Tom Fisher sent you. That's me, Tom Fisher's the name. He'll fit you up—but cash, mind, no credit cards, you get me." The little man gave a conspiratorial wink.

"That's mighty obliging," Bell said. As he paid for the

fishing rod, he slid an extra ten-dollar bill across the counter. "Don't take it wrong," he added. "I'd like for you to have a drink on me tonight. You don't know how helpful you've been."

It was as the little man had forecast. Bell drove the fifty or so miles to Flagstaff, found the gun fair on a patch of open ground next to some trestle tables where somber-faced Indians were selling Navajo rugs, beads, and silver-ware and bought the Browning nine-millimeter Hi Power off the fat Mr. Richards. He went through the rigmarole of saying that Tom Fisher had sent him, but for all the notice that the phlegmatic, gum-chewing dealer took, he reckoned that he could have said that Ronald Reagan had suggested it.

Darkness had fallen by the time he was back in Prescott, and now he was ready to complete his stores.

When checking in at the motel, he had noticed that, a hundred yards or so behind it, there was a small housing development for what seemed to be blue-collar workers, judging by the lines of washing in the backyards and the state of the cars parked outside. There were street lamps on the development but they were wide spaced. Once it was dark he changed into his denim suit, took the sack and the hunk of fish, and moved like a ghost across to the houses. He put part of the fish out behind one backyard where he had seen cats playing earlier, and then stood back in the shade of the fence. In a few minutes, a large tabby cat came out to sniff the fish. In a flash, Bell had it by the scruff of the neck and flung it into the sack he held in his left hand. After one startled yelp, the cat stayed silent. It had little choice, because from the outside of the sack Bell's right hand was gripping it around the neck.

He waited patiently like a statue in the shade of the fence for another ten minutes until a second, smaller cat came wandering along and stopped to sniff at the fish. Once again, he moved like a snake striking, and the second cat was in the sack. Unhurriedly, he scooped up the fish and dropped it into the sack—mustn't be unduly cruel to animals, he thought—and then he vaulted across a low wicket gate and went over to a stout clothesline pole, which he had spotted earlier that afternoon in his reconnaissance. He removed it from the line it was supporting and silently moved back to the motel. He opened the trunk of his car, tied a loose knot in the top of the sack, and dumped the cats into the trunk. He reckoned that enough air would percolate through the fairly open weave of the sack to keep them alive—at least, as long as he needed them. Next, he took out the roll of strong adhesive tape and lashed the clothesline pole to the underside of the car, avoiding the risk of its getting burned through contact with the exhaust pipe. Now, all was ready.

He waited quietly in his darkened motel room for a party of revelers, carrying a crate of beer cans, to go into the next room but one, shouting and laughing as they went. Then, gathering up the rest of his equipment, he left the room, unlocked the car door, and drove at moderate speed north toward Chino Valley. He parked the car under a different clump of trees, two or three hundred yards away from the site he'd used the night before. Then, with all his gear, he moved slowly and silently through the night toward the Minter estate. In the distance, he could see pinpoints of light every few minutes, like the circulating lamp of a lighthouse, and he knew them to be the floodlights on the fence around the estate. What a giveaway, he thought.

The night before, he had seen that there was one area of dead ground within about thirty yards of the fence that remained in darkness even when the floodlights were on. Whoever sited the fence had been either clumsy or not very smart. The dark space was about fifteen feet long and perhaps eight feet wide, more than enough for his purpose. So the next time there was a long pause before the floodlights came on again, he moved himself and his gear into the dead ground. Now he had to be patient and wait for the next five-minute gap to come around. While waiting, he undid the button of the top lefthand pocket of his denim blouse and fingered the SAS cap badge for luck.

When the moment was right, he slipped over to the outer fence and attached the three-foot length of wire to it with the dog clips. Then he took the strong fishing rod and began to cast over the outside fence at the electric wire running along the inner fence. Each time the hook fell short, he jerked it back like a fly fisherman to avoid contact with the outer fence. On the fourth attempt he hooked the inner wire and began to take up the slack by reeling it in. The wire suddenly pulled tight—it must have hit a snag on the fence—and for a moment he wondered whether the fishing line would take the strain. But hold it did, and after he had waggled it gently to and fro a few times, the wire loosened and he continued slowly but inexorably to reel it in toward the bridge he had made with the other wire and the dog clips. He maneuvered all three lengths of wire until they touched. The bridge was complete, effectively giving him a gap in the wire. There was a smell of burning rubber, and a few seconds later, a light came on in the ground floor of the Minter house. Was it coincidence, Bell wondered, or had someone already spotted that the warning system on the fences was suffering a slight voltage drop? Always safer to assume the worst, he thought. So—no time to hang around—let's go!

He slung the sack with the cats still in it over one shoulder and picked up the clothesline pole. He chose a level run up and vaulted easily over the outer fence. So far, so good, but the next one was a real bitch. The fence might be low but the run up was shortened and the six-foot-wide pressure pad beyond it also had to be cleared. He took a few deep breaths to steady himself, worked out the approach that would give him the longest run up without his coming at the fence at too acute an angle, then picked up the pole. Go for it, he said under his breath, ran up to

the fence, dug the pole in and hurled himself up and across
the gap. His left heel landed three inches inside the pressure pad and for a second he teetered dangerously, almost
falling back onto the pad. With an immense effort, he held
his balance and then slid forward facedown on the ground.

As he did so, he unhitched the sack from his shoulder.
There was no time to lose. The cats were getting restless,
mewing and writhing in their dark prison. Just as well,
because he could hear across the stillness of the night
voices coming from the kennels and the excited yelping of
the Dobermans. He released the cats and gave them a
shove toward the house. They needed no further instructions but dashed off into the night. They'll keep the
Dobermans busy for the next ten minutes, he thought, as
he lay absolutely rigid. He did not want to distract the
dogs by sound or movement from their quarry, the cats,
though he knew from experience that the dogs would never
catch them. The Dobermans rounded the corner of the
house like a pair of fighter aircraft in close formation.

He kept his gaze steady on the house, to mark the
ground-floor room where the light had come on. That
meant it must be excluded from the warning system for the
house itself. A few minutes later the light went off, but he
had memorized the position of the room. There was still
just a chance that the room where the light went on and off
was a kind of decoy—and that it really was wired up to the
rest of the warning system. So he studied it quickly but
carefully, finding the gain of his image intensifier very
effective for the operation. He reckoned it was safe.

Away to his right, he could hear one of the cats howling
in fright. There was not a moment to lose. He ran lightly
across the two- or three-hundred-meter gap between the
inner fence and the house, jinking as he went in case there
was someone inside the house taking aim at him through
the nightsight of a high-powered hunting rifle. But as he
ran a snipe's course, he watched his target, the safe room.

He tried the door handle. Locked. He had expected that.

It was a matter of seconds to attach strips of the sealing
tape to the window. Then he took out the glass cutter and
scored a circle on the pane close to the doorknob and
around the sealing tape. He gently pressed the circle of
glass. Then he slid a hand through the gap, found the key
in the lock on the inside—someone was a real idiot to have
left it there—and turned it. A quick shove and he was
inside. He closed the door quietly behind him, switched on
a table lamp, and looked around.

It seemed to be the library, judging from the rows of
leather-bound books on the shelves. There was a marble
fireplace—Adam? he wondered—and a painting above it
that yelled Old Master at him. There were big leather
chairs, just like those at the Athenaeum, over on one side
of the room and a polished mahogany table alongside,
bearing drinks and cut-glass tumblers. A nice sight, he
thought, wall to wall money.

On a side table near the fireplace, he saw, there was a
telephone with instructions printed alongside the buttons.
He picked it up, dialed ''0'' and when a voice answered,
said abruptly, ''Tell Mr. Minter to come at once to the
library. It's very urgent.'' He rang off, went and sat down
in one of the leather chairs facing the door into the room,
took out the Browning automatic and the hunting knife and
placed them softly on the gleaming surface of the table.
Then he waited.

He had not long to wait. A few minutes later, a burly-
looking man charged into the room, followed by a tall,
thin man in glasses and a shorter, swarthy man with
crinkly hair. Bell sat back in the armchair, knees crossed,
gently swinging the foot that was in the air. ''Doctor
Minter, I presume,'' he said. ''Well, if you won't answer
my telephone calls—''

''What the hell are you doing in my house? And who
are you? Go and get him,'' Minter shouted to the burly
man.

''I wouldn't if I were you,'' Bell said softly. ''Not if

you don't want blood—his blood—on your nice Persian carpet. Tell him to go away. I've eaten better men than him for breakfast.''

Minter hesitated. The coolness and confidence of this apparent burglar took him out of his stride, as Bell had intended. As he wavered, the third man said something softly to him and, somewhat sheepishly, he told the body-guard to leave the room. Round one to me, Bell thought. Keep going while the advantage is with you.

''Let's all sit down and be friends,'' he said. ''You're going to find that you need me, and I don't mind admitting I need you and all your money.''

''This is pre-preposterous,'' Minter said agitatedly. He was pacing up and down, cracking the joints of his long bony hands as he went. ''You come busting into *my* house, unannounced, uninvited, and have the gall to sit there and talk about being friends? It's like a nightmare!''

''Relax,'' Bell said soothingly. ''Just relax. Look, I tried to do the decent thing and call you up for an appoint-ment. Twice yesterday and twice again today. What hap-pens? I get the bum's rush. 'Mr. Minter does not make appointments with strangers.' So if you won't see me the ordinary way, I have to find another way, don't I?''

He hurried on before Minter could protest again. ''And just think of this. What did all the security here cost you? You're probably too grand to notice a dirty thing like money, so I'll give an educated guess. Somewhere be-tween a million and a half and two million dollars. That pressure pad alone cost a buck or two, I'll bet. And what happens? It didn't take an army with a lot of sophisticated equipment to get through your defenses. It took just one man, and all he needed was bought in the shopping mall down the road in Prescott. Is the message getting through to you?''

The swarthy man tugged Minter by the sleeve and mo-tioned to him to sit down. Minter obeyed, which interested

Bell. Then the swarthy man said, "You're English." It was more of a statement than a question.

Bell said, "Yes."

"And I suspect you are, or were, in the SAS."

Bell nodded.

The man turned to Minter and said, "You must have heard of the SAS, Gene. Remember that Iranian embassy siege in London, which was televised as it was happening? Those men in black assault suits throwing stun grenades through the windows? Well, that was the SAS. It's a special *corps d'élite* taken from all ranks in the British Army and trained to do almost anything in the line of fighting."

He went on talking to Minter, patiently, slowly, almost as an adult might talk to a young but promising child. "In spite of his—ah—unorthodox entry, I think we should hear him out, Gene. Look, I don't suppose he took all this trouble and risked a savage mauling from your dogs just to win a bet. And he's already done you one kindness. Proved that your security needs overhauling quickly. It can't hurt us to listen to him for a while." He turned to Bell, "My name is Abu Sayeed. Yes, I'm a Palestinian, a graduate of Cairo University and Professor of Arab Studies here at Minter College. Would you like a drink?"

"That's very civil of you," Bell said. "Yes, I'd like a Scotch. On the rocks, please, but with a dash of soda, if you've got it."

"We have everything," Sayeed answered. "And then some more as well." He busied himself at the drinks table, while Minter sat motionless, seemingly stunned, clasping his chin and leaning forward like Rodin's statue.

Sayeed went over to Bell and handed him the cut-glass tumbler. Bell took an appreciative sniff. It was a straight malt. There was something to being rich, he thought. He noticed that Minter was not drinking and that Sayeed had poured himself a token Perrier water with the inevitable slice of lemon.

"Before we get cozy, as you might put it—oh, yes, I lived in London for several years before coming West," Sayeed said, "don't you think it would be a nice gesture to remove the—the hardware?" He gestured at the Browning automatic and the hunting knife on the table. "I promise you we're not fighting men. Besides, you could easily deal with an elderly fat Arab and an unfit American with your bare hands, I'm sure!"

Bell smiled and slipped the gun and the knife back inside his belt. This man is pretty smooth, he thought, with a mingled sense of admiration and suspicion.

"That's better," Sayeed said. "I have always preferred butter to guns." He patted his ample belly. "Besides, it mars a peace conference if one comes armed to it. Now, without being insulting, may I ask you a few questions?"

Bell nodded, sipping his drink the while.

"First, would you confirm that you are, or were, in the SAS?" He saw Bell hesitate and went on quickly, "You might as well tell me the truth. There's one thing about enormous wealth—it buys information very quickly. If we wanted to, we could find out almost everything about you in seventy-two hours at the outside. It will be quicker and easier if you would kindly tell me the truth."

"Fair enough," Bell said. "I'm thirty-six years of age. I spent the last seventeen of them in the Regiment. I'd reached the rank of captain and wasn't going to go any higher. Northern Ireland is a dirty little war and there wasn't much happening elsewhere, so I took my discharge— just the other day. An honorable discharge, of course."

"Of course. And your name?"

"Bell. Tim Bell—short for Timothy."

"Yes. I may not be a Christian but I do understand Christian names! Now the question that's been on my mind since our dramatic confrontation just now. Why the break-in? It can't just be because someone put the phone down on you. This is an unmannerly country, Captain Bell. You would be extremely busy breaking into every house where the occupant had slammed down the phone on you. What do you want of us? And, more to the point, how did we become of interest to *you?*"

Bell noticed how Sayeed had taken easy command, not only of the situation but of Minter as well. Minter had still not uttered a word, but he was no longer clasping his chin. His head was turning from one to the other as they spoke, like a spectator at a tennis match. He appeared to be utterly shell-shocked.

Bell said, "It's a long, involved story. Besides, your host looks as though he needs more time to take all this in. I've an idea to put to him—and you—but I need to know more about Minter College and what it really stands for before I tell you my secret. If then. You've already got some idea of what I can do if I put my mind to it. And I haven't come all this way from England, at *my* own expense, to waste your time, let alone my own. So what I suggest is we break it up for now and I come back tomorrow for a longer spell."

"That makes good sense," Sayeed said. "Don't you think so, Gene?" Minter managed to nod and say a croaky "Yes." Sayeed went on, "Where are you staying, Captain Bell?" When he saw Bell hesitate, he added, "You might as well tell me. It must be in the state of Arizona and we have means of checking every hotel and motel from the Grand Canyon to Tombstone inside twenty-four hours. I am learning quickly not to underestimate you, so please do not underestimate us—or the power of money."

"Fair enough. I'm staying at the motel just this side of Prescott, the Desert Ranch."

Sayeed said, "I suggest you check out tomorrow. You can come and stay here with us. Can't he, Gene? There's a guest wing that's unoccupied."

"Would I be a guest, or a prisoner?"

"Come, come, Captain Bell, that's an unworthy suspicion. I assure you our intentions are the friendliest. Besides, if you can break in here so easily, what's to stop you breaking out again if you felt—shall we say?—that you had exhausted your welcome? I take it you have a rented car parked somewhere out there.''

Bell nodded.

"Again, I suggest that you check it in tomorrow. We have a fleet of cars here. I will send a driver to pick you up at the Desert Ranch at—what shall we say? Let us make it two o'clock in the afternoon. That means there will still be an hour or two of daylight if you want to have a look at the college itself. Though, being a good soldier, I expect you've done that already!''

This guy's no fool, thought Bell. He needs careful watching. Aloud, he said, "You're taking a great deal of trouble for a stranger.''

"What's that saying they have in Yorkshire, England? 'Cometh the hour, cometh the man.' '' Sayeed did a passable imitation of a broad Yorkshire accent. "I have a feeling you may be the man.''

SWOLLEN WITH CUNNING OF A SELF-DECEIT.

151

THIS IS THE life, Bell thought, twenty-four hours later, as he was once again sitting in the library with Minter and Sayeed. This time, he was fondling a balloon glass of cognac—Delamain Frères—after a splendid dinner. Money can't buy you happiness, he thought, but at least it gives you the run of Harrods and Neiman-Marcus. There had been maids and a manservant in attendance from the moment of his arrival. His grip had been taken from him, his few clothes and spare shirts unpacked, and his bed turned down in readiness for the night. He had not been in his room in the south turret for five minutes when the bedside telephone purred. He picked it up and the voice of Sayeed came into his ear. "We thought you might be traveling light, so I took the liberty of sending one of our helicopters into Phoenix this morning and buying several suits and shirts from the best outfitters there. I hope they're more or less your size. The suits are hanging in the wardrobe alongside the bed. I'm not sure where they've put the shirts but no doubt you'll find them."

"I don't know what to say," Bell said.

"Please. As they say here, be my guest."

That afternoon, Minter had not been on view when he had arrived. Still getting over the shock, he supposed. But Sayeed had been on the steps leading up to the main door and had greeted him warmly, like an old friend and not a strange intruder. They had spent the afternoon touring Minter College and had sat in on one of the lectures for some twenty minutes. Bell could hardly make head or tail of the lecture. It had been delivered at breakneck speed by a middle-aged black man—an African, Bell reckoned, from his accent and tribal scars—and, from what he could vaguely pick out, the theme was that force is acceptable, even desirable, in a situation in which democratic means had either failed or were nonexistent. Bell recalled the old mercenary joke—"Me freedom fighter, you terrorist!"—and wondered why the young audience was listening so intently to this old black windbag.

And now, after a fine dinner and a choice of exquisite wines, it was time to get down to brass tacks. Gene Minter had appeared a different man during dinner, at ease and dignified, but it had largely been small talk as the soft-footed servants had moved to and fro behind the magnificent oak table in the dining room.

Bell said, "This is where I start singing for my supper, I suppose. But before I tell you anything of my plans, I need to know more about you. Oh, I know quite a bit already. I didn't just stick a pin in the map to hit on this place. You, Mr. Minter, are one of the richest men in the world—"

"Anyone who can read knows that," Sayeed interrupted.

"Granted. But the readers don't know this next bit. You didn't leave the State Department with a great career in front of you to run your father's businesses. That may have been the official reason but it doesn't wash. There was that girl in West Berlin, for example." He paused and looked hard at Minter. Somewhere in a cheap novel, he had read the phrase "a guilty start," and now he realized that life does imitate bad fiction. It was exactly what Minter did. His whole body jerked like a fish the moment it is hooked and in the dim light of the dining room he appeared to blush.

"I'm not sure I like the tone of this conversation," Minter said and turned to appeal to Sayeed.

There was a brief pause, then Sayeed said slowly, "You are remarkably well informed, Captain Bell. This is not the kind of information, I think, that gets bandied around the officers' mess in Hereford, England. May I ask who briefed you?"

"You may, indeed. I was coming to that. Minter College and you, Mr. Minter, are under surveillance by the FBI. Surely you must have guessed that?"

Sayeed nodded his head slowly. "We have had a vague suspicion—nothing firm but an uneasy feeling. And what you say explains various small incidents. Yes, I accept you're probably right."

"Damn sure I'm right! You see—and I want you both to take this in—I've had access to the CIA files. I'll tell you how. It's a small world in the Special Forces. There are only a few hundred of us in England and the States put together. And we often share training facilities and swap secret information. Why, I've been assigned to Fort Bragg four or five times in my career and quite a few Delta Force officers and men come over and do some training with us in Europe. I called in at Bragg only a few days ago and had a long session with an old mate of mine. He shouldn't have done but he did—he showed me the file on you."

"But we've done nothing wrong," Minter said in a blustering voice. "It's no crime to leave the State Department. People do it every day. And it's no crime to set up a college with particular departments and faculties. What's wrong with that?"

"Nothing, in my book," Bell said. "But look what you're teaching. This country's gone farther right under Reagan's presidency. The people waiting to take over later this year are farther right still. Some of them make him look distinctly pink! And here you are, preaching the gospel of the far left. That stuff I was listening to this afternoon from that African National Congress guy, or whatever he was. Back there in Washington, D.C., they don't like that kind of talk. Look, don't get me wrong. The Seventh Cavalry isn't about to ride in and arrest the lot of you. But the CIA know all about that brother of yours, Mr. Sayeed. He wouldn't talk but the other two arrested with him sang to Shin Beth, who passed the file on to the CIA. So you're a marked man. And with him on your staff, Mr. Minter, what do you expect? At Bragg they call you a bomb without a fuse. That's why I'm here. I'm the fuse!''

"I wonder whether your friend at Bragg may not have missed the whole point. Forgive me,'' said Sayeed, ''but we do have our own plan, and there's nothing illegal about it. The students here are carefully screened and inter- viewed in great depth before they are admitted to Minter College. They have to be of a superior IQ—we test them for that—and with positive personalities. Here, they take all the regular courses, but we also have an essential course on political philosophy, in which we influence them—you would call it indoctrinating them—toward Marx- ist beliefs. When they leave here, most of them will go into the professions or into government positions. Many will take up politics at local or state level. They will all be young and upwardly mobile men and women, many of whom will go far, and some may rise to the very top. And they will all have gone underground when they leave here. Beneath the surface, they will be burrowing away like a pack of moles. What do you think of our plan?''

"Very neat, as far as it goes. But isn't it going to take an age? Tell me, how many students graduate from here each year?''

"At present, around five hundred. We have plans to double that number over the next five years.''

Bell said, "Let's call it an average of seven-fifty in the near future. And how long has the plan been in operation?"

"It started about six years ago, but that was in a very small way. We just picked out half a dozen promising sophomores and tested the scheme on them. To be precise, it is only a couple of years since we got into full swing."

"They leave here in their early twenties? It's gonna take them at least another twenty years to get into positions with power and influence. So you're looking well into the next century before the revolution arrives! With respect, you and Mr. Minter here could be dead by then, and I'll be thinking of applying for my old age pension.

"And if you are still around by then," he went on, "what happens? Do you give the signal—and they all throw their ballpoint pens at the secretary of state? Or if they're lawyers in court, do they start being rude to the judge?"

"Please, Captain Bell," Sayeed said. "Forgive me, but that's a rather cheap joke. There will be moments when a future president is about to have a summit meeting with his Soviet opposite number. There will be memoranda produced, summaries of the arguments pro and con, briefings for the secretary of state so that he can in turn brief the president. If we have one or two, maybe more, moles inside the White House at that moment, just think how they could influence things. A short paragraph slanted in a certain direction, a summary that left out a vital point—don't you see the possibilities?

"And another twenty years ahead," he continued, "one of those men assisting the secretary of state will himself occupy the position. Or even be inside the Oval Office itself."

"And by that time we'll all be dead."

"One learns to be patient in the revolutionary business, Captain Bell. Why, it took even Lenin over thirty years and a world war before he brought about the October Revolution. And look at my own people in Palestine—

many of them not in Palestine. They have been forty years in the wilderness—yes, just like the Jews—and they're no nearer getting back to *their* promised land. It's a slow business."

Bell gave Sayeed a cold stare. "Where do your Islamic Brothers figure in all this?"

For the first time, Gene Minter broke into the conversation. He had seemed to be in a world of his own, gazing dreamily at the flames dancing in the open log fire, but he must have been listening intently. "You've seen fit to ridicule our plan, Mr. Bell, but we've heard no detail of yours. Is that fair?"

"Not ridicule, Mr. Minter, please believe me. In fact, I admire it. Your plan is very ingenious and I can see how it might well work. But you both seem content to sit back for at least twenty years and wait for it to happen. That's not my style. I have a plan—the details are not yet fully worked out but the whole thing's broadly there—to take effect inside the next three months."

Minter sat up in his armchair. "Will you tell us your plan?" His tone was level and almost detached.

"In a moment. But first I must get to know you better. If we're going to be partners, I've got to know you well. You already know quite a bit about me—now it's my turn. Let's take you first, Mr. Sayeed. How do you happen to be sitting right here, drinking brandy with a multimillionaire? It's an awful long way from the Middle East."

"You have a forceful way with you, Captain Bell," Sayeed answered. "But may I suggest—if we are going to be partners, as you say—that we drop these formalities? May I call you Tim? And you must call me Sayeed. My full name in fact is Sayeed Abu Sayeed. All it means is Sayeed, the son of Sayeed. The equivalent in your country would be a man named John Johnson. John, the son of John. And Mr. Minter here—Doctor Minter, I should say, because he has several doctorates to his name—is Gene, short for Eugene. Is that all right with you, Gene?"

Minter nodded.

"Well, Tim," Sayeed said, "you want to know about me and my background. I'll try to make it brief. I was born in 1938 in a small town—you would call it a village—a few miles outside Jerusalem. My father was the mayor and a man of some influence. I was his eldest son. Even then, Palestine was in a state of unrest. The Mufti of Jerusalem was a fascist, conspiring against the British Mandate, and your Palestine Police were often brutal toward us.

"My father was not himself an educated man but he made many sacrifices to see that his sons were taught properly. After the Israelis took over our land when I was ten years old, my father managed to smuggle my younger brother and me over the border into Lebanon—to Beirut, where we attended the American College. My brother Hassan was more hot-tempered than me. He flunked out of school at seventeen and joined the PLO. He was shot by the Israelis five years ago. My father never recovered—he just pined away and died. As for me, I won a scholarship to Oregon State University, took my master's degree, saved up enough to take a doctorate at Columbia and then went back to the Middle East, to Cairo, and taught at the university there. Gene here heard of me through a mutual friend at Columbia, and when he decided to found his college, he invited me to advise him. Which I've done ever since. It was useful that we both shared the same political outlook."

"I can well understand your being anti-Jewish," Bell said, "but why Mr. Minter—Gene—here? What's he got against the Jews?"

"What we all should have, Tim. Hate. Hate and fear. What propagandists! Superb is not a strong enough word. Do you know that in one year alone before the war, when Stalin began to collectivize the farms, six million people died in Soviet Russia, either through execution or by famine? *Six million in one year*. The so-called Holocaust claims that number in the whole of the war—six years of it—and most statisticians consider that number a gross exaggeration. But do you see the difference? Only a few of the intelligentsia know about the Russian deaths. The whole world knows about the Holocaust—and keeps on being reminded. That's propaganda for you. Look at the movie industry. Most of the studios are and have been run by Jews. Television the same. The newspapers—Ochs, Sulzberger—not very Aryan, are they? And book publishing—almost totally run by Jews over here. The law. Do you know that over half the lawyers in this country are Jewish? Zionism is like an octopus gradually throttling the United States!''

Bell could see little bubbles of white froth at the corner of his lips. The suave Sayeed had vanished; in his place was this ranting obsessed Arab. But the switch suited Bell perfectly.

"That is my story, Tim," Sayeed continued in a more rational tone. "If you had lost your country to an invader, had your brother murdered, your father dead of grief and the rest of the family dispersed, you too might feel bitter. But you asked about Gene. Many of his memories are still too painful for him to talk openly about them. Gene, do you mind if I give Tim some idea?''

Minter said, "You go ahead." He was holding his left hand in the air, palm away from him, and gazing at his knuckles and fingernails as though he had never seen them before. If Bell had not known otherwise, he would have considered the man a half-wit.

"You have seen his background from those CIA papers, so I'll be brief," Sayeed said. "Gene's father, like Armand Hammer before him, made a fortune trading with the Russians when the rest of America thought they had the plague. Still does, in fact! And he branched out into oil and then real estate. I never knew old Mr. Minter but he wasn't just a money machine. He genuinely believed in the comradeship of nations—that the Soviets had something to teach us in the West—and Gene took it all in as he grew up. That's why he joined the Foreign Service, wasn't it, Gene? He thought he had a contribution to make. And it was all going well up to the time he was posted to West Berlin. There was a girl interpreter attached to the American embassy. Her name was Heidi. Gene didn't need her help—his German was almost as good as hers. But he got to know her and they fell in love.

"He applied through the head of mission in West Berlin to the ambassador in Bonn for permission to marry Heidi. Gene followed the proper protocol in all his dealings with the authorities, even if they didn't follow suit. And what happens? A few days later, it was reported to the head of security at the mission—another Jew, as it happens, Zilliacus—that Heidi had been snatched. She was walking along a street near her home in the suburb of Spandau when a car drew up, two men got out and hustled her inside, and the car drove off at speed. She has never been seen again!"

"God, that's tragic," Bell said. Privately, he thought that she must have been an East German spy. She had sucked Minter dry and now there was this embarrassing talk of marriage, the time had come for her to do a disappearing act.

"The Americans got her," Sayeed said. "Gene's own countrymen headed by a Jew, wouldn't you know. They were grooming Gene for other things. They didn't want him tied down to a German girl, maybe taking a German point of view. They don't deserve men like Gene in the Foreign Service. So he resigned. Even then, it was officially put out that he had resigned in order to look after his father's business interests. Absolute nonsense! His father had already been dead two or three years—hadn't he, Gene?—and several capable trustees were already looking after things with great efficiency. This is Gene's revenge on the system, and I've been proud to assist him. When the system goes rotten, you have to dig the rot out. There can be no half measures. Gene sincerely feels my people have been similarly betrayed by his country's politicians."

"But we come back again to the question of timing," Bell said. "Your method's gonna take twenty years at least before it even begins to show results. Then another twenty before it's really in the big time. I've told you the CIA won't allow you that time. Okay, I hear what you're saying about the long view. But what if something dramatic were to happen—soon? Wouldn't that help to speed up the program?"

"It depends what it was," Sayeed said. "If it were very dramatic and symbolic . . ."

"It's both," Bell said. "But before I tell you what it is, there must be an understanding between us. If you don't want it, we forget this discussion and go our separate ways. Is that agreed?"

"Agreed," said Sayeed promptly.

"What about you, Mr. Minter—Gene?"

"I agree," Minter said. "Do you expect us to cut our wrists and mingle the blood?"

Bell ignored the jibe. "This is my plan," he said. "This coming May—the fifteenth, to be precise—Israel celebrates the fortieth anniversary of the founding of the state. A big celebration dinner has been arranged in New York on the evening of the big day. The guest list is limited to the leading Jews in the arts, in business, and on Wall Street. My plan is—we hijack the dinner!"

16

THE ROOM WAS stilled. A charred log, falling back into the embers in the fireplace, sounded like the crash of a tall pine.

Minter said, "You must be mad!"

"I'm as sane as you are."

Sayeed spoke. "Let's not get into a psychological discussion. It's very ingenious. What my pupils would call 'wild.' But I don't see how it would ever work, Tim. All right, I accept that you might—just might—manage to hijack the dinner party but how do you get away again afterward? Or were you thinking of dying a martyr's death?"

"Not me. I want to live to a ripe old age! In the Regiment they have a saying: Anything you can get into, you can get out of. I haven't worked out all the details as yet, I'd need to spend a day or two in New York and walk the course, but I know that, given ten very fit and trained troops, I can do it."

"You sound very self-confident," Minter said with a sneering edge to his voice.

"I have to be. You see, when it comes to action, I *know* I'm good. In my time, I've fought the Viet Cong, I've fought in Oman, I've fought the Argies, and I've fought the IRA—and all of those were tougher than a bunch of soft, overfed Jews. You want proof I'm good? Just take last night. Who went through your security fences, on his own, like a knife going through butter?"

"He's got a point there, Gene," said Sayeed.

Bell pressed on. "It would be a perfect fail-safe position for you. Okay, I need financing—I don't pretend otherwise. But money's nothing to you, Gene, and you could always pay me in untraceable notes. Take the worst scenario. *I'll* be carrying the can. There'll be nothing to trace it back here. No one would suspect a middle-aged academic running his own college."

"But you said just now that the FBI has a watch on Minter College," Sayeed said quietly.

He's too damn smart, thought Bell. Aloud, he said, "Yes, but it's only general surveillance. They don't suspect any violent action coming out of Minter College. They're more interested in what's taught here and who the tutors are. Which could be a big negative for *your* plan. What's to stop the FBI putting a tag on all your bright boys and following their careers after they graduate? Ever thought of that?"

"You also said just now that you needed ten—was it?—fit and trained troops to help. You can hardly put an advertisement on the noticeboard at Fort Bragg! And it's under three months to May fifteenth. So where do you find your men in that short time?"

"Easy. I need a possible forty to pick from—men who are young, healthy and determined. I can whittle them down to the number I need through rigorous testing. That'd take a couple of weeks, maybe three, and then I need another month—six weeks—to train 'em up. Oh, I could do it all right."

"But you still haven't said where you're going to find them."

"I could start with your football squad. They ought to be fit and healthy."

"But that would pinpoint Minter College. You said you'd keep us out of the picture," said Sayeed.

"You're right. I accept that. Okay, what about this? Gene here owns a lot of real estate in Idaho. Most of it heavily forested."

Sayeed interjected, "Ah, yes, Tim, that reminds me. You're very well informed."

Bell went on, "There's a very rich man named Holliday—calls himself 'Doc' because he claims to be descended from the gunfighter. His company—one of his companies—has a lease on the timber on Gene's land. Now, Holliday is the power behind the Anglo-Saxon Brethren. You must have heard of the ASB? They're further right than Attila the Hun and they're very antiblack as well as very anti-Jew. According to the FBI files, their headquarters is around Hayden Lake in Idaho. I don't suppose for one moment Gene knows Doc Holliday but I'm damn sure he could arrange an introduction for me. There've got to be high-level contacts between his real estate company and Holliday."

"My SAS friend," Sayeed said, "we have a meeting of the minds here." He glanced at Gene Minter, who nodded. "Yes," Sayeed said, "I think that could be arranged. But there is still one question you haven't answered. As they say here, what's the bottom line? Or, to put it more crudely, what's in it for us?"

"It's 'heads you win, tails you can't lose.' Gene here owns several TV stations. Well, if it works, and it will, we can demand that Gene be given equal media time to broadcast his own case. Don't look blank! I tell you, once we've got those famous Jews at gunpoint, most likely with TV coverage, do you think the White House is going to argue? And if it does want a show of strength, we only have to shoot a Nobel Prize winner or a top violinist in front of the cameras to make the president sit up and beg. You seem to forget it's election year, and no one's going to risk the Jewish vote.''

"But if Gene were to make a broadcast, it'd be a public admission he was involved.''

"Not so. As the leader, I'd announce we had done the hijacking in sympathy with Gene Minter's views but he had nothing to do with the plan. And then he would come on the air, denounce me and my band as violent activists, then say his piece. The authorities might suspect but they could never prove a thing.''

Sayeed turned toward Minter, who was gazing at the fire as though he had never seen flames before. "Gene, you're very quiet. What do you think of all this?''

"I find myself in a complete quandary. Part of me is very tempted to go along with Captain Bell's ingenious plan. The chance of speaking to the whole nation, to win them over to our cause—that appeals to me greatly. Another thing. You and I know that this present regime, this so-called government of ours, is impotent when it comes to countering terrorism. But the American people do not realize this. What an opportunity to show up this dithering government on television! They rose to power through manipulating the media, now let them perish by the weapon they created.''

"Then you're in favor, Gene?''

Minter half shook his head. "No. That side attracts me enormously—but there is a reverse side. It comes down to the age-old question of ends and means. If I—we—back Captain Bell, we are advocating terrorism, in a sense, we become terrorists. And terrorism is evil.''

"With great respect, Gene, are you not being just a shade naive?'' Sayeed asked. "Terrorism is a point of view. Today's terrorist is often tomorrow's statesman. Take the very state of Israel whose existence we both abhor. Menachem Begin was refused entry into Britain, declared 'persona non grata' because of his activities with the Stern Gang at the end of the war. A year or two later, he was prime minister of Israel, hobnobbing with all the great and the good. When he goes he hands over to Shamir, another Stern and Irgun man. If the British Army had caught either of them in 1946 or '47, they would have been hanged as terrorists. Two or three years later, they have become patriots, thirty years later they are statesmen.

"Or an even more dramatic case is Jomo Kenyatta in Kenya. One moment, he is the Mau-Mau leader responsible for vicious atrocities on the white settlers, the next he is the revered leader of his independent country. A quick-change artist, indeed! And, more recently, what of our friends in the African National Congress? When Winnie Mandela advocates violence to put an end to apartheid, how do you judge her? Gene, I tell you, it is the end we must always keep in view. The means are the tools to achieve that end. Captain Bell here must forgive me if I say he is our tool. The nail cannot knock itself into the wood. It requires a hammer and a controlling hand. Don't you realize, Gene, you will be that hand?"

Like hell, Bell thought. He was going to be nail, hammer, and hand, all in one. But he said nothing as he gazed without expression at Minter, who took off his spectacles, rubbed his eyes wearily with the knuckles of both hands, replaced the horn-rims and at last said gruffly, "I trust you, Sayeed, old friend. And I trust your judgment. Perhaps our deliberate emphasis on nonviolence has made our progress too slow. The more I think of it, the more attracted I am by the thought of that nationwide publicity. Can you imagine—the whole of America being told the truth at last! It could be a blow the capitalist system would never recover from." Behind the spectacles, his eyes were bright, dilated. "That broadcast—what a moment, what an opportunity! Why, it would advance our cause as nothing else would. And if the siege lasted long enough . . ."

"I'd make it last," came from Bell.

". . . there would be satellite transmissions to Europe. With all my money, I just couldn't buy that kind of publicity," Minter said eagerly.

"But is that the kind we want?" Sayeed asked. "What of our plan to build slowly and surely?"

"Tim here is right. J. M. Keynes put it well. 'In the long run, we are all dead.' No, I like it. And so should you. Sayeed, old friend, you have suffered if any man has. Your beloved younger brother tortured and then shot by those Israelis. Your father dying of his grief. You an exile, wandering the world everywhere but in his own homeland. My sufferings are nothing compared to yours, but at night, when I can't sleep, I keep thinking of Heidi and the way she smiled and waved at our last parting. I was watching her go and at the corner of the road she turned again to catch a glimpse of me. The last one ever. The Jews were behind her disappearance, the way they've been behind every bad move here in our own country. Once I thought that the Democrats might have the answer. There was Adlai Stevenson—but the Jews with their newspapers and their television finished off his campaign before it really started. Now under Reagan, that superannuated actor, the country has lurched ever further to the right in the last seven years. The rich keep more of their riches while the poor despair. Production should be for distribution, not buying and selling shares in Wall Street! The capitalist system is doomed. With Tim's help, we can roll a boulder down the mountainside that may help to crush it."

He had jumped up in his agitation and was pacing up and down the vast room, waving his arms like a Hyde Park orator. Bell could see that his eyes were dilated behind the horn-rimmed spectacles and that patches of crimson suffused his face and neck. You had to hand it to old Gene, he thought. The guy usually sat there like a moron but once the right button was pressed, he was a real raver.

"Do you want to sleep on it?" Bell asked. "The only thing is, if you're not on, I'll have to be up and away early

tomorrow. There are other people to see—maybe I should
have gone straight to Doc Holliday—and I can't hold the
offer open indefinitely. Right now, I'm using my own
cash, and that's not elastic.''

There was a moment's silence. Sayeed stared hard at
Minter, who had sat down again and who for once looked
him straight back in the eye. Then he gave an almost
imperceptible nod. Sayeed turned to Bell and said, ''We're
on. It's a deal.''

That same day, over fifteen hundred miles to the east,
another meeting had taken place. The venue was Bob
Yardley's training office inside Fort Bragg. There were
just two men there, himself and his closest CIA contact, a
man named Joe Dodds.

Dodds had served in Vietnam, heavily involved in covert programs with exotic names like Sigma and Omega.
On his discharge, he had joined the FBI. He was a smart
and straight agent, a not entirely usual combination, and
had risen within a few years to higher ranks. One of his
bosses had mentioned him to a senior friend in the CIA
and after the regular training Dodds had taken his transfer.
He was a big, powerful man but it was a pity, Yardley
thought, that he had gotten so unfit driving a desk. His
belly bulged over the waistband of his trousers like a
Pacific wave about to break.

Dodds was slow spoken and he tended to listen more
than talk. He had the typical cynical attitude of a man
scarred by the dirty secret war in Vietnam. He said, ''I've
asked this before and I'll ask it again. You positive this
room is clean?''

''As a whistle. It's swept at irregular intervals every
week.''

''That still leaves time to plant a bug between sweepings.''

''Sure, Joe. But it was swept this very morning—and
I've not been out since.''

''Okay,'' Dodds said. ''Last time we met, you were

telling me about your friend from Hereford, England." He looked at his notes. "Yeah, that's right—Captain Bell."

"Yes. Do you want a recap?"

"No, thanks, I have it right here. He turned up at Bragg, you took him on a parachute jump, thinking he was still an active soldier, word came through that he'd been kicked out of the SAS and your CO gave you a going over. You met him briefly that night, good as told him to get lost and then left. That about the size of it?"

"Yeah, that's it. I'm beginning to wonder if I didn't act a bit hasty. Never gave him a chance to tell his side of the story."

"There isn't another side. We've had more details through from an MI6 contact. Boy, those Brits are smart! They keep their press and TV right where they want them. Here, it'd have been a front-page, prime-time scandal. Seems he was in charge of two IRA suspects in Northern Ireland. Oh, sure, there'd have been heavy charges against them as long as your arm. But your friend didn't hang around for a trial. He let 'em both have it right between the eyes. The guy must be pathological."

"The SAS always hates scandals. They just rid themselves of him nice and quiet. Lucky Bell, he could have been up for murder. What you just said about him being pathological—you know, that figures."

"What do you mean?"

"I've known him for years. He's usually a relaxed guy but this time he was kind of edgy. Acting the hard man, which isn't like him. He beat up one of our sergeant instructors in a bar, for example. The sergeant probably gave him some lip—they'd run across each other before— but again, it's not like Bell to invite a fight. Those SAS men are trained to be inconspicuous. They'll walk out of a pub rather than get caught up in a fight."

"Did he tell you what he was going to do, Bob?"

"I didn't give him the chance, dammit. I told him to enlist as a merc for the Contras. It was a putdown, really."

"Well, he sure as hell didn't. At least, we think not. There's been a possible sighting. You know we keep a watch on Minter College in Arizona—trying to count the Reds under the beds. One of our local help reported that a man answering to Bell's description—with a little dressing up, dummy spectacles and so on—turned up in Prescott, Arizona, three days ago. Prescott's a small town ten or fifteen miles south of Minter College. He hasn't been seen—if it *is* him—over the last two days but he could've gotten inside the college or gone to ground someplace else. But the big point is, how come he knows about Minter College? It can't be a coincidence."

"If it really is Bell. Lots of guys look like him."

"Oh, we reckon it's Bell all right. He bought some interesting stuff, a hunting knife, camouflage clothes, glass cutters, and that, at stores in the Prescott shopping mall."

"Could be a keen hunter."

"In Arizona? At this time of the year? No, there's been a leak somewhere. Over Minter College, I mean. You sure you never mentioned the place?"

"Oh, for God's sake, Joe. Sure I'm sure. The whole meeting didn't last five minutes. So what happens next?"

"That's the point," Dodds said. "What *does* happen next? It's not like a game of tag—our man goes up to him, touches him on the shoulder and says 'Gotcha!' No, sir. This is supposed to be a free country. We can't stop Captain Bell visiting sunny Arizona."

"You couldn't lean on him a bit? You know, get the local state police to harass him, keep stopping his car for supposed speeding, that sort of thing?"

"That might frighten your maiden aunt, Bob, but it wouldn't make a hard man like Bell burst into tears. And it would only alert him. We want to catch him unawares, if there's anything to catch."

"So what's the drill? I can see an idea building up in that head of yours," Yardley said.

There was a short pause. Dodds began slowly, as though

he were picking his words with infinite care. "Through sources in the UK—don't ask me which 'cause I can't tell you—we managed to get all the details of Bell's career, official and unofficial, faxed through to HQ. He's a helluva fighting man, I grant you that. And we are told the man is angry. But one interesting point stood out. Nothing to do with the regimental side. He had a girlfriend, and later on you married her."

Yardley exploded. "What the fucking hell is all this about? You creeps are worse than the Gestapo. Prying into a man's private life . . ."

"Change the tape, Bob," Dodds said. "No one in this game has the luxury of a private life. You ought to know that. You volunteered, no one stuck a gun to your head."

"Even so, I'm saying, back off my private life. So what if he and Angela were—were friends before I came along? How does that figure?"

"Well, we had half a thought on that. Clearly, you can't suddenly turn up in Prescott, Arizona, or Minter College and just bump into your old friend accidentally. But what if—"

"I know exactly what you're going to say, and the answer is a flat No. Angela is *not* going to act as bait. I'm not having her fly out to Arizona and do a Mata Hari act with Bell. No, sir."

"But if you trust her?"

"I trust Angie all the way, and then a bit further. But it's no go."

"Look, she wouldn't have to go to bed with the guy! Just flutter her eyelashes a bit. All we need to know" —and he ticked the points off on his stubby fingers—"is, A, why he's there, B, what he's trying to achieve and, C, what his next move is."

"And you think he's gonna spill that lot to a pretty girl off the Greyhound bus? You're out of the ballpark, Joe, this is the most naive idea you people've come up with since the Iranian abort. It stinks."

"That one hurt. Right below the belt. So you don't think it would work?"

"Damn sure it wouldn't. I hate talking about my own wife like this, but if there ever was a spark between those two, it sure has burned out. The other night, he and Angie were like brother and sister. Next day, you know, I had to go to Washington, and I did just wonder whether he might take the opportunity to call on Angie. No way. She told me he called up to say goodbye—and that was it. He hightailed off West that same day, she said."

"Well, if there's nothing between them now . . ."

"Don't keep pushing it, Joe. The answer's still a flat No. My wife is my wife, not one of your operators. And she's going to stay that way. Besides, she wants to fly back to England pretty soon and visit her parents. Her mother's been none too well."

"Oh, well," Dodds said, "it was worth a shot. I wish to Christ we could get a tail on him one way or the other. We'll have to do some more brainstorming."

"Is there nothing else I can do?"

"Not for the moment, Bob. Either the whole thing's just a coincidence—Bell's got friends in Arizona and decides to visit them, nothing wrong with that—or it's sinister. In that case, sooner or later he's got to show his hand. Which means all we can do right now is keep a close watch and wait for his next move."

That evening, Yardley went back to his married quarters, flung his briefcase at the sofa, where it bounced off a cushion and landed on the floor, and went over to the drinks table to pour himself three thick fingers of Scotch. Angela, who was tending to the fire, looked up and said, "Temper, temper."

"Sorry, darling, but if you'd been to the kind of crazy meeting I've just had . . ."

"Bad, was it?"

"Bad? It was bloody dreadful. I sometimes think these

CIA guys should be strapped up and taken away! The crazy ideas they come up with.''

"What's it this time?'' she asked. "Hey, go steady with that Scotch. There's still plenty left in the PX.''

"The hell with the PX—I need another now. That's better. You won't believe this. That headcase Joe Dodds—you know him—actually had the gall to suggest that *you* of all people should go and look up Tim Bell and see what he's up to.''

"What?''

"Exactly what I said. The man's a nut.''

"But what's all this about Tim? Why should the CIA be interested? Tim's gone to look for a job. He called me up next morning to say goodbye. I told you when you came home that evening. You remember?''

"Well, it didn't work that way. He flew all round the place—to put the CIA off the scent, I suppose—but he ended up in Arizona.''

"Why Arizona?'' she asked.

"Exactly. Why Arizona? I'll tell you why Arizona. There's a very rich leftie there named Minter who owns a college—and we reckon Tim's gone to see him.''

"And why shouldn't he?''

"Because Minter College is under CIA surveillance. They teach some real hard left stuff there. There are guys with terrorist experience teaching there. I shouldn't be telling you all this, it's hush-hush stuff.''

"And who would I be telling it to? These stuffy Army wives hardly pass the time of day, as it is. And how could Tim get hold of your secrets?''

"That's what I'd like to know.''

"If it *is* Tim, it could just be a coincidence. Maybe this rich man needs a bodyguard. But what's made my little Bobbie all angry? You came storming in just now like Pooh-bear with his little black cloud.''

"I was trying to tell you,'' he said. "Dodds wants you

to go and play Mata Hari in Arizona. Rather, he did. He had the message by the time I finished.''

"It's ridiculous. Bloody ridiculous. Tim means absolutely nothing to me these days and—it's not flattering to say it—I mean nothing at all to him.''

"Let's keep it that way," Yardley said.

"Oh, for Heaven's sake, Bob! We've been over this a thousand times. Okay, so we were lovers for a short time, but that was before you came along. I loved you and I married you. What more do you want? You had lots of women before we met. I don't keep throwing them up at you. That was then—this is now.''

"I'm sorry.''

"You damn well should be. It was *you* Tim wanted to see, not me. Oh, that hand-holding bit when you came in—is that what's bugging you? He said something funny and I just grabbed his hand, that's all. And when he called next morning to say goodbye, he couldn't get off the phone fast enough. Tim's just a ship in the night, believe me.''

"That's what I told Joe Dodds. I also told him if you went anywhere it would be to England to see the family.''

"I was going to tell you, Bobbie. Daddy called this afternoon—it must have been suppertime in England. Mummy's not getting any better. They've called in another specialist and are going to do further tests. It's all a bit worrying. He was trying to put a brave front on it but I could tell he was worried. He'd like me over there pretty soon.''

"I'll miss you, but of course you must go. No problem over the flights—as an Army wife, you're due at least a couple of concessionary flights this year. How long d'you reckon you'd be away, love?''

"Not a moment longer than I need. I suppose it would be at least a week, to be realistic, but I would hope two weeks at the outside. I might have to sort Daddy out if she has to go into hospital for a spell—you know, find him someone to do the cleaning and some cooking. The old dear's quite useless, left to himself! But I'd come back as soon as I could.''

''And you'll go when?''

''Really, the sooner the better. On the phone, Daddy sounded as though it was quite urgent.''

He said, ''Tomorrow may be too short notice. Let's aim for the day after. First thing when I get to my office tomorrow morning, I'll check out the MAT flight availability and make the reservations for you—open-ended for the return flight.''

''No, you won't. It's terribly sweet—and I love you for it. But you're far too busy. You just give me the Fort Bragg number to call after breakfast tomorrow and I'll make the bookings. Now for Heaven's sake, finish that Scotch and we'll have supper. Why, oh why, did I fall for an alcoholic?'' She went over and hugged him.

Bell was shaving in his palatial suite when the telephone purred softly. He picked up the receiver and heard the equally soft purr of Sayeed's voice in his ear.

''Good morning, Tim. You slept well, I trust? Gene will not be in evidence today. One day a week he spends on his own, fasting and meditating. He says it clears his mental and physical system. He has left a message. He wants you and me to have a meeting and mull over more of the details of the plan. There's a lot to be filled in, don't you agree?''

''Of course. I'd be delighted to talk it over. When and where?''

''Shall we say the library at ten o'clock? That'll give time to read the papers and have that extra cup of coffee. I hope they're looking after you well in the guest wing.''

''Couldn't be better. The library at ten, then.''

''Things are moving forward, Tim,'' Sayeed said, beaming and rubbing his pudgy hands, as Bell walked into the library. "I've been in touch with Mr. Holliday and he's agreed to meet us in Salt Lake City this afternoon."

Bell sat down in one of the leather armchairs. "Why the hell Salt Lake City?"

"Psychology, Tim. Just psychology. Neither party's going to fly the whole way to the other guy's backyard. That would be a sign of inferiority. Holliday knows that Gene is even richer than he is, so he certainly wouldn't come all this way to meet us. His place in Idaho is about eight hundred miles north of here. Salt Lake City is about five hundred miles north. So if we meet there, it gives him the slight advantage. On the other hand, it's we who are going to ask the favor—and he guesses that. He is no fool, is Mr. Holliday."

"Do you know him personally?"

"No, we've never met. But I've been doing my homework, as you would say. He pretends to be a cowhand who hit it lucky. In fact, he passed out of MIT with high grades. It should be an interesting meeting this afternoon. If you wouldn't mind an early lunch, I've arranged for the company Gulfstream to be ready for takeoff at one o'clock."

"Suits me fine. Formal dress?"

Sayeed looked blank for a moment. "Oh, I see what you mean. Yes, lounge suit and a tie. I expect Mr. Holliday will turn up in a ten-gallon hat and chaps, but I think we ought to dress formally. Now, Tim, talking of business, that's the other reason I wanted us to meet. We really must work out some financial arrangements for you. To put it bluntly, what do you want—for yourself?"

"I take it either Gene or Mr. Holliday, or both, will look after all the other costs—gear, equipment, weapons, transport, everything like that?"

"Yes, there's no problem for you there. If we can convince Mr. Holliday, you and your men will get the best of everything. How it's paid for and who pays is something we'll work out on the side. Gene will not be ungenerous. So it comes down to your personal arrangement."

Bell was ready for him. "Simple. I want half a million dollars."

"That seems rather a lot, Tim. Once that money had been paid over, you could disappear out of our lives forever! Gene may be a recluse and a visionary, but he's shrewd with money. Few people know that since he inherited his father's vast fortune, he's actually increased it by clever investments."

"Then he can all the more afford to pay me properly! Look, Sayeed, it isn't you or him that's going to be up there at the sharp end of the operation. This is my stock in trade, you're buying the best. And let's say I'm looking for a return on all the time I invested in becoming the best. When they take their countermeasures, it will be me, and only me, who will know the game.

"I want a cash draft deposited with Credit Suisse in Zurich. The first installment to be payable on the completion of training. We'll fix that date after our meeting with Holliday. The second half of my payment is to be released the day we go operational. I'm to be given a bank contact and test key number to confirm this arrangement is in place before we begin the little exercise. And on top I want twenty thousand dollars in cash up front to cover expenses. If you're worried about me absconding, I can tell you I've no intention of looking behind me for your Palestinian brothers or expecting my mail to blow up in my face for the rest of my life."

Sayeed rubbed his dark chin and gazed into space. Then he said, "Frankly, Tim, it's more than we had expected to pay. Gene and I had reckoned on paying you about half that amount. And we thought that was generous enough."

"I'll say it once more. This is going to be a life or death mission. So far, I haven't even worked out how we're going to get away afterward. It's *my* life on the line up there. I've got a better idea what it's worth than you or Gene have. Think yourself lucky I didn't say a whole million."

After another short silence, Sayeed said, "All right, Tim, you persuade me. But we must dress it up a little for Gene's benefit. Would you accept one hundred and fifty thousand at the end of the training period? As you said, the second installment can be payable in Switzerland once the hijack has started."

"And at that stage I'm trusting you! But you'd be silly to take a chance and not pay it. I'd get you and Gene wherever you hid out. And remember, once I'm prime media up there, I could easily denounce you both if you don't play ball. Okay, on the first payment, I'll take it the way you say—a hundred and fifty at the end of training. But the twenty thousand cash comes across now!"

"I think we can stretch a point, Tim! I'll have the money for you later today. I'm glad we've got that settled. Would you like to shake hands on it?"

He held out his chubby paw. Bell grasped it—and was surprised. He was expecting a soft handshake, like squeezing a down-filled cushion, but he could feel strong bone and muscle under the plump flesh. He made yet another mental note.

NOR IN THE POMP OF PROUD AUDACIOUS DEEDS.

17

THE GULFSTREAM GRACEFULLY touched down at the Salt
Lake City Airport and the pilot, following radio instructions, taxied along the perimeter toward the hangar sheds in
the southeast corner. The aircraft pulled up alongside the
Lear 35 Executive jet that had been pointed out by the
control tower. Sayeed and Bell descended from the Gulfstream and, as they did so, the Lear jet's door opened, the
steps came down, and a short, bowlegged man stepped
out. As Sayeed had forecast, he was wearing a tall Stetson,
high-heeled leather boots, and a cord tie around the neck
of his check shirt. He walked toward them and a black
stretch limo with smoked black windows and a pair of
white bull's horns attached to the radiator came gliding
from behind the hangar and drew up a few yards away
from them.

Bell expected Holliday to say, "Howdy, folks," and
then spit a stream of tobacco juice into the dust. Instead,
he said, "You're Mr. Sayeed," staring keenly at him for a
moment under bushy eyebrows. "And you're Mr. Bell—do

I call you Mister? Mr. Sayeed here says you're some kind of English army officer.'' It sounded like an insult.

"Mister will do fine."

"Okay, son. Now this here is what I propose. That's one of my limos right there. I sent it on first thing this morning to give us some comfort and privacy on the ground here. What say we step inside and drive around a piece? Then there's nobody around to hear us or see us. I guess you folks haven't come all this way excep' for something private to chew over. Right?"

"That will be perfect," said Sayeed. Bell thought, nothing fazes our Mr. Sayeed, not even this Western vulgarity. They climbed into the imposing vehicle, which looked more like a single-decker bus than a self-respecting automobile. Bell noted that the driver's hand not only covered the door handle but also showed the hardening marks of a martial arts devotee. Holliday sat on the backseat, which was so deep that his little legs hardly touched the floor. Sayeed sat alongside him and Bell on a jumpseat facing them both. The long car drifted off silently; Holliday pressed a hidden button and a panel slid back, revealing a well-stocked cocktail cabinet and glasses in racks. He had already closed the glass partition, after telling the chauffeur to drive into Salt Lake City, cruise around, and be ready to return to the airport when he gave the word.

"A drink?" he suggested. "It's dry work flying around the place."

"Not for me, thank you," Sayeed said.

"Oh, I suppose you guys aren't allowed to. Religion and all that."

"It's not the religious side that bothers me. It's just I don't awfully like drinking before the evening."

"Suit yourself. They say it's a free country. Not from where I sit it ain't! How about you, son?"

Bell thought, If he calls me "son" once more, I'll clobber him. Aloud, he said, "Scotch for me. If you've got it."

"If that's meant to be funny," Holliday rasped, "give a kinda grin when you say it. Then we'll all see the joke. Have I got Scotch? I've got enough Scotch to drown Scotland."

Bell could sense Sayeed's eyes on him and he decided to sit back and not score points off this odd little man. He took the proffered glass and smiled in thanks. Holliday helped himself to what looked like a bourbon and branch water.

"Well," he said, "now it's all nice and friendly like, what can I do for you good folks? You didn't fly all this way just to take my pulse."

Sayeed and Bell exchanged glances and then Sayeed said, "Perhaps I should be the spokesman. Much of our plan—all of it—depends on Captain Bell here. I feel he might be too modest and not put the case strongly enough. So let me try."

Fluently and in logical order, he ran through the sequence of events from Bell's break-in at the Minter house and the audacious details of his plan to a biographical sketch of his military career to date and the fact of Gene Minter's enthusiastic backing. Holliday did not interrupt his speech but when he was finished, smacked a hand against his thigh. "Well, I'll be darned! To get me a Jewboy or two before I die. I hate Jews. I hate rattlesnakes, I hate a woman who keeps her legs crossed, I hate a man who deals off the bottom of the pack, but worst of all, I hate fucking Jews! Take me. I *love* this country of ours. I make things grow. I grow millions of trees that turn into wooden huts and furniture and pit props and even the paper the government prints all that shit on. And I pump oil out of the ground to keep America moving. What do those Jews make? They make fucking money. They buy it and sell it and every time they take a turn. That insider trading back in the winter of '86—you think it's a coincidence the villains had names like Levine and Boesky? You have a plan to sort them out, I'm with you."

"Well said, sir," came from Sayeed.

"What are you," Holliday went on, "some kind of A-rab, I guess. You've no cause to love them either."

"That could be a massive understatement," Sayeed murmured.

Holliday either missed or ignored the irony. He went on, "Now lemme get this clear. We hit the Zionist dinner and give 'em a dose of indigestion. Captain Bell here would be in charge. Your man Minter would put up the dough for the guns, equipment, training, transport—all that side. What you want from me is the men and a big desolate area to train in. Yeah, I got that. Now tell me, how many men and for how long?"

Bell said, "I want forty men to start with. No one over thirty-five and no one under twenty-five. No one with any physical defects *including* wearing spectacles. And I want them for a minimum of six weeks."

"You don't want much, do you? And why the six weeks?"

"To train them."

"My guys are trained already. They go out weekends hunting and stalking in the woods."

"I don't want to get into an argument with you, Mr. Holliday, but in my book that's not training. They've got to be hair-trigger fit for what I want."

Sayeed could sense a row developing, so he smoothly cut in. "I'm sure we can work all this out. From what we hear in Arizona, you've got a fine body of young men in the Anglo-Saxon Brotherhood, Mr. Holliday."

"Say, call me Doc, everybody else does. And what name d'you go by."

"That's easy, Doc. The first and last names are both the same—Sayeed. Sah-yeed."

"I got it. Long as I don't say the last bit as 'yid'!"

"Well, Doc, I was saying—you've got some fine strong young men up there in Idaho, doing forestry work and so forth. I'm sure you'd have no difficulty in selecting forty. And the winter must be a quiet time of the year. Six weeks isn't all that long. If need be, we could help out and hire some stand-ins for you.''

Holliday said abruptly, ''I'll have you know I do my own hiring and firing. That's no problem. But what I don't get is this. You said the actual assault would be done with maybe ten-twelve men. So why start with forty? Why not fifteen?''

''The dropout rate is larger than you think, Doc,'' Bell said. ''Besides, the more you have to pick from, the better your final team is. Why, in the SAS, out of every hundred who apply about five get taken on. On that basis, I'd need you to supply two hundred.''

''You two keep talking about this SAS. I tell you, it don't mean a thing to me,'' Doc Holliday said. ''The only SAS I ever heard of is some airline over there in Europe. Which reminds me. I don't take nothing and no one on trust. I didn't get where I am through believing what folks tell me. As that little sonofabitch Truman said, you gotta show me.''

''What are you saying, Doc?'' asked Sayeed.

''Just this. If the leader's no good, the team's no good. You tell me this guy here is Rambo and then some.'' Bell winced. Unheeding, Holliday went on, ''You may be right. If I'm gonna invest in the plan, you damn well gotta be right! But how do I know? To me, he's just some youngish guy in a gray flannel suit sitting in a limo drinking Scotch.''

''It's a good point,'' Bell said. ''You want me to prove I know what I'm doing. Fair enough. What do you suggest?''

''This.'' He turned to Sayeed. ''We drive back to the airport, and then I borrow your man for a day. Tim here flies back to Boise, Idaho, with me and you take your plane back to Arizona. Tomorrow morning we'll give him a few tests. If he passes, I'm your man. I'll find the fit young guys you need. If he fails, then forget it! Either way, I'll have the Lear or one of my other jets fly him back to your place tomorrow afternoon. Have we got us a deal?'' He stuck out his right hand. Bell noticed that, incongruously, the fingernails were manicured and polished a soft pink. He shook hands and so did Sayeed.

"One thing I must ask," Sayeed said, "is that whatever happens the plan remains a top secret. If you come in with us, and I already know Tim well enough to be confident that he'll pass any test you devise, then in your own interests you must keep it secret. If you decide not to come in, then you must give us a fair chance of success by keeping quiet. After all, both of us have good cause to hate the Jews. So give us the chance to hit them swiftly and secretly, like the plague out of Egypt.''

"Well said. I'll shake on that." And once again Doc Holliday held out his manicured hand.

After an excruciatingly boring evening during which Holliday became increasingly drunk and rambled on over every detail of his successful business and love life, Bell woke early next morning. He knew he must keep his feelings in check but he felt resentful that he had to bow and scrape to this foul-mouthed, foul-minded little jerk.

The house was built ranch-style with exposed wooden beams and interminable rooms. The contents were like a magpie's treasure trove. What Bell took to be a Monet hung alongside a Navajo rug of the kind you could buy at most airports in the West of the U.S.A. There were bullfight posters with Holliday's name printed in, moroselooking elk heads on the walls, two grand pianos, one at either end of the lounge, which must have been nearly a hundred feet long, and what Holliday referred to proudly as "my hand-painted Rembrandt" hanging over the roaring fire, and no doubt being ruined in the process, Bell thought.

And there were young women everywhere, with enameled faces made up in a permanent simper, long legs and scanty clothes. They were about as real as the contestants in a Miss World competition. They seemed to be interchangeable as waitresses and callgirls. Before dinner, two of them, Annie-Lou and Honey, served the drinks while Sukie nestled on the sofa alongside Holliday, who from time to time slid his spare hand up her thigh and between her legs. At dinner, it was Annie-Lou's turn to fondle the boss while Sukie was relegated to the soup-carrying role.

After dinner, Holliday said to Bell, with all the finesse of a thundering herd, "If you want either of these little lovelies to warm your bed tonight, just whistle. Not Annie-Lou, she's mine tonight, aintcha, baby? Either one'll do you proud. Boy, are they a pair of little hoovers!"

Bell declined, saying something about needing to be fit for tomorrow.

"Not a fag, are you, son? If I had my way, I'd treat all fags the way they did one of your English kings way back. Rammed a redhot poker up his ass! That'd teach 'em."

Bell dressed in the camouflage suit and rubber-soled combat boots he found laid out in the dressing room alongside his bedroom. It was all a good fit. You had to hand it to the Yanks, he thought. They might be a bunch of overloud and oversexed people but they believed in equipment. When he got down to the dining room, Holliday had already finished his coffee and was sucking on a long black cheroot.

"Help yourself to whatever you want," he said, "but I kinda prefer it if you don't hang around. I gotta busy day ahead. This is the routine. Five miles north, I had a clearing made in the woods and we set up this here snap-shooting range. You know what I mean? You run along, a target pops up—it could be a woman carrying a child or a terrorist pointing a gun at you—and it stays up so many seconds. With beginners, we keep each target up maybe five or six seconds. Once a guy's trained, we reduce the time to maybe two and a half or three seconds. The man taking the test don't know just where the targets will pop up because we have different positions wired up. Do they do this kinda thing where you come from?''

''Yes. We call them 'friend or foe' targets. How long is your range?''

''Couple of hundred yards,'' Holliday said. ''And with a few obstacles scattered around. It's not just a gentle stroll like going duck-shooting. The record is eighty-four seconds—with all the right targets hit. My range master did that last month.''

''He sounds quite a guy.''

''Sure is. Arthur Fields—ex-lieutenant in the U.S. Marines. He took part in that Grenada operation. Did well, too. He took an early discharge from the Forces and he's been with me three years now. Well, what say we make a move? I've got business and you've got a long flight back. This don't need to keep us more'n half an hour. I don't kid around. With me, you're either in or you're out. There's no middle bit.''

It was a dry day—a good omen, Bell thought—but with a chillness in the air, a heaviness that forecast a snowfall later on. Drawn up outside the main door was a long black limo with the white bull's horns fixed to the top of the radiator. Either it was the same limo that had met him and Sayeed at Salt Lake City, which meant that the chauffeur had driven back half the night, or Doc Holliday had a whole fleet of identical Cadillacs, each flaunting his special insignia.

''Hop in, son,'' he said. ''Let's go.''

Ten minutes later, after lurching and wallowing up a forest track, the limousine drew up at the outdoor range. A man was waiting by a table at the near end of the range.

Holliday and Bell got out and the driver then moved two hundred yards away and parked away from the butts—a thick earth bank to absorb the flying rounds of ammunition.

"Arthur," said Holliday, "meet Tim Bell—or do you wanna be called 'Captain Bell'?"

"Tim is just fine." Fields took his hand and they stood there for a moment, sizing each other up. Bell saw a man an inch or two taller than himself, with broad shoulders and a strong neck; gray-eyed, capable-looking. He noticed that Fields' eyes did not hold his for long but slid sideways and down. It might mean nothing but he added the item to his mental store.

There were several covered tables in front of them. On one of the tables a pistol and clips of ammunition had been laid out. Bell went over, picked up the pistol, and hefted it. It was a Browning nine-millimeter Hi-Power. He pulled back the action and then ejected the magazine, which was empty.

"You know the Browning?" Fields asked.

"Sure. How does this one throw?"

"It's been zeroed in. All our weapons here are zeroed in."

"I'm not criticizing. I just wanted to make sure. If I'm going to take the test, I want to be sure the gun shoots straight! Would you mind if I took a couple of practice shots?"

Fields said, "Be my guest." He took two nine-millimeter rounds from his side pocket and tossed them to Bell, who caught them and slipped them one after the other into the magazine clip, which he rammed back into the butt of the pistol. There was a tree behind him with a white bole. He swung into a crouch position, legs apart, aimed and fired, aimed and fired. Splinters flew from the tree trunk. He walked over to the tree and inspected the bullet holes.

"Typical Browning Hi Power," he said, as he walked back to the group. "Slightly high and right."

"If you hold it tight, it shoots straight enough," Fields said with a deadpan look on his face. Bell knew the technique. Before a test, get the other man worked up, get him angry. Accuracy goes if the adrenaline's pumping too hard.

"If I stuffed it up your ass and pulled the trigger, it'd probably hit something. Most like, your brains," he replied.

"Come on, come on," Doc Holliday said testily. "I don't have all day to watch you two locking horns. Tell him what he's gotta do, Arthur, and then for Chrissake, let's get on with it."

"Right, sir." He turned to Bell. "Listen good, because I don't want to have to say it twice. There are two magazines on the table in front of you. They're each full, thirteen rounds apiece plus one in the chamber. On the signal, you put one magazine in the butt, the other one in your pocket or wherever you like—it's up to you—and then you run over to that nearest oil drum. You see it? It's filled with concrete, so you can't knock it over. You crouch behind it, a target will pop up, you fire two rounds— get it? *two* rounds, not one and not three—and then you move on to that next oil drum twenty feet on. Same thing again—and so on to the third drum. The enemy targets show a terrorist in a black balaclava-type face mask. The friendly ones should be obvious. After the third drum, there's a kind of short assault course, you gotta go under those strands of barbed wire and over that pile of logs. There are three more sets of targets in that area—and again we want a couple of shots at each. By now you'll be down to two rounds in the first magazine and will have thirteen rounds in the second. You then run the last fifty yards toward the butts and thirty feet short of them you come to a deep trench. Slide into it and on the butts side there's a parapet. Stand on that, look out and you'll see a single white dinner plate stuck up in front of the butts. You're allowed two more shots. If you smash the plate with one of those two, you've finished the course. You with me? Oh, the signal to start will be me giving the table one tap. Okay?''

"Sure. But why the second mag?"

"You might get a blockage or waste a few," was the dry answer from Fields.

"What's the course record? Did I hear it's eighty-four seconds?''

Fields nodded and Holliday said, "Don't be too cock-sure, son. Arthur here's done the course a hundred times. You just concentrate on getting through it in one piece.''

Fields tapped the table once. Bell picked up the first magazine and balanced it in the palm of his hand before sliding it into the butt of the Browning. It felt a little light. He had hefted the weapon's thirty-two ounces enough times to know. He added the point to his subliminal regis-ter. He took up the other clip and tucked it into his waistband, making sure that the blouse of his camouflage suit did not impede it. Then he was off on a loping run to the first oil drum, instinctively checking that the safety catch was off as he went. Up came the first target—a woman carrying a child in her arms. He ignored it. Just alongside, a terrorist target flipped up. He fired two shots in a blur of sound and then was on to the next oil drum. This time, the target was a postman followed by a terrorist target. Two more quick shots at the latter and he was off again. The third set was the trickiest, a terrorist holding a woman in front of his body with just his head and pistol arm protruding. Bell loosed off his two shots before the target flipped down again.

The Browning felt too light. It should still have eight rounds left in the first clip. He suspected trickery on the part of Fields or Holliday. As he loped toward the barbed wire, he slid out the magazine and saw that it was empty. The sods! If he'd tried to fire at the next batch of targets, there would have been a dull click and the target would have disappeared before he had time to change magazines and take fresh aim. Holding the gun in front of his body so that the two men behind him could not see what was happening, he thumbed the ejected magazine into his belt, and in one flowing movement pulled the other from his waistband and rammed it into the butt of the Browning, without breaking step.

I'll show you bastards, he thought. He palmed the action and went under the barbed wire without pausing, over the pile of logs, took out the next three targets, instinctively noting they had tried to trick him again—in one target the terrorist was not wearing a balaclava—vaulted down into the trench and up onto the parapet, smashed the plate with his first shot and looked at the sweephand on his wristwatch. His pulse pounded in his ears. Holliday and Fields came strolling up, having inspected each group of targets as they passed.

"I make that seventy-three seconds," Bell said. "You agree?"

"You could be cheating yourself," Fields said. "When that plate went, I had you clocked in at just over seventy-two."

"Which reminds me," Bell said. "You talking about cheating." The Cadillac was drawn up some thirty feet away, its engine already running and a long feather of smoke jetting from the exhaust onto the chill air. Bell swung around, crouched, aimed, fired—then again, swiveling, crouch, aim, fire. One bull's horn on the front of the radiator just disintegrated in a flurry of bone dust; the other went spinning like a boomerang to the rutted ground.

"What in hell's name you do that for?" Doc Holliday shouted. "You gone crazy?"

"I don't like cheats, Mr. Holliday. If I go into a fight

with a guy on my side, I may have to trust him with my life and he may trust me with his. *Trust*, Mr. Holliday. That's the operative word. Guys who play dirty little tricks, like pretending a magazine's full when there's only six rounds in it, deserve to get their fucking horns shot off. You're damn lucky it's not your own balls!''

"Okay, okay, okay. That was wrong. We shouldn't oughter done it. Boy, you're some shot. You got each of those targets plumb smack in the head, ain't that right, Arthur? And now this?'' He gestured toward the Cadillac. The driver had stepped out and was looking pale in the frosty morning air.

Holliday went on, "How do you rate him, Arthur?'' Bell felt that he might as well be a prime carcass of beef.

"The best, Mr. Holliday. I have to say it, the best.''

"That's good enough for me. Here, Tim, we're in business, shake hands on it. Arthur ought to know. If he says you're the best, you're good enough for me. I'll have you flown back to Arizona this morning—you'll welcome a break from our winter—and when you're airborne, I'll call your Mr. Sayeed and tell him I'm with you all the way. But what's the program from your angle?''

Bell said, "I need about a week for my final recon. It's now Thursday the third of March. Let's reassemble here first thing Monday the fourteenth. Say nine o'clock sharp. That gives you ten days to get your forty men together. Remember, I don't want anyone over thirty-five and, preferably, no one under twenty-five, though I'd stretch a point on the younger side. But let's have one thing clear right from the start. Come that Monday morning when I get them on parade, they're not going to be your men, Mr. Holliday, nor yours, Fields—they're going to be *mine*. Got it? They don't take orders from anybody but me. From that point on, I'm the boss. Agreed?''

Fields looked at Holliday, who looked searchingly at Bell. At last, he said, "You drive a tough bargain, Tim, but I sure ain't gonna argue with a guy who's that good with a gun! Okay, you have yourself a deal. Shake.''

Sayeed took the call in the quietness of the library.

"It's on!" Holliday paused. "That's quite a boy you have there," he said, "I like his style."

"So he acquitted himself well?"

"Are we on a secure line?"

"Of course."

"Good. I'll say he did! I've never seen shooting like it. Boy, I'd rather have him on my side than against me.''

"You think he'll do what we want him to do?"

"In spades. There's a kind of deadliness about him. We played a stupid trick on him—my man Fields suggested it. Told him he had a full clip of ammo when it was only half full. And did he spot it? He didn't go angry, he just went cold. One moment, I thought he was going to shoot us both, but instead he took those bull's horns off the front of my Caddy—bang, bang—the neatest bit of shooting I ever did see. I tell you, I could have shat myself!''

"Can we control him?"

"We'll damn well have to. When you're holding a tiger by the tail, you gotta hold tight. But that's not all I want to say. Lemme say I kinda like your style as well. You and me talk the same language. I hear tell that Minter's a sort of soft egg, great on ideas but no action. Do I read him right?''

"Gene's a fine man, a real old-fashioned gentleman, and pretty clever, but you're right, he's not a man of action.''

"Will he go along with what you say, once you've convinced him?''

Sayeed paused slightly. "Yes. I can genuinely say he usually heeds my advice.''

"Usually ain't good enough in my book.''

"Perhaps I was falling into that Anglo-Saxon trap of modesty. To be blunt, I cannot think of one case where he has refused to follow my advice. Once he trusts someone, he trusts them entirely. And I'm happy to say he trusts me.''

"That's good," Doc Holliday said. "Real good. This is the big-money table, you understand? We'll be rolling high once the plan gets going. Bell gets my vote, and so do you, but I've gotta be 105 percent positive that Minter's not going to swoon when it comes to the point.''

"Rest assured, my friend. We Palestinians live in a world in which you are liable to die quickly and nastily if you can't assess a man's real character. I *know* my Gene Minter.''

"That's a great relief. Boy, I haven't been this excited about anything since my daddy took me to my first whorehouse in Amarillo!''

AND LADIES' CHEEKS WERE PAINTED RED WITH WINE,
THEIR TONGUES, AS SHORT AND NIMBLE AS THEIR HEELS,
UTTERING WORDS SWEET AND THICK; AND WHEN THEY ROSE,
WERE MERRILY DISPOSED TO FALL AGAIN.

▮8▮

WHEN BELL GOT back to the Minter enclave and walked through the long hall, Sayeed was waiting for him. He grasped Bell by the elbow, steering him into a small, book-lined room. "I use this as a study from time to time," he said. "We can't be disturbed here."

"What's all the secrecy?" Bell asked.

"You may well ask! If Gene got to hear what's happened, he'd call the whole plan off. As it is, if you haven't a proper explanation, perhaps we should think again—or wait till things cool off."

"Well, what the hell *has* happened, Sayeed?"

"This. Around ten o'clock this morning, there was a telephone call for you. From a woman. Luckily, the servants transferred it to me and not to Gene, who's still meditating, Allah be praised! I was very cool with the woman, who sounded English, by the way. I said we'd never heard of a Captain Bell and suggested she had the wrong number. She persisted. She said she damn well knew you were here and you'd better call her back today without fail. Since then, she's called twice more. Tim, what *is* all this? How does some strange woman know just where you are?''

Bell had never thought as fast before. "That's okay," he said reassuringly. "It's only Angela Yardley. Something urgent must be happening at her end for her to break security like that. I'd better call her back at once. What's the number?''

"Not so quick. That's no explanation. Who is this Angela?''

"I'll tell you, Sayeed. But let's make it snappy. If she's called three times, it's urgent. You're right, Angela is an English girl. She and I were friends—good friends, you understand?—back there. When we broke up, she married an American Special Forces officer, Bob Yardley, who was a mate of mine. I'm not boasting when I say she's still carrying the torch, and she'll do almost anything I ask. Now, Bob Yardley's in charge of special antiterrorist operations, and she's his loving little wife, who does her duty by discussing his plans with him. Get it? She's my Trojan Horse.''

"Why didn't you mention this earlier, Tim? When you first told us your plan. It might have had a real bearing on the decision.''

"I looked on it as my own private insurance policy. Let me just remind you once again, Sayeed, of one big difference between you and me. When the operation starts, you'll be back here, nice and comfy, watching it on television in front of a warm fire. I'll be the one at the sharp end. Now if I've got a mole in the enemy camp, telling me what's happening at that end, I'll keep one jump ahead, and more likely to come out of this in one piece. You follow me?''

"That makes good sense—up to a point. How do you know she's not a double agent?''

"Working both sides of the street? Not my Angela. She hasn't the brains, for a start. And there's always something inward about real spies and agents. They live behind a kind of mask. Not Angela. She's too impulsive, too outgoing. She's no double agent, I'd stake my life on it.''

"You may have to,'' Sayeed said. "Frankly, I'm not altogether happy—but why don't you call her and find out what's up? It's a New York number—area code 212—and it sounds like a hotel. I have the number here in my wallet—555–1344, extension 611. Have you got that?''

"I'll call her right away.''

"You do that. I'll leave you alone to make your call, but I have to warn you—I'll be listening on an extension in another room. By the way, I should have said this earlier—congratulations on passing Holliday's test. He sounds highly impressed, though none too pleased over having those ghastly horns shot off the front of his car.''

"He told you that, did he? Let me see, New York must be two hours ahead of us. So it's just on seven o'clock in the evening there. I'll give you half a minute to be listening on your extension and then I'll make the call.''

Angela must have been sitting alongside the telephone in her hotel bedroom for there was only one ring after the hotel operator had switched the call through before he heard the breathless voice almost in tears say, "Hallo, hallo.''

"Angie,'' he said, "it's Tim.''

"Oh, Tim, where've you been? I've sat here for hours and hours, I thought you'd never call back.''

"Sorry, I've been out all day on a job.''

"How's it going? And how're you feeling? Oh, there's so much I want to hear about!''

He steered the conversation away from the thin ice. "Darling, what the hell are you doing in New York? What's happened?''

"You remember my mother back home? She's not very well. Actually, it's nothing at all serious but I exaggerated a bit with Bob, who was very sweet and insisted on me flying back to look after her and Daddy. I was supposed to catch a plane from Kennedy this evening but I postponed it when you didn't call me back."

"Angie, you've given me a great idea. I've got to fly to New York myself—honest to God. Normally, I might have left it over for a few days but there's nothing to stop me flying tomorrow. There are one or two jobs I must do but we could have a few days together. Can you square Bob?"

"No problem. I'll call him tomorrow and make out I'm already in England. You know, with direct dialing you could be calling from anywhere. I'll tell him not to worry and I'll call him back in a day or two. That should fix it."

She had clearly rehearsed her little deception plan and was pleased with herself for being smart. Bell was not so sanguine. Inside, he agreed with Sayeed; Angie could be a real threat to the operation. Aloud, he said, "That's great. Now, I tell you what. You stay on where you are for tonight—you've got enough cash to pay the bill? What's that? You'll settle by American Express card? No, do it in cash if you can, darling—I'll pay you back when we meet. Don't you see? When they send you the monthly account, the details are going to be on it. What if Bob checks through your Amex expenses? He'd catch you out in a lie right off."

She said she'd never thought of that. Bell went on, "Anyway, you settle up there tomorrow morning and then take a cab to the Waldorf. It's on Park Avenue. You must have heard of it."

"Of course, I've heard of it. Who hasn't? But it must be frightfully expensive—are you sure you can afford it, Tim?"

"Would I suggest it if I couldn't? Well, when you get there, there'll be a suite booked in the name of—let me see—why not Hereford? Mr. and Mrs. Hereford. No, that's a bit too obvious. Let's make it Ford.

"I'll take the first plane out of Phoenix tomorrow morning and should be with you by midafternoon. So you just sit back in that suite and wait for me, okay? After you've called Bob, no more phone calls, understand?''

"Oh, Tim, I can hardly wait to see you. Get here just as fast as you can, won't you?''

"If I don't think the aircraft's going fast enough, I'll get out and push.''

"Silly—but do come quickly, if you know what I mean. Love you.''

Bell hung up and a few moments later Sayeed came back into the room.

"I suppose you heard all that?'' Bell inquired.

"Yes. It seemed all right. But I still think this could be a possible weak link. You say she's not clever enough to be a double agent. I accept that. With respect, Tim, I imagine you didn't pick her for her brains. But what if this man Yardley, her husband, started to grill her? Would she stand up under pressure?''

"Well, if that's the way you're thinking, perhaps she ought to be eliminated.''

"Just like that, Tim?''

"Yes, just like that. Of course, I'd be sorry. She's a nice enough girl and it's not her fault she got in the firing line. But nothing—and no one—is going to stop us. You and Gene want value for your money. I'll damn well see you get it.''

"Wouldn't her—her disappearance—cause more problems than it solved? Her husband would discover soon enough that she wasn't in England, hadn't even gotten beyond New York. Doesn't that point the finger at you?''

Bell said, "Not if I cover my tracks. Anyway, we don't have to apply the solution right now. Let me study the position once I'm in New York. Which reminds me—could I have a chopper or the Gulfstream to fly me to Phoenix at first light tomorrow? There must be several nonstops to New York from Phoenix.''

"There are. I'll see you're booked on the first flight. Not a word of all this to Gene, by the way. I expect we'll see him at dinner tonight. As far as he's aware, you're off to New York for a few days to reconnoiter the target and see that explosives expert with the colorful name. Let's keep it that way.''

Bell paid off the cab at the awning of the Waldorf-Astoria. He waved aside a porter and carried his own grip up the flight of steps into the first of several vast lobbies. To him, the hotel was like a gigantic ocean liner moored alongside Park Avenue, with its gleaming dark woods, its lush carpets, and what could have been promenade walks for the rich and unhurried. All this should knock Angela for a loop, he thought as he checked at the desk for his room number and was told that Mrs. Ford was waiting for him in the suite. He was also told to have a good day for the umpteenth time.

The suite was on the forty-eighth floor. He let himself in with the key from the desk in the lobby, and there was Angela, just as she had been after their lunch—was it only six days ago? Naked except for a light wrap. She had been gazing out of the window at the string of colored lights moving up and down Park Avenue; those white lights on the left as you looked were the headlights of cars driving south down the avenue and those parallel red beads on the right going up were the taillights of myriad cars. Angela swung around and almost spilled the contents of the large glass she was clutching.

''Oh, it's gorgeous,'' she said, ''simply gorgeous. You are sweet to me, Tim. Here, let me give you a kiss''—and she grabbed him with her free hand and planted a gin-tasting smack on his mouth. ''I could hardly wait for you,'' she went on. ''This town does things to a girl. Oh, come on, Tim, let's go to bed, for God's sake!''

They made love like rutting animals, he thought, grabbing and tearing and biting at each other—more like an act of hate than an act of love. And she was moaning all the time, as though she were in pain that could never be healed. It would be easy, a cold inner voice whispered to him, to stop nuzzling her arched throat and squeeze it in his hands.

Afterward, they showered and dressed and helped themselves to drinks from the cabinet next to the enormous television set. Bell said, "Now, we've got to make a big decision. Rather, you have. Do you want to have dinner here in the hotel—there's quite a good restaurant on the ground floor the other side of Peacock Alley—or have dinner sent up, or go out to a restaurant? There are quite a few within a short walk."

"You decide, Tim love. You're the man."

"Feeling more like half a one right now. Okay, we could both do with a breath of fresh air. I vote we have dinner at the Laurent. It's only a few blocks north of here—smashing French restaurant, you'll love it."

"And I bet it costs the earth! Why are you doing all this for me, Tim?"

"Do you really have to ask?"

"Oh, you are sweet!" She gave him an impulsive hug. "Talk about waving a magic wand. There I was—was it only yesterday?—sitting in those dreary married quarters, Army furniture, Army decorations, bored out of my skull, and here I am now, high above New York in a posh hotel, debating whether to dine at this wildly expensive restaurant or that one. And with the man I love." She looked at him wide-eyed over the rim of her glass, her face reflecting the excitement of an expectant child.

When they were sitting at a corner table in the Laurent, drinking a predinner Scotch, Angela said, "How come you know New York so well? I know you're not a country boy but you mention places like Saks and Macy's, and judging by this gorgeous place, you know quite a bit about New York restaurants. Seems odd for a man who's supposed to spend most of his time crawling around ditches with his face blacked up."

"Simple answer," he said. "On my last attachment at

Bragg—you and Bob must have been stationed somewhere else right then—I got friendly with a guy in Delta Force who had a stinking rich daddy. Whenever we had any leave coming, we would hotfoot it up to li'l ol' New York and have ourselves a whale of a time.''

"Like chasing all the girls, I suppose.''

"Now, now, Angie. Green eyes don't become you. There might've been a woman or two drifting past but I was usually too smashed to notice.''

"The day you're too smashed to notice a good-looking woman, they'll be doing open heart surgery on you!''

They made love again that night back at the hotel—and in the morning, too. Angela seemed insatiable and Bell wondered secretly how long he could keep going at this rate. There was something pathetic in her eagerness to please and be pleased. Being in bed with her was like riding a runaway roller coaster; he had never known any other woman so driven by her urges. Out of bed, she could only prattle away about fashion and makeup and the kind of barroom political theories she must have picked up from Bob and his friends. Bell again wondered if he could stand the next few days—in more senses than one.

Realizing that she hardly knew New York at all, he ran her off her feet for the next two days. The first morning, they worked their way down Fifth Avenue, starting at the Metropolitan Museum and taking in the Frick, the Guggenheim and the Museum of Modern Art just off Fifth. As a sop, he let her gaze into the windows of Tiffany's and Van Cleef & Arpels and even take a turn around Bonwit Teller and Saks Fifth Avenue. Lunch at La Caravelle restored her drooping energies, and then it was off downtown to the Empire State Building. After that, a cab down to the Battery and a ride to Staten Island and back on the ferry. Even Bell was moved to see the lights coming on in the downtown skyscrapers. The energy, the sheer wastefulness of New York; he loved it. A chill wind was whipping across the Narrows and he put his arm around Angela as they stood in the prow and gazed at approaching Manhattan. He pointed out, slightly to her left, the twin towers of the World Trade Center.

"I hear they've got a restaurant up near the top of one of those towers," he said. "The view must be fabulous. What do you say we dine there one night?"

"Love to, Tim. But not tonight, *please!* My feet are killing me after all that walking around. It sounds silly, but I think the New York sidewalks are harder than the London pavements."

"Could be," he said. "It's built on a thousand feet of granite, they say. Okay, tonight we'll have something sent up to the room and sit there watching TV, if you like."

"No, I'll be all right once I've soaked my poor feet in a hot bath. But pick something nice and close to the Waldorf, won't you? None of your forced marches."

"I can see you've got your eye on the Four Seasons. If they'll reserve a poolside table in the main dining room, you can even bathe your feet while we eat."

"Idiot," and she hugged him again, kissing the lobe of his ear.

The following morning, he told her that he had a couple of business engagements that would take up most of the morning. He said that she should either potter around the suite or, if she preferred, go down to the lobby and have coffee or a drink in Peacock Alley—but on no account to leave the hotel.

"What are you worried about, my love? I'm a big girl now, hadn't you noticed?"

"New York's a bad place for a woman on her own. Even in daylight."

"Oh, Tim, you are gallant—and an old-fashioned fool! But okay, if you want me to stay in the hotel, of course, I will."

"That's my girl. Anything you want, just ring the desk and get them to send it up. I won't be too long—promise."

Out on the sidewalk, he refused the doorman's offer to get him a cab and walked a few blocks down toward the Pan Am Building before hailing a cruising cab. He didn't want some doorman with big ears hearing the destination and remembering him and it. A minute chance indeed, but now's the time to take no chances, he thought, as he directed the man to an address off Washington Square. He thought again of Angela and what he should do. He realized with some surprise that he was getting quite fond of her. Over a long stretch, she would probably drive him mad with her pathetic urge to please and her tongue like the clapper of a bell. But she had a good heart and she was one of the few people alive who really cared for him.

Even so, should she be got rid of? What were the pros and cons? He had told Sayeed that eliminating her now would only draw Yardley's attention to them. But would it? That she had not flown to England, had only got as far as New York, would be easy to trace. But from then on? The next step would be to check all the hotel registers, and that would take some time. And even then, would anyone spot Angela Yardley hidden behind "Mr. and Mrs. Ford"? Detectives from the NYPD would have to go around to every hotel reception desk, showing photographs of her and asking the desk clerks if they recognized her. That could take some weeks, or they could strike it lucky within a few days. And if she was identified by the Waldorf staff, there could be a description of himself, which Yardley would quickly recognize. They would get to that first call to Minter's eventually. But by that time, he would be miles away in the depths of the Idaho forests. He needed the heat off for these next eight weeks. After that, his name and likeness would probably be on the front pages of newspapers across the world. Then he would have another problem—how to disappear into obscurity after all that.

But what if he let Angela live? She would fly to England, spend a week or two with her family, and then fly back to Fort Bragg. Would she be strong enough to tough it out with Bob, if he asked any awkward questions? There was one thing in her favor. Bob was clearly very much in love with her, and men in love don't want to rock the boat by asking too many questions. Or do they? Men in love can be madly jealous of the loved one, as Bob had already shown after that episode with the failed parachute. And was Angela the kind who might get the confessional urge, wanting to make a clean breast of everything, or even deliberately telling Bob, to set up a crisis and force him to free her? Christ, he hoped not. Perhaps it would be safer to get rid of her on this trip. He felt the impatience growing from within and recognized the familiar buildup of combat adrenaline. A deadly mindset putting all the ducks in a row. He paid off the cab driver at the destination off Washington Square, then strolled, apparently aimlessly, down a couple of streets until he saw a vacant cab. He asked the man to drop him on Delancey Street, not far from the Williamsburg Bridge. He would then be within a mile of his destination, which was Flamer Brown's hideyhole, but he was not risking the cab driver's memory, if he was ever questioned by the police.

He had the professional soldier's trick of mentally photographing an area of the map. He had bought the Hagstrom map of Brooklyn and Lower Manhattan at the airport on his arrival in New York and he knew exactly where Forsyth Street was. So he walked smartly along East Broadway until he came to the junction with Canal Street. He went into a liquor store on the corner of the street and bought a pint bottle of Scotch. He buttoned his coat and slipped the bottle inside, so that it was concealed and also left his hands free. Then he walked slowly down the street toward the address he had filched from Bob Yardley's files. He hoped to God that Flamer was there and would be alone. There was a good chance, because as a recluse he probably stayed indoors on his own until darkness fell, one of New York's night people.

He stood on Orchard Street and thought he had come to

the end of the world, the place where dreams finally shatter against the hard facts of reality. Orchard Street— what joker had ever named it that? There was no blossom, no fragrant fruit, no sense of ripeness and the seasons. Rusty fire escapes clung to the grimy walls, shop windows were either smashed or boarded up, doors hung at a drunken angle from their hinges. On a whitewashed wall at the corner of the street was a notice that said it all:

LOFT SPACE FOR RENT

NO LIVNG.

Damn right, Bell thought. No living—that's the motto. It was equally ironic that, a mile away beyond East Broadway, you could see the twin towers of the World Trade Center, symbol of wealth and prosperity. And nearer still, just across the street, in fact, was Chinatown, quiet, discreet, and prosperous too in its own way. Orchard Street was the rodent ulcer on the face of Midas.

He walked a short way farther and came to Forsyth Street. It was worse in its dirt and decay. It ran almost beneath the overhead line of the IND subway; every minute or so a train would go chuntering past with a rumble and a shaking of the bridge that almost straddled the street. The sidewalk was lined with derelict cars rusting away in the filth and stink. What had once been warehouses occupied the other side of the street. The windows had long gone; the gaps were boarded up with planks. Iron fire escapes hung crazily against the walls, their red rust-stains marking the walls like new scars. There was a triangular space at ground level, where the first warehouse jutted out farther than its neighbor. There were old iron pipes and a rubber-tired wheel lying in the gap. The wall behind had once been painted white. It was now gray and grimy and there were childish scrawls at waist height made with a spraygun. One Bell noticed was FUK THE PIGGS. He agreed with the sentiment but felt a touch of horror that a child of seven or eight, judging by the height of the graffiti on the wall, should feel that way.

On Flamer Brown's front door an adult had written in chalk, DON'T KNOCK. DON'T ENTER. The door hung an inch or two ajar. Recalling Flamer Brown's expertise at setting booby-traps, Bell found a broken plank among the rubbish in the vacant area and then, flattening himself against the front wall, used the end of the plank to prod the door back on its hinges. It creaked back with a groan, but there was no explosion. The street was deserted except for two black men leaning against a wrecked auto fifty yards away.

So far, so good. He slipped through the doorway and then stood stock still, running his eyes over every inch of the walls and floor of the dusty passageway. There was a ragged-edged mat on the floor in front of him and, using the end of the plank again, he cautiously pushed it aside. The floorboards had not been tampered with. He moved forward very slowly, eyes alert for an innocent-looking loose wire or a bulge in a wall, until he reached the foot of the rickety stairs. He guessed that Flamer would not dare use a lot of explosives in any booby-traps he set for the unwelcome visitor. In a built-up area, even one as squalid as this, sudden loud explosions are difficult to explain away. He tried to remember all the kinds of booby-traps the U.S. Special Forces had used against the Cong, and vice versa. Yes, it would most probably be a crossbow bolt or a *panga,* a sharpened stick, fired by a small explosives charge—or even very strong elastic. He felt that prickly sensation, his inheritance from Belfast days.

Sure enough, on the first bend of the stairs, where the light from a cracked windowpane high above the front door hardly penetrated, his sharp eyes caught the glint of a thread or thin wire stretched across the corner tread, two inches above it. He was still carrying the plank. Lying flat against the stairs, at full arm's length, he pressed the end of the plank against the wire. There was a noise like a whip-crack, something burst out of the wall opposite and, flying faster than the eye could track, penetrated the wall alongside the stairs, quivering as it came to rest half-buried in the woodwork. It was a *panga* stick, Bell noticed, a sliver of hardwood polished and sharpened into a kind of spearhead, the kind that the Viet Cong had used when ambushing the Americans and that the Special Forces had themselves copied. If he had trodden unwarily on that step ahead, he would now have lost his kneecap or had the back of his calf sliced off. His anger swelled against Flamer Brown and with a conscious effort he lay still on the stairs, slowly counting up to fifty until the rage subsided and he was back in icy control. The fucking madman! Some perfectly innocent visitor—the mailman or an inquisitive child—could be lying on the stairs screaming and spouting blood. If the Flamer did not fit his scenario so perfectly, he would have taken him out in the next five minutes and felt some gratification over the deed.

There were no further booby-traps on the stairs and he reached the upper landing. There were two doors to the right and two to the left along the bare boards of the grimy corridor. The walls were dark with dirt and grease. No self-respecting rat would live here, he thought.

"Flamer, where the hell are you?" he shouted into the gloom of the landing.

There was a pause. Then a surly voice came from behind the nearest door on his left, "Fuck off, willya?"

"Hey, Flamer, don't be like that. I'm an old friend, Tim Bell."

"I don't know no Tim Bell, so fuck off."

"Oh, yes, you do. Tim Bell. British Special Forces. We met on the Laos border in '72. And just a few years back, you gave an explosives demonstration at Hereford. You must remember. We got pissed out of our minds that night!"

"Maybe I remember you, maybe I don't. Here, stand against that wall—right at the edge where it goes down the stairs. Stand still now."

Bell did as ordered, thinking furiously, what is the crazy fool up to now? Is there another *panga* stick in the wall opposite, aimed between my eyes or, knowing him, straight at my balls? He tensed himself. A small searchlight came on, dazzling him with its brilliance. He could just see that the door had opened a crack. So the Flamer was inspecting him, just to make sure who he really was.

The light was abruptly switched off and Bell was left with a flickering radiance behind his eyelids. The croaky voice said, "Yeah, well I do recognize you, though I couldn't have put a name to it. In the fucking Services, they all come and go, come and go. Okay, you can step inside."

Bell was careful to keep both hands in view, fingers open and palms to the front. "I've brought you a present," he said. "A bottle of the good stuff. It's inside my jacket. Mind if I get it out?"

"Be my guest. Or do I mean—my host?" He gave a cackle that ended in a liquid, wheezing cough. "Come on in, it's cold outside."

The door was flung back and Bell walked forward, clutching the bottle of Scotch by the neck in his left hand. The room was dim and Flamer Brown had sat down with his back to the window with the shade pulled down. Flamer sat in a creaking basket chair; the only other chair was an upright wooden one with copies of *Soldier of Fortune* piled on the seat. Brown picked them up and looked at Flamer questioningly. The latter pointed to the floor and cackled again. Gradually, Bell's sight was losing the dazzle of the searchlight and growing accustomed to the gloom of Flamer's sanctum. It was one of the filthiest rooms he had ever seen. There was a heap of chipped dishes in the sink with scraps of congealed food on them and what looked like a green mold growing at the side. A rusty faucet dripped monotonously into the sink. In the far corner of the room was a pile of rags that Bell suddenly realized was Flamer's bed. The only clean things in the room were the tools of his trade, switches, timers, pincers, and drills, set out neatly on the shelves behind Flamer's head. He put the bottle of Scotch on the uneven floor and looked around for a couple of glasses. Flamer Brown's thumb indicated two grimy and chipped enamel mugs on the draining board. There was only a trickle of brown, rusty-looking water from the faucet, so Bell took out his handkerchief and polished the mugs as clean as he could. Then he poured a large slug into each and handed one to Flamer, who gulped the drink down at once and held out his mug for more, as he wiped his mouth with the back of his hand.

Bell poured less this time. He felt his fingers were sticky with something off the mug; he sniffed them and smelled gelatin. At once, his mind was tuned to booby traps and he looked sharply at the wooden bench between the draining board and the shelves holding Flamer's equipment. There he saw two samples of the man's diabolical art. Flamer had taken an M47 pineapple hand grenade, coated it with gold paint, removed the striker mechanism, neatly sliced the top of the grenade off like a man about to eat a hard-boiled egg, and repacked the grenade with seismic explosive and extra metal fragments. An electric detonator had been pushed into the explosive mix. Then he had broken a light bulb, making sure that the filament was intact, and had soldered the filament end to the detonator. The fragile combination had then been stabilized in a covering of gelatin carefully topped off at the neck of the grenade. The screw-type bulb fitting protruded and the whole contraption looked like a decorated light bulb. It could indeed be screwed into the usual light socket. But when someone switched on the light, the filament would glow brightly and initiate the detonator, setting off the explosive charge, and hundreds of lethal shrapnel needles would burst out with a bang. In a confined area, it would be murderous. And Flamer had made a couple of these toys for unwelcome visitors. Others were in various stages of construction.

"Up to your old tricks, I see," he said.

"And tell me why the fuck not? That little baby is one of my best sellers. You Brits have a good saying—'An Englishman's home is his castle.' Well, it ain't much but this here is *my* castle. Anyone comes here comes at his wish, not mine. If they keep well away, they won't get hurt."

"Sounds fair," Bell said. He sipped from the mug and then remembered what had struck him the first moment he had entered the room—a sweet, almost sickly stench. He had been trying to recall where he had smelled it before, and now it came back to him. One night, when he had been on leave in Saigon, a South Korean Special Forces sergeant had taken him and a few others on a tour of the Saigon the casual visitor never saw. They had ended up in an opium den and had watched the preparation of the pipes, the lighting, and the deep inhaling. That had been the same smell. Christ, he thought, apart from all else, Flamer's on the smokes these days. Would the guy be up to the skillful and precise job he wanted?

"Well, here's to old times," he said, as he raised his mug aloft.

"I'll drink to that," Flamer said and emptied the mug again.

Bell poured only a little Scotch this time. He didn't want the man getting drunk on him—and have to risk another journey to this filthy, stinking rathole.

His eyes had become adjusted to the twilight in the room: He could see that Flamer had grown his hair long—or perhaps it was a wig?—and had draped one hank across the left side of his face. Bell had recently seen a television program of Hollywood stars of yesterday and he suddenly realized that the Flamer's attempt to cover the ruined side of his face was a grotesque travesty of Veronica Lake's peekaboo style. Even so, he could see the scar-swollen eyelid of Flamer's left eye, so that just a thin glint of the eyeball itself was visible, and the inflamed weals of the surgical stitching down his cheek and chin. Christ, you poor sod, he thought. He tried to recall how Brown had looked as a young, jokey sergeant. A good-looking guy, as far as he could remember, always laughing, eyes bright, fun to be with. And here was this poor bloody hermit in this shithouse of a place, looking like the Hunchback of Notre Dame. Made you think.

"Say, what's it all about?" Flamer Brown asked in that cracked voice. "You didn't come all this way for my autograph."

"Damn right. I've got a proposal to make. Before I mention it, you know who I am, don't you?"

"Sure, I know you. It's a small world in the Special Forces, and I ain't been out long enough to lose touch. You were a so-called observer in 'Nam—probably did more fighting than the real troops!—and you were in Oman, I guess, and the Falklands. I know you all right, Captain Bell. When I was on detachment, slogging up and down those fuckin' Welsh mountains, there were times I'd cheerfully have cut your throat with a table knife!"

"So you know I don't kid around?"

"Sure, I know it. So what do you want?"

"This," said Bell. "But let me fill you in quickly first. I got in a spot of bother in Northern Ireland, killed a couple of IRA prisoners, and the Regiment gave me the heave. I'm over here to carry out a nice little caper and I need an explosives expert. That's why I've come to you."

"Where is it and what would I have to do? And what would I get paid?"

"The 'where' I can't tell you yet. Need to know, and all that. The 'what' is this. Is there some way you could put a device together so that a heavy rectangular object could go safely past it, but if the object was moved back again, the mechanism would trip an explosive charge?"

Flamer did not pause. "Easy, boy, easy," he said. "In

the business, we call it a nonreversible arming switch. No sweat. That and a shaped charge would do the job nicely. No complaints. But, say, what moves this rectangular object?''

"Steel cables, maybe two inches in diameter.''

"Sounds like an Otis elevator cable to me,'' Flamer said.

Bell took a chance. "Flamer, you're not as big a fool as you look.'' He leaned forward and poured some more Scotch into the other man's mug. Flamer's good eye narrowed for a moment, and then he started laughing. Bell joined in.

He went on talking. "This is the plan so far. I'm not telling you yet which building it's going to be but I can say it's in the New York area. One of my backers is enormously rich and he happens to be a major stockholder in the company that services most of the elevators in that area, including this one. The maintenance is done at night so as not to have the elevators out of order when the public want to use them. Now, we're going to infiltrate a couple of guys in as maintenance men—they'll be properly trained and know their stuff—and you'd be the third. I take it you could fit a device that could be kept in position harmlessly for even a few weeks, and could be armed just before the operation started?''

"Nothing simpler.''

"Well, the idea is—I can't tell you when but certainly in the next few weeks—the two other guys would go to work and do the usual maintenance. The nighttime security guards in the building would get used to them. At that point, you'd be brought in as a supervisor, checking the other men's work over several nights, however long it took you to set the devices. Once they're in place, you'd just melt away. Your job would be done.''

"I'm pretty damn conspicuous, Tim. Have you thought of that?'' Flamer Brown rubbed his left cheek. "Even a dozy night guard's gonna remember me.''

"Makeup and tinted glasses would do it. Or you could have a big scarf round the lower half of your face. Pretend you'd got toothache. We'll work something out. There's an alternative. You could turn up just as you are and let the security guards get a good look at you. Then, the moment your job's done—and you'd be the first one finished—I could easily arrange for you to go to the best plastic surgery unit in the country and see if they couldn't improve that left side. That would keep you out of circulation if and when the heat came on. And when you came out, any description the cops had wouldn't fit you."

"You're a fucking little Santa Claus, aren't you?"

"If I can help a mate, why not? And it's not my money, anyway."

"Talking of which," Brown said, "what's in it for me?"

"What do you say to five thousand bucks and all your out-of-pocket expenses covered?"

"Not much. You shouldn't have mentioned your rich backer."

"Look, Flamer, I'm not asking you to take any risks. The worst they could get you for would be trespassing and passing yourself off as authorized."

"And for carrying explosives."

"So what? With your war record you'd walk it, the most you'd get would be a fine. Look, I'll go to ten grand, but that's the absolute limit. I don't want to be tough with an old mate like you but just think about it. The job lasts maybe four nights, it's under cover and in the warm, and the risk is minimal. I'd only have to stand outside the gates at Bragg and whistle and half the explosives experts would come running on those terms. And you damn well know it, Flamer. Tell you what I'll do. I'll give you a couple of grand before I leave, another couple when you start and the rest the morning after you've set the devices and finished the job. Fair enough?"

Flamer Brown nodded. Bell stuck out his right hand and

they shook, formally. Then Bell said, "Couple of other things. Do you know a good chopper pilot? Someone who'll take a risk or two?"

"With the law? Or his life?"

"Maybe both. He'd get well paid."

Brown pointed to a poster stuck alongside the filthy sink. It showed an expanse of unnaturally blue sea and a lighted-up skyscraper, rising like Aphrodite from about high-tide mark. In the foreground a helicopter hovered like a giant dragonfly. The inscription read: RESORTS INTER-NATIONAL, ATLANTIC CITY. Scrawled diagonally across the lower left-hand corner of the poster were seven figures, quite obviously a telephone number.

"That's your man," Flamer Brown said. "Harry Ginsberg. He was one of those quick-pick-up pilots in 'Nam. You remember, the ones that went in after deep penetration patrols and lifted them out. He might well have gotten you out once or twice."

"I was usually too busy getting out to pass the time of day with the pilot! Still, he sounds the right guy. Is that his phone number?"

Brown nodded. "But take it easy, man. Don't just go busting up to him and yell out your name, rank, and number. That guy's got problems—real problems. There's a lot of real good stuff, Colombian gold and that, moving in and out of the big C and Harry's been known to stash some in that chopper of his. Just doin' a good turn to a friend, you know. But there're a bunch of hard guys around the gaming tables, and they don't like gamblers who can't pay their debts. And right now I hear tell Harry's in the shit for some big notes. So he'd grab your dough right out of your hand."

"If he doesn't answer the phone, how do I find him?"

"Easy. The Resorts International chopper makes regular flights between Atlantic City and the heliport on the West Side in Manhattan. He's one of the pilots. Your best place to find him would be around the city heliport or at the casino. He's a crazy mad gambler, that one. And he's always spouting poetry and stuff.''

''You're a real help, Flamer. Thanks. Now one last bit of the plan. I'll need some diversionary tactics. Can you make some small incendiary devices, timed to go off on a particular day, with some adhesive on the outside to stick them on? Like under a table or the wall of a cupboard?''

''Nothing simpler. A bit of plastic with a phosphorous cover and a mechanical timer. Nothing to it.''

''How big would they be?''

''Oh, the size and shape of a pack of cigarettes—slightly bigger perhaps. But what's all this about?''

Bell thought quickly. How far could he trust Flamer Brown? Hell, he'd have to tell him something. ''It's like this. The big one comes off on a Sunday evening and it could run on through the Monday. Maybe longer. I want those incendiary devices to be planted the week before in a number of big stores, like Saks and Bloomingdale's and Bonwit Teller, timed to go off on the Monday morning when the stores are full of shoppers. That'll stretch the Police and the Fire departments, and get some panic going.''

''And who does the planting?''

''You do.''

''Like fuck I do! Take a good look at me, Tim, baby.'' He pulled back the long hank of hair and held his wounded face up to the light. ''I'm a marked man. You want *me* to wander round those stores in broad daylight, planting my little fire bombs? You're crazy, man.''

''I'll make it worth your while. How about another five thousand bucks for a morning's stroll?''

''How about another ten thousand?'' Flamer said.

''Okay, I won't argue. That's twenty thousand in all. You can do it. Wear dark glasses, a hat, and a raincoat with the collar up. And hobble around with a stick. Shoppers don't look closely at other shoppers. All they're looking for are the things to buy. You'd be in and out like a dose of salts!''

"You make it sound fucking easy, but you won't be there to get caught."

Bell said, "Okay, if you're chicken, I tell you what. You make up half a dozen of these devices and I'll pick 'em up off you and do it myself. But I don't pay a guy ten thousand bucks to do the job myself. Your take drops to a thousand, and that includes the cost of the materials."

"Not so fast. I didn't say I wouldn't do it."

"Well, are you on or aren't you?"

Flamer Brown paused and licked his lips. Then he said, "Right, I'll do it."

"Great. One last thing. Would you like to make a really big bang?"

"Like what?"

"Like blowing up the subway under Rockefeller Center."

"Holy fucking Christ! What's gotten into you, Tim? You tryin' to flatten New York?"

"Kind of. I want New York to know it's been taken. That subway area carries a lot of traffic. I can't give you the details—yet—but that Monday morning the whole city's gonna be on edge. Panic in the streets, that kind of thing. And just to top it off, we get these big stores mysteriously bursting into flames and then—whoosh—the subway blows! You get the picture?"

"Jesus, Tim. Like they say, you go for it."

"And you're the trigger man. Tell you what I'll do. I'll round it up to a neat twenty-five thousand if you'll plant a device in the subway—under Rockefeller Center—that Monday morning."

Flamer Brown said, "It could be a giggle. Pack it in a suitcase, thirty-minute timer, leave the case somewhere handy and then just stroll away. What a bang! That'll teach 'em."

"You're my boy. Well, are we on for the lot?"

"You bet."

They shook hands again. Bell took a wad of notes out of an inner pocket. "There's a couple of grand there. Count it, if you like. But now I'm gonna lay it on you. Hard. For Chrissakes, get a grip on yourself. This place is like a fucking pigsty. Clean it up, clean yourself up, and for Jesus Christ's sake, cut out the opium pipes. I don't want you seeing green snakes in the sky when it comes to placing the devices. If they don't go up when we need 'em to, I'm personally going to find you and cut off one of your fingers every day until you're left with ten bleeding stumps. And no local anesthetic. Do you read me loud and clear?''

Bell and Angie took a cab down Fifth Avenue. Approaching Washington Square, the driver turned right, then eventually left onto West Street, down past Pier 40 and up the short ramp to Two World Trade Center, the southerly tower block. He had already booked a table for dinner that night in the other tower and had suggested to Angie that they arrive in the afternoon and spend two or three hours looking round. She had agreed eagerly; he occasionally wondered how far he would have to go before she drew herself up and said No in a loud voice.

He had been on a brief tour of the center when on furlough in New York but he had not observed the place seriously. This time was operational and, while his eyes moved everywhere, his mind clenched itself in concentration. While Angie was ooh-ing and ah-ing at the size and height of the atrium and the mirror glass fronting the elevator doors, he was privately pacing out the internal measurements. He made each wall to be seventy-five paces across the red carpet. He took several of the free illustrated brochures at a desk near the main bank of elevators. He leafed through one of them and saw that it contained some of the vital points he needed to know; that each tower was served by twenty-three high-speed express cars, seventy-two local elevators and four giant freight elevators. The whole system was computer-controlled. The elevators traveled at up to sixteen hundred feet per minute and it took fifty-eight seconds to whisk the passenger from the ground to the 107th floor in the nonstop express elevator.

They took the escalator up to the mezzanine floor. Here there was a plaza connecting the towers, a stone expanse with a huge bronze globe set on a marble platform in one corner. To the front there stood a strange piece of metal sculpture, an angular contraption that rose thirty feet in the air like a rectangle pushed over on one of its sides. And to the left, midway between the towers, the only piece of nature in the whole man-designed, man-created Babylon— half a dozen plane trees that would come into leaf in the spring.

Bell had imagined that the two towers would have been set on the same axis and was surprised to see that it was otherwise. The east side of the northerly tower, if continued in a straight line, would constitute the west side of the southerly tower. This meant that the line would have to be fired at an angle of up to forty-five degrees. Not impossible, but not as simple as he would have wished. He told Angie that he needed a breath of fresh air and wouldn't be away for more than a few minutes—indeed, he'd be in her sight all the time. He went out of the door on the mezzanine floor and walked across the plaza toward the other tower, counting under his breath as he went. He stopped at the near corner, turned and waved to her; he reckoned that it had taken him forty-five paces from corner to corner. He retraced the journey and this time made it forty-six paces. The infantryman's pace is thirty inches but Bell reckoned that he opened it up to thirty-three when measuring for distance. He would do his detailed sums later but a quick mental calculation showed him that the distance was about one hundred and twenty-five feet—forty yards plus. He would need to allow a little more for the downward angle and for the fact that the trajectory would be fairly flat and would be aimed into the center of the opposite tower and not at the corner. Even so, he was not displeased. He had been allowing for up to two hundred feet.

"Sorry, my love," he said, "but it was worth it. I've won a bet with a rich friend."

"How on earth? You looked just like a sentry marching up and down out there."

"You remember me telling you about that rich friend I came here with? Well, he bet me a hundred bucks that the distance between the two towers was more than a hundred yards. In fact, it's under fifty. Now I'm a man of wealth, I can afford to treat you to the observation floor."

The observation floor ran around three sides of the building, the fourth side being a souvenir shop and a fast-food "servery." Just in case the idle visitor needed reminding, the internal walls depicted the history of capitalism from the days of barter through "the Lure of Gold" to J. Maynard Keynes, who apparently saved capitalism when it looked as though the wicked socialists, communists indeed, might have won the day. Angie loved the murals but Bell was more concerned to gaze through the wide windows at the tower almost opposite. He saw another problem. The observation area was on the 107th floor of Tower Two. The main restaurant where the Zionist dinner was to take place was on the 107th floor of Tower One. He needed elevation for his firing position. With the excuse that he wanted to take another look at the murals on the farther wall, he walked swiftly around the floor. Then he breathed again. There was an elevator running up to the roof, three floors higher. That day, it was closed to the public because of the high winds but he could see at a glance that only a flimsy wooden partition sealed it off.

He rejoined Angie and they spent the next ten minutes gazing down on the length of Manhattan, picking out landmarks like the Empire State Building, the Pan Am Building, and the Chrysler Building from the silhouettes on the windows. Angie said, "Oh, it makes me feel sort of religious."

"Religious?"

"Yes, religious. Do you remember that bit in the Bible where the Devil took Jesus to the top of a high mountain and showed him all the wonders of the world? I somehow know how Jesus must have felt."

"Which makes me the Devil."

She laughed. He took her arm and steered her toward the servery, where they had a coffee each. There was an off-duty attendant at the next table, who was looking for a light for his cigarette. Bell flicked open his lighter and started chatting with the man. He learned that there were no offices between the observation floor and the roof, only a service area for water tanks, the electricity grid, and the various other necessities that kept the tower working. It was really like a vertical town, the man said; twenty-five thousand people worked in Tower Two, and the same again in Tower One. In any one day, up to another thirty thousand visitors came to the two towers. "Eighty thousand," he said, "that's a helluva lot of folks. Comin' and goin', comin' and goin'. Ants, that's all we are. Thousands of ants."

Angie's spirits fell when he said there was no way they were going to hack fifty blocks uptown to the Waldorf and fifty blocks all the way back again, just so that she could shower and change into an evening dress for their dinner at the Windows on the World restaurant. But they rose when he grasped her firmly by the elbow, guided her down in the elevator to the shopping concourse under the plaza, insisted on her buying a new dress, and then steered her across to the Vista Hotel, which joined the twin towers along their outer edges. There he booked a room, shot the bolt in the door, stripped her clothes off and aggressively took her to new sexual heights. When she had stopped gasping and moaning, he gave her a dig in the ribs and said, "Woman, there's the bathroom. You have exactly forty minutes to take a shower, put on your new dress, put on your warpaint and be standing ready. Get me?"

"Yes, sir. Under that hard exterior there beats a heart

equally hard. God knows why I love you so much, you shit!''

A corridor joined the northern side of the Vista Hotel to the lobby of Tower One. They walked past the airline booking desks along the wall to the mirror-fronted express elevators—two of them—that soared nonstop the quarter of a mile up to the Windows on the World restaurant. The girl who had taken his telephone booking had asked him to be there precisely at seven and had added the polite reminder that gentlemen must wear jackets and ties—and positively no jeans, please.

The elevator comfortably took twenty people. If both of them were working on the night of the Zionist dinner, as he expected they would be, the 120 guests could be transported up to the restaurant in fifteen minutes, allowing time for the elevators to disgorge at the top and come back down again. That would be the crucial period and he was privately glad that it would be no longer. Six rectangles of wrought iron made up the ceiling of the elevator, with a gentle diffused light behind them. Bell made a mental note that time would be needed for dismantling and then replacing them.

The internal walls of the elevator were in the same semifrosted mirror glass, as was the long corridor that led to the restaurant. Even Angie, whose mouth was a permanent O from each successive wonder of the world that caught her eye, pronounced that the effect was very chic. Bell gave the names of Mr. and Mrs. Ford to the maître d'hôtel who presided over an enormous list spread out on an easel and they were soon led to their table by a waitress in a creamy white two-piece costume. There, over a Scotch, he took stock while Angie enthused about the view, which was indeed dramatic.

The restaurant extended the whole length of the north side and into a dogleg on the east side. So that all diners would get the same view, it descended in three steps toward the windows that ran around the floor. The tables for two were on a fairly narrow corridor furthest away from the windows. A broader middle section, perhaps five feet lower down, was occupied with banquettes for four except that—close to the junction with the east side—there was a raised dais with a low rail round it, which could supply space for twenty diners. Bell would have placed a large bet that this was going to be the "high table" for the speakers and the most distinguished guests; he made a mental note to ask Sayeed to try to get a seating plan for the celebration dinner.

He asked Angie to excuse him for a moment. On his way back to the men's room and in the guise of an enthusiastic tourist, he gazed at everything en route. His mind, trained to absorb and retain significant details, took in the fact that beyond the swinging doors where the restaurant area ended there was a bar and a sitting area. He assumed it would be closed on the night of the dinner because no one sitting there could see or hear what was going on in the restaurant but again he would feel happier if Sayeed could have the point checked out. The rest of the east and south walls were taken up by an observation area and, farther on, rooms for private dining clubs. The kitchens must occupy the northwest corner.

In the middle of dinner, he excused himself again. Angie said, "What's the matter, darling? Cracking up in your old age?"

"It must be the white wine," he said. "Goes through you like a dose of salts."

"How elegantly put."

"Well, you know me, sweetie," he said as he rose. "Just a plain honest soldier."

"I'll buy the soldier bit—that's all."

He took this second opportunity to study angles of fire and blind areas that would need flushing out. There would be at least one Israeli security man stationed in the corridor leading to the restaurant and probably another by the lobby this side of the elevators. He or they must be dealt with fast, before they could take cover in the observation area or the private rooms. The same went for the chef and his cooks. They had to be rounded up and herded into the dining area. His team were too few to stand spreading out over such a vast area. Besides, a kitchen is a dangerous place, with sharp knives and the hard edges of plates and boiling water. Everyone there was a hazard; Israeli security men could be infiltrated as chefs. So anyone who blinked out of turn would get it. The thought reminded him of what a vulnerable edge he and his men would have.

When their dinner was over, Bell took Angie to the observation area and showed her the Statue of Liberty shining down in the black waters of the bay and Ellis Island alongside. Even Angie, whose family had lived in Shropshire on the edge of the Welsh Marches for over ten generations, could picture the romance, the excitement, and often the tragedy of leaving Europe with what you stood up in and one battered old trunk to make a life in a New World, exchanging the mild tyranny of the czar for the fierce tyranny of the market and the sweatshop. Bell, meanwhile, was observing the heliport on the extreme southwest edge of Manhattan, not far from the Fire Department Pier and next to Battery Park. It was half a mile away from the foot of the tower.

One other problem had caught his attention. Presumably to withstand the buffeting of the winds at this height, the windows were narrow vertical strips with a marble-faced rounded pillar supporting them on either side. It would have been too conspicuous to go over and measure them by hand, so he had to rely on his practiced eye; he reckoned they were between three and three and a half feet across. It would have to be an accurate or lucky shot to be on target first time and Flamer Brown's frame charges must cut perfectly. Fortunately, the pillars were rounded, so a near miss would be likely to skid off the pillar and through the gap. He hoped so—Christ, he hoped so.

The momentum of surprise will be our only edge, he thought. The reaction delay of the security guards will be minimal, seconds. My best gun hands have to be there.

The telephone rang on Bob Yardley's desk in the Fort Bragg stockade. His assistant's voice said, "Would you pick up on red, Major? It's a scrambler call, personal to you."

Yardley lifted the red telephone and said, "Yardley."

With a slight echo on the line, as though he were talking from a deep cave, Joe Dodds came through. "Bob, that you? Fine. Has our friend been in touch at all?"

"Not a damn thing. Like I said, the last time I saw him was nearly two weeks back. He called my wife next day to say thanks. That's the last we've heard from him."

"You're positive? There's no way he could have called her again—or she called him—without you knowing?"

Yardley said coldly, "I don't know where you're coming from, Joe, but I don't like it. Let's get this straight once and for all. Anything that happened between Angela and Tim Bell *before* our marriage is long gone. I love her and I'm damn sure she loves me. And I resent that kind of personal innuendo."

"I'm sorry, Bob. Honest to God, I'm sorry. I don't like prying into another man's life—you must believe that. But how come there were three telephone calls made the same day last week from a New York hotel to Dr. Minter's unlisted number in Arizona?"

"How the hell would I know?"

"It was a woman's voice, Bob. And she gave her name as Angela Yardley. You see, after that Bell sighting, we put a twenty-four-hour tap on Minter's telephones. I'm afraid it was your Angie, all right."

"But what the hell would she be doing calling Minter?"

"She wasn't calling him. She asked each time to speak to Captain Bell."

"*What?*"

" 'Fraid so, Bob. If you don't believe me, listen to the tapes yourself. How did Bell get to know about Minter College? And how did your wife get hold of the unlisted number? Do you ever take classified documents back to your married quarters?"

Yardley said, "Doesn't everybody? Come off it, Joe, don't get starchy with me. I keep them under lock and key."

"Well, someone borrowed the key. I don't have to guess who."

"Are you trying to tell me my wife's in league with that shit? That's fighting talk. Besides, now I think of it, she flew to London that very morning. Her mother back in England's been none too well, so Angie flew over to be with her. Yeah, that's right, she caught a British Airways flight that morning. Why, I remember, she called me from a hotel at Heathrow where she stayed the night."

"Bob, I sure hate to say this, but you're positive she really is in England?"

"Sure. She called me from one of those hotels on the Heathrow perimeter. That's right, the Excelsior. She was going to rest up a while and then take a cab to Paddington Station to catch the Shrewsbury train. What are you getting at?"

"Well . . ."

"Oh, I see. She tells me she's going to England and then hotfoots it to Arizona instead, to shack up with the boyfriend. Christ, did you start with a dirty mind, Joe, or do they teach it to you in the CIA?"

Dodds ignored the remark. "Well, all I can say is we've lost track of Bell. Either he's gone to ground inside the Minter fortress and won't emerge for a while or he's slipped out through the cordon."

"Knowing Tim, you'd have to have a pretty tight cordon to hold him inside."

"Tight cordon! Two old dugouts and a kid who's still wet behind the ears. There's a lot of big talk up on the Hill about the security budget always being on the increase, but you should see it from where I sit. There's plenty of fat asses polishing seats in Administration, but out in the field, it's another story. Still, I better not keep you listening to my woes. Lemme know when your wife calls again, Bob, won't you? Just for the record, you know.'' He hung up.

Yardley glanced at his watch. A quarter of eleven. That made it midafternoon in England. He picked up the telephone again and tapped the button for an outside line.

That same morning, a few hundred miles north in the Waldorf-Astoria, Bell had made love to Angela before breakfast—tenderly, almost sacramentally. He had balanced the pros and cons in his mind and had decided not to kill her. It would have been simple to rent a car, make some pretext—he knew she would now accept almost anything from him—and drive a few miles north up the Taconic Parkway, go for a stroll, kill her, and leave her body hidden in the dense woods. But he had decided that disposing of her would create more problems than it solved. Besides, in an odd sort of way, he found himself becoming more fond of her as each day passed. She was probably the only person in the world who believed him to be far better than he knew he was. If he walked into a room where she was sitting, even if he had only been absent a short while, her face really did light up. He had never mattered that much to anyone before. The force of her feelings frightened him a little.

When he told her that she would have to call the airline and rebook her flight to England for that night, she cried. ''Oh, Tim, can't this just go on forever? I've never been this happy in my life. Let's stay another day or two!''

''Can't, sweetheart. If you don't go and see your family soon, they'll be sending out a search party. Besides, I've got to get back to Arizona. No, as my stepfather used to say, the doll's done dancing.''

"Some doll," she said and slid a hand across his thighs.

"Some dancing," he replied, as he grabbed her hand. "I've got a real treat for you this last day. A magical mystery tour. So get off that sexy bum of yours and grab a shower. I'll order up some breakfast."

After breakfast, they took a cab to the West Side heliport, a short distance from the World Trade Center where they had dined the previous night. Bell had already booked them on the regular forty-minute flight to Altantic City's Steel Heliport. She had never been in a helicopter before and she marveled at everything, the rearward glimpse of the receding towers of Manhattan, the vast stretch of water where the Hudson River joins the Atlantic Ocean, even the flat grimy shore of industrial New Jersey. She sat there, squeezing Bell's hand and gazing out the window as the helicopter clattered southward. She had a great capacity for enjoyment; once again, he almost loved her for it.

On arrival, they walked along the jetty and then across the boardwalk to the casino in the hotel. Although it was still midmorning, nearly all the one-armed bandits were occupied and the din was deafening. Fat women and desiccated old men stood guard in front of their particular machines, clutching handfuls of quarters and feeding them into the hungry maw. Lights flashed, the handles clanged, the dials spun, over and over in a nonstop torrent. Bell knew the machines' entrails were adjusted in favor of the house and that for every ten quarters put into the slot, five at least never came back to Joe Public. All the same, he changed a ten-dollar bill for himself and one for Angie; they started playing adjacent machines. He tried to explain that you won if four of the same symbols came up in line and that you were able to "hold" certain columns if the "Hold" light came on. She hardly took it in, more intent on watching the patchwork of humanity, but all the same she won twice—two dollars the first time and a dollar fifty the second. She screamed with delight and kissed him full on the mouth. Bell went on losing steadily and had to change another ten-dollar bill.

After about half an hour, he shouted to Angela above the din, "It's a bit noisy in here, don't you think? What do you say we find a quieter spot?"

"Whatever you say, darling. It's not that you're jealous of my winnings, is it?"

"Big deal," he said. "Let's go through to the main casino—the blackjack tables."

"Blackjack? That sounds sinister. Isn't that what you hit someone on the head with?"

"It's not that kind of blackjack, sweetie. This is a card game. You must have played pontoon as a kid—vingt-et-un, whatever you call it."

"Is that where you twist and bust?"

"Absolutely right. You have to try to get as close to twenty-one as you can without going over. Court cards count as ten, aces as one or eleven."

"I remember. We used to play it at Christmas with matches."

"It's a bit more expensive here, but you've got the right idea. Here, let me go and buy you some counters and then we'll watch for a bit before you start playing. To get your eye in."

"What about you, Tim? Aren't you going to try your luck?"

"Not right away. Just remembered a couple of phone calls I must make before lunch. You go ahead, love, and I'll join you in a minute. Remember—always stick on eighteen!"

It didn't take her long to find out that blackjack is a boring game. She watched the listless faces of the other players around the banana-shaped dealing table and wondered why they did it. There was no secret, no surprise, no finesse. It wasn't anything like the fun she recalled from those long-ago Christmas games with the matchsticks. She won a few dollars, then lost a few dollars, then had quite a good winning streak in which she doubled the original pile of counters, and then gradually they were whittled away until after playing for about half an hour, she had lost everything. A pang of guilt welled up inside her, and it wasn't for the money. She decided to ignore it.

She got up from the table and looked around the huge room. No sign of Tim. The permanent artificial lighting and the lack of windows to let in the daylight gave the place a sinister timelessness, or so she felt, and the sense of warm stale air all around her made her want to get out of the casino and feel the ocean winds on her face. So she walked out past the glittering rows of coin in the slot machines into the lobby.

She stopped abruptly when she saw Tim Bell over by an ornamental fountain talking earnestly to a short, dark-haired man with a thin, lined face, who nodded every now and then. She was about to go over and say hello, but something in their attitudes, in the deferential way the other man stood alongside Tim, made her hesitate and then turn back into the main casino. They must be talking serious business. For the hundredth time, she wished that she could get closer to Tim's thoughts, that he would confide in her more. More!—that he would confide in her at all. He was such a man of mystery. What on earth was he doing in the States and where did all these dollars come from? A captain's pay in the SAS didn't let you starve altogether, she knew, but it didn't run to suites at the Waldorf, dinner in all the best New York restaurants, and losing a couple of hundred dollars at the gaming tables. What was he up to?

A few minutes later, Bell joined her and took her off for a prelunch drink at one of the restaurants in the huge building. He teased her over losing all his dollars at black-jack and seemed to be in the best of moods. After lunch, they took the helicopter back to the West Side heliport in lower Manhattan.

Angela had a vague idea that the pilot was the same short, dark-haired man Tim had been talking to but, as he was wearing large headphones that hid part of his face, she

could not be certain. But he certainly went out of his way
to keep the passengers entertained. He was a bit of a card,
she thought, always coming up on the intercom with some
quotation or other. He must have read the insides of a box
of Christmas crackers. As they lifted up over the New
Jersey shoreline, with the sun going down to their left and
making red streaks low in the sky, the pilot's voice pro-
claimed, "See, see, where Christ's blood streams in the
firmament"—a bit on the blasphemous side, she thought
privately. And again, as they were approaching the Hudson River and all the lights of New York came up on the
skyline, he burst out with

" 'Is it not brave to be a king, Techelles?
Usumcasane and Theridamas,
Is it not passing brave to be a king,
And ride in triumph through Persepolis?'

"Ah, Persepolis! You folks can call it New York, Manhattan, what you like. To me it's always Persepolis."

"That guy's some kind of nut," said a surly-looking
male passenger alongside her and Tim. "Hope he knows
how to drive this thing."

Instead of making a direct line for the heliport, the pilot
flew a few degrees to the northwest and made a sweep two
or three hundred feet above the twin towers of the World
Trade Center, making sure to avoid the tall mast that stood
on the roof of the northerly tower. He appeared to hover
awhile so that the passengers could gaze straight down at
the giant buildings.

"There they are, Tim," he said, "the topless towers
themselves.

" 'Was this the face that launch'd a thousand ships,
And burnt the topless towers of Ilium?'

"Take some burning, those babies would. That poor

guy Marlowe. Supposed to be a secret agent, got himself stabbed to death in a tavern. But what a poet.''

Angela saw that Bell's face was tight, brooding. She said, ''Did you hear? He called you Tim.''

''It couldn't be me,'' he said. ''Must be some other Tim on board.''

She was about to say that surely the pilot was the same man she had seen him talking to at the casino, but something about his closed-down face stopped her. If he wanted to have his little secrets, let him.

She cried when the time came late that afternoon to pack her bag—and again at Kennedy Airport when they were waiting for her flight to be called. ''I'm so sorry, Tim,'' she choked, ''I hate embarrassing you in public. But it's been so lovely, and when shall I ever see you again?''

''Soon,'' he said, ''soon. You'll have to spend two, maybe three weeks with your family and I'm going to be tied up on a job at least that long. Maybe longer. I'll expect you back at Fort Bragg by the end of the month— first week of April, to be on the safe side.''

''But how'll we get in touch?''

''Leave that side to me. Here, let me have your parents' phone number. Scribble it down on this little notepad, why don't you? There's just a chance I'll contact you while you're still there. And if anything goes badly wrong with Bob when you get back to Bragg, and you have to leave sharply, I'll always know where to get in touch.''

''You *will* get in touch, Tim?'' She looked at him earnestly, almost a little sadly.

''Cross my heart. Hey, that's your flight they're calling. Safe journey and see you soon. That's a promise.''

. . . BUT WHERE WE ARE IS HELL,
AND WHERE HELL IS, THERE MUST WE EVER BE.

19

BELL FLEW BACK to Phoenix next day. On the flight, he
thought about the reconnaissance trip he had just completed and decided that it had worked quite well. He would
need to make at least one more flying visit to New York,
to be sure that Flamer Brown was sobering up and getting
down to work. He would also need to keep in touch with
Harry Ginsberg, the chopper guy. Ginsberg was one of
your "gamblerholics"; even standing there in the lobby of
the casino, Bell sensed that the little man was getting a
hard-on at the thought of the tables so close by. And he
was into the heavy mob for a bunch of gambling debts.
That could be a big problem, because he was a major link
in Bell's own plan. On the other hand, he would not have
come that cheap or been that desperate to pick up illegal
bucks if he had been a churchwarden at the local church.
So, on the whole, it had been okay. Angela was still a
problem—what if she went back to Bob in two or three
weeks and told him the lot? Apart from kicking her out,
what the hell could he do? All she could say was that

they'd had fun here and there, eaten at half a dozen different restaurants, seen every damn painting and statue up and down Fifth Avenue, and done the usual hick's tour of Manhattan. Nothing suspicious in that. And he, Tim Bell, would be under cover in the Idaho forests until the time came to strike. Up yours, Bob, he thought.

Once back in the Minter residence, he briefed Sayeed on the main points of the New York visit and told him that he would like to move on to Boise, Idaho, the following morning. The first meeting with the "troops" was set for nine o'clock next Monday and he needed the long weekend to work himself up to peak fitness and get to know the local terrain. He told Sayeed that he preferred not to stay at Doc Holliday's palatial ranch house but to be independent. Sayeed agreed that it would be better to use Minter's Gulfstream executive jet to fly Bell to Boise and not risk scheduled flights. He explained to Bell that he had already had several long telephone conversations with Holliday and had exchanged telex messages; all the details were in hand and under control.

That night at dinner Gene Minter was unusually eloquent. It was as though, deep down, he was beginning to enjoy the fact that the threat brought to his ivory tower by the presence of Bell would not be with him for more than a few hours. He talked quite amusingly of his early days in the State Department and of the gaffes and scandals that occur through the spoils system, when ambitious young professionals are continually thwarted because the top posts in diplomacy so often go to the rich amateur who backed the presidential campaign or to the awkward politician who may do less damage several thousand miles away in a European capital.

Then he waxed solemn. "There's one thing I'm not altogether happy about, Sayeed—and you too, Tim, you come into this. It's the fact that you propose to use these Anglo-Saxon Brethren, or whatever they call themselves, to carry out the plan. They are white trash, fascist trash.

I've read articles about them, seen photographs. They swagger about with their pseudo-Nazi insignia, wearing guns like phallic symbols—they're the scum of the earth. They have no ideals, no political code to follow. They just want to be bully-boys stamping on people with their jack-boots, worshiping force because they know inside that without force and the power of the gun they are nothing!"

Sayeed cut in smoothly with, "Of course, you're right, Gene. We and they are poles apart. We have nothing in common. We believe that the force of reason will ulti-mately prevail, they believe in the force of the bullet. But let's keep in mind, Gene, what Tim said the other day. These young men are expendable. If blood is to be shed, I would rather know that it belonged to some gun freak and not to one of our splendid young men."

"All the same . . ." Minter began.

"No, it's not the same," Sayeed talked over him. "It's a question of ends and means. It always is. We Marxists know that the Jew must be suppressed and finally eradi-cated. The whole Jewish race is too individualistic, too *different,* ever to fit into the overall pattern of Marxist life. Look at the career of Trotsky, who could not stay in step with the majority. The Anglo-Saxon Brethren approach the problem from the other end. They know deep down that the Jew is too clever, too ambitious, too well supported by other Jews, not to thrive and not to push them down—where they really belong. They sense that the only way they can ever beat the Jew is by force. That's why they strut around with guns strapped to their belts like Nazi storm troopers. With a gun, they feel they are somebody. Without a gun, they go back to being gas-pump attendants or the boy who carries your groceries to your car."

"But I still don't see why we should make use of them," Minter said testily.

"Because of the eventual goal. Because the end is more important than the means. Think back, Gene—nearly fifty years. There was a great outcry when the Ribbentrop-

Molotov pact was announced. All the political thinkers, even convinced Marxists, thought that Stalin had either gone mad or sold out to the Nazi thugs. And if Hitler had not felt that his eastern flank was then secure because of the pact, he might never have risked invading Poland. We shall never know. But what we do know is that Stalin bought himself more than eighteen months of precious time in which to train and equip his forces. Without that vital breathing space, Moscow might well have fallen when Hitler did finally attack Soviet Russia in 1941. Don't you see, Gene, we are using these Nazi-type thugs just as Molotov, directed by Stalin, used that champagne sales-man, *von* Ribbentrop?''

''What do you think, Tim?'' asked Minter. ''You're very quiet.''

''Political history's not my field, Gene. But I agree with Sayeed here. Think of these fellows as bullets. It's the man with brains and ideas who puts the bullet in the gun, then aims and fires it. The bullet is just an object. It can do nothing by itself. If the aim is straight, the bullet will hit the target. If not, it won't. The bullet can't aim itself or fire itself. Like I say, it's just an object. That's what these guys are. Objects.''

''Tim sums it up neatly, don't you think, Gene?'' Sayeed said. ''We can't make him a professor at the college and I'm sure he wouldn't accept if a post were offered, but at least I can offer him another glass of your excellent port. And perhaps he can explain a point that I have never understood. Why is it *de rigueur* to circulate the port in a clockwise direction?''

It was lunchtime the following day when the Gulfstream executive jet touched down smoothly at Boise Airport. Bell thanked the pilot and strode across with a suitcase in each hand to the car-rental desks, where he signed for an inconspicuous standard model. He had a leisurely drive through and around the town of Boise and eventually picked a quiet motel with a lit-up VACANCY sign. It was as cold as he had remembered from his visit the week before, with brooding slate-gray skies and a sharp-edged wind from the northwest licking one's extremities. Arizona had been in the mid-seventies, balmy and warm. This lumber town was at least thirty degrees cooler, and he shivered slightly inside the sheepskin coat that Sayeed had thoughtfully included in his wardrobe.

For three days, he drove himself mercilessly toward peak physical condition. He knew that he would need to be not just as good as the best athletes in the training squad, but better. One man trying to dominate forty can leave nothing to chance. So every morning and every evening in the quiet of his motel room, dressed in a tracksuit padded with towels and a thick jersey, he flung himself into an hour of the severest gymnastics. With the sweat pouring down his face and muscles standing out like bars, he attempted, and achieved, 150 continuous fling-ups. He then switched to a hundred press-ups on the fingertips of one hand only; then another hundred on the other hand.

In the daytime, he would cram stones and earth into an SAS-type backpack, until it weighed thirty pounds. With the pack slung on his back, he would lope off into the forest with an effortless running action, covering seven or eight miles of uphill soggy ground and drifts of snow, crossing icy streams or weaving to and fro between the trunks of the forest giants—all inside one hour. He wore heavy boots and thick underwear and sweated away every surplus ounce of flesh until he knew himself to be as hard and fit as he had ever been in his life. And all the time as he panted and grunted and drove himself to the edge, and then beyond, he was thinking how he would handle that first meeting with the squad.

On Monday morning, he arrived early at the rendezvous in the forest. It was alongside the firing range, where there had already been a couple of sheds and a small hut for the range warden. Doc Holliday had had two large prefabricated barrackroom huts erected as sleeping quarters and a dining hut put up alongside. Bell commandeered the range warden's hut for himself. To maintain the mystique, a leader has to be aloof. Fields, the ex–Green Beret rangemaster, might resent the loss of his privacy when he had to bed down with the rank and file—but that was his problem.

The men began arriving in ones and twos, many in four-wheel-drive Jeeps or small trucks. They stood around talking, their breath in plumes on the cold still air. A few dragged away at cigarettes. Bell smiled grimly to himself. Those lungs would soon be too tortured, too straining for every gasp of air, to stand the luxury of a deep drag of nicotine.

Sharp on nine o'clock, he strode out of the range warden's hut and stood in front of the men, who were in little groups. "Right," he said in a loud clear voice. "Fields, I want you here as right marker. The rest of you fall in in two lines. The front rank alongside Fields here, the rear rank three paces behind. Got it? Okay, on the double!"

Someone in the second-nearest group muttered, "Who the fuck does he think he is?"

Bell marched over and thrust his face within six inches of the face of the man who had spoken. He looked him straight in the eye and said clearly, "I talk, *you* listen. Got it? If I want an opinion from you, *I* ask the question, *you* give the answer. Remember that and we'll have no trouble."

The men fell in in two ragged lines. They were dressed in an odd variety of outside clothes, lumber jackets, weatherproof blousons, a few plain overcoats. Most were carrying weapons, ranging from shotguns to hunting rifles to long-barreled Colt revolvers. In the middle of the front row, Bell noticed two men lounging, one well over six feet and the other about his own height. They were dressed up as German Waffen SS officers, with the double lightning insignia on their epaulets and tunic fronts, the silver cording around the caps, whose peaks came straight down over the eyes, and the black polished leather high boots.

Bell went over and stood in front of the taller man.
"I'm looking for men," he said, "not kids in fancy dress.
You two are out—as of now! Leave the parade and get the
hell out of here."

He turned contemptuously but he could see what was
happening reflected in a window of the hut opposite. The
bigger man stepped forward and aimed a rabbit punch at
the back of Bell's neck. As the fist came through the air,
Bell swiveled, grasped the man's wrist, and using his own
momentum, pulled his arm at full stretch across his own
shoulder. He ducked sideways and the heavy body slid
over his right shoulder to crash on the ground in front. Still
holding the man's right wrist in his own right hand, Bell
jerked his opponent's head back and with the edge of his
left hand, gave him a smart clip below the left ear. The
man grunted and went limp.

It had all happened in perhaps a second, not more than
two. Bell swung round again and stared at the other man.
"Are you looking for an argument?" he said.

"No."

"No, what?"

"No, sir."

"Right. You drag him off the parade. It's okay, he's not
dead, just out for a while. And I don't ever want to see
hide or hair of you two, ever again. You can go and wank
in front of Hitler's portrait!"

"Stand at ease," he commanded the rest of the squad.
"I'll keep this brief. My name's Bell. There are forty of
you—thirty-eight now the Gestapo has left. It's my job to
whittle you down to twelve—two teams of six. I'm going
to see what you're made of and you're going to hate my
guts before we're finished. So if anyone wants to quit right
now, he's welcome. I'll give you one minute." He glanced
at his wristwatch. "If you want to go, just get into your
car and get the hell out of here. And don't ever come
back." He looked at his watch again. "Okay, minute's
up. No takers? Right, let's see what you're made of.

"For the moment, I'm appointing Fields here as my second in command. First off, we're going for a cross-country run. It's a triangle. Out along the forest track northwest to where the wooden bridge crosses the creek. Fields will be there to check you off. Then northeast through the woods to the lumber pile at Prairie Meadow. And then back here the fastest way you know. I'll be moving around in the forest—any man cutting corners is out. You've got seventy minutes to run the whole circuit. Anyone taking longer is out. He can pack his things and go. Any questions?"

"But that must be over seven miles, Mr. Bell," a voice said from the rear rank.

"You don't call me Mister—call me boss. Got it? All together now—Yes, boss. That's lousy, a girl's school would sound louder. Once again now—Yes, boss. That's better. Right, who asked that question?"

"I did."

"I did—*what?*" He ended on a shout.

"I did, boss."

"Well, you're damn right. It's seven miles one furlong on the most direct route. And seventy minutes is the limit. If you can't average a mile in ten minutes across country, you're no good to me. Any other questions?"

There was a shuffling of feet and someone, again in the rear rank, muttered a word or two, but no questions.

"Right," Bell said sharply. "Fields, you trot on ahead to the bridge across the creek. You know the one I mean? Good. You know all these guys by sight or name?"

"Yes, boss," Fields said.

"Fine. There are thirty-eight on parade, thirty-seven not counting yourself. Check 'em all across the bridge, will you, and then follow them round the course. You don't have to bring up the rear, if you feel like a good stretch. Carry on. The rest of you, into your huts, strip down to your undervests and underpants—keep your boots and socks on, for Chrissake—and back here within three minutes. On the double!"

"In this freezing weather, boss?"

"You heard me. Once you're running your guts out, you'll soon get warm!"

For a moment, he thought there was going to be a rebellion. There was a further shuffling of feet and louder muttering from the rear rank. He knew that if they all rushed him together, the best he could do would be to take two or three out with him before he went under the rolling wave of boots and fists. The ringleader appeared to be a thick-necked, red-faced man in jeans near the end of the front rank. He was turning around and whispering loudly to someone behind.

"You," Bell spoke incisively. "You, showing your fat backside. If you've got anything to say, you say it to me. Got it?" Bell walked closer as he spoke, until he was a yard away from the man. "Don't any of you jerkers understand simple English? I said double over to your huts, strip down to your underwear and back on parade. Sharp! Come on now. No one's gonna bugger you while you're not looking. So get on with it."

The parade broke up, none too happily, and the men dispersed toward their huts. Fields asked Bell, "Do you want me to strip down as well, *boss?*" There was heavy sarcasm in the way he emphasized the last word.

"No, not you. You'll have to hang around maybe ten minutes at the creek. I don't want you getting warmed through and then cooling off too fast while you're waiting."

"Very thoughtful. I suppose you know what you're doing with these others?"

"I know what I'm doing. On your way now."

The men were beginning to clatter back from the huts across the crisp earth of the parade ground. Bell counted them as they arrived and ordered the early arrivals to jog up and down to keep warm. They looked a forlorn bunch with their white exposed arms and legs. Once the numbers were complete, Bell ordered them off with a shout. They ran in a ragged line toward the edge of the pine trees and

up the rutted track. As soon as the last man disappeared,
Bell was away in a loping run, sliding through the trees as
he kept a course roughly parallel with them. Away to his
left, he could hear heavy panting and a loud curse as a
man tripped over a tree stump. Noisy bastards, he thought.
They're supposed to be men of the wilds, hunters, most of
them. They sound more like a panzer division on the
march.

He headed in the direction of Prairie Meadow but weaved
left from time to time, to make sure that no one was
cutting a corner after being checked in by Fields at the
bridge. There was no official check-in at Prairie Meadow
and it would be simple enough for the laggards to work
their way through the forest and turn south without ever
getting near the lumber pile. They'd regret it if they tried
that stunt, he thought.

There were still drifts of snow piled up in the hollows
and on the west side of tree trunks. Aloft, the branches
creaked and whispered as melting snow slid off to spatter
against the ground many feet below. He noticed that the
ice was quite thick in places against the banks of the creek,
although open water flowed fast in the middle. He ran
easily along the bank of the creek until he came to a
narrow point about ten feet across, measured out his run
up and then leaped clean across the stream. He felt great,
breathing easily, his whole body like a well-tuned engine.
He ran lightly through the trees toward the lumber pile and
waited for the leaders to come panting and plunging through
the mud toward him. He allowed the first half dozen to
pass him and, when there were another twenty in sight,
strung out over a furlong and more, he turned for home
and accelerated past the snorting leaders.

He was back on the parade square, wristwatch held in
front of his face, as they came stumbling into camp.
"Well done," he shouted to the first bunch, "sixty-four
minutes plus. Off you go for a hot shower. After that,

you'll find camouflage combat suits laid out in the next hut. You should find a set to fit you. On you go.''

He repeated the same message to the next bunch of arrivals, and the next after them, until the minute hand on his watch indicated that the seventy minutes were up. One man came bounding up a few seconds late and Bell waved him in toward the showers. Fields had rejoined him by then and together they checked off the numbers. Thirty-one had completed the course on time; the man Bell let through made thirty-two. The six stragglers took another five to seven minutes to turn up. To each one, Bell said, ''Sorry, you flunked. Get your gear together and go.''

One of them replied, his panting breath condensing in spurts on the chill air, ''You sonofabitch! I'll get you for this.''

Bell stepped across to him. ''Would you like to start now?'' he inquired softly. The man stumbled off toward the barrack huts.

''What's the drill now, boss?'' Fields asked.

''Let's give 'em an hour's break. Then they can load their packs up with—let's say twenty pounds' weight and do the cross-country run all over again. Fully dressed this time. And we'll cut the time limit down to sixty-five minutes. That should sort a few out.''

''Aren't you driving them a bit hard? They're not Delta Force, you know.''

''And they never will be. I've got to drive them. There just isn't the time to take it slowly.''

''What's the rush, boss? And what's it all about? You want to get down to a team of twelve—what for?''

''Fields, I can't tell you right now. I will as soon as I can. Don't push it.''

''But it's something big?''

''Yeah, you could say that. But, like I say, don't push it. There'll be proper briefings when the time comes.''

Later that morning, the thirty-two survivors went off for

their second run with the weighted packs on their backs. This time, Fields did his checking in at Prairie Meadow and Bell acted as whipper-in to the stragglers. He jogged to the top of a hill in the forest, which commanded a wide view along the length of the creek. Six men were trotting along together, quite obviously friends. Bell saw one of them, attempting to leap across the creek, crashing down on the very edge of the far bank and landing awkwardly with his left leg doubled underneath him. "Christ!" he yelled in pain, "reckon I've broken my leg." The sound floated to Bell across the still forest.

The other five hunted round in the undergrowth, found a couple of straight saplings, which one of them cut clear with a hunting knife, and then, using their belts as straps, fashioned a rough and ready stretcher for their friend. They lifted him tenderly onto the contraption and taking turns, four of them at a time carried the injured man like stretcher-bearers toward the Prairie Meadow checkpoint.

Bell ran back to the parade ground. He timed the leaders in and told them to put on greatcoats and come back on parade. The first twenty-six all got back within the sixty-five minutes, though several were ashen-pale and traces of vomit on the front of one or two camouflage jackets showed how physically stretched they had been. The carrying party of five with the injured man on the improvised stretcher arrived four minutes late.

"Okay," shouted Bell, "gather round, all of you. This is lesson number one. You're out, anyway"—he pointed to the injured man still on his stretcher—"that leg won't heal in the time we've got. Anyway, it's largely your own fault. You should have jumped the creek cleanly. Yeah, don't look surprised. I saw it all.

"As for you other five, I ought to dismiss you as well." He paused.

"What the hell for, boss? We took care of our own guy, and brought him back safe."

"That's the lesson I'm coming to. Now, listen carefully, all of you. What was my order? I'll tell you again. It was—run the full course and get back here inside sixty-five minutes. Okay? Now what if this had been for real and we had a carefully timed attack planned? It's no damn good guys wandering in three, four, five minutes late and saying, 'Gee, boss, I just saved someone's life. Pin a medal on me, willya?' If the other guy comes a cropper, that's just too bad. We'll try to pick him up when the action's over. You stick to your orders.''

He went on, ''As this is first time out, I'll give you five guys one last chance. You can either drop out now, collect your gear and get the hell out of here, or you can do a penalty speed trial.''

''Meaning what?'' one man asked.

''Meaning this. And when you speak to me, you call me boss. Get it? That's the last time I remind anyone. The penalty speed trial is this. The weight in the packs will be increased to thirty pounds. You'll run the same circuit as before but this time you'll do it in *fifty-five* minutes.''

''That's fucking impossible,'' someone said.

''We'll see. I know what most of you are thinking. You're saying to yourselves, 'It's okay for this limey to talk. He never shows us what he can do.' This time I'll show you. Fields, go and find me a pack, will you. Fill it with *forty* pounds' weight, not thirty like the others. I'll run you round the circuit—if there're any prepared to have a go.''

Grumbling among themselves, the five collected their backpacks. Fields came back with the one he had prepared; hefting it, Bell sensed that he had added a few pounds overweight for luck but he said nothing. He told the others to take a break until the speed trial was over. When the five men came back, Bell commanded Fields and another man who had been pointed out to him, an ex-corporal named Clyde who had served in the Eighty-second Airborne Division, to act as joint timekeepers. On the word "Go," the five, with Bell making the sixth, set off at a run into the forest.

Bell enjoyed himself. He felt strong and secure in his physical hardness. Although the track was now muddy and churned up with all the previous footmarks and scuffle marks, Bell felt that he was skimming along the surface. He was soon ten yards in front of the next man, then twenty and thirty until he had almost lost sight of them as they wallowed along behind him. But he could hear their anguished breathing in the distance and their shouted curses as they slipped and stumbled along the forest track.

He waded through the creek instead of trying to jump it clean—an extra forty pounds on your back will affect the distance you can jump—and the icy wetness refreshed his pumping legs. He was probably seventy-five yards ahead of his nearest pursuer when he ran up to the lumber pile in Prairie Meadow and deliberately slowed a little on the segment of the run leading back to camp. Glancing at the minute hand of his watch as he loped along, he timed himself to reach the parade ground in a few seconds over fifty-three minutes.

The sweep hand moved inexorably around the dial. With half a minute to go, the first of the other runners burst through the trees and in a weaving, stumbling course aimed for the knot of onlookers. He swayed as he reached them; two of the men grabbed him before he keeled over.

"Well done," Bell said. "You've made it. Now go and have a shower and rest up. You've got guts."

Two minutes went by and the next two appeared, trotting side by side. Bell went over and shook them both by the hand. "Sorry," he said, "you had a good go, and you didn't quite make it. But you tried—and I like that. Thanks for being good sports."

Finally, the last two turned up. Knowing they were way over the time limit, they had given up the struggle and walked into camp. One of them had flung his pack away to ease his journey. Bell stared at them coldly. He said nothing. Avoiding his gaze, they walked straight past the group into the barracks hut. A few minutes later, he could hear the noise of engines starting up and the rejects drove slowly out of the camp.

"Right," he said. "That's enough for one morning. We'll knock off for food now and a short break after that. We'll reassemble here at three o'clock—*sharp*. Anyone late without an excuse is out, finished. Don't any of you forget, there are still twenty-seven in the running, and I'm only looking for a team of twelve. So more than half of you are for the chop. Sorry, but that's how it crumbles."

"What's on this afternoon, boss?" one man asked.

"Obstacle training."

"When are we going to get down to some shooting? That's what I like."

"All in good time. There was a big general in World War II who had a motto: 'Fighting fit and fit to fight.' That's going to be our motto. By the time we've finished here, you'll all be fitter than you've ever been in your whole lives. Then it's up to you. I can make you fit, but I can't give you the guts to fight. That bit's up to you."

"There will be some fighting, then?"

"You bet your life!"

Six days went by. The first three days were spent in obstacle training. Bell formed two squads, one of fourteen and the other of thirteen, with Fields and Clyde in charge of their respective squads. He told them to break up the squads into smaller units of four each. Then he mapped out a lozenge-shaped course through the forest, full of natural and man-made obstacles—piles of stacked timber, the creek that meandered across the course to be navigated both ways, a blocked defile where a storm must have brought down several pine trees that lay across the steep banks on either side. The idea was that each team of four should pick up a heavy pine log, twenty-four feet in length, and somehow maneuver it around the perimeter of the lozenge-shaped course. Half of them would travel the course clockwise, the other half counterclockwise. There was more than a sporting chance that the most difficult obstacles would be approached simultaneously by teams of four arriving from opposite directions. Bell determined to be out of sight but able to observe when that happened. It was a quick and simple test of how the men worked together, which were the dominant personalities, and how Fields and Clyde acted in their roles of encouraging and exhorting their teams.

He watched while one man fell off a pile of stacked timber and lay groaning on the ground. He had either sprained or broken his leg. But the lesson had been learned. The other three men in the unit went on maneuvering their clumsy log across the stack of timber and only then did one of them call to Clyde to report the accident. Behind the tree that was his hiding place, Bell nodded in silent appreciation. It was beginning to work.

Also as part of the obstacle training, he taught them rope work, abseiling and crossing from one tall pine tree to another by means of a rope slung between the two. Three of the men could not stand heights, he discovered, and they had to be discarded, along with the man who had fallen off the timber stack. That left twenty-three survivors.

On the fourth day, Bell switched them over to assault course training, scrambling under tightly laid nets, across barbed wire, up and over wooden walls, swinging by ropes across deep drops. To give it a competitive edge, he kept them in teams of four vying with one another. At first, they tried the assault course in their camouflage uniforms and boots, then with packs on their backs, and finally in full equipment including gas masks, carrying unloaded submachine guns. And all the time, he was driving them on to be swifter, neater, more purposeful in everything they did. He instituted a prize of a bottle of Scotch for the winning team. When one of them asked him shyly if he would take a drink from the bottle himself, he knew that he was beginning to get across to them. These young men would not have joined the Anglo-Saxon Brethren if there hadn't been a gap in their lives, an urge to dress up and share the power. If they were beginning to want him as their little Hitler, so be it.

At irregular intervals, he would give them a speed march through the forest, on each occasion traveling that much farther in that much less time. He drove them and drove them, keeping up a running barrage of insults and gibes. And yet they could see that he drove himself just as hard, and did everything quicker, better, more efficiently than they did.

He was beginning to get a feeling for their individual characters through what they did or failed to do. He had reservations about Fields; the man had been a good soldier, no doubt of that, and was physically tough. But Bell could sense that he was desperately jealous. Once, he had been the young men's natural leader, Doc Holliday's rangemaster, who taught them how to shoot at snap targets. Now he had been demoted, number two to Bell's number one. Sooner or later, there would be—there would have to be—a showdown.

Clyde was a quieter, more rigid personality. Bell felt that he would be loyal under pressure but limited. Given clear orders, he would carry them out faithfully but, left to himself with the need to improvise, he might well dither and end up doing nothing. Bell reckoned that if you could take the two of them, Fields and Clyde, extract their better qualities, and build them into one guy, you would end up with a helluva fine soldier.

He was getting to know the rank and file as well. A few he had picked out already as men who were likely to "go for it." There was the tall blond Swenson, clearly of Scandinavian stock, who was always chuckling over some private joke; and Ellis, a dark-haired chunky fellow, with the look of a gypsy about him; and Geoghegan, a Roman Catholic who wore a small silver crucifix around his brawny neck. The others were all confined to camp throughout the training period but Geoghegan' asked permission through his team leader, Clyde, to talk to Bell privately. Bell saw him in his own small hut and asked what the problem was. The young man said he would like permission to leave the camp and drive to a church nearly ten miles away, where he knew that the priest heard confessions every Saturday night.

Bell pondered for a moment. He wanted to keep the security loop closed the whole time. And if he allowed one man to break bounds even for a reasonable excuse, would that lead to wholesale requests? Yet Geoghegan appeared sincere enough. He chatted to the man for a few minutes, trying to find out more about him. It turned out that he was the second-youngest of nine children, six girls and three boys. The father, who had fought in the British Army in World War II, had emigrated from County Galway to Massachusetts in the early 1950s and had soon married a girl of Irish descent. He had lost his job as a construction worker in downtown Boston some ten years back and had moved west with his family until he had ended up as an overseer at a lumber camp fifty miles northwest of Boise. The family had been raised as devout Catholics; Geoghegan's father had encouraged him to join the Anglo-Saxon Brethren on the strange grounds that they must be worthwhile if they were against Jews and black Southern Baptists. Hearing all this, Bell decided to let him go out of camp to have his confession heard—but he arranged for Clyde to accompany him and wait at the back of the church.

After the evening meal, there was not much to do in the camp at night except drink or play cards or sit around chewing the rag and telling unlikely tales of sexual exploits. Bell drove them hard in the daytime, not only to stretch their muscles and their minds but also to make them so tired that after they had eaten, they would slump on their barrack cots and sleep for ten hours or more. But he made a practice of inviting them in ones and twos into his hut at night after the meal. Over Scotch or bourbon, he would get to know them better by encouraging them to talk about themselves. He had to know what made them tick, their strengths and their weaknesses. If you met a stranger in the SAS, you knew automatically he must be good, and tough. A weakling would never survive the rigorous testing. And he might be a stranger to you but his reputation would have gone ahead. In a handpicked squadron of a hundred or two, you soon heard on the grapevine who was who—and how they measured up. But now he had to find out for himself. You had to get to know a man well—your life might depend in a few weeks on his guts and his speed of reaction.

Two men who interested him in particular were Elliott and Macrae. The squad called them the Heavenly Twins, and they were indeed inseparable. They always wanted to be on the same team in all the trials and off duty they stuck together. What was more, they looked alike. Both were lean, slow-speaking, with lined faces and Zapata-type drooping mustaches. They were older than the others. They had given their ages as thirty-four and thirty-three respectively but Bell reckoned privately that you could add three or four years to each total and be nearer the mark. He discovered one night over several glasses of bourbon that they had met in Vietnam, in the same infantry unit. Elliott had been wounded in the arm—a clean "through and through," luckily—and Macrae had helped him back to safety. They had stuck together ever since. On their discharge, they had bummed around the States, working long enough in one place to build up a grubstake and then moving on, always looking for something they couldn't describe, and wouldn't know if they found it. He knew instinctively they were not homosexual—Macrae had a wife in a small town in Minneapolis he occasionally sent money to when he had some to spare and Elliott had been married and divorced. He realized from his Army days that there always were some straight-up men who just preferred masculine company.

These two could go for hours with hardly a word exchanged but he sensed there was a bond there that it might take death to break.

They were a bitter pair, bitter about the whole Vietnam screw-up and the way the American people didn't want to know when the "heroes" returned. They had learned from their Army days that if you said "Yes, sir," and "No, sir," the authorities just kicked you around. If you carried a gun and didn't mind using it, people quickly stood to attention and gave you respect. So when they found jobs, as tractor driver and mechanic, with one of Doc Holliday's lumber camps, they had joined the Anglo-Saxon Brethren, although they secretly despised most of the slobs who were their fellow members.

Bell came to the conclusion they would be part of his team if they got through the final tests. He had them provisionally selected to accompany Clyde in fixing the elevators at the World Trade Center and then carrying out the vital break-in at the dinner itself. He needed quiet, steady men for the job, men who could lie up patiently waiting for the exact moment. Clyde would be reliable, and so would they be, he reckoned.

Geoghegan looked another likely starter. He was physically strong and sharp, a real Irish "mick," with his dark curly hair, blue eyes, and fresh complexion. He still had a touch of the brogue, too. There was something about him, though, that left Bell a shade uneasy. He was almost too keen, too ready to push himself to the limit and beyond. It was as if he were acting the part of the ideal trainee, the model soldier. The others would sweat and swear, but Geoghegan carried out every nasty gut-wrenching task with a willing nod and a smile. Maybe it was that fervent Catholicism of his. Bell mistrusted religious fervor instinctively, but then he recalled that one of the early heroes of the SAS, a living legend, Major Roy Farran, had been a staunch Catholic. He hoped Geoghegan would turn out to be one-quarter as good when it came to the sharp edge.

• • •

Doc Holliday turned up unexpectedly one afternoon to watch the men jumaring up pine trees, abseiling down, or swarming across on a rope from one tree to another. Bell had them competing in time trials. Each man had to jumar up a fixed rope by putting one foot in a loop attached to the fixed rope and swarming up by shifting the jumar (a ratchet that could slide upward but, if pulled, gripped the rope at that point) upward until he reached the top. Then he had to tie a ribbon to the highest branch of the pine tree, slide along the next fixed rope that was stretched to the top of another pine tree forty feet away, tie another ribbon to the highest branch of that tree, and abseil down to the ground. The moment his feet touched the earth, the next man in the team repeated the exercise, and so on until all four had done their rope work. The teams flung themselves into it with a will, yelling encouragement to one another and flinging insults at their rivals. And Bell was everywhere, shouting, cajoling, insulting, goading them on to ever quicker efforts.

That night, back at his mansion ranch house, Doc Holliday said to Annie-Lou, who was ministering to him as he lay on his back, "Say, Annie-Lou, y'ever see a shark's eye?"

"Can't say I have, Doc," she mumbled.

"Hey, a bit slower, girl. Let's not rush things. Yeah, a shark's eye. I seen plenty, out there off Bimini with the game fishing. It's an evil-looking thing, a shark's eye, I'm telling you. It don't show anger or hate or friendship—it sees everything but it don't show nothing. You can kill it an' it still gives you that cold stare. Every time I see that guy Bell, somehow I keep thinking of a shark's eye. He's just a killing machine, that one."

Annie-Lou raised her lovely head. "You sure he ain't kinda faggy, Doc? He didn't touch one of us girls when he stayed here."

"Who knows? But I'm damn sure of one thing. I ain't." Gently, with the palm of his hand on the back of her neck, he pressed her head down again.

• • •

Bell decided the men were ready now for night operations. Nearly a week had elapsed since the intensive training had begun and the numbers had dwindled. Three men had dropped out through severe cuts and bruises, the result of overenthusiastic Tarzan efforts in the high pines. Another man had a bad attack of dysentery and became too weak to keep up with the others; two more came privately to Bell and told him they couldn't take it any longer—they just couldn't face the unending physical pressure and the nervous strain of having to compete against and beat their friends. Bell thanked them for being honest and for their efforts. He shook hands and wished them well. One of them had tears in his eyes as he turned to leave.

Bell kept rearranging the seventeen survivors in their teams of four. He was getting close to his final selection, as he had decided to pick, unknown to themselves, two reserves along with the team of twelve. He was going to taper off the training by the end of April, two weeks before D-Day. There was always the risk that a team member might have an accident or fall ill in those run-up days, so it would be more than useful to be able to slot in another trained and highly fit man at the last moment.

Keeping to their teams of four, he started the night operations by ordering each team to march by compass bearing to a different fixed point five miles away in the forest, set up bivouacs, take turns in doing sentry duty, prepare themselves a field breakfast at first light, and then return to camp not later than nine-thirty. No lights of any kind were to be taken, no torches, and no matches. Nightscopes were strictly banned. The moon would set well before midnight but way above the tops of the pine trees there would be stars to guide by—if any of them, he said sarcastically, knew the Pole Star from the Milky Way. They were to be as silent as possible, to move quietly and only talk in the merest whisper when it became necessary to pass on directions.

He sent the four teams off at five-minute intervals. With the track running more or less straight to the bridge over the creek acting as the dividing line, he ordered two teams to the west of the track and the other two to the east, each with its own destination set down as a map reference. He realized well enough that skill at map-reading was not a qualification for the planned assault but he thought he might as well turn these youngsters into the nearest facsimile of a trained soldier that was possible in the limited time. He instructed Fields and Clyde to move around the western half of the forest area, keeping an eye on their two teams, while he roved the eastern side.

With years of practice behind him, he slid into the trees, moving silently from one to the next while his eyes grew accustomed to the dark. He hardly needed eyesight; ahead and to his right he could hear a noise like the crashing of young elephants on their way to a waterhole. There was the sound of a cracking branch and an angry voice said, "Oh, shee-it!" There was hardly any wind and the night was still, apart from the slight creaking and soughing of a million pine branches. The curse could have been heard a good hundred yards away.

Bell had slung a pack at his side and had filled it with thunder-flashes and nonlethal stun grenades. He circled around the noisy team until he was ahead of them, hidden behind a clump of undergrowth. As they came stumbling past, he tossed a stun grenade into their path. He ducked his head and put a gloved hand over his eyes to avoid being dazzled but the team panicked, running to and fro like headless chickens, shouting, falling over tree stumps and bracken. Bell waited for them to collect themselves and then silently moved out of his hiding place and confronted them.

"That's lesson number one," he said. "You're not off to a tea party or to go screw a few girls. This is enemy territory—get it? When you're on an operation, *everywhere* is enemy territory. You should be taking it in turns to have a man out front and a man at the back, watching both ways. And move strung out, not in a little bunch. Not frightened of the dark, are you? Strung out, it's more difficult to get the lot of you in one burst. The way you are, you'd all have been dead men by now. Remember that.''

The whole night, he moved around the forest, creeping up on different teams and harassing those that seemed at all careless. He found one sentry leaning against a tree, half asleep, and gave him the fright of his life when he felt the sharp tip of a commando knife just touching the soft flesh behind the angle of his jawbone. Another time, Bell managed to infiltrate behind a sentry and wriggle up to a two-man bivouac, which he demolished by slashing the guy-ropes. The men inside struggled and heaved as they felt themselves enveloped in the folds of the tent. When the sentry swung round, he saw the deadly shape of Bell moving into him with the knife poised.

Back at camp next morning, he had them all on parade, weary, unshaven, and in most cases hungry, as their ingenuity did not stretch to an uncooked breakfast. He went through every mistake and every weakness with them, taunting and goading them for being little kids frightened of the dark.

"There's nothing sinister about the dark," he shouted. "Everything's just the same as before. Darkness is only the absence of light—got it? Most of you were crashing around like a fart in a bottle. So tonight we'll go again— and tomorrow night, if need be, and the night after that. I'm gonna get you fit for night fighting if I have to give you all insomnia.''

"I've got to talk to you, Joe," Yardley said to Dodds.

"So what's wrong with now? These two phones are scrambled.''

"No, I need to see you. We've got to talk—and think something out. Hey, can you organize this? Wednesday,

Thursday, Friday, I've got to take a squad down to South Carolina. We're doing a tactical scheme with some of the SEAL boys offshore near Hilton Head.''

"Hilton Head? That's how the taxpayer's money goes. What's the scheme? Ordering up dry martinis as you loll in your suite?''

"Ha, ha. You're as funny as a crutch. You ought to know by now the sand and vegetation just north of Hilton Head are like what you get on the North African coast.''

"Sure, I know. The old 'let's kill Qaddafi' plot. When are you Army types gonna grow up?''

"I'll duck that question,'' Yardley said. "But I've got to see you. It's that urgent. Tell you what, we could combine business and pleasure. Let's meet in Charleston, South Carolina. It's an easy drive for me up the coast from the Head, and there'd be regular flights for you. The Miller House there's great. An old Southern mansion they turned into a hotel. We could meet Saturday afternoon, have a quiet dinner, and go our ways on Sunday morning.''

"Great. Another weekend fucked up for me. Mary's gonna have my head served up with a green salad. She reckons I ought to wear a name tag when I come home, so's the kids will know who I am! Bob, this had better be worth the aggravation.''

That Saturday evening, they sat on the marble-floored balcony of the old Miller House, having a predinner drink. Spring had already arrived in balmy Charleston; scattered around the hotel were large wooden tubs with young magnolia bushes blooming. Yardley thought that Scarlett and Rhett might come round the corner any moment.

Dodds cut into his reverie. "Do we talk now, or what? If it's that urgent . . .''

"You're right. Let's talk. Which are the main terrorist groups we're watching?'' He ticked them off in turn on each finger of his left hand. "There's the Spanish ETA crowd in Southern California, the new Black Panthers in Chicago, the very far-out Jewish organizations, a few Arab embassies, and the Anglo-Saxon Brethren. It struck me when I took on this job that infiltration would be the best way of knowing what they were up to. To cut a long story short, I knew there was no way to infiltrate ETA—our Hispanics can't play Basque. The black guys in my unit are reluctant to join their brothers on the street, and I only have one Jew in the outfit. He pretends he's a straight-up Gentile, anyway. So that really left just the ASB.''

"Well?''

"Well, this. I got one of my young guys, who was brought up in Oregon, to take a phony discharge. I sorted it out with a special friend in the A and Q Department. My man's having his pay continued but put in a special bank account. He went off to Idaho as a civvy, got in touch with the ASB, pretended he was a raving freak like the rest of them, and was soon asked to join. Nothing happened for a while, they'd just strut around toting their six-shooters and looking for the OK Corral. My man was mainly feeding some strong info to me on some of the wealthy political backing behind the group. Then, a couple of weeks ago, forty of them were asked to volunteer for special duties. My boy joined in. Who should be in charge but Captain Timothy Bell, late of the Special Air Services!''

"What?''

"Right. *Our* Mister Bell. My guy only managed to get a brief gabbled message out. Security's pretty tight—they've taken over a big lumber camp northwest of Boise and no one's allowed out of camp. But it seems Bell is giving them a crash fitness and endurance course, like the ones we run in Delta Force and the SAS course at Hereford. And there's special emphasis on tree-climbing—you know, jumaring, abseiling, swinging from one tall tree to another on a rope.''

"Jesus,'' said Dodds. He put down his bourbon and looked Yardley in the eye. "Are you thinking what I'm thinking?''

Then they said in unison, "Camp David!''

"That's what it sounds like," Yardley said. "When I first got the message, that struck me. Then I thought it was too farfetched. But you hit on it at once. Why?"

"Coupla good reasons. This president is far enough to the right for most people but to the ASB he could be Joe Stalin. They'd reckon Attila the Hun was a fellow traveler! The other thing is I've never thought Camp David was all that secure."

"Why not?"

"Simple. It's the one place the president can go to and relax. He can drive that electric buggy around the paths, wander about in an open-necked shirt or just put his feet up. There's no special protocol, no ceremony. That makes it all the tougher for the security men."

"Who does provide security?"

"The Secret Service in close. Oh, they're pretty good these days. That Hinckley fiasco shook them up real good. A bunch of Marines cover the grounds. But it's easier to protect a president if he sticks to fixed arrangements. You know where he is at any given hour. It's when he's having a break, doing things his own sweet way, that it gets more difficult. Say, just how good is this Bell?"

"Tops. You won't find a better fighting soldier anywhere. I mean it. There's an old SAS saying about 'going for it.' That describes a guy who's that bit more determined, puts that extra bit of effort into it. All I can say is, Bell goes for it."

"Could he put a team together that'd be a serious threat to Camp David?"

"Knowing him, the answer's yes! Seems from what my guy got through, Bell started with forty trainees and he's already eliminated half of them. I don't know how many he'd need on his assault team—eight, ten?—but if it's a one-target operation, he could get them in good shape in a couple of months, say."

"And so far, he's been training them for—how long?"

"Must be two, three weeks. My guy's last routine check-in was mid-March," Yardley said.

"So, on that reckoning, he wouldn't be ready to go for at least another month?''

"Yeah, but let's keep the timetable fluid. With a guy like Bell, you never can tell. The ball's in your court, Joe. You must have an in with the Secret Service. I'd alert them right away, if I were you. If I can help at all, you know where to get me."

"Well, thanks, Bob. How about we go and eat? Dinner's on me, even if you've ruined my next few weekends as well!''

Over Southern shrimp and a bottle of dry white California burgundy, they chatted, seemingly jumping from one subject of gossip to another, although Yardley was secretly amused to see how Dodds was maneuvering the topic toward home life and family and married bliss. Finally Dodds came out with "And how's that nice wife of yours? Angela. She back yet?''

"Nice of you to ask. No, she's still in England with her parents. The mother's been in the hospital—just out now—but she's still too weak to run the home and look after Angie's dad, who's a bit feeble himself. She should be back within the week. I hope so. Mary in good form?''

"The best, thank God. Coming back to Angie, I suppose . . .''

"No way, Joe. Positively no way. For the last time, get it clear in that bonehead of yours. I'm not—repeat not—having my wife doing a Mata Hari act for the CIA. No, sir!''

"Could be very useful right now. Find out just what's in Bell's mind. I'm not suggesting she get into bed with him, you understand.''

"I don't care what the hell you're suggesting, Joe. And if you think Tim Bell's the type who tells a girl all if she flutters her eyelashes at him, you underestimate him. You and I—we're friends and that's good. But don't lean on it too hard, Joe, you get me?''

•   •   •

Bell was about to move into the third and crucial stage of the training. He ordered Clyde and a party of five others—Ellis, Swenson, the inseparables Elliott and Macrae, and a silent man with a broken nose, Purdy—to call at his hut for secret instructions. The next morning, when all the teams returned from an all-night exercise, tired, wet through and hungry, Bell's special squad grabbed four of the others, Page, Newman, Corder and Granville, and shackled them to one of the internal wooden walls of a hut. Their arms were stretched above their heads and they were trussed up so that they were supporting their whole weight on tiptoe. They were told harshly to keep silent, and when one of them started blustering, he was punched in the face.

The other men, coming back from the night exercise, were told to have their showers and then go off for a hot breakfast. They went off, laughing and joking and teasing the four who were trussed up like Thanksgiving turkeys, each wondering what the hell he had done to get into this fix. Every time one of them tried to ask questions or complain, he was hit viciously by one of the guards.

They were left like that, cold and wet and hungry, for three hours—well into midmorning. They could hear their comrades, refreshed by a hot shower and dressed in clean fatigues, trooping off for breakfast. The tantalizing smell of bacon and sausages cooking wafted across their famished faces. And all the time they had to hang there, wrists numb and pains shooting up the backs of their aching calves from the toes that were carrying all their weight. Then, suddenly, they were released, and all four of them slumped to the floor. At once, the guards grabbed them again, tied their hands behind their backs, tied their feet together at the ankles, shoved hard hoods down over their heads and faces and pushed them down on the floor in a huddled group. They were told to keep absolutely silent for one hour. Corder, who was short and inclined to be bumptious, started to argue. He was grabbed, hauled to his feet, punched viciously in the stomach and balls, and then deposited back on the floor, gasping and retching. The others took the hint and kept quiet.

Then the guards started harassing tactics, prompted by Bell, who stayed in the background and indicated the next move by making gestures. They would punch two out of the four ''prisoners'' at random, or order one man to get to his feet. Having lost his sense of balance through being blinded by the hood and encumbered through having his hands and feet tied, he would somehow manage to sway and stumble upward. He would then be told sharply to take a pace forward and would hop into position, standing there, apprehensive, off balance, wondering what was going to happen, not daring to speak. And then it would happen. One of his tormentors would come over, swing his leg, and kick the captive hard in the crotch. Down he would crash, moaning and gasping, and the others would tremble under their hoods, not knowing quite what had happened and wondering when it would be their turn.

They received no consideration. If they needed to urinate or defecate, they had to do so on the spot and sit with the discomfort and the stench, which would also affect the rest of the squad. The ordeal stretched through the afternoon. In the early evening, they were moved to another room, still hooded and tied up, and still having to keep silent. Then, one by one, their hoods were removed and they were taken over to a large tub. Inside, it was full of butcher's offal, the entrails of sheep and cattle, guts and saclike stomachs, still reeking and warm. Again in turn, each prisoner found himself being grabbed by the shoulders and his face and head plunged into the loathsome mess of blood and grease. The hood was then rammed back over his head, which left the residue of the offal to congeal slowly on his forehead, eyelids, and cheeks. He was then bundled into a separate cell under bright strobe lights. His tormentors stood around and over him as he knelt on the floor, taunting and shoving him, giving him no peace. Earlier, each of the ''prisoners,'' while still shackled on tiptoe to the wall, had been told by Bell that, whatever happened, he was not to give his own name or the names of his comrades to the interrogators. Now, they started pressing each of the men in turn, kicking them, tumbling them around and around the floor, threatening them with unmentionable tortures. Every now and then, as an encouragement to break down and tell all, they were taken back to the vat of offal, their hoods removed, and their faces and heads plunged yet again into the filthy, congealing mess, after which the hoods were rammed back again. They would then be pushed back into the communal room and made to huddle together on the floor, still not allowed to talk or even whisper to one another. Anyone attempting to do so was viciously thumped.

At three o'clock in the morning, the hour when resistance is at its lowest and sick men die, Bell had Corder called out of the group and taken to a smaller interrogation room. The other three were resisting pretty well, he reckoned, but Corder showed every sign of being about to break down. Bell told the guards to untie his wrists and ankles and remove the hood. Someone even got a warm, wet towel and gently wiped his face clean of the streaky blood and grease that was smearing it. Bell said softly in Corder's ear, "Come on now, kid. You've stuck it out okay. Why go through with more of this? Just tell us your name—and the names of the other three guys. There's nothing to it. You'll be doing them and yourself a favor. Sooner or later, one of you's gonna sing. Why not make it sooner?"

"I don't think I should, boss," Corder said hesitantly.

"Come on—why not? I can keep this going for days if I want to. You're in a mess now. Just think what it'll be like trussed up like a turkey for another three days—maybe a week. No food, no clean clothes, nothing but harassment all the time. And there's worse in store, and that's a promise. A wise man knows when he's beaten. Come on, four names, that's all I want. Simple."

There was a moment's pause. Then Corder said, "Well, if that's an order, boss, my name is—"

But before he could get the name out, Bell gave the prearranged signal to the guards, who grabbed him. One shoved a hand across his mouth, two others lashed his hands and feet, and the fourth jammed the hood down over his head again. He was bundled fast over to the vat of offal and this time dunked for nearly a full minute. Gasping, he came up for air, the hood was jammed back again, and he was tossed like a postal package back into the bigger room with the others. He sat huddled with the group, whimpering like a baby.

And there they stayed until dawn broke and the rest of the camp began to stir. Then Bell signaled to the guards to release them. Gently, like nurses tending the wounded, the guards untied their hands and feet and rubbed them to restore the circulation, removed the hoods and washed their faces, helped them to their feet, and stood there supporting them as they trembled with fatigue, drained of all resistance. Bell said, "Page, Granville, Newman, you've done well. I'm proud of you." He shook hands with each of them in turn. "Now go off, have a good soak in the showers, change into clean things, and you'll find a special breakfast waiting for you. Then go and sleep. Take it easy for the rest of the day. Tonight—but don't tell anyone—you'll get your turn to beat the shit out of another squad! On your way—and well done."

He swung round to face Corder. "You tried your best, son, and I'm not faulting you on that score. But it wasn't good enough. Go and change and have a rest, then pack your things and check out at the office. I'm not keeping you in the team, but Mr. Holliday has something else in mind for you until it's over."

Corder rubbed his eyes with the backs of his knuckles, like a small boy. "You're a hard bastard," he said. "You never give a man a second chance."

"True. And can you blame me? That interrogation a

few hours back. If that had been for real and you were being grilled by CIA goons when the rest of the bunch was still on the run, how long would they have survived? You'd be singing like a canary. In Northern Ireland the IRA has a neat little trick. They run an electric drill through your kneecap to encourage conversation. And SAS men are trained to expect that and worse and keep quiet. Goodbye and good luck.''

It took another three days with intervals for resting to put all the men through the interrogation tests. All the time, Bell was getting to know them as individuals and to gauge their capabilities and their weaknesses. And it was interesting to see how the men came to look on the tests as a kind of ordeal by fire. They walked around with that much more of a swagger and felt secretly proud of themselves for not having succumbed. What was more, he could see that turning the tables by making the prisoners of one day become the guards of the next brought out their sadistic instincts. He did not have to encourage them to kick and punch their mates. They did so with a will. They were not much of an advertisement for manhood, he thought, as he heard the continual jeering and guffawing that passed for humor and their almost moronic views on politics, race, and the world about them, but by God, he was whipping them into shape as fighting men. And he also noticed, as the days passed, that their initial skepticism and dislike of him was slowly turning to a form of hero worship. The word had got round camp that he had fought in several actions; men like Newman and Granville would sidle up to him in an off-duty moment and ask, "Was it real tough down there in the Falklands, boss?" and expected to get "Rawhide" or Superman stories of mowing down a dozen Argies with one well-aimed burst. Most of them, if they read at all, read comic books and *Soldier of Fortune*. Each, no doubt, secretly saw himself as another Clint Eastwood, drawling "Make my day," as he aimed his

Magnum at the wounded bank robber. And yet he had a kind of amused affection for their eagerness to shine in his eyes.

Having completed the interrogation tests, he at last put them on to weapons training. But it was not, as they had hoped, prancing around firing bursts from the hip. Bell had made them hand in their personal weapons, which were mostly either shotguns, hunting rifles or fancy Colt long-barreled revolvers. Instead, they were now issued an Uzi submachine gun each and a Browning nine-millimeter Hi Power as a sidearm.

Before they ever fired a round from either weapon, Bell had them stripping and reassembling the working parts, stripping and reassembling, first taking their own time, then, as they grew more adept, under time trials and finally blindfolded. "Why this, boss?" Cooper, the most slow-witted, was foolish enough to ask him.

"Are you just a natural-born cunt, Cooper, or do you work at it? However well you maintain it, a gun will sometimes jam. It could be at night—in the dark, you slob. All of you've got to be able to strip a weapon, correct the fault, and put it together again, at speed. If you can do it blindfolded, you can do it in the dark. Come on now, once more, all of you. Christ, Purdy, stop fumbling with that bolt. Get the first and second fingers of your left hand around the breech and then guide the bolt toward them. Jesus! You'd find that hole fast enough if it had hair around it."

Gradually, they became more adept and he began to teach them the correct method for aiming and firing, first with the pistol and later with the submachine gun. They spent hours on the range until the light failed; if there was heavy rain or an occasional flurry of snow late in the season, the firing practice went on. Bell told them that war was not like an open-air tennis match. Rain never stopped play. They were training for fighting, not playing a game.

The first couple of days were spent on orthodox station-

ary targets. Each man was positioned in front of the twenty-
yard range with the silhouette of a man's head, chest, and
waist as the fixed target. On the command, "Draw-aim-
fire," he had to pull the Browning pistol out of its holster,
bring it up using both hands until it was level with his
shoulders, and at the same time place his feet half a pace
apart, crouch forward slightly, and fire three aimed rounds
at the center of the target. To prevent monotony, the men
were put into two teams, one under the command of Fields
and the other under Clyde, and Bell made them compete
against each other. He deliberately loaded Fields' team
with the worse shots so that Clyde's team consistently
won. He had the hunch that Fields' jealousy of him was
like an angry boil on the neck; it was slowly coming to a
head and would soon need lancing. There was not much
more than a month left before the operation—and somehow he would have to sort out Fields in that time. To kick
him out now might risk prejudicing Doc Holliday, whose
protégé he was. Besides, if he could be turned into a loyal
subordinate, he would be a very useful fighting soldier.

Once the men had become competent at hitting station-
ary targets, Bell moved them on to the snapshooting range,
where weeks before he had broken the local record and
then shot the horns off the radiator of Doc's Cadillac. But
he instituted a major difference in the targets, unknown to
the men. They were told that the enemy targets would all
be carrying a weapon of some sort; the friendly targets
might be carrying a shopping bag or a baby but never any
kind of weapon. What he did not tell them was that he had
radically altered two targets. Instead of snarling terrorists
in balaclava-type headgear, he had two U.S. Army soldiers in helmets carrying semi-automatic rifles.

As he suspected would happen, on the first time through,
his men froze when these targets popped up. Clyde was in
the know and so did not take part in the exercise. Of the
other dozen, only Fields and Macrae got a single shot
away—and then only as the target was flipping back out of
sight.

Bell at once called the practice to a halt and told the men to gather around. "Okay," he said. "That shook you, didn't it? It's all right to fire at a target showing some dirty Arab terrorist coming at you. But you don't fire on your own side—isn't that the message? Like firing at the flag, ain't it? Well, you've got to learn a lesson right now. And learn it so it sticks good and hard. Once you're ready, we're going to fight a short, sharp war. And it's not a war against Arab terrorists in nightshirts. The target could be—will be—your fellow Americans. If the U.S. Army comes out against us, we've just got to shoot at them. They'll sure as hell be shooting at us! So you've got to decide right now just who you are. You're either Bellforce or you're Americans. You can't be both."

There was silence for several seconds. One or two of the men shuffled their feet and looked at each other. Purdy with the broken nose cleared his throat and spat the phlegm at the nearest oil drum. Then Fields said, "That's sick! The sickest thing I heard in years. I didn't serve my time in the U.S. Marine Corps to end up shooting at my own guys."

Bell said, "Well, there's a simple answer to that, Fields. You can dismiss right now, pack your bags, and get the hell out."

"And why don't you get the hell out—*boss?* We had a nice thing going here—didn't we, fellas?—until you came along. All this forced marching and tying up and interrogations—what are you, some kind of sadistic freak?"

There was a muttering in the ranks. Bell could not interpret its meaning. Were the men behind him or swinging over to Fields? There was only one way to find out.

"Okay, Fields," he said. "If that's the way you want it. I'll go. No hard feelings. Will you shake on it?"

He walked forward, right hand outstretched. Fields extended his own right hand, as he took a pace forward. Then, with his left hand, Bell hit him hard on the side of the jaw. Fields staggered back, caught his heel on the edge of an ammunition box, and fell on his back. He twisted around as he landed. There was a stout piece of planking lying nearby; Fields grabbed it in his right hand.

Bell came sliding in like a shark through the water. As he moved, his right hand whipped out the commando knife he wore slung low on his thigh. He stabbed down in one movement and the knife sliced through the back of Fields' hand, nailing it to the plank. Fields screamed.

Bell put his left foot across Fields' left wrist and his right boot hard against the back of his knees. Fields was transfixed. He lay helpless, wincing while the blood welled out of the back of his right hand.

"You're the one that's out," Bell said softly to him. "We'll be finished by the time that hand heals. If it ever does. Clyde, get a field dressing, will you? We'll bandage him up and you, Ellis, go start up one of the half-ton trucks. You can run him to the main house. They'll call Mr. Holliday's private doctor to see to that hand. I'll call them up to say you're on your way."

He leaned down and tugged his knife free. Fields yelled again. Bell wiped the blade on a tussock of grass and slid it back into the sheath. "The rest of you can take a twenty-minute break," he said. "Then we'll get back to target shooting." To Fields, he said, "Next time I'll kill you."

MOST WOMEN HAVE SMALL WAISTS THE WORLD
  THROUGHOUT;
  BUT THEIR DESIRES ARE THOUSAND MILES ABOUT.

▌10▐

"IT'S TIME WE had some straight talking," Bob Yardley said to Angela. She had returned from her English trip that afternoon.

"What do you mean, darling? That sounds an odd way to greet your long-lost love."

"Oh, cut the crap. I couldn't ask you on the phone in front of your family, but there's something I don't understand. You left here on a Tuesday and you should have been home with your people by early afternoon on Wednesday at the latest. The flight wasn't delayed, I checked it. But you didn't turn up home until Saturday. So where the hell were you on Wednesday, Thursday and Friday?"

"But, sweetheart, I remember distinctly—I called you from Heathrow that Wednesday morning. I had breakfast and a wash at the Excelsior and I called you from there."

"Like hell you did! You certainly called me but it wasn't from London or anywhere in England. Look, don't try to brazen it out. I called your home number in England and spoke to your father the very next day. I changed my voice so he didn't recognize me and pretended to be the husband of one of your American friends. He said you'd postponed your visit and wouldn't be there till the weekend."

"Spying on me, were you?" she said.

"There seems to've been something to spy on. Where were you, for God's sake? For three days and nights . . ."

"I'm sorry, darling, I really am." His direct onslaught seemed to lift the burden of how to confess her dilemma. The words just burst from her head. "I was with Tim!"

"Christ," he said. He felt breathless, as though he had been kicked hard in the guts. "With Tim?"

"I had to tell you sooner or later, Bob. You see, I never really got over Tim. Looking back, I should never have married you. Oh, it's my fault, not yours—you've been as sweet as a man could be. And I have tried, I really have tried. But when Tim came around here, it was as though he'd never been away. I'm sorry, darling, I'm so sorry." Head down, shoulders rounded, she started crying, long hopeless sobs.

Yardley found himself clenching and unclenching his large fists. Part of him felt a strange sympathy for her and part of him a strong revulsion. "My God," he said, almost to himself, "talk about ironic. There was Joe Dodds trying to get me to have you spy on Tim Bell and all the time you're shacked up with that shit. Joe was smarter than me. I thought you were faithful to me."

"I couldn't help it," she said through her sobs. "I did sort of try. I never got in touch with him, not once, since we got married."

"And then he comes along and crooks his little finger and you fall down on your back. Jesus Christ!"

"I tell you—I'm sorry. I do love you, I really do. You're the best thing to happen to me, much better than Tim, who'd lie and cheat you without turning a hair."

"But he's got something I haven't got. Is that it?"

She hunched her shoulders and said nothing.

"Well," he pressed on, "we'll have to talk about all

this another time. Right now, I've got to know where you were and what you did those three days with Tim." He felt himself retreating from the emotional confusion and allowing the cold professional in him to take control.

"Oh, Bob," she said, looking up at him.

"Forget that side," he said. "I don't want to know how many times he fucked you—and what way. Christ, I don't. It makes me feel sick to the pit of my stomach just imagining you in bed with that bastard. I want to know what you did and where you went with him when you weren't in bed. Get me?"

"We met in New York," she started to say.

"Go back a stage. How did you and he fix things up?"

"It was my fault, really. I rang him up in Arizona. I guessed somehow he'd make for Minter College or whatever you call it and I found out the number from your secret papers."

"Smart of you. And then?"

"I was in New York on my way to England. He said he had to come to New York on a business trip and booked us in at the Waldorf-Astoria."

"The Waldorf?"

"Yes, the Waldorf."

"Tim has gone up in the world. On a captain's pay?"

"Well, we did stay there, really."

"Where you met the next day. Right?"

She nodded. "It was early evening when he arrived. So we only went out to dinner that night. At some smart restaurant with a French name, a few blocks north, just off Park Avenue. Then the next day we did the usual kind of tourist stuff. You know, the museums and the Empire State Building and the Staten Island ferry."

"Did you visit the United Nations Building?"

"I think so," she said. "It's all a great jumble."

"I suppose you were gazing into his eyes most of the time."

"*Please*, Bob," she said.

"Okay. You'd remember the United Nations Building if you saw it. Over on the East Side—it looks like a matchbox stood up on its short side. And it has all those flags outside."

"Oh, yes, we certainly saw that."

"And what about the World Trade Center?"

"Yes, I remember that distinctly. We had dinner there one night, in the restaurant near the top of one tower."

"Did you spend long in either place?"

"Not really. I seem to remember we had a conducted tour round the UN Building. And the World Trade Center—we just caught a cab downtown, went up in the elevator, saw the view, and had dinner. Then we came down and went back to the hotel. No, sorry, one other thing. He bought me a dress at a shop in the concourse there. But what do you want to know all this for?"

"That's my business. What else did you do?"

"That's about it, really. I never realized how many museums there are in New York." She gave a wan smile. "By the time we got down to the Museum of Modern Art, I could have screamed for mercy."

"I never knew Tim Bell was an authority on art."

"I don't think he is. But he certainly dragged me round every statue and every painting he could find!"

"And that's the lot, is it?"

"Just about. Oh yes, we did do a spot of gambling my last day in New York. We both lost."

"You're not the only ones. You never went on the shuttle down to Washington during the trip?"

She shook her head.

"And did he talk at all about Washington or the president? Or mention any of the places in or around Washington? You know, like the Lincoln Memorial or the White House or the Pentagon or Arlington or Camp David?"

"I don't think so. In fact, I'm pretty sure he didn't. We didn't talk much about politics and stuff."

"I bet you didn't! Did he make any phone calls, or receive any, while you were at the Waldorf?"

"Not as far as I know."

"And did he go off on his own at all?"

"Yes, once. He told me he had to see a man on business and I wasn't to leave the hotel."

"Where did he go?"

"I've no idea, Bob. He didn't tell me and he made it pretty clear by his manner I wasn't to ask."

"And he didn't say what kind of business?"

"No."

"How long was he away for?"

"It must have been two or three hours. He left not long after breakfast and was only just back in time for lunch. Nearer three hours, I suppose."

He kept at her relentlessly.

"So the meeting must have been somewhere in or near New York City. You've no idea at all where he went or who he saw?"

"No, Bob. I'd tell you if I could, really, I would. I just don't know. What's more to the point—what's going to become of us? Is Tim more important than me, you, us? Do you want me to pack up and get out?" She was visibly shaking but in control.

He moved his big shoulders as though he was shifting a great weight from one side to the other. "Christ, I don't know," he said. "Give me time to think."

"That's the problem, Bob," she said sadly. "You could have thrashed me, knocked me around the room. Or told me to get the hell out. Instead, you ask me a whole load of questions. I don't understand all this. Either you don't bloody care or . . . ."

"Oh, shit!" he said.

Bell started his teams on their final phase of training. By now, they were all better than average shots with a pistol but he still had to yell and curse them when it came to single-shot and short-burst practice with the Uzi submachine gun.

"Do you want to be a bunch of dumb fucking heroes?" he would shout. *"Controlled fire*—that's the password. Shoot to kill. Got it? SHOOT—TO—KILL. How many times do I have to tell you? You've all been watching too many TV news programs. Like in Beirut when some guy pops up from behind a wall and starts hosepiping the street. That's bullshit—done for the benefit of the camera. One well-aimed shot will kill a man. You don't need a whole long burst.

"And remember," he would add. "On our op, we'll be traveling light. The most you'll have is a couple of spare magazines. Guard them with your life. When you run out of ammo, you've had it!"

"When are you going to tell us the details, boss?" Geoghegan asked.

"All in good time. But not long now, I promise."

With Clyde's help, he had rigged up a converted structure for their final practice sessions. It was a two-story hut with a criss-crossing of passageways on both floors, six or seven rooms with movable walls so that the shape and size could be altered at every session and various obstacles scattered inside the rooms. "This, gentlemen, is the killing house." The men, acting in pairs, would take their turn in, "clearing" the house, rushing down a passageway, one on guard with submachine gun aimed while the other kicked in the door and lobbed a stun grenade through the gap— and so on from room to room. To make things more realistic, Bell had rigged up machine guns of his own, firing on fixed lines, at the end of some corridors and in one or two of the rooms. They were loaded with blanks and fitted with a remote control, so that at irregular intervals he could let off a burst in the direction of the attacking pair. The shock and the shattering noise in such a confined space at first numbed and disoriented the men. They froze in temporary panic.

The "killing house" was also fitted up with targets that jumped into view for a couple of seconds and then disappeared. Several were "innocent"—a woman with a baby in her arms or an old man with a bent back and a walking stick. Many were "hostile"—terrorists in balaclava-type headgear or U.S. Army troops. The leading member of the assaulting pair had to choose in a split second whether to fire or hold fire; those whose inbred reactions stopped them from firing at their own people were sent back into the killing house again and again until they would unhesitatingly treat a U.S. Army uniform as hostile.

Sometimes, to keep the pairs all the more alert, Bell himself would slip unnoticed into the back of the killing house and hide behind an obstacle. On those occasions he would present himself fleetingly as a real live target and loose a couple of rounds at the assaulting pair, making sure to miss but be close enough to shower plaster or splinters of wood on them. He smiled to see them drop on their bellies in consternation, hole up for perhaps a minute and completely lose the smooth momentum of their progress. As he would point out afterward to the whole team, it was one thing to go waltzing through a building when you know the enemy is rectangular and made of wood. The big test came when the enemy fired back! The pause would get them killed. They had to fire by reflex.

Four more days went by in intensive training, including an uncomfortable introduction to CS gas, at the end of which even Bell had to admit to himself, a shade grudgingly, that, if not up to SAS standard, his six pairs were pretty damn good. Doc Holliday had turned up to see the final days of training and, somewhat to Bell's surprise, had brought Sayeed with him. It was now late April and a balmy spell of weather had settled over Idaho. Bell had his men in shirtsleeves demonstrating what they had learned—going on ten-mile pressure runs through the forest with packs on their backs that Holliday found to his secret chagrin he could barely lift off the ground, jumaring up pine trees, sliding across from one tree to another on inclined ropes high above the forest, unarmed combat, and weapon firing. And Holliday could see for himself the physical change that had come over the squad. Instead of the lounging, soft-bellied mob they had been two months earlier, they were now lean and hard, with a glint in their eyes. And they clearly worshiped Bell. As Sayeed said in an aside to Doc Holliday, "With respect, Doc, you may be paying for them but he *owns* them. I have a nasty feeling that if he ordered them to kill you and me on the spot, they wouldn't hesitate."

"Son of a gun," said Holliday. "Just don't put ideas in his head is all."

At the end of the session, Bell called the men around him in a group and in front of Doc Holliday and Sayeed said, "That's it, lads. You've passed through Bell College and taken your degree. God knows what in, but you've got it. When I think what a shower of shit you were when I first laid eyes on you—now you'd almost pass for human beings, in poor light, of course. It's Friday night—and Friday night is party night.

"Now a party's no good without booze and broads. And your host, Mr. Holliday, is going to do you proud both ways. There are two large trucks on their way from Boise. One has enough beer on board to float a battleship, the other's full of some gorgeous talent.

"There are only two rules to this party. We reassemble at oh-nine-thirty Monday morning. The girls must be out by then and the camp looking shipshape. That's rule one. Rule two is this. Those girls will be here for the screwing, not to hear all about your training and how well you can shoot. Any guy gets smashed and spills anything to one of the girls, he's out so fast his feet won't touch the ground. That's a promise."

The men dispersed to their huts and Bell walked over to his own private hut with Doc Holliday and Sayeed. The latter said, "Do you think that is altogether wise, Tim? Bringing strange girls into the camp, I mean. Word could get around."

"What word, Sayeed? They don't have a clue what the target is. They really don't."

"But even so . . ."

"Look, with respect, I *know* soldiers. And these guys are getting to be real soldiers now. You never saw what a mob they were to start with—but you did, Doc. They've never been fitter or felt tougher in their lives. But soldiers are like athletes, they can go stale if you keep'em at it too long without a break. No, it's a calculated risk on my part, but it'll work fine, you'll see."

"Well, you're the boss," Doc Holliday said.

"That I am. While we're all here, let me check into your side of things. That office I asked you to rent high up in the other tower?"

Holliday made a ring with his right thumb and forefinger. "In the bag. It's on the 104th floor, exactly where you wanted it. I rented it through a couple of nominee companies, one of 'em in the Cayman Islands, so no one will be able to trace it back to any of us. It's a three-year lease, like you said, with an option to renew. Big waste of money but I suppose you're right. It would have looked suspicious to take it just for two or three months. And, also like you said, we got some genuine clerks and their boss shipped in from a company I'm connected with in Illinois and they've been using it as a proper office. The Chicago Import Company, it's called—and they've even done some real business! It's costing me an arm and a leg but at least their operation could break even."

"Right," said Bell, "that sounds fine. Now on Monday, May second, they're to be told by head office that the experiment hasn't worked out. Setting up a New York office, I mean. They will be given that week's notice to clear their desks and close down the business side, which will be transferring back to Illinois. And then they are to have two weeks' paid vacation as from Friday, May sixth."

"Oh, boy—do you do things in style! And with someone else's money. That's going to cost me another ten thousand bucks at least."

"Doc, you want a good operation planned. So let me do the planning. I need the whole of that next week to get the weapons and explosives bit by bit into that office. *And* to assemble the team there without causing suspicion. *And* all the time to make like a real office, so any nosy mailman delivering the mail won't think it strange. You followed my instructions and got only men to run the office? Plus a reliable girl as receptionist in the outer office?"

"Sure thing. It'll be my Annie-Lou. I trust her."

"That's good. Now I need your help on the other phase. The elevator maintenance men—what's the score there?"

"Smooth as silk," Doc Holliday said. "Turned out Gene Minter and me both had the right clout. He's got a large nominee holding in the corporation that controls the real estate company that—you know the kind of thing. And I've got friends of friends. Yessir. Give us the two guys for a week. Even if when they start they don't know how to switch on the light in a room, we'll turn 'em into real trained elevator maintenance men."

"I can do better than that, Doc. I'm nominating Elliott and Macrae. Macrae worked for a bit as an electrical engineer, which helps. Besides, those two are inseparable— real good friends—and it's a tough assignment ahead of them. Impossible to stay cramped up like that for twenty-four hours unless you get on with the other guy real well."

"Not a pair of gays, are they?" Holliday asked.

"Is that all you ever think of? I don't go around asking my men about their sex lives. I'd say those two are just damn good friends and that's all there is to it. Christ, what's the world coming to? A man can't just get on with another man without everyone thinking they're a couple of fags."

"Okay, okay. I get the point."

"We'll need a third man with them. In charge. That'll be Clyde. There'll be plenty of room for him."

Bell turned to Sayeed. "What have your contacts managed to find out about the Zionist dinner?"

"A lot. Quite a lot." He explained to Doc Holliday, "Gene Minter owns several TV stations and a chain of newspapers, mostly in the West and Midwest. It was Tim's bright idea that we should get one of the top TV executives and one of the newspaper editors—without knowing the real reason—to make an approach to the organizers of the dinner for exclusive coverage. It was never really on—those Jews were smart enough to know they had what I think you would call a hot property and they stood out for a cable network deal. All the same, our people found out a good deal about the dinner."

"Such as?" Bell asked.

"Let's take the timing first. The date we all know—Sunday, fifteenth May. The dinner is seven-thirty for eight o'clock. Guests have been asked to be as punctual as possible."

Bell said, "So, allowing for traffic, the capacity of the elevators, and what have you, they should be sitting down at least by eight-fifteen?"

"Agreed. There are to be only two speeches. The toast to the state of Israel is to be made by a very old doctor named Chaim Aranson. He is in fact a Nobel Prize winner for having discovered some special immunization drug. He is now eighty-eight, born at the turn of the century, and his parents brought him over as a refugee when he was four or five. He represents the old generation at the dinner. The response to the toast is to be given by Avrik Stern."

"Who's he?" asked Holliday.

"You may well ask. I only got the information through our sources. Avrik Stern will have his fortieth birthday on May the fifteenth. You've got it. He's exactly the same age as the state itself. So he'll be representing the younger generation at the dinner. The fact that he and his father are very rich Wall Street brokers, who have endowed hospitals and a university wing in Israel could also have something to do with it." He rubbed his pudgy thumb against his forefinger. "The Lord giveth and the state of Israel taketh away."

"Fuck 'em all, I say," said Holliday.

Bell cut in with, "Have you any word on who's been invited? More important, who's accepted?"

"It's a little early to know the acceptances but our people got the very firm impression that there won't be many refusals. It's *the* dinner of the year for the Jewish top crowd. The invitations are limited to 120—and there must be at least ten times that number who would fight to get in. Isaac Stern's been invited—the violinist, you know—and Yehudi Menuhin. There was some talk of their playing the Israeli national anthem as a violin duet but that got dropped. On the writing side, there's Saul Bellow and Philip Roth and Norman Mailer. Somebody called Tom Guinzburg has been asked to represent book publishing—oh, and of course there'll be Lord Weidenfeld from England. He never misses a function like this."

"You're convinced that there'll be enough newsworthy names there on the night?"

"Absolutely. It's a gathering of what you English would call 'the great and the good.' Top scientists, bankers, artists—they'll all be there. But positively no women."

"Fine. We must get the publicity—and those names will guarantee it. What do you hear about the security? If anything?"

"Glad you asked. Our TV delegation automatically checked with the New York Police Department over likely facilities and found them very put out. The Israeli ambassador will attend the dinner and there may be one or two cabinet ministers who've flown in specially. So the ambassador has insisted that all security from the lobby of the tower up be carried out by his own men."

"Which means Mossad, dressed up as waiters."

"That's the impression I get, Tim. We couldn't possibly find out how many there will be."

"Of course not. You've done very well, Sayeed. That helps a lot. My thanks."

Sayeed said, "About those two young men you mentioned just now. Tim, you gave Gene and me a general idea of the plan when we first met but now I'm lost. What are these two young men going to do in those cramped conditions?"

Bell looked at Holliday, who gave the slightest of nods. Then he said, "Sayeed, this is for your ears only for now. Not even for Gene to know—yet. Promise?"

"I promise."

"Elliott and Macrae have the key role. If they fail, we've all had it. During that week, the week starting May ninth, they go into the World Trade Center to give the elevators a check-over. The work's done at night, so there's no inconvenience for the daytime workers and visitors to the center. The regular maintenance men will have been given a special vacation for long service and good conduct, courtesy of the Doc here. My two guys will be carrying those big canvas workman's bags and they really will have the tools for the job inside. But they'll also have Uzi submachine guns, broken down, and several loaded magazines. Okay so far?"

Sayeed nodded.

"Right. Now, every proper elevator has a detachable lid in the roof. If something's wrong with the cables, the engineer's got to be able to go up through the roof and find out the problem. So during that week, Elliott and Macrae will quietly be storing their submachine guns and ammunition on the roof of one particular elevator. You still with me?"

"Yes, I follow you."

"One important bit I've left out. There's an ex–Special Forces man named Brown—Flamer Brown—who's an explosives expert. Doc here knows about him because Doc has paid him an advance in cash, through me. Flamer will go in at night with Macrae and Elliott as a kind of supervisor. But while they're storing the guns and ammo on top of the elevators, he'll be booby-trapping the cables. I won't go into technicalities but there's a nonreversible switch, which, when you arm it, will allow the elevator to go up or down—just the one way—but if it returns beyond a certain point, the switch is tripped and the explosive charge blows.''

"You mean . . ."

"You bet your sweet life I do! Once that last Jew guest has arrived for the dinner, Macrae will arm the switch. That means the elevators will be able to travel four floors up and down—from the top to the 104th floor. But if anyone tries to take 'em lower, that's it. They'll go off with a real bang.'' He gave a thin grin. "Oh, yes, I nearly forgot. Flamer will have booby-trapped the three sets of fire escape stairs as well, so there's no point anyone trying to storm us that way."

"Why the nickname Flamer?" Sayeed asked.

"Yeah, I wondered about that," Holliday chimed in.

"He had a nasty accident with an incendiary device a few years back. Burned part of his face off."

"He won't be too conspicuous?"

"No, I've thought of that. Don't forget he'll only be going in at night. There's no bright daylight to contend with. And those night security men usually aren't all that alert. Anyway, this is the scenario. During the week of the ninth, the rest of us will be arriving in New York in ones and twos and putting up at various midtown hotels like the Mansfield and the Royalton on West Forty-fourth. Nice places but nothing too ritzy. In the daytime, we'll be attending the office you've rented, sticking to normal office hours. I asked you to arrange for an extra-big safe, and in it we'll be storing, not cash, but our weapons and ammunition and the special device."

"What's that?" Sayeed asked.

"Don't look worried. I'll come to it in a moment, but I promise it's not nuclear! To go back to the schedule, by the afternoon of Saturday, May fourteenth, we'll all be installed in our office high up across the way from the tower the restaurant's in. Elliott and Macrae and Clyde will be armed up and living on the roof of their elevator in the restaurant block. When the last guest has arrived at the dinner, they come down off their perch, burst into the dinner, shoot the Israeli security men, and then give us the signal. While Macrae and Clyde have their submachine guns trained on the guests—and they're still feeling the shock—Elliott will trigger Flamer's charges, which'll blow out two of the plate-glass windows facing our side.

"At that point, I fire the device. It's just like one of those things they use at sea called a breeches buoy. It doesn't have a grappling iron at the far end but an explosive anchoring head attached to a length of rope. The propellant charge will send it two hundred feet and more through the air. I fire it into the gaps where the plateglass windows were, it anchors itself on the far wall, and then—with me leading—we go like bats out of hell across the ropes and into the other tower. Shouldn't take more than a minute, two at the outside, to get the whole team of ten across, and all the time there's a buildup of men in the restaurant to help out Clyde and his two men."

"Jesus H. Christ, I love it! I love it," Doc Holliday shouted. "So that's why you've been concentrating on that monkey stuff up in the pine trees."

"Right. It's no good me taking a guy along who's going to suffer from a fear of heights. Timing and height are second nature to them now."

Sayeed said, "To my untutored mind, it seems an excellent plan. By the way, I have some news for you, Tim. It has been confirmed that Cable News Network will be televising the speeches at the Zionist dinner."

"Terrific. That guarantees the publicity side. Couldn't be better."

"Let me ask what I hope is an academic question," Sayeed went on. "So far, it all sounds excellent. According to one of the laws of nature, what goes up must come down. I see how you are going to get up there, but have you worked out how to get down again?"

"Sure. That's the first bit I thought of! Don't forget the full house we'll be playing. All those famous Jews as hostages—Nobel Prize winners, great musicians, big bankers. And just six months away from a presidential election with the Jewish vote to reckon with. When I snap my fingers, do you reckon the White House isn't going to play ball? I've only got to shoot one of those great Zionists in front of the TV cameras—maybe the Israeli ambassador would be fine to start off—and the National Security Council will give me everything I want."

"Such as?"

"Such as a Chinook helicopter at the West Side heliport to fly us to Newark. And then a comfortable jet to take us to South America. You see, we'd take at least half a dozen of the most important hostages with us for insurance. They'd be wired up to explosives, so I'd only have to press a switch to blow them to hell and gone. And the other side would damn well know that. We disperse my team among the hostages to confuse any attempt to snatch them back or pick us off. I have someone talking to friends in Colombia who would welcome our Jewish guests for a short stay. They will then trade with the U.S. government. The Colombians want some of their people out of jail over here. They'll use the hostages ruthlessly and keep this whole thing in the public eye for weeks."

"Haven't you forgotten one thing? That nonreversible switch on the elevators?" Sayeed asked.

"Thought of that. One elevator will be rigged to make a descent over the trip switch—and only Flamer and me'll know which one it is."

"Can the other side disarm the switches?"

"The switches are placed on the cables themselves four floors below the restaurant. To disarm them, you've got to climb up the elevator shaft and tackle it with your hands while suspended on the cables. Do you think we're just going to sit there twiddling our thumbs and let the opposition walk up? They can't use the fire escape stairs, anyway, because they'll be booby-trapped—and I have more surprises in store to keep them busy.''

"You really have thought it through. One last question from me. What's Gene's role in all this?''

"The way I explained it when we first met. Gene owns several TV stations—right? Once we've got things under control up there, I go on the air or speak on the telephone to whoever's in charge at ground level and state our conditions. One is that Gene's given a coast-to-coast link and the chance to make his own speech. They're bound to accept. If they don't, then a hostage gets it—in front of the cameras. This is going to make great television! Anyway, Gene gets the go-ahead. He can say that he's never heard of us before and is totally against our methods blah-blah-blah. That covers him. Then he goes into his song-and-dance act about how corrupt the dear old U.S. of A. has become, we need a new spirit, true democracy, 'vote for me'—and all that stuff.''

"Please, Tim. Some of us actually believe in that 'stuff.' ''

"Sorry, Sayeed. If that's what turns you on . . .''

Doc Holliday had been silent all through this exchange. He now came out with, "That's great for Gene and his A-rab friend here. They've got their kicks laid on. How do I score?''

"You're best off of the lot, Doc. Let me tell you. One, you keep your head down all the time. If it goes wrong, which it won't, you may have let some guys use your land for training, but you didn't know what the hell they were up to. If you had, you'd have stopped it at once. Two, you hate the Jews. Like the rest of America, you'll get the chance to see their top people humiliated, maybe shot. If I tell one of those big bankers to get down on his belly and eat shit—and I hold a gun to his head—he'll get quite an appetite for the brown stuff! And, three, those friends of yours in the Senate are certainly going to show their gratitude, and you know it. As a bonus, Doc, you end up with a small army of trained troops who've been under fire.''

"Fat lot of use they'll be to me down in South America.''

"Come on, Doc. That defeatist talk's not like you. Ever heard of plastic surgery? And remember Mengele in Paraguay? He moved around pretty freely. Made one or two trips to Europe and nobody stopped him. In a few months, the heat will be off your boys and you can slip them back over the border in ones and twos whenever you like. Think of it, Holliday's private army. All hard men. Why, you'd be like one of those robber barons in the olden days.''

Bell could see Doc Holliday's eyes gleam and his little pigeon chest swell. Christ, he thought. I used to be a soldier and now I've turned into a bullshitter.

"What say we go off and tie one on? Private celebration?'' the Doc asked.

"Wish I could. But there's a party here in camp tonight and I must be with my men. Will you be staying with Doc tonight, Sayeed? I'd like to see you tomorrow and sort out my next slice of pay. And arrange to draw some more for Flamer Brown. The moment their leave's up, I want to take Macrae and Elliott to New York to meet the Flamer. I'll only be gone a couple of days and Clyde can keep the training going that long.''

Sayeed said, "I want to thank you, Tim. I'm sure the Doc will join me in saying you've done a great job already. Here's wishing you all the luck in the world. I see your regimental motto is 'Who Dares Wins.' Let us all believe in that.''

GOOD, HAPPY, SWIFT: THERE'S GUNPOWDER I' THE
   COURT,
WILDFIRE AT MIDNIGHT.

■ 11 ■

THERE WERE A thousand similar rooms in and around Wash-
ington, D.C.; gray, anonymous, functional—even the air
filtered into the room seemed to have been breathed twice.
Joe Dodds had brought Yardley to meet "the General."
"You remember that ruckus back eighteen months ago?"
Dodds had said. "When Poindexter resigned and your old
friend North got the chop. All that stuff about Iran and
Israel and the Nicaraguans. Well, this is the guy who
put the 'Security' back between the words 'National' and
'Council.' He's a real hard-nosed sonofabitch, I'm telling you."

The General was just as gray and functional as the
room, Yardley thought, when he and Dodds were ushered
in. He used words as though they were ten-dollar bills. He
didn't get up, offer to shake hands, mention the weather.
He merely pointed at the two chairs across from his desk
and regarded them across the tops of his half-moon glasses.

Joe said, "Dodds and Yardley, sir. CIA and Special
Forces."

"If I hadn't known that already, you wouldn't be here. Cut out the waltz-time, Dodds. What do you two want?"

"Leave to speak, sir? Major Yardley, Special Forces, attached to Delta Force at Fort Bragg."

"I know all that, Major. Get on with it."

Yardley told him in short, sharp sentences all he knew of Tim Bell and his movements since he had arrived at Fort Bragg two months before, except for the fact that his own wife had been with Bell during the New York visit. He did not think the fact was germane. Even if he had, he secretly wondered whether pride would not have stopped him from telling. But he did mention that he had managed to infiltrate one of his men into Bellforce.

He glanced up to find the General's eyes focused on him. "Good, Yardley, that's good. What's the name of your man?"

Bob Yardley took a deep breath. "Sorry, sir. Not even Joe Dodds here knows."

"And if I give you a direct order to tell me?"

"I'd have to take the consequences, sir. You know it's not that I distrust you, of all people. But you've got clerks and typists and juniors. That Bell is a killer, take my word for it. If he found out there was a traitor in the camp, my guy's life wouldn't be worth a broken matchstick. It's need to know I'm thinking of. And you don't really *need* his name, sir."

"I'm beginning to like you, Major. You've got balls. And you're damn right. Why the hell should I know? Okay, to sum up. Bell's an SAS hotshot. He came over here after the Regiment gave him the heave, got in with some funny rich types, hiked off to the Idaho woods, and started training the local talent to be like Special Forces. And now he's about ready to start something. That correct so far?"

"Yes, sir," they both said.

"You *think*—there's no proof either way—his prime target is to kill or kidnap the president when he's at Camp

David. I don't buy it. Let's talk off the record, okay? Don't look cynical, Dodds. You know I know there's a voice-activated tape running the whole time in here. Sure. But who's able to cut and resplice the tape if he wants to? They didn't pull me off the last train from Montana, you know.'' He gave a laugh that sounded like ice cubes dropping into a glass.

''Lemme give you the downside of that scenario,'' he went on. ''There's a presidential election in six months' time. This one can't run again. He's not a lame duck, he's a dead duck already. So somebody kills him. So the VP takes over for the last few months. Not even a Libyan would reckon there's any percentage in that. If Qaddafi wants to get Reagan—and he's waited all this time—he's only got to wait until the man's out of office. Sure, I know. All ex-presidents have bodyguards. But the security's nothing like as tight as when they're in office. And it's bound to get slacker as the years go by. A killer could get Ford any day on the golf course. No, I don't buy the assassination theme.''

''What about kidnaping?'' Dodds asked.

''I don't like that one much, either. Not where a president's concerned. It's just too big, too outrageous. Like kidnaping the pope—or maybe the queen of England. So you catch yourself the president. Then what? Do you treat him badly, pull out a few fingernails? Make tapes of his screaming and send them to the White House? Along with an ear or two to show you're serious? Or do you fetch him three hot meals a day and his favorite bourbon? And what happens if the White House or Congress doesn't accept your demands? Do you then shoot the president in front of the TV cameras? It's too unwieldy, too many overtones. Here, Yardley, you've known this Bell a long time. He sounds a bright guy. Is he?''

''He's plenty bright, sir.''

''How do you read him? Is he the type to make a

grandstand play and the hell with the consequences? Or does he want to live to fight another day?''

''Put like that, sir, he'll want to move on when all this is over. Why should he die on the barricades? He couldn't care less who's president of the U.S.A. or what kind of government we have here. He's an Englishman, and basically a mercenary. So he'll want to be light on his feet, not toting an aged president around the countryside. I think you're right, sir. Camp David's not the target after all.''

Dry as a withered stick, sarcastic, the General said, ''Nice of you to agree with me, Major. Sure makes my day. So what do you two *want* with me? I can give you five more minutes, and that's it.''

Dodds said, ''We would like your permission, sir, to stop Bell in his tracks.''

''Meaning?''

''Meaning that the civil power, backed up by Major Yardley here and a squad of his trained men, go into Idaho and arrest Bell and his team.''

''On what grounds?''

''On good suspicion that they intend to disturb the peace and commit a serious felony.''

''Nice try, Dodds. But it wouldn't work in a hundred years. Look, this isn't like turning over a bunch of Mafia hoodlums or raiding a laboratory where you know they're manufacturing LSD. Has Bell got himself a criminal record? No. Have any of his men got a record, except maybe a drunk driving charge? No. To a judge and jury, especially in those uncivilized parts, they're just red-blooded young men being trained to look after themselves and their loved ones. Don't forget, in this country it's every man's *right* to carry arms for self-defense. Right now, we can't afford to arrest men with clean records on suspicion alone. There's an election in six months, remember.''

Yardley said, ''So we just sit by and wait for him to strike first, sir?''

''That's it, Major. That's exactly it. You think I like it?

You think I wouldn't run those fascist shits out of town if I had the slightest chance? Do you know who's behind them? It's a nut named Holliday. Calls himself Doc, for Christ's sake. Hey, don't look surprised, the pair of you. I've got my contacts too, you know. Anyway, this Holliday owns most of Idaho and a good chunk of Colorado and God knows what else. He's Mister Republican in those parts, and boy, does the party need his machine from now till polling day! You think anyone on Pennsylvania Avenue and surrounding parts is going to upset the good Doc this side of November—or after? Grow up, you guys."

Yardley said, "Well, at least we told you of our suspicions. We did warn you."

"You did. And I'm grateful. But it's not going to get you any medals. Once you're both out of this room, which you will be in one and a half minutes flat, that voice-activated tape gets destroyed. You and Mr. Dodds weren't ever here. You don't exist in my book. And if anyone was able to connect us, I'd merely say that you'd gone behind your colonel's back, which you have, sort of, with some outrageous suggestion. I told you where you got off but, so as not to have it on your Army record—one Army man always sticks with another—I wiped the tape clean. Okay?"

They both nodded.

The General said, "Do I have both your direct lines? If not, leave them with the desk outside when you go. And I want day and night numbers. Don't worry, Yardley. I know that colonel of yours. He'll be happier polishing the medals on his chest and his ass on a nice soft chair. These next few days, get your rush squad up to full numbers and on permanent twelve-hour notice. If things look like breaking fast, we'll bring that notice time down fast—but I don't want good troops kept on edge too long. I've seen 'em go off the boil. You, Dodds, I'll be in touch with your boss and ask for you to be assigned full time to this Bell project. Beef up your men and your contacts around Boise. For the next two weeks, I'll put an aide of mine, a Major

Thornhill, to act as liaison with the two of you. You'll have his round-the-clock numbers, and if things look like breaking, get onto him fast.

"That's all I can do for you," he went on, "as the bishop said to the actress." He removed his spectacles and rubbed the red marks on either side of his nose with finger and thumb. "It ain't much, as the bishop also said. Democracy means that the other guy always has the chance of shooting first."

Annie-Lou having been sent tearfully away at lunchtime, with a pat on her neat rump and an extra fifty dollars for her reception work, at three o'clock on Friday afternoon, up on the 104th floor of Two World Trade Center, Bell called the staff of the Chicago Import Company together for a final briefing. He said, "Right, you, Geoghegan, you stay on the reception desk. Not likely we'll get any callers this late but you never know. The rest of you—in the conference room right now. We'll keep the door open, Geoghegan, so at least you'll hear what's going on.

"Now listen carefully, the lot of you, for this is the last run-through, and you've all got to know by heart what the other guy has to do, as well as your own task. Clyde, Elliott, and Macrae will be off for a rest any moment 'cause they'll be on the go for the next couple of nights. You all know the intention—we hijack the Zionist dinner on Sunday night. Now for the method. It breaks into two phases.

"Phase one: Clyde, Elliott, Macrae—you go off and do your elevator maintenance tonight, meeting Flamer Brown in the lobby of Tower One at nine o'clock. Flamer will finish booby-trapping the emergency stairs and will set up the claymore mines in the express elevators on floors 104 through 106. Once they're armed, opening the elevator doors will trigger them. You've all trained with the claymore. You know what damage it can do. It's one of the best antipersonnel devices in the Army's inventory. When those babies go off they are going to need a nail file to scrape what is left of you off the walls! Once Clyde has armed the system, anyone can ride up and down in the main elevators okay, but once the doors slide open—whoof! The doors opening actuate the claymores. He's an ingenious bastard, that Flamer Brown. So don't any of you go near those damned elevators once we're inside Tower One.

"Anyway, tonight, Clyde and you other two, you get up onto the roof of the elevator you've picked and stay there for the next two days, nearly. There's plenty of room but for Christ's sake don't move about more than you have to. The restaurant is open for lunch and dinner tomorrow, Saturday, and again for lunch on Sunday, before they close to get ready for the big dinner Sunday night. We don't want you trampling around like a herd of elephants, so stay put. You've got food, water, blankets, and a latrine bucket? Fine. Here are some antinausea pills the SAS use for seaborne ops. Just in case any of you feel sick with the elevator rushing up and down. Any questions so far?"

No one spoke, so he went on, "Right, that completes phase one. Now for phase two. It's Sunday evening. The dinner guests start arriving at seven-thirty and they should all be in by eight-fifteen. Dinner is served and my guess is that speeches will begin by nine-thirty. There are only two speeches but you know how people yack when they get the chance. There'll be some really old men at the dinner and they'll want to get away by half past ten. That's their first mistake! Now, dead on nine-fifty, Clyde, you and the other two come down off the elevator roof—last one out arms the switches. Remember that. I'll say it again slowly. Last one out arms the switches. Clyde, you'd better nominate one of them to do the job, okay?

"We know that the Israeli ambassador is bringing in his own security men. Mossad guys, no doubt. Now let me tell you a fact of life, and listen well. Mossad men are good—real good. They don't hang around. First sniff of danger and they'll come out firing both barrels. You've got just a few seconds of surprise, and you've got to make the most of them. With luck, by that time in the evening and with everything going smoothly, the security men will have lost their edge. That's why I'm timing the attack for nine-fifty. But don't bank on it.''

''Any idea where they'll be, boss? I mean, in a bunch or spread around?'' Clyde asked.

''All of you, take a good look at the plan here on the wall. You can all see it? I reckon there will be around six security men, give or take, probably dressed up as waiters. You'll be able to spot them. A real waiter is always on the move, bringing dishes in, taking dishes out, all that stuff. These guys will be standing still in places where they command a good field of fire. There's bound to be one in the lobby—here, where the elevators open—and another near the end of this corridor where it opens out into the restaurant. And probably another out in the kitchens, making sure no one's poisoning the chicken soup. You've got to get 'em all, and you've got maybe ten seconds. *So take no chances*. Shoot to kill. If you get an innocent waiter or two, it's a big shame. But we can't have any Mossad men on the loose. Same goes for the kitchen staff. They've all got to be rounded up and brought into the restaurant. Any chef who's slow putting down his carving knife or his meat chopper, he gets it—zap! The guards, the cooks, the waiters—they're all expendable. Remember it. Any questions so far?''

No one said anything but Bell noticed that Purdy and Ellis were running their tongues across dry lips and that Newman's Adam's apple bobbed up and down as he swallowed. Each could see his moment of truth moving closer all the time.

''The other nine of us will be on the roof of Tower Two by then. While Clyde and Elliott are dealing with the security guards, you, Macrae, will move fast with those framed charges Flamer's made up to fit the windows and attach them here and there. You arm the ten-second fuse immediately and back off to one side to cover our entry. You stay there until we're all in. And for Christ's sake, keep clear of the gaps. That rope propellant would take your head clean off.

"When we see the windows go, I shall fire the ropes from Tower Two. There'll be four ropes and at least two of them must go through the window gaps. I'll go first and the rest of you know your order of entry. Clyde, when you hear me hit the floor, go for the kitchen. There could be Israeli security men in there. If there are, shoot them. You'll be last across, Swenson, and for God's sake make sure there's some slack in all the ropes."

"Boss, wouldn't it be easier to cross if the ropes were good and tight?" Granville asked.

"Oh, sure, that's what you'd think. But just remember we're quarter of a mile up in the sky and there's always a high wind blowing. The top of either tower can easily move six feet or more to and fro, according to the breeze. They're built that way specially—with enough give to take the wind. Same principle as nature and a tall tree. So we need some give in the ropes as well. What's more, they'll give better braking action.

"Which takes me on to another point. You've all done damn well on your abseiling and high work in the forest. This is exactly the same, just a bit more so. If you're cool at a hundred feet, you'll be cool at thirteen hundred. You've all crossed a seventy-foot gap time and time again. This one will be just twice as wide—that's all. Don't forget—it's all downhill the moment you're attached to the rope. From the top of the roof into the restaurant is a twenty-degree incline. You'll be across in no time. The night will be dark but many of the offices will be lit up—and particularly the restaurant. Remember the wind, and correct your run. And for God's sake don't hit your snap release till you're through.

"Now get this next bit, and get it good. From this moment until we're safe in South America, real names are out. We'll take our details from playing cards. Here, get in a line, will you, it'll make things easier. I'm Ace, Clyde, you're King, sorry about this, Ellis, but you're Queen, Swenson Jack and the rest of you Ten, Nine, Eight, and so on. Geoghegan, can you hear all right out there? You're Two. From now on, there'll be trouble if I hear any one of you call another by his real name. Get those numbers drilled into your memories—your own number and all the other guys'."

"Can we still call you boss?" Page asked.

"Sure, that's no giveaway. Boss or Ace, either'll do. Well, that's just about the lot. Remember, it's balaclavas on all the time. That goes for everyone. There's no point in hiding your names if your faces are recognized on television.

"Once we're all inside the restaurant, I'll be issuing new orders. Then you'll go on a proper roster, so many on duty and so many off. Don't forget the siege could last several days. At least, we've picked a smart restaurant where there's plenty to eat and drink. Not that you'll be hitting the wine and spirits—no, sir. It's club soda only until we fly out down south. Right, King, Nine, and Ten need their rest, so for the last time, any questions?"

It was Granville again. "That all sounds great, boss, but how do we get out again? The elevators are mined, the stairs are trapped, and there's the whole of the New York police force down on the street. What happens then?"

"Very good question. We've got all these rich, powerful Jews in our hands. I'll threaten to shoot one every hour on the hour—and by God I will, too—if the president doesn't accept our demands. So he supplies us with a large chopper to fly us to the nearest big airport and another plane from there to South America. We take some of the hostages with us and don't release them until we're safe in South America, probably Nicaragua. And once the heat dies off, we'll slip you back over the border into the U.S. of A. Trust me."

"Do you reckon it'll work, boss?"

"Would I be sticking out my own neck if I didn't? They talk about Jesse James and Wyatt Earp at the OK Corral and Capone and the Brinks job but the story of Bellforce and the way we took those snipcocks of Jews on their big celebration day will top the lot. Every step covered by TV. You'll be heroes, each one of you. Mark my words. Legends in your own lifetimes." Poor fools, he thought.

It was around midnight on Friday. A black security man named Sidney was strolling toward the bank of express elevators in the northerly tower of the World Trade Center when Flamer Brown emerged. An unrecognizable Flamer Brown; his hair was cropped short, he had grown a bushy mustache almost as compensation, and a grease-proof amber makeup softened the red weals on his left cheek. He was dressed in workmen's overalls and was carrying a holdall. He had in fact watched Sidney perambulating slowly around the lobby from the shelter of the elevator and when he was out of sight had slipped out, popped the three checkout cards for Clyde, Elliott, and Macrae through the glass-fronted slot alongside the security desk, and returned to the elevator.

"Thank God for that," Sidney said.

"For what?"

"Friday the thirteenth—it's just over." He looked at his calendar watch. "There you are. Three minutes after midnight. It's Saturday morning now. Boy, am I always glad when Friday the thirteenth is over."

"You don't reckon there could be worse to come?"

"Oh, sure. There always is. You off early tonight?"

"Early, me? I'm the last to leave. Just giving that baby over there one last up and down."

"I never saw your mates leave," Sidney said.

"When did you come on? Half an hour ago, was it? They must've gone at least ten minutes before that. Guys these days got no conscience. I told them there was a

slight judder on that west elevator. Nothin' serious but
worth investigating. Did they take a look? Did they—shit!
Said they were off for a quick beer before goin' home. My
bet is they were looking for a quick bunk-up with a woman
or two. Then they go back to their wives and say they've
been doin' overtime. Like fuck!''

"You could be right.''

"Damn sure I'm right. Look, there are their checkout
cards. In the box. I really ought to report them to the
supervisor.''

"So you're off now?''

"You bet. Monday night should just about see the job
finished. Will I see you then?''

"No,'' said Sidney. "We do three on and four off. This
is my third night in a row. I'm not back on till—let me
see—Wednesday.''

"Maybe we'll still be here. Well, I'm off for the
weekend.''

"Have a nice time.''

"Thanks.''

1030 hours Saturday morning: Carefully dressed in a raincoat, scarf and wide-brimmed hat, even though it was a
balmy day, Flamer Brown left his rat's nest and caught a
bus uptown. His dark glasses were in his breast pocket and
he carried a walking stick in his right hand. In his left he
held an old plastic shopping bag containing the incendiary
devices. He had slipped each one inside an empty King
Edward cigar container. If some nosy security man in a
store took a close look at the contents of the plastic bag, he
knew he was a goner, but the cardboard cigar boxes might
pass casual scrutiny. Fuck that Bell, he thought. Pity he
wasn't the one with his balls suspended over the circular
saw. Still, it could be worth it for the extra bucks—and his
mind gloated at the thought of the mayhem, the fierce
flames and the smoke, that would rage through the stores
on Monday morning. He had set the timers at fifteen-

minute intervals and reckoned that if he spread three apiece—
there were nine in all—between Bloomingdale's, Bonwit
Teller, and Saks Fifth Avenue, there'd be enough to set
the lady shoppers peeing their pants when the fireballs
went off. He hadn't had a woman in all of two years, ever
since his accident, and Christ knew when he'd next have
one, with his face looking like a butcher's slab. There'd
been one girl in some dive who'd made a pass but he
reckoned she was one of those psychos who got a kick out
of screwing oddballs. Women were shit, the lot of them.

He was as nervous as hell when he entered the swinging
doors at Bloomingdale's, but it proved as easy as pie. He
kept well away from the lingerie and dresses but with the
adhesive backing planted a device in the jewelry section
and another among the handbags and gloves. He stumped
through the store, limping heavily. Bell was right. Shoppers didn't look at other shoppers, they looked at the
goods on display. Once or twice, a store assistant would
come up to him and ask if she could help but he managed
to say he was just looking around for an anniversary
present for his wife. The trick, he soon learned, was to
walk purposefully through the store as though he were
aiming for a particular department. That way, no one
stopped him with offers of help.

In Bonwit Teller, growing bolder, he asked if he could
use the staff lavatory. Once there on his own, he planted a
device behind the cistern and another under the second
washbasin from the left. The third went into a storage
cupboard containing lightweight suits. In Saks Fifth Avenue, he planted his next-to-last package in the three-inch
gap between the bottom of the modern jewelry counter and
the floor. He had to lay his walking stick on the ground
and crouch as though he needed to tie his shoelace. He had
the almost-empty plastic bag alongside him on the floor
and it was a simple matter to slip the King Edward case
out when no one was watching him, remove the device

and press it with his fingers to the underside of the counter. Then he undid his shoelace and did it up again.

He was flushed when he regained his feet and began to limp away. A pretty young assistant came up and said, "Can I help you, sir? Would you like a chair? You must be tired."

He was about to snarl something at her when the irony struck him. "That's very nice of you, my dear. Shopping is a tiring business. I left most of this leg behind me in Vietnam."

"Oh, I'm so sorry. Here, let me find you a chair. This way, sir."

He followed her to a vacant corner and sat on the chair she proffered. He smiled his thanks and she walked back to her counter. Luckily, it was sited so that her back was to him. He sank down gratefully. His legs were twitching with the strain and the unaccustomed exercise. When he was sure the girl was not looking over her shoulder and that no one else was watching him, he put his left hand into the plastic bag, removed the cigar container from the last device, which he palmed as he took his hand from the bag. Crossing his legs for cover, he slipped his hand around the underside of the seat and pressed the device against it.

He was smiling as he limped out of the store and lined up on Fifth Avenue for a downtown bus. Anyone sitting on that chair come ten-thirty Monday morning would end up with a hot ass! It had been easy, like shelling peas. Now he must get back to his bolt-hole and start packing that cheap old suitcase he had bought with HE and primers and a thirty- to forty-minute fuse. Rockefeller Center, here I come, he chuckled to himself as the bus trundled him down toward the Flatiron Building. Christ, if he timed it right, he could hide the case in the subway and be out in time to see Saks, almost opposite, go up in flames. Flames! The guys in the old mob—at Bragg and Hereford—would soon put two and two together. No one could prove a damn thing but the men who mattered would know. They'd shake their heads in wonder and take another drink and say, "It must have been old Flamer. No one else coulda done it. What a guy!"

At three-forty-two on Saturday afternoon at the Special Forces signals office in Fort Bragg, two buck privates were on duty, Bancroft and Snyder. Bancroft was concentrating on a magazine quiz, Snyder was picking his nose with his feet up on the desk.

"Just my fucking luck," he said. "That's twice in a row I caught weekend duty. And there's a big game on up the road, too."

"Do you have to keep interrupting? I could win a prize here."

"And what's the wonderful prize?"

"First prize is one week in Miami, all expenses paid."

"One week in fucking Miami with all those Cubans ready to cut your balls off. I suppose the second prize is two weeks in Miami."

"Ha-ha. You're as funny as a dose. Now you've broken my concentration, you might as well help. Which famous American president had a favorite saying: 'You gotta show me'?"

Snyder said, "Fucked if I know. Probably the one who went to the strip show."

"You get worse every day. Don't know why I bother to consult you. Here, this is an easier one. 'Which is the tallest building in the USA?' "

"That's easy. The Empire State Building."

"Wrong. It was the tallest—but that was a good few years ago."

"Then it's probably the Sears Building in Chicago. I read somewhere that was very tall."

"Wrong again," Bancroft said.

"Well, if you know the fucking answer, why ask me?

Go on, show us what a clever little prick you are. Which is the tallest building—as if I cared?''

''The World Trade Center in New York. Don't argue, I looked it up.''

Snyder wrinkled his forehead. ''That's funny,'' he said. ''Looks as though one of the officers is doing that same quiz. And he's getting some help from outside. Just like an officer!''

''What the hell do you mean?''

''Look, in the tray over there—the incoming messages.'' He swung his feet onto the floor and reached across the table, then riffled through the various buff forms in the wire tray. ''Here you are. Telephone message, time of origin fourteen-ten.'' He read aloud, '' 'Tell Major Yardley it's the World Trade Center.' I knew I'd seen something about the World Trade Center before you mentioned it.''

''Do you reckon we ought to pass it on?''

''Like hell. One thing is he wouldn't thank us for discovering his secret. I wonder who's helping him on that quiz? Probably some ass-kissing junior officer.''

''The signature here looks weird. 'Geo-something.' ''

''Here, gimme a look. You ignorant twat—that's an Irish name. Pronounced 'Ger-hay-gan.' I remember that little cocksucker. Always playing up to the officers—'yes, sir, no, sir, whatever you say, sir.' Funny thing is he never made corporal. Something musta gone wrong. He left in a hurry just before you were transferred into this shitbag.''

''Still, don't you think we ought to get it around to the major?''

''No way. He's probably in bed right now with that gorgeous wife of his. Boy, could I ram it right into her!'' He held out his rigid left forearm and punched the bicep with his other hand. ''She'd be howling for mercy before I was finished.''

''She'd suck you dry in ten seconds. But she certainly has a sweet ass on her. Maybe I ought to take the message around. I might catch her on her own.''

"Forget it. Monday morning's soon enough."

"But it's marked 'Urgent.' "

"When you've got as much service in as I have, you'll know there's some cunt always goes around stamping messages urgent or top secret or your eyes only. It don't mean a thing. If it had come from somewhere important or some senior officer, maybe we shoulda told the major. But that prick Geoghegan—he's not even in the Army these days."

"You sure?"

"Damn sure I'm sure. What's urgent about telling the major the answer to some quiz question? I tell you, he'd have you on extra fatigues soon as look at you if you spoiled his Saturday afternoon. I know the major too damn well."

"Well, if that's what you reckon. . . ."

"That's what I reckon. Come on, ask me another one."

O LENTE, LENTE, CURRITE NOCTIS EQUI!
(O TROT SLOWLY, SLOWLY, HORSES OF THE NIGHT!)

▌12▐

SO FAR, SO good, Bell thought, as he eased himself down behind the parapet on the roof of Tower Two. It was a perfect night for the operation, dry, balmy, a slight breeze blowing from the northwest. He had fought in all kinds of weather: desert temperatures well over a hundred degrees when the metal of a submachine gun would be too hot to handle with the naked hand, the sleet and snow and biting cold of the Falklands heights, the pitiless rain of an Irish countryside, the prickly heat and drenching monsoons of the Laotian jungle. This was the kind he preferred.

He had the two rope dischargers alongside him, loaded with Propac Rappelling kits. Two reloads lay prepared, the ropes out of the bags and carefully coiled. His eight men were spread out along the roof, four on either side. His last word of command before they had left their 104th-floor office and tiptoed along the empty corridor had been "No talking—not a word—till we're inside the restaurant." Manhattan was glowing hundreds of feet below and in the diffused light, by raising himself on his elbows, he could see the taut profiles of his men as they lay and waited. It was nine-thirty-three, seventeen minutes to go.

It pleased him to see them preoccupied with checking their equipment. He enjoyed this moment—just before going in. He always had. The load-bearing vests each man wore carried extra magazines and stun grenades. The quick-release mechanism, not unlike an inverted parachute release, was positioned high on the vest, giving a high center of gravity and thus stability during the wild ride down the rope. The small precision-tooled device would be the man's only contact with the rope and by gripping it in one hand he would control his rate of descent to the target.

For the hundredth time, he wondered how they would make out. At that moment, he would gladly have swapped half his payoff for a couple of SAS Pagoda teams alongside him. Boy, they'd go through that restaurant like the proverbial dose of salts! But his lot weren't too bad, considering. He'd only had them for a couple of months, all told. Given as much time again, he might have worked them up to that sharp point where in action the conscious mind gives way to the trained reflex. Still, they'd do— they'd have to do. The only two he had any reservations over were Ellis and Geoghegan. It was a neat coincidence that Ellis had been lined up to get the "Queen" tag. Bell had wondered for some weeks whether there might be an effeminate streak to him, almost unknown to himself. You never know with queers, he thought; they might turn out to be icy-cool brave or screamingly terrified. In training, Ellis had been as good as any. In less than a quarter of an hour now, we'll know what he's like in action, Bell thought.

And what of Geoghegan? He had been outstanding in training. So much so that Bell had asked him if he'd served in the Forces and he admitted he had done a couple of years in the U.S. Infantry but had been discharged on compassionate grounds as he was the only support for his elderly parents. He did everything with a will—and did it all well—but there was something about him that stuck in

Bell's craw. Perhaps it was his fervent Catholicism; he had
been the only one allowed to break bounds in order to have
his confession heard by a local priest. Perhaps it was that
"too good to be true" air about him on and off parade. He
always seemed to be on stage, never relaxed. Well, it was
too late now. If Ellis or Geoghegan, or anyone else in the
team, for that matter, was going to fall to pieces, there was
nothing he could do about it now.

He glanced at the luminous dial of his wristwatch, from
long practice cupping his right hand over the dial—although
there was no one higher in the sky right now except for the
passengers and crew of aircraft taking off from Newark
Airport and flying off out to sea as they gained height.
Nine-forty-six—four minutes to go. Clyde and the other
two must be standing by across the gap, getting ready to
lift the lid from the elevator roof and drop down to wreak
havoc with their Uzi submachine guns. A good man, that
Clyde. Quiet but dependable and tough. The other two,
Elliott and Macrae, were okay as well. They'd go for it.

He nudged Swenson, who was lying on his left side and
who was to be anchorman on the crossing part of the
operation. Swenson nodded in the gloaming and rolled
backward to keep clear of the others. Bell peered over the
parapet. He could see the lit-up restaurant forty-five yards
away and three floors lower; the night was so clear he
could even see the shadows of the waiters moving to and
fro. Come on, he thought, come on—let's go!

In the tower across the way, the elevator doors slid open.
The sinister black cylinder of a stun grenade lobbed out in
a slow arc. It landed by the smoked-glass partition and,
milliseconds later, exploded with an eardrum-breaking crash.
Splinters of mirror glass cascaded in a crazy fountain.
Three dark figures in balaclavas emerged in a crouching
run, with Clyde leading. The three Mossad security men in
the lobby were momentarily stunned, all breath expelled
from their lungs and all messages from their alert brains

refusing to transmit to the hands. Too late, they grabbed for their weapons. Clyde took out two with aimed head and heart shots, Elliott just behind him killed the third, whose body draped across an ornamental urn like a Victorian etching. The pistol shots reverberated down the long passageway leading to the restaurant.

Moving in a practiced choreography, Clyde and Elliott ran diagonally down the passage; Macrae, carrying the frame charges, brought up the rear. Clyde reached the short flight of stairs leading to the main restaurant, rolled down them in a somersault, and came up off the floor by the viewing rail. In one flowing movement, he aimed and fired at a Mossad man with a bushy black mustache who was taking aim at him. At short range, he pumped two bullets into the man; the second smashed his jaw and opened up the side of his face in a bloody raw splash of bone and muscle. The impact sent the man skidding across a serving table, which collapsed in a crash of cutlery.

Clyde yelled "Grenade!" On cue, Macrae from behind leaped forward and, left-handed, threw a second stun grenade into the main restaurant. As he did so, a shot cracked out from a security man over by the windows. The bullet scored through the fleshy part of his underarm and he staggered backward. The diners, already aghast at the din of battle and the whip-cracking of bullets across the confined space, fell sideways in confusion when the stun grenade went off with a flash and a roar. Like the dead after a cavalry charge, they littered the floor of the restaurant, white dress shirts gleaming incongruously in the smoke of the action.

Clyde knew instinctively that anyone with the nerve to stay on his feet must be Mossad. He took one out with two aimed shots. The man's head burst open as if a cleaver had slashed through an overripe melon. His forefinger had stiffened on the trigger in a reflex action and the random bullet smashed into a large bowl of fruit salad, which sprayed outward in a fountain of pineapple cubes and passion fruit. Elliott opened up with his Uzi submachine gun in rapid selective bursts, dropping two of the security men. One was stitched up from groin to throat by the burst. With his jugular spouting an arc of glistening blood, he was thrown backward, his own submachine gun spraying the ceiling with bullets in his death throes. One of the diners began to wail hysterically, an age-old lament for salvation in the face of imminent death.

Ignoring his wound in the heat of action, Macrae moved toward the windows with his frame charges. Clyde yelled to Elliott, ''Cover the kitchens!'' and then, gripping his pistol in both hands in a crouch, he slowly fanned it across the room from side to side, searching for additional Mossad men. The Browning was slippery between his palms and he felt a bead of sweat rolling down the side of his nose from inside his balaclava. He yearned to disengage one hand and wipe the sweat away but he knew his life depended on searching his front.

He glimpsed rather than saw the back of a shoulder from behind one of the pillars to his far left. Suddenly, the last Mossad man emerged. He had grabbed a waiter as he ducked for cover and, using the wretched man as a shield, loosed off a snap shot at Clyde from behind the terrified waiter's right ear. In a reflex action, Clyde dived to his left and found himself crouching behind a serving trolley. It was a standoff. He was out of the Mossad man's field of fire but could not get an aimed shot off without the risk of hitting the waiter. The few seconds that ticked by seemed an eternity. Then the frame charges went off and the windows blew out with a massive roar.

Two windows in the other building disintegrated. Shards of glass went sailing out into space, the light glinting off them as they turned over and over on their way down.

Bell, with his elbows on the parapet, took careful aim through the night vision sight and fired the discharger. The first charge was a shade too far right and low; it skidded off a pillar support, exploded harmlessly and dropped toward the ground with its trailing rope.

He scooped up the second launcher, took aim, and fired again. This time, a bull's-eye. The charge went snaking through the blown-out window across the way, across the bar, and buried itself in the opposite wall. Bell swung to his left, aimed the reloaded launcher again and fired a third round at a window ten feet further along the building. Another bull's-eye. The second rope held fast. Now there were two lifelines—or deathlines—to the other tower. Bell leaped to his feet. He yelled, "Swenson, anchored off?" "Anchored off, boss." Bell straddled the parapet, hooked himself onto one of the ropes, and shouted, "Okay, let's go! Use both ropes. Never more than three men on the rope at a time. Knave, you keep 'em separated. Got it? And for Chrissake, keep a little slack in the ropes. You come when you see the last one go through the window. Right, guys, go, go, go!"

He felt great as he slid across the abyss, the wind catching his face under the balaclava, the sense of space and light and movement dazzling one part of his mind while the sober side concentrated on the task ahead. Clyde and Company would have to hold the situation over there for at least another minute. As he swung through space, the wind clawing at him, he sensed rather than heard one, two, three isolated shots from the restaurant. It was the deeper crack of an automatic pistol, he decided. No, fuck it, Clyde was not in control.

The rope lurched as he closed on the window and he needed all his skill and experience to stop it from yawing wildly from side to side. Now he was on the window ledge; he thumped the quick release and in a coordinated move detached himself from the rope and landed in a practiced crouch position on the floor. He was primed for action. He rose in one smooth movement and, as he came up, the Browning semi-auto slid into his right hand.

Even as he moved forward past Macrae, who was

strangely inert behind an overturned table, he sensed Clyde moving toward the kitchens. He went fast around the bar, eyes flicking to and fro, pistol held forward like a pointing stick. There was a rising hubbub on his right and as he hugged the left hand wall across from the bar, he saw Elliott crouching behind a pillar.

"It's Ace," he shouted. "Are we clear?"

"Macrae—Christ, sorry, I mean Nine—has been hit. Through the left arm. We got all the guards 'cept one. He's grabbed a waiter to shield him. The bastard's over there."

"Where? Point to him!"

"Over there." He pointed. "The other side of the raised platform."

Bell moved fast. He snaked behind the dais where the startled diners gazed at him stupefied. He peered around the side and saw the big dark-haired security man, who was crouched with his left arm holding the waiter around the throat in front of him. In his right hand he held a pistol. He was keeping his head well behind the waiter's and with one visible eye was quartering the room.

Bell rose to his knees and fired two shots, so quickly the reports almost merged into one. It was the "head and heart" aim he had used a thousand times. The waiter's head almost burst open like an overripe melon. His body arced to one side. The guard, now exposed and with streaks of the waiter's blood and brain tissue across his white shirt, came to his feet. Bell shot him twice, head and heart again, and the impact thumped him against the window wall. He slid downward and the pistol fell out of his hand, clattering against the marble pillar.

"Too bad about that waiter," Bell said to Elliott. "Where the fuck are the others? Go round 'em up as they arrive. Three, is the kitchen secure?"

"Kitchen secured, boss."

"Get the staff out here. The rest of you spread around

the dining room. You know your jobs. Eight, you know anything about first aid?''

"A bit, boss."

"Fine. Go look after Nine. I'll be over soon as I can. Move." He ran up the steps behind the maître d'hôtel's desk and, shielding his eyes from the arc light, pointed his Browning in the direction of the television cameraman and his assistant. "Did you get all that on film?" he shouted.

The man nodded, too frightened to speak.

"Well, keep it rolling. I want all this in glorious technicolor, you hear? Got plenty of film to shoot?"

The man nodded again.

"Right. Do your job properly and you'll come to no harm. Try anything funny and you're dead. It's your choice." Bell turned to the assembled diners, some still numb with shock, and said in a loud voice, "Gentlemen, I'm the Thing from Outer Space. This is a hijack!"

2201 hours: In the bedroom of their married quarters at Fort Bragg, Angela was saying to Bob Yardley, "Look, we just can't go on like this. You sit there, never saying a word, hour after hour. It's gone on for weeks now. You treat me politely, standing up when I come into the room, that sort of thing, but I might as well be a total stranger wished on you. I can't take it much longer."

He said, "Hell, Angie, what can I do? You started it, for God's sake!"

"I know. And I'm sorry. I've said I'm sorry, over and over. I'd give anything to be back where we were three months ago. That Tim! The thought of him makes me feel dirty. He used me, that's all there was to it."

"It was you who showed him my secret files, wasn't it?"

"Yes. What a bloody fool I was! But he took me in. I thought then he was genuine, down on his luck, looking for an honest job. If I'd known what I know now, what you've told me . . ."

"That's Tim, all over. Looking out for number one the whole time. I could kill the bastard! I bet he never told you I saved his life on that parachute drop we did. His chute candled and I had to grab him and get him down in one piece. Christ, I should've let him drop!" He smacked one big fist into the palm of his other hand. "It would've saved us all this."

"But what's going to become of us? I can't—"

The telephone rang. Yardley said, "Who the hell can that be at this time of night?" He went over to the bedside table and, on the third ring, snatched the instrument off its cradle. "Yardley."

It was Thornhill, the General's liaison man. "They've hit. The World Trade Center."

"Christ Almighty!"

"Yeah, we think it's your mate Bell."

"*What?*"

"It's on the box. Tune into cable news if you don't believe me. They came over on ropes from the other tower and snatched that Zionist dinner. And the hijack leader is making the TV crew go on filming. We daren't cut them off the air 'cause he's threatened to shoot the whole crew. He's already knocked off a waiter and the security team. But I can't stop chatting. This is your sixty-minute warning. There's a C130 on the Flight Line at Bragg field right now. Be ready to take off at twenty-three hundred. Blue team, Second Squad is being alerted. Got it?"

"Right."

"First stop is Newark Airport. You'll RV with a CH53 out of Andrews—ETA Newark oh-oh-thirty. It'll lift you to the West Side heliport, half a mile from the World Trade Center. On arrival you report to the tac room set up at the base of the tower. The New York commissioner of police and the mayor are expecting you. The FBI are still putting their team together. By the way, there'll be a U.S. marshal to meet you at Newark. We'll keep you briefed en route."

"Jesus, is this a civilian op?"

"So far. Defense hasn't even gotten permission for your force to fly in as yet. Not into New York, that is. Someone got the mayor of Newark, New Jersey, on the phone at home and he's given verbal permission for the C130 to land at his airport. He's worried about that civil liberties crap. We reckon to have authority for the chopper to land on Manhattan by the time you're airborne. Anyway, Bob, hustle your ass over to Bragg field and get that task force of yours in the air. Oh, and good hunting."

2215 hours Sunday—0100 hours Monday: On the island of Manhattan and on the far sides of the East River and the Hudson River pandemonium set in. Of those in that area who were watching the television cable news, over a thousand viewers got into their cars and drove toward the scene of the action. Mingling with the usual late-night traffic coming into the metropolitan area, they turned the Triborough Bridge route, the Midtown Tunnel, and the Holland Tunnel into a sweating, carbon-monoxide-laden, blaring cacophony of static nose-to-tail traffic.

Several hundred of the more fanciful inhabitants, either mistaking Bell's shouted remark to the television camera that he was the Thing from Outer Space or hearing the rumor spread on the phone by friends and neighbors, decided that Orson Welles had only been some fifty years early in his prophecy; this time, the Martians really had landed. They roused their children from bed, wrapped them in blankets, emptied the iceboxes for emergency rations and drove out of the New York area—anywhere, as long as it was away. They added considerably to the fear and confusion—and fascination—that were gripping Manhattan.

By 11:15 P.M. the mayor of New York and the commissioner of police had managed to work their way separately into the siege area. They took over several suites of rooms in the Vista Hotel, linking the two World Trade Center towers, and established a joint Tac HQ. They were just in time. Half an hour later, West Street was blocked solid throughout its length and there was hardly standing room on Vesey Street, Liberty Street, or Trinity Place. Ten fire trucks, summoned to the scene as a precaution, were hopelessly blocked on West Broadway.

In the hubbub of the Tac HQ room, a voice shouted, "The commissioner wants to know if the NYPD hostage negotiation team has made it here."

Someone answered, "Yeah, they're setting up their telephone links in Room 202."

"Great. Tell 'em full briefing here in five minutes."

Even the imperious Outside Broadcast TV crews from the networks were making slow going. They had been smart enough to approach from the other side, down the FDR Drive and along Fulton Street or Wall Street, but they got through only because the police cleared a path for them. The police were realists: They knew there was such a thing as bad publicity, and had no desire to get on the wrong side of the TV networks.

At 10:55 P.M. a senior vice-president of one network sat in his sumptuous apartment on Sutton Place. He could hardly take his eyes off his bank of television sets, all of which were blank except one, which showed the cable news. Turning the sound low, he reached for a telephone and called one of his important Washington contacts, a senior senator.

"Hal, it's Evan. Yeah, that's right—how many Evans do you know? Sorry to call you so late. What's that?—you won't get much sleep tonight. Me, neither. Yeah, right on, it's fantastic, isn't it?

"But one thing I want you should know, Hal. And when you get the chance, let the president know. Sure, sure, he's a busy man, aren't we all? We're having a formal statement given at every news bulletin tomorrow that we strongly deprecate—no, deprecate, Hal—all this giving publicity to hijackers. It's playing right into their hands. Sure, it's great television. You're watching it, I'm watching it. We've both *got* to watch it because we're the opinion-formers and the decision-takers. It's our job to *know* what's going on. But it's only working up the average viewer in the worst possible way.

"What's that, Hal? You admire my sentiments. I'm glad you do. Let's not forget you may need some air time next time around and a camera shooting you from tactful angles. No, I'm not getting nasty. You know me better than that, Hal. I just like looking facts in the face and stating them. Well, it's mighty good of you to pass the word around, Hal. I appreciate that. And a word in the president's ear—maybe the VP. Yeah, that would be nice, real nice."

He dialed another number, this time that of an important "fixer" in the network. "George, it's Evan. Sure, it's great television—I'm watching even as we talk. So are you, I know it. Why the hell didn't we cover that Zionist dinner? We decided not to bid? Jee-sus! What's come over us? It would have interfered with a regular prime-time series. So what? What's that you're saying? We have a high rating in the South and Midwest and they don't awfully like Jews in those parts. Now you're making sense. Yeah, I agree. Until this happened, it was just a boring old dinner with a lot of old Jewish farts telling their life stories. No, I'm kidding. I'm no anti-Semite. Pity that hijacker didn't tip us off in advance. That's kidding, too. Where's your sense of humor?

"But, talking of hijackers, you were with that cable news company, weren't you? Great. And still have friends there? Better still. I want you to call the most senior friend you have there—yeah, right away—and let's buy into this exclusive of theirs. Will they sell us the sole right to run up to ten minutes in the hour of newsflashes? Ten minutes maximum. Ah, yes, and the right to show four times a day at peak hours an edited update of the action. And we'd like to keep syndication rights in our own edited versions. Sure, I know that would be confusing to overseas viewers, but so what?

"How much will we pay? I dunno. Two hundred thou a day? Christ, George, this hijack could run for weeks. You reckon we need to go higher? Two hundred and fifty thou—that's murder. The board'll have my head on a platter if it goes wrong. We've got to have it absolutely exclusive. Remember that. We won't share a minute, not ten seconds, with one of the other networks. Drive that home when you talk. And get onto them fast, George. Our rivals could be creeping up right now. Call me back, will you? I'm not getting much sleep this night the way things are going.

"What's that? Playing into the hands of the hijackers? Responsibility to the public? Let me tell you, I've been onto Washington already and pledged that we'll do nothing to glamorize those evil men. But that's good thinking on your part, George. We'll preface each bulletin—let's use that guy with the grave voice—with a solemn statement, something about we'd never aid the hijacker by filming him direct but as it's our responsibility to bring news to the public, good or bad, we do so with a heavy heart. That sound right to you, George? Well, go to it, baby."

All the telephones in the restaurant began to ring, a startling lowpitched cooing like the inside of a monstrous dovecote. It had not taken the smart American public long to realize that if they called the number of the Windows on the World restaurant, they might even get the chance of talking to the chief hijacker. What a story to tell their friends!

Bell strode over to the telephone switchboard and gave it a sharp burst. Electronic bits and pieces flew through the air. The telephones stopped their ringing. He had noticed a television set in the bar and another in the suite of private dining rooms. He ordered numbers Three and Five to fetch the sets and plug them in at the high area behind the maître d'hôtel's desk. Then he turned to face the cable news camera and said, "I know that out there someone big in the government is watching us. So get this. We're going to close down soon and take a rest till the morning. But before then, I'm going to switch both sets to Channel Seven. Got it? Channel Seven. You can't talk to me on the phone and I would advise you to tell those heroes in the NYPD not to use the elevators. They're booby-trapped. But by eight tomorrow morning, you will arrange for a senior spokesman to be standing by in a Channel Seven studio. That way, I'll know who I'm talking to. Right, that's all I have to say for now." He turned to the cameraman. "Okay, switch that damn thing off. Like I said, we're going off the air for the rest of the night. You two—and that third guy back of you who's jumping around like a fart in a bottle—get some rest. Here, Four, we've got a couple of blankets to spare. Go get 'em, will you? The crew can bed down right there."

2331 hours Sunday: At Tac HQ in the Vista Hotel, two senior policemen were talking softly in one corner. One said, "Did you hear that arrogant sonofabitch on the box just now? Ordering us around like school kids. I reckon he's bluffing."

"How do you mean, sir?"

"Talking about rigging the elevators. Do you know how many elevators there are in that tower? Must be close on a hundred if you include the local ones. Now how the hell could someone go around in broad daylight laying explosives in elevators that are constantly stopping, with people getting in and out? That ain't logical. Must be a bluff."

"He didn't sound to me like he was kidding."

"Course he didn't. These guys are actors deep down. That's why they do it. They just like being center stage. Are there any EOD teams standing by?"

"EOD, sir?"

"Yeah, for Chrissake. Explosive Ordnance Disposal teams."

"Oh, I'm sorry. I could hardly catch what you were saying. That noise over there. Sure, we've got a couple of teams standing by."

"Which is the best one?"

"Well, there's Sergeant Kelly's team. He must have a good twenty years' service in. Good guy, very dependable. The other sergeant is pretty new to us—Littwak. Transferred recently. Seems a good guy."

"Sounds a fucking Polack to me. Let's pick Kelly, he sounds like the man," said the senior policeman, whose name was O'Reilly. "Tell him to do a reconnaissance— just him and one other, we don't want to risk the whole team. Here, there's a plan of the elevators on that table. Here we are. Tell 'em to avoid like the plague the express elevators running up to the restaurant. On the other side of the block are the express elevators serving the offices up to the top. Tell them to scout around there. If they can find a back way in to approach the restaurant, fine. But no heroics. It's just a scouting job is all."

"Right, sir. I get it."

The junior police officer went off and briefed Sergeant Kelly. He selected his best technical officer and together they walked with their equipment along the corridor of the Vista International Hotel and into the lobby of Tower One. There were uniform and plainclothes police everywhere, almost falling over one another. Kelly was continually being stopped and ordered to show his pass. His technical officer, cumbersome in his protective bomb suit, cursed every delay. It took them nearly four minutes to walk the two hundred feet to the far side of the elevator block.

Sergeant Kelly said, "You go in first and keep the 'Open' button pressed. I'll inspect the outside and then come and help you inside."

He scrutinized the floor, the outer edges of the door arch, and the internal edges of the two doors themselves.

"That's all clear," he said. "No wires, no suspicious bumps. How about your side, Tommy?"

"Not so good. Come in a moment, Sarge, and I'll show you. See that mark there, where the paneling's been forced? There's a device behind it, for sure. Looks as though it's been done in a hurry. No attempt to restain the paneling."

"Amateur job?"

"Could be."

"Could be a double bluff, too. No sign of any other devices?"

"Not that I can see, Sarge."

"Let's take the elevator up to a higher floor. Then we can sit down quietly and deal with that device with no one interfering. What do you say? The 104th floor—that's as far as this baby goes."

The elevator whooshed up to the 104th floor. The doors slid open. In the last few seconds of his life, Kelly recognized the squat concave shape of the antipersonnel mine on the edge of the landing. His lips formed the word "claymore" as he died. The blast made the surrounding floors tremble and shake. The reverberation ran deep down the shaft like booming thunder. The doors of the elevator hung crazily open and inside it was an abattoir. Gouts of blood and shreds of flesh spattered the walls like a hellish surrealist painting. A belt buckle ricocheted across the walls of the elevator, clanging as it flew. A pall of black smoke eddied out into the corridor on the 104th floor. The sergeant had taken most of the blast. His head had been neatly severed from his neck and it lay in one corner of the broken elevator, the face a shapeless blur of raw flesh.

The senior police officer made no comment when the news got back to him some minutes later. It had been worth trying, he thought. At least, it proved that sonofabitch terrorist was not bluffing.

2352 hours Sunday: The senior police officer had something really serious to worry about. A captain of police,

one of his oldest and most trusted friends, reported that his
cops on the street had sent a deputation. They had managed to unload their blue barriers and squeeze the spectators back off the streets and onto the sidewalks. Reinforce-
ments had arrived to start a new spell of duty and somehow keep the sluggish flow of traffic moving to make
room for essential vehicles. The fire trucks had finally
made it and were parked in a line on the roadway spur
beyond the Vista Hotel.

The police deputation posed a fresh problem. Their shift
was due to come off duty at midnight; because of the
emergency they had been ordered to keep going until at
least eight o'clock the following morning. They wanted
double pay for that additional eight-hour spell, and triple
pay for every hour thereafter. Otherwise, in less than ten
minutes' time, they would leave their posts and go home
to their wives and families.

The SPO called it fucking blackmail and wondered where
their sense of civic pride was. Then he went to talk to one
of the mayor's confidants in another hotel room along the
corridor. There was further swearing and private threats to
make life hell for the ringleaders once this crisis was over.
Two minutes before the deadline expired, the SPO returned and told the captain of police to give in and agree
but to find out who was behind it all, as he, the SPO,
would personally twist his or their balls until they came
away in his hand.

An hour and a half earlier, up in the restaurant, Bell had
begun to reinforce his control. He knew that his captives
represented the top stratum of intelligence. There was thus
less chance that a psychological transference would take
place, with the prisoner gradually acquiring respect and
even affection for his guard. These men didn't become
hotshots in business or Wall Street or argue intricate legal
cases or become great violinists without having a special

amount of drive and determination. So he had to keep up the pressure of fear and confusion.

"Listen to me," he shouted. "No talking. See this?" and he raised the butt of his Uzi high in the air. "I hear another word out of anyone and he gets this in the face. And, believe me, I don't bluff. Now, I want each one of you to empty out his pockets—every pocket—and put his things on the plate in front of him. Yeah, everything, down to your last few cents' loose change. Everything, I said. Wallets, pens, pencils, letters, whatever.

"We're not thieves. You'll get 'em back. All except pocket knives or nail scissors or anything that could become a weapon. Here, you, Nine, and you, Seven, grab a cloth off one of those empty tables and hold it by the corners. Go around every table. Don't touch the wallets or the ordinary stuff but take anything suspicious, including pens and pencils. Someone stabs you in the eye with a ballpoint pen, you'll soon know it can be a weapon!"

He turned back to the diners. "Don't play games with me and hold anything back. I'm going to have random strip searches done. Anyone I find holding back anything at all will get badly hurt. A rifle butt hard against the back of the knuckles doesn't help a pianist play his scales properly, does it, Daniel? So none of you try to be clever. Go on, empty your pockets."

Doctor Chaim Aranson, the eighty-eight-year-old main speaker at the dinner, rose a little shakily to his feet. Bell said to him, "Where the hell do you think you're going?"

"Hell is the right word, young man. I must answer the call of nature."

"You must—what? You *mustn't* do anything. You do what I tell you to do. And that could mean sitting in your chair and shitting in your pants if you can't control it."

Doctor Aranson stayed on his feet. "You do not understand," he said slowly. "Oh, yes, we are your prisoners now. You can wave your gun and order us about. You, sir, are not qualified to be our jailer. You can't win.

You'll never win. I am old enough to remember the thunder of the horses' hooves in the streets of the Russian ghetto when the Cossacks rode in to take us. But we survived. And there was Mr. Mosley in London before the war. And Hitler and Himmler and the SS and the Gestapo and our folk herded like sheep to the slaughter. And still some of us survived. And then there was the British government and the British Army on the side of the Arabs—but here we are this evening celebrating the survival of Israel. You'll never crush us. The Jew goes through history like a gold thread in an ancient tapestry.''

He began to move away from his chair and Bell raised the Uzi. "Go on," said Doctor Aranson, "shoot me if you want to. I am not playing the hero. I may be approaching second childhood but I do not intend to act like a baby, messing his diaper. I despise your kind.''

Bell lowered the submachine gun. "I like your guts," he said. "You're a brave old fool. Okay, Three, you take him to the men's room. If he does want a crap, then leave the door wide open and you keep a close watch all the time. Go on, get moving. The rest of you sit tight—and, remember, no talking.''

As the C130 droned toward Newark, Bob Yardley sat in silence. He was concentrating on getting his mind—his "mindset," as they called it in the Special Forces—fully operational. He had coldly to eliminate all distractions, his jealousy and rage over Angela's infidelity, his own childish behavior of only a few hours ago, the whole idea of what, if any, future there would be for the two of them. Bell, if it was Bell, and the hijack team were now the sole target.

The next essential was to get all the rest he could manage on the two-hour flight. There would be precious little sleep for the rest of the night and he expected to be on his feet throughout the whole of Monday. There was no point in trying to work out a plan: The information on which to base decisions was as yet far too scanty. Rest was the thing. He pulled his beret down over his eyes to keep out the cabin lights, let all his muscles go slack, and tried to doze.

He came fully alert at once when he sensed the rumble of the undercarriage dropping into place as the aircraft made ready to land. Once on the tarmac of the runway, the plane rolled along to a far corner of the airfield where a small hut was lit up. Drawn up to one side of it was a CH53 helicopter.

While his team was disembarking and sorting out their equipment with rehearsed precision, Yardley marched over to the hut. Inside, there were three men sitting on wooden chairs, drawn up to a wooden trestle table. Two of them were the helicopter pilots. At a word from the third man, they rose, saluted Yardley, and went out of the hut to prepare the CH53 for flight.

The third man was tall and very thin with black hair and two thick bars of eyebrows above a beaky nose. He stood up and held out his hand. "Hughes," he said, "Lister Hughes, U.S. marshal. You must be Major Yardley."

They shook hands. Hughes flicked a cigarette from his pack and stuck it between his lips. He offered the pack to Yardley, who shook his head with a smile. "Wise man," the marshal said, "it's a stupid habit. Wish I could break it." He tore a match out of the book, struck it, and blew a plume of gray smoke across the hut. "Right, let's get down to business. No point in hanging around New Jersey when the action's across the river."

"No wish to be rude," Yardley said, "but just where do you fit in? My orders were to report to the mayor of New York and the chief of police on arrival. Are you here to brief me?"

"In one sense. You know Joe Dodds, don't you? Good guy, that Joe. I thought he would have filled you in. Well, this is the drill. This isn't England. Our government can't deal direct with troubles wherever they occur—and hand things straight over to the military when things get too hot for the ordinary police. You know our Constitution. Here the feds and state and municipal authorities all try to run the ship. That hijack is taking place in New York City, so that means the mayor has to be involved. He has to consult his chief of police, who enforces law and order. But New York City is inside New York State, so that means the governor has a finger in the pie. And hijacking is a federal offense, not least when you've got foreign nationals— Israelis, in this case—being shot up. So that brings the White House in. And when the White House gets in an OK Corral situation, they call on the Agency, they call us Wyatt Earps, to step over a few heads on their behalf. Let's just say, anything you and I agree on will be legally agreed to by our mutual friend Joe Dodds, at the CIA.''

''Are you my boss?''

''I won't kid around. If we go down to the bottom line, the answer's yes. This may be a lousy democracy but it's the only one we have. The state can never finally hand control over to the military. But in practice I'm not going to interfere. You're the expert, you've done the training for this very thing. I'm not going to try to tell you how you attack this problem.''

''But when I come up with a plan, I have to get your approval?''

''Oh, sure. But, like I say, if you reckon it's the only way to proceed, who am I to argue? I want you to know I was a Green Beret once myself. And let me put another thought to you, Major. What's the alternative? When you make your plan to flush out those hijackers, you go to the mayor and get him to rubber-stamp it, which he may or may not do. But, of course, he must consult the chief of police before he says yes or no to you. Let's say the mayor okays it. Then you have to go through the whole process all over again with the governor. And he may want to consult the senators and congressmen. By this time, the eldest of those Jewish guys who've been hijacked will be dying off from old age and the chief hijacker will be getting desperate! So it may all work out well in the end, but the end could be a long time coming. You read me, Major?''

"Loud and clear. What do I call you? Mister Marshal?''

"What's wrong with Lister? And you're Robert—is that what they call you?''

"Bob, usually.''

"Okay, Bob, let's go to work. They'll have the choppers ready in five minutes. Let me give you a quick briefing before we move on.''

He stubbed out his cigarette in an old tin on the wooden table, then almost at once lit up another. Succinctly, he brought Yardley up to date, mentioning how the attack had taken place, that the Israeli security men had been either killed or overpowered and one of the waiters had been murdered in full view of the TV camera. The leader had insisted that the cable news team continue filming, obviously to maximize the publicity. He was wearing a camouflage combat suit, as were the rest of his men, and a balaclava head cover that concealed his face, except for the eyes and mouth. But he was of medium height and his accent sounded like an English one, maybe Canadian.

"That's no Canadian,'' Yardley said, "that's Tim Bell. Captain Bell, MC, late of the SAS.''

"You know him?''

"Too well. It's a long story and we've no time now. Let's just say I've served with Captain Bell here at Fort Bragg and across the pond in his country. You get to know a man when you go on maneuvers.''

"That could be our first break,'' Hughes said. "You knowing him well. At some point he has to make his first big move. I mean, since the hijack, which was big enough, for Chrissake. What's he after? If you can read his mind, it puts an ace in our hand. God knows we don't have the big cards right now.''

One of the helicopter pilots stuck his head around the

door of the hut and reported that the troops and their gear were all aboard. Everything was ready for takeoff. Lister Hughes told him to give them two more minutes. Seeing the impatient look on Yardley's face, he added that the chief hijacker had destroyed the telephone system by firing a submachine gun burst into the switchboard and had closed the television coverage down till eight o'clock next morning, so they were not missing any action.

"What beats me," Hughes said, "is the efficient way they've mined the elevators and the emergency stairs. Joe Dodds gave me a quick briefing before I flew up from Washington. If it is Bell—and it must be—seems they've spent all their time training out in Idaho. So who rigged up the mines and the booby-traps? Whoever it was was a hell of a pro. Seems that a New York police EOD team—and those guys are no fools when it comes to explosives—was blown to hell and gone by what sounds like a claymore in one elevator. And another squad looking for medals went storming up one lot of emergency stairs, set off a booby-trap that did for the two guys in the lead and then set off another on the way back, which they'd missed as they went up! Six guys go up, two and a half live ones come back. What with the Israeli guards and that poor dumb waiter plus five trained cops and another who's lost a leg and half an arm, the score is something like ten–zip to the hijackers right now."

Yardley stood up and shrugged on his combat vest. "Let's go," he said. "Time we were off the bench and on the field."

The giant helicopter lifted off and flew fast and low over the Hudson River and diagonally down toward the West Side heliport. Yardley noted with silent amusement that the pilot steered a wide course away from the World Trade Center and made a low tactical approach to the heliport. Bell—and now he was certain it was Bell—might have left a rear guard on the roof of the southern tower, armed with a ground-to-air missile launcher. Or even a 0.50-caliber heavy machine gun. Either would be capable of knocking an inquisitive chopper out of the air.

There was no time to think about Bell on this short flight. Looking around the chopper, Yardley could feel the rising eagerness, the alertness, of his team. It would be close on 3:00 A.M. by the time he and his men reported in to the Vista Hotel Tac HQ. Yardley was an old hand; he knew that the energy and endurance even of highly trained troops is limited. Some inexperienced officers would have their men prancing around in the small hours carrying out unnecessary tasks, spreading the old bullshit to impress their seniors. Eighteen hours later, they would be drooping, and six or ten hours further on, out on their feet. He and his guys would report in, set up their own night watch system alongside the nerve center of Tac HQ, and then relax. Why stay at a smart hotel and sleep in a bedroll on the floor? He had once had a commanding officer whose motto was "Any damn fool can be uncomfortable."

He felt the massive helicopter shudder as the pilot began reducing power on his collective and raising the nose in a rapid transition to a tactical landing. As Yardley instinctively leaned into the increasing pitch of the floor he observed men coming to a state of readiness. Silent and determined.

The wheels had just made ground contact when the crewman actuated the rear ramp. They disembarked at the West Side heliport, running low to the waiting transport— some police trucks, parked outside the heliport to take the team the half mile to the Center. As they had been cooped up in one aircraft or another for the past three hours, he was tempted to "scrub" the transport and take the men at the double up West Street. But he quickly decided the discreet approach was the best and ordered the men into the trucks.

The night was now dry but there had been a short but sharp rain shower in the past hour. The streets were still heavy with traffic but the police had it moving in a steady, if sluggish, stream. Most of the pedestrian spectators had gone home. There was no percentage in gazing up a hundred stories into the sky when you could see nothing happening. Better to stay at home in the warm and watch it *as* it happened on the box.

Yardley and Hughes reported to the Tac HQ room at the Vista International Hotel. There was a hubbub of telephones ringing, men talking in low tones, huddled in corners, a blue haze of cigarette smoke pervading all. The police commissioner and his entourage occupied one corner of the suite. Alongside was the FBI bureau chief with his assistants and representatives of the governor. Yardley marched up to the most likely desk, saluted, and said briskly, "Major Yardley, OC Special Forces detachment. On site and ready to go."

A weary, gray-faced man looked up at him and said, "Welcome aboard, Major. Good to have you with us. It's what you'd call a SNAFU. The terrorists refuse to talk to our NYPD negotiation team, EOD have lost five men, the building's been declared unsafe and uncleared. It's going to take us at least two or three hours before we know where we stand. You and your troops have been allocated rooms on this floor, I reckon. Best thing would be for you to stand down till we know the score. Okay, Major?"

"Suits me," Yardley said. "We have plenty to do. Where can I get a floor plan of the building and how soon can I be briefed on the current position up there?"

The FBI chief agent approached the table. "Here's your plan. I'll be along to brief you in ten minutes. We're still waiting for some data to reach us on those bastards."

Yardley summoned Lieutenant Vaughan, his second in command, and said, "We've got a standoff. They don't know what the hell's happening, and it'll be a couple of hours at least before they have a job for us. Once the guys have their equipment sorted out, let 'em stand down and take a rest. Have 'em ready to go at oh-six-thirty. I'm going to get the picture from the FBI and consider our options.''

When the briefing was complete, Lister Hughes said, "I'm too tensed up to sleep. I'll sit around the Tac HQ. Until they infiltrate some surveillance up there, we have to suffer Bell's standoff. Here, take this spare bleeper. I know you won't go off site without telling me, but just in case anything breaks in the next hour or two. . . .''

"Thanks. If you want to sit around, good luck. Shut-eye is my order of the day.''

He had been allotted a twin-bedded room with Lieutenant Vaughan. Once he knew the men were comfortable, he went back to his room, undressed down to his undershirt and underpants, and lay between the cold clean sheets. He had acquired the knack of catnapping, of being able to switch off and fall asleep at once for a spell that he could subconsciously predetermine—one hour, two hours, even as little as ten or fifteen minutes. He needed to be wide awake at six o'clock but first he wanted the luxury of some private thinking.

He concentrated on Tim Bell, trying to recall the first time they had met and working slowly toward the present. He could remember back-breaking exercises across the Brecon Beacons and those Welsh mountains that are much steeper than they look, fording icy, rushing streams with Bell and others, rope work across gulleys, HALO drops by parachute, nights out in the open without a bivouac but with the wind tearing through the valleys and blasting the exposed crags behind which they vainly tried to shelter.

There had been times when they sat quietly in a Hereford pub, drinking the flat sour beer that the English seemed to prefer to a foaming Budweiser or a bubbly Michelob. There might be a little gentle ribbing, jokes about Yanks, but deep down a sense of real comradeship. Any professional soldier who had been through the toughest tests the Army could throw at him and come out the other side would respect and feel kinship for someone else who had done the same.

He had first met Tim Bell when the latter attended a course at Fort Bragg. That must have been a few weeks after the abortive Iranian operation, run by Charlie Beckwith, which he himself had been on. He could still remember that feeling of bottled-up frustration and rage, the lingering suspicion that they had been set up by a conspiracy in the Pentagon that wanted Carter out and a Republican in. So it must have been the fall of 1980, seven and a half years ago. Bell had done a six-week course on that occasion and he himself had been attached to the SAS several times, for a month each time, since then. On the second occasion, he had met and become engaged to Angela—but that was a different issue. Let's keep personal feelings out of this for now, he thought.

And he had met Bell again after a two-year absence just a few weeks ago. The guy had changed—Christ, he had changed. He had always been something of a loner, sociable enough in company if never the life and soul of the party, and you sometimes had the strange feeling that he would be just as happy on his own. And, to be honest, there had always been something a shade grudging, a little on the mean side, about him. Not that he didn't stand his round of drinks or share the expenses of a night out, but you felt somehow that he had it all weighed up, was keeping careful track of who spent what so that he wouldn't be hit for more than his share.

But this last time had been a real eye-opener. Leaving aside—and he knew it was nearly impossible to box away his jealous rage—what he had since learned about Angie's affair and what he had picked up from that briefing by the British Military Mission, how Bell had been kicked out of the SAS for murdering two IRA suspects, he had been secretly surprised by the man's conduct on arriving at Fort Bragg. Breaking the soldier's little finger and beating up Sergeant Drucker, who had been released from military hospital only a week or two ago, was completely un-characteristic behavior on Bell's part. It was almost as though he was signaling a deep change in his makeup. But that would not be typical of the usually secretive Tim Bell. So what did it mean? Had he really become a psychopath? He was a trained killer through his SAS career, but a killer with all the checks and balances applied by strict moral training. If those restraints had been jettisoned, and they must have been, Bell was a killing machine out of control.

No, that was wrong. He might have gone ape—but apes are full of cunning. He must have had it in mind when he left England nearly three months ago that Fort Bragg held the secrets of terrorist cells. It wasn't just a case, as he'd maintained, of visiting North Carolina to look up an old friend. Bell must already have decided to try to wheedle the facts out of him, Bob Yardley. And when he'd gotten the brush-off, he switched to his old flame, Angie. Get her in bed—and all would be revealed. The shit! The cold-blooded bastard! It would almost have been better if he still had been carrying a torch for her. At least, there would have been real feelings for her. My God, I wish I'd let him drop on that HALO jump, Yardley thought. It would have saved all this, and I might have kept my wife.

He felt himself go stiff with rage, teeth and fists clenched hard. Deliberately, he relaxed his big frame, breathed deeply in and out for a few minutes until he had cooled off and could adjust his mindset. Now, what had there been in those secret files that Angie had opened up for Bell? Just after she had opened her legs. Christ, he said to himself, cool it—stop thinking about that. He wrenched his mind back to the files. No need to recall the details of subversive organizations and likely targets. Open a window and he could virtually toss a pebble onto the foot of the target from his hotel room. And Bell's team was made up of the Anglo-Saxon Brethren. That at least was known. What other notes were in the files?

Bell knew more than most about explosive devices but

even he would not have had the skill and experience, or indeed the opportunity, to set those mines and booby-traps in both towers of the center. That would have needed a real expert with up-to-date technical equipment and time to spare. Someone in the New York area, too. You couldn't come into town on the Greyhound bus carrying all that stuff with you. God Almighty, of course—it all fitted. Flamer Brown! There *had* been a memo on Flamer in one of the files. He remembered now. Only an expert like Flamer would have been up to it. And he'd have done it, too. Willingly. Apart from the money, he'd grab the chance to shove two fingers up at the great American public. He would reckon he was owed one for the way the U.S. Army had rid itself of him after the accident to his face.

Sandy Vaughan, his number two, was snoring away in the other bed. Yardley picked up the bedside telephone— Tac HQ had taken over the hotel switchboard—and asked the police operator to switch the call across to his own man. He ordered the new guy to get on to the duty officer at Bragg, say it was Major Yardley's instructions, and get him to check ex-sergeant Brown's civilian address from Records. It was operational priority, he told the man. Details must be through by oh-six-hundred at the latest. No, he didn't want to be awakened when the facts were known, but by God he'd expect to have them when he called up at six.

That was enough for one night, he thought. He turned over on his right side and composed himself for two hours' sleep.

THE STARS MOVE STILL, TIME RUNS, THE CLOCK WILL STRIKE.

▌13▐

YARDLEY WAS SHAVED and dressed in combat gear by oh-six-thirty on Monday morning. He reported to Tac HQ, a couple of floors below, which was awash with paper coffee cups and blue with the rank smoke of a hundred cigarettes. Lister Hughes was sitting in one corner, his long legs thrust out. He was red-eyed with fatigue.

"Couldn't sleep," he said. "More I tried, the wider awake I was. So I've been hanging around here in case anything breaks."

"Has it?"

"No. As quiet as the grave."

In urgent undertones, Yardley sketched out how he had worked out that Flamer Brown must have laid the charges— and that Flamer's address, if you could call it that, was less than a mile away. He wanted to go now—right now— while Flamer was probably still asleep and have a little chat with him.

"Bob, you mean arrest him under suspicion?"

"If you like. But I want a talk with him first. Just him and me."

"So you can beat him up a bit if he gets tongue-tied. Is that it?"

"Look, Lister, if we play it by the book, we'll get nowhere—fast. You arrest Flamer on suspicion, some smart lawyer bails him out—Vietnam war hero and all that crap, wounded in the service of his country—and the next thing you know he's skipped bail and is sitting in the sun at Acapulco. Meanwhile, Tim Bell up there is laughing his head off when he isn't knocking off a few Jewish dinner guests!"

"Okay, then let's try it your way," Hughes said. "What's the plan?"

"Right. Here's a large-scale map of lower Manhattan. See where Park Row runs into East Broadway? That's it. Canal Street intersects from the left—just there, below where Division Street is marked. Now run your eye ten o'clock from the intersection. Got it? That's Forsyth Street where Flamer hangs out. It's not a mile as the crow flies."

"Okay. So what do you do?"

"This. I take myself, a sergeant, and two other men. All good men. We get into Flamer's place. Either he lets us in or we'll force an entry. Then he and I'll have a little talk. He knows me, don't forget. We've soldiered together and we always got on well."

"Okay, let's try it. But I'm going to attach one, maybe two, of New York's finest to your team," Hughes said. "No, don't frown, I don't mean for them to do anything more active than keep watch outside while you soldiers are inside. With them on patrol, it'll keep any other inquisitive cop out of your hair."

"Good thinking. I'll go with that. Don't suppose the old Flamer is an early riser, but I want to hit his pad before he's wide awake. Can you fix up the two cops to be ready in thirty minutes—right here?"

"Done."

• • •

They left the underground garage beneath the Vista Hotel in a half-ton truck, Bob Yardley, a sergeant, and two men and the two cops who would stand guard outside. A crowd of reporters and cameramen surged forward as the truck cleared the ramp and high up on ready-made platforms the TV cameras whirred away. Little good would it do them, thought Yardley. If only they knew his destination and could come along, they might get a few exciting shots.

The traffic was flowing reasonably well; in under ten minutes, Yardley signed to the driver to pull off and park on Ludlow Street, fifty yards from the target. One of the cops stood guard over the Army truck. It was the kind of neighborhood, Yardley thought, where if you yawned too wide, someone would steal the fillings in your teeth.

He had never seen anything so squalid in any of the major cities in the world. Back there over his shoulder, caught in the dazzling rays of the rising sun, were the towers of wealth and affluence, wall to wall money. Here in front of him was the dead end, the grim, hopeless underside of the glittering coin.

He carried out a quick reconnaissance from behind a pillar of the bridge. The warehouse that was Flamer's pad looked filthy and deserted, with its crumbling rust-red fire escape and windows either boarded up or with a sack loosely nailed to the rotting wood frame. But he guessed that Flamer Brown would be there. When danger threatens, a rat always goes back to its hole.

Leaving the second cop as a sentry outside, Yardley moved his men silently on their rubber-soled boots across the street and up against the wall of the warehouse. The street was empty, flung into dark shadows by the sun behind the bridge. On the drive to the target, Yardley had already briefed his team. They knew that Flamer was an explosives expert with a nastily ingenious mind for booby-traps. "Look everywhere," Yardley had urged, "inside, as well as outside, on top and underneath—the lot. And be very, very careful. This guy could outwit the Cong—and you don't get smarter than that.''

He ordered one of his men, Wade, to scout ahead up the tilted stairs but to wait on the landing to one side, aiming at the door. He would come second, the other soldier third, and Sergeant Taylor would bring up the rear.

There was enough diffused light from one of the boarded-up window sockets for Wade to see where he was going as he made a gingerly crawl on hands and knees up the rickety stairs. And then it happened. He must have pressed against the wire that set off the *panga* booby-trap. There was a twang and a sudden thud as the *panga* stick sliced open Wade's buttocks and buried itself in the wood paneling alongside the staircase. Wade screamed and pressed his hand against his right buttock. It came away red with blood and he held it in front of his face, looking at it in wonder.

Yardley rapped out his orders. The other private was to use his own field dressing to stanch Wade's wound as best he could and then take him in the truck back to the casualty station set up at the hotel. One of the cops was to go with them in case of problems with the civil authorities. He and Sergeant Taylor would remain.

"Now, Taylor," he said, "you stand guard at the foot of the stairs. Anyone tries to get in or get out, stop 'em. Minimum of force but use your own judgment. I'm going up to sort out Mr. Flaming Brown!"

"I don't like for you to be up there on your own," the sergeant said. "How's about me coming, too, sir?"

"That was an order, Taylor. If I have to get rough with him, I don't want you involved. Down here, you'll be out of it. Right, Sergeant?"

"Right, sir."

Yardley picked up the submachine gun Wade had dropped on the stairs, released the safety catch, and fired a burst through the banisters at the door of Flamer Brown's pad. The tearing noise rocketed through the building. Splinters of wood burst out in all directions. The door, split through in places, sagged back on its hinges.

He sprinted up the stairs, risking the presence of other booby-traps, and went through the doorway at a crouch, the muzzle of the submachine gun swiveling from side to side as he looked for his enemy. There was Flamer, barefoot and wearing a stained undershirt and an old pair of Army fatigue pants, standing by the cluttered sink. This was a very different Flamer from the one he had last seen. This one had close-cropped hair and a bushy mustache. But he would have recognized those livid scars on his face anywhere.

"Christ, I ought to kill you, Flamer," he said, as he poked the gun toward Brown. "You and your fucking tricks. You've probably maimed a good man for life with that *panga* thing on the stairs."

"And who the fuck are you? Busting into someone else's home. There's a law of trespass, I'll have you know."

"Trespass my ass! No self-respecting cockroach would call this a home. You and me are going to have a little talk, Flamer."

"You have the advantage. You keep calling me Flamer, but who the hell are you?"

"Yardley. Bob Yardley. Remember me?"

"Sir!" Flamer sprang to attention with exaggerated deference, thumbs down the seams of the trousers, head up, chin tucked in, eyes gazing into space at their own level. "Major Robert Yardley, as I live and breathe. And what brings you here, sir?"

Yardley took a pace forward, reversed the submachine gun, and swung the butt hard against Brown's left cheek. He staggered back with the impact and slowly brought his left hand up to massage the scarred left cheek that had taken the blow. A thin trickle of blood ran down from the left corner of his mouth.

"Let's cut the kidding," Yardley said softly. "I need

answers to some questions and I need 'em fast. First, you did that job for Tim Bell, didn't you?''

"What job and who's Tim Bell?"

This time, Yardley drove the muzzle of the MP5 straight into Flamer Brown's belly. Gasping and retching, Brown went down on the dirt-stained floor, holding his guts and rocking to and fro in agony with his knees drawn up.

"You should damn well know who Tim Bell is. You served with him up on the Laotian border back in '72 and you've seen him regularly since then. The last time no doubt a week or two back. Captain Bell, SAS."

"Oh, that Tim Bell! Why didn't you say?" Flamer Brown managed to gasp out as he fought for air in his tortured lungs. "Is he looking for someone to do a job?"

"For the last time, Flamer, drop the jokes. I just don't have time for witty byplay. I need answers fast. Half the world knows it's Bell up there in the World Trade Center with those Jews he's hijacked, so don't get coy with me. You have seen Bell recently?"

"Oh, sure, I've seen him. No crime in that. He called on me couple of months back, brought a bottle of Scotch, talked about old times. That's what old comrades do when they meet, Major, sir."

"And he asked you to do a job for him. To fix those elevators in the World Trade Center and booby-trap the emergency stairs."

"He did say something on those lines but it struck me as illegal so I declined."

Yardley suddenly placed his right foot across Brown's left wrist, pinning that hand against the wooden floorboards. He cocked the MP5 and switched the lever to single shot. Then he placed the muzzle an inch from the second joint of Flamer Brown's little finger. "Now hear this, and hear it good," he said. "You screw me around any more and I blow the top half off that little finger. And then it'll be the third finger and after that the middle finger. There's not much call for a one-handed explosives expert, they tell me. And if you keep me going, you'll be a fucking no-handed expert when I've done with you. Now talk.''

"Funny, that's just what Tim said. Okay. I did that job for him. But this won't stand up in a court of law, Major. It's evidence obtained under duress.''

"I'm not the DA, I'm Special Forces, remember? I don't give a damn about a court of law, I want to stop the hijack.''

"You've got your work cut out, Major. I shouldn't boast, but those top floors are tighter than a duck's asshole.'' He explained how he had armed the ''triggers'' on each elevator so that the carriage, once past the 104th floor, would explode, the cables would be cut, and the whole apparatus would plunge over a thousand feet to the bottom. ''They're sealed off, Major. There's no way you can get at them.''

"How about landing a helicopter on the roof?''

"Tim's sharp, Major. He has a ground-to-air missile launcher. His rich friend in Idaho borrowed a Stinger from the national armory. He only has to take twenty or thirty of the hostages with him for cover—you're not going to risk killing them, are you?—and pot your chopper like one of those ducks in a shooting gallery. No, sir, Major, I wouldn't try landing a helicopter up there.''

"So you can't attack from the elevators and you can't fight your way up the emergency stairs and the roof's out and a sniper from the other tower picking them off one by one would be too risky. What's left?''

"Prayer, Major, prayer.''

Flamer Brown suddenly squirmed on the floor, tore his left hand free, grabbed Yardley around the shins with both hands, and shoved. Yardley went down on his back with a thump and the rebound flung the submachine gun clattering into a corner. He managed to get to his knees but Brown maintained the relentless shove and Yardley found himself backed up against a wall with a half-open door alongside. He sensed, rather than saw, that it was the bathroom, just as dirty and decayed as the rest of the apartment. He realized that Flamer Brown was trying to push him through the door.

Getting some leverage from the doorjamb, he raised himself on one leg, feinted by pretending to go limp, and as Flamer momentarily slackened his grip, Yardley swung him around and bulled him through the doorway. Flamer tripped and fell backward.

There was no shade on the lamp and one glance was enough for Yardley to spot that the light bulb was no bulb but a grenade. It was an M47 pineapple grenade. The bastard, he thought. In that split second, he saw that the light switch was on the outside of the door. He shoved Flamer right into the room, slammed the door shut and, as he fell away behind the protecting wall, flipped on the light switch.

There was a giant slamming noise. The door disintegrated in a mass of splinters. There was a sound like hailstones on the internal walls, as the antipersonnel grenade exploded into hundreds of steel needles that pocked the walls. A dark cloud wafted through the shattered door.

Sergeant Taylor came sprinting up the sagging staircase, submachine gun at the ready. "What happened, sir?"

"An accident. Or maybe suicide. We'll never know. I was questioning him when he suddenly made a bolt for the bathroom, banged the door to, and that was that. He may have been caught short. Stupid cunt shouldn't forget where he puts his own booby-traps!"

Yardley felt no remorse. He had already realized that Flamer Brown had intended to kill him in the way that he himself had died. Yardley kicked the remnants of the shattered door aside and peered in. The sergeant, looking over his shoulder, said "Christ Almighty!" ran to the kitchen sink, and convulsively threw up. Yardley himself had to swallow twice. Flamer had been no beauty in life; in death he looked disgusting. He had been lying almost directly under the "light bulb" and had received the full impact. His good cheek was slashed into strips and his right eyeball hung down an inch below the red raw socket. His lower jaw was missing. You live by gelignite, you bloody die by gelignite, Yardley thought.

He had meant to find out more from Flamer and cursed himself for coming off his guard long enough to let the man have a go at him. There must be something in this room, some clue, that would tell him more about Bell's plan as he discussed it with Flamer. He ordered Sergeant Taylor to return to the outside of the building and brief the cop, just in case a squad car had heard the explosion and came around to investigate it.

Then he quartered the room, stripping the bundle of ragged blankets that had served as a bed, pulling out drawers in the ramshackle desk, rummaging through the paperback books and old copies of survivalist magazines in case there were any secret papers hidden away between the leaves. He found nothing. He stood in the middle of the room, the stink of cordite in his nostrils, and tried to read Tim Bell's mind when he had first called on Flamer. They would have discussed the feasibility of arming all the elevators and booby-trapping the stairs. That, incidentally, must have taken several days—more likely, nights—to carry out. Someone pretty high up must be behind the operation, someone with enough clout to infiltrate Flamer and a helper or two into the World Trade Center as bona fide operators.

He saw in a corner to the right of the shelves holding equipment a battered old suitcase with the lid half open. He looked inside and then jerked back in surprise. There were rows of gelignite, neatly bound up and packed, with the primers already inserted. One wire was inserted in a timing device, the other—and he let out a breath of relief—was still loose. Peering closer, he saw that the timer was set for forty minutes. Where the hell had Flamer been expecting to dump that lethal load? And that very morning

from the look of it. The gelignite was already sweating a
little. There was enough there to blow the building apart.
Not even an old hand like Flamer would have constructed
a mobile bomb unless he expected to use it in a few hours.
Well, his death had saved a piece of New York. Yardley
made a mental note to get an EOD squad over to dismantle
the thing.

Once Flamer had given it the nod, they would have
discussed money. Money. Yardley's eyes searched the
room for likely hiding places. The walls, though dirt-
streaked, were unblemished, and the ceiling as well. Gingerly, he switched on the overhead light in case there was
a telltale shadow on the once-white bowl. Nothing. He
rummaged through the shelves of equipment, coils of wire,
detonators, clockwork mechanisms. Again nothing. Then
his eye lit on a strip of burlap that seemed too neatly
aligned, parallel to the angle where two walls joined. He
gently shoved it to one side, using the muzzle of the MP5
at full stretch. The floorboard had been sawn across; one
of the screws holding it looked too bright and new.

Taking a screwdriver from one of the shelves, Yardley
delicately removed the two screws. He doubted whether
even a nut like Flamer Brown would booby-trap his own
treasure hoard so that, even if the intruder was badly
maimed, the notes would end up as a bunch of confetti.
All the same, he exhaled his pent-up breath in a sigh of
relief when he eased the section of floorboard away and
saw in the aperture a tightly rolled wad of dollar bills that
would have choked a horse. You couldn't take it with you,
Flamer, baby, he thought, as he replaced the board.

But something else must have happened in this room
between Bell and Flamer Brown. Angie—and he felt a
small twinge of pity—must have been just a decoy duck.
Bell might have come to New York after her phone call to
silence her—he would not have put it past a cold loner like
Tim to consider murder as a means of shutting her
mouth—or at least to play along with the phony romance,

but he would have had to make the trip anyway to meet Flamer Brown. And who else?

Yardley looked closely at the chipped and stained sink, stacked with unscraped dishes. His nostrils wrinkled when they picked up the sour stench of Sergeant Taylor's vomit. Alongside the sink, a gaudy poster was stuck up. It advertised some gambling center. He peered more closely and saw it was a picture of a skyscraper near an improbably white beach. In the foreground, there was a helicopter against an equally unnatural blue sky. The caption read: RESORTS INTERNATIONAL, ATLANTIC CITY. Someone had scrawled a telephone number across the bottom left-hand corner.

An idea suddenly came to him. Over by the desk on the bottom shelf there was an antique-looking telephone. He hoped to God it worked. It did. He dialed the number at his married quarters in Fort Bragg.

It rang four times before Angela's sleepy voice answered. "Angie," he said urgently, "it's me. Bob."

"Bob! How's it going? I've been asleep. What's the news?"

"Okay so far. But I don't have time to talk. This is important. When you were in New York with Tim—"

"Please, Bob, do we have to go all through that again? Stop torturing yourself."

"Hell, this is not about *us*. I need some facts, fast. It's about the hijack."

"So that makes it important."

He ignored the jibe. "There's something missing. You met Tim one evening at the Waldorf. Next day, you did the usual rubbernecking tour. The following morning he leaves you in the hotel and goes off on some business appointment—he didn't tell you where. That afternoon and evening you two spent down at the World Trade Center. The following evening you took a night flight from Kennedy to London. But that left the whole morning and afternoon blank. What did you do?"

"I told you."

"No, you didn't."

"Oh, Bob, let's not argue. But I remember telling you we went gambling that last day in New York."

"Okay, I remember now. Sorry. Where did this take place? Some private club?"

"No. Atlantic City. At a huge casino there. We went there and back by helicopter. The pilot was very nice. He flew quite close to several tall buildings and quoted bits of Shakespeare and things."

"Did you find out his name?"

"No. But I saw him talking to Tim after we got to Atlantic City. It looked quite a serious talk."

"Anything else you remember?"

"Not really. I won quite a bit at blackjack and then I lost it all."

"That's the way it goes. Angie, you've been enormously helpful."

"I don't see how," she said.

"Never mind. Just take my word for it. Look, I must rush. Have you enough food in the icebox? You have? Good. Stay put the whole of the day, you hear me? I may need to call you back."

"Look after yourself, Bob. Darling. Don't do anything rash."

"As if I would." He replaced the receiver, took his Army message pad from the pocket on the front of his camouflage trousers, scribbled down the phone number on the poster, and then, with one last glance around the sordid room, shut the door behind him and tiptoed down the rickety stairs.

Back at Tac HQ, he saw Lister Hughes, who had washed and shaved and looked more alert. In front of him on the table were half a dozen empty plastic cups that had once held coffee and an ashtray overflowing with crushed butts. He reported briefly the events at Flamer Brown's hideout, still maintaining the fiction that Flamer either had killed himself deliberately or had been upended by his own device. He knew that a court of inquiry would eventually clear him if the truth came out but he also knew that these things are a waste of time and mental energy; that even if he came away blameless, the fact that there had been a court of inquiry would always be a mark on a career officer's confidential record.

Their part of Tac HQ occupied what had been a suite in the hotel. The intervening door was wide open and Yardley could see that powerful lights were being installed and a TV camera set up on a tripod.

"What gives?" he asked.

"It's your big chance for stardom. You're going on the air."

"I'm what?"

"You're going on the air. Orders from the White House. Your chum up there is opening up again at oh-eight-hundred and first of all one of the hotshots from the National Security Council is gonna try and talk him out of it. 'Don't be an idiot, lay down your arms'—that kind of crap. Bell's bound to tell him to stuff it and then it's your turn. The idea is that when he hears your voice and sees your face on the box, he'll burst into tears and repent his wicked ways." Hughes gave a lopsided grin and lit another cigarette.

"That's crazy. And you know it. We stand a better chance of getting them out if Bell *doesn't* know I'm involved. Don't forget he's done several attachments to Delta Force. He knows exactly how we operate, just as I know from experience his mindset. Don't you see it?"

"Of course I see it. It's not my idea, Bob. Lucky we haven't had the president on television, going down on his knees and begging Bell to be a good boy."

"D'you want to bet that won't happen?"

"No takers."

"What do I say to him if they put me on?"

"That's up to you. What the hell *can* you say? He holds all the cards. All you can try to do is chat him up and see if he lets anything slip."

"I still think it's a fucking stupid idea."

"No comment."

At nearly eight o'clock on Monday morning, the Windows on the World restaurant was a shambles. The hundred diners, weary, unshaven, deeply scared in spite of trying to look nonchalant, were a strange bunch in their evening dress, with bow ties askew and creases and stains across the once immaculate linen of their shirts. Bell had allowed them to go, a few at a time under armed escort, to the lavatories, but spending the night dozing in a sitting position had left the middle-aged and elderly among them stiff and cramped.

His own men, he was glad to see, had fitted quite well into the routine. He had meant to tell them that the worst thing about war was not the actual fighting. That was when the adrenaline flowed and the impossible might be tackled in the heat of the moment. The worst thing was the boredom, the stupid routine tasks that took up 95 percent of the time. The waiting, the inaction—they were what sapped morale in an insidious way.

He had personally dressed Macrae's arm wound. He did not say so to the wounded man but he reckoned that the security guard's bullet had smashed the main bone in the upper arm. Luckily, it had been a "through and through" —the bullet had gone clean through the arm and out the other side—but he privately doubted that Macrae would ever use that arm again. He strapped the arm tight against the man's body, put his wrist in a sling so that no sudden movement would grate the edges of the bone, and gave him a good shot of morphine.

He had set up spells of two hours on and four hours off for the eleven fit men remaining. He himself had catnapped during the night, leaving Clyde in charge, and was now feeling alert, wary like a prowling animal, and determined. He had arranged for one of the cooks under armed guard to go to the kitchens and produce coffee and hot rolls for himself and his men. To keep the spirits of the hostages low, he allowed a jug of cold water for each table but no food. It would do some of those fat bellies good, he thought, to be put on an enforced diet.

"Boss, it's two minutes short of oh-eight-hundred," Swenson said to him.

"Right. Is that set adjusted to Channel Seven? It is? Good." He turned to the cameraman, who was still drinking his coffee. "Stand by to shoot, or whatever you say in your business. You ready?"

The cameraman quickly put down the coffee cup and nodded. He felt it was not the right moment to discuss union rules and overtime pay with this hard guy in a balaclava who was nifty with a gun.

"Okay," Bell said. "Let's go." He turned to the camera and said, "It's eight o'clock and I'm back on the air. Is there anyone out there representing the government? If so, come on now."

There was a quick snatch of the theme tune and the face of a senior announcer appeared on the set. In grave tones, he announced that an important member of the National Security Council had agreed to speak to the leader of the hijackers but this was only to avoid the risk of further bloodshed and was not to be taken as a sign that the president and the two Houses would be prepared to negotiate in any way with criminals.

A quarter of a mile below in the Vista Hotel, Bob Yardley was sitting in the annex to Tac HQ, feeling like a cross between the village idiot and a San Francisco gay in his TV makeup, which felt greasy on the skin. He was surprised to see that the face that came up next on the screen was that of the General. Christ, what an act to follow, he thought.

The General looked straight out of the screen and said,

"Good morning. I always like to know just who I'm talking to. I take it you are Captain Bell, late of the Special Air Services in England?"

"You're well informed. I am. And who the hell are you?"

"Let's just say I'm a member of the National Security Council."

"Let's not. *I* like knowing who I'm talking to as well. You look like an Army type. Come on—name, rank, and number."

"No."

"You say No to me?" Bell whirled around, grabbed the nearest hostage by the coat collar and yanked him to his feet. He drew his Browning automatic and held the muzzle an inch from the man's right ear. The victim closed his eyes and winced.

"Okay," he said, "I don't know who the hell this guy is. Could be Einstein for all I care. But he's obviously someone important or he wouldn't be at this dinner. And he has a wife and loved ones, I bet, out there. Expect they're watching the screen this very moment. Now, are you going to tell me who you are? Or do I zap his brains all over the floor? You think I'm bluffing? Go on, take a chance. Call my bluff."

There was a pause of perhaps five seconds. To Yardley, watching below, it seemed an eternity. In that space of time, he sensed that the General's face was crumpling; he had become an old man.

He said, slowly and haltingly, "My name's Bradford. Ephraim Bradford. Rank of brigadier general. I think the number was 176795 but I can't properly recall. It's a long time since West Point."

"Okay, General, screw the number." He shoved the hostage back into his chair with his left hand and slipped the Browning back into its holster with the other. "You were smart then. Let's keep it smart, you hear?"

"I am instructed to tell you to surrender at once and

release all the hostages unhurt. If you fail to do so within one hour, I cannot answer for the consequences.''

"No, but I can, General. You can't attack us up the elevators, you can't use the stairs unless you want to get blown to hell and back, we'd shoot down any helicopter that tried to make a landing on the roof. In my book, that only leaves rocket-firing—or sniper teams from the opposite tower. And don't you think I wouldn't line up the hostages by the windows so they'd be hit first? Consequences! Don't try to kid me. I'm the one holding the gun, remember?''

"I repeat, you are to release the hostages unharmed, leave your weapons up there, disarm the devices on the elevators, and surrender in the lobby of the building.''

"And if I don't, the president will come and slap me on the wrist! Let's stop this fooling, shall we? I'm a Hereford graduate in negotiation techniques. And you don't have an Arab martyr scenario up here. *I'm* holding the cards. Now I want to make one thing absolutely clear—to you and the NSC and the White House and all those millions out there watching us. I'm going to give you till twelve noon to set up what I say. If you don't, at one minute after twelve, I'm going to shoot one of these hostages. It could be him—or him—or even that gutsy old doctor. And every thirty minutes from then on, I'll shoot another one. And so on. At the rate of two an hour, a hundred hostages'll last just over two days. And each one gets it in front of the camera. Don't worry, I'll start with those Wall Street slobs first. Shoot a money man and there'll always be another to take his place. But once I run out of bankers and money-lenders and inside dealers, I'll start on the Nobel Prize winners and the artists. You read me?''

"I read you," said the General.

"Well, aren't you going to ask me what my conditions are?''

The other man said wearily, "I'm not empowered to trade with you.''

"Get fresh instructions or find someone with the authority." He held up his left hand to the camera, showing his wristwatch. "It's nine after eight. I'm closing down now for exactly fifteen minutes. The camera will open up here again at eight-twenty-four. If there's no one on Channel Seven to listen to me then, I'll shoot the first hostage." He pointed at random; his forefinger aimed at a fat man who had tried to balance his bald pate with long sidewhiskers. "You'll do nicely." The man buried his head in his hands, as if that would hide him. "Okay," said Bell to the cameraman, "switch off, or whatever you do."

Lister Hughes walked into the annex and said to Bob Yardley, "All right, you can wipe that goo off your face. You're not going on the air."

"Thank God for that. Why the sudden change of plan?"

"God knows. The word just came through on the blower."

"Bloody typical. You know, they have a saying in the British Army—I heard it at Hereford. 'Order, counterorder, disorder.' Is nobody thinking straight down there in Washington?"

The telephone rang. Hughes picked up the receiver, listened for a moment, and handed it to Yardley. "It's for you, Bob."

"Who?"

"Someone high up. The call's coming through from the NSC."

Yardley said, "Yardley. Yes, this is Major Yardley. Morning, General, just seen you on the box."

The dry voice said, "Let's cut the crap, Yardley. Time's running out. You know that man up there, that Bell?"

"I do, sir. I told you when we met."

"You did. But do you know him well—real well?"

Yardley felt like saying, If his seducing my wife helps me to get to know him, I damn well do. Instead, he said, "Yes, sir. I reckon to know him pretty well."

"This is the big one. Is he serious? Those threats . . ."

"He's serious, sir. And he's a killer. If you're thinking of calling his bluff, he'll shoot that first hostage and then the next one, and the one after that, and he won't give a damn. I know him. You've seen the video when he blew away the Mossad security man."

"I was afraid of that. You reckon he's got us by the short and curlies?"

"Yes, sir. We'll get him in the end—I've got a plan—"

"Look, Major, I've got no time to discuss it. There's seven minutes to go. Just think of Lord Nelson and his blind eye. You hear me?" He rang off abruptly.

"I followed that all right," Lister Hughes said. "But what's this about a plan? You might have told me."

"Relax, it's only come to me in the last few minutes. Tim Bell is basically a loner. He's trained those men of his damn well—you have to hand it to him. But, deep down, they're just cannon fodder as far as he's concerned. The only thing that matters to Tim baby is his own skin. He'll sacrifice the lot of them and not turn a hair, just so long as he gets clean away. I'd lay a big wager he has a neat little private getaway plan all worked out."

"So what are you going to do? Call him up and ask for the details?"

"Ha-ha. I think I *know* what the plan is. All I don't yet know is the timing. We'll know more when we hear what conditions he's going to lay down."

Hughes interrupted. "Hey, watch that screen! The General's coming back on the air."

"D'you reckon he's the one calling the shots? If he isn't, he must be very close to the top. It's not five minutes since—"

"Hush up," said Hughes. "This could be the vital bit."

The General's crumpled features came up on the screen. He peered out, little gray eyes moving from side to side. "Are you there, Captain Bell? We are ready to talk."

"And very sensible, too," came from Bell, as he faced

the cable news camera. "Are you prepared to hear my conditions?"

"We are."

"And who is 'we'? I'm not wasting my time on some junior bloody officer—begging your pardon, General. Are you talking with the full authority of the president?"

"I am, sir."

"Right. Then listen to this. I have just two conditions. The first is that you provide a Chinook-type helicopter at the West Side heliport, fueled up and ready to lift me and my men to Newark Airport. There you are to have a 747 jumbo with sufficient fuel to fly us to Nicaragua. Don't expect it back—it'll be a gift to the people of Nicaragua!"

"I hear what you're saying. But we can't guarantee Nicaragua will take you."

"Don't worry about that. They're expecting it, courtesy of our sponsor. We shall be taking the ten most important Jewish hostages along, including the Israeli ambassador. Each of them will have a neat little explosive package strapped to his heart. One false move, I press the remote control switch and that gentle beating heart will be blown right out through someone's backbone! You hear me loud and clear?"

"Yes."

"Once we've landed in Nicaragua, I'll hold those ten hostages for another forty-eight hours, while my men disperse. Then I'll release them. You have my word on that."

From one of the dining tables, a voice shouted—it was Doctor Aranson's—"Don't do it! Don't play his game."

Bell swung round. "King, shut that old fool's mouth! If he opens it again, shoot him." To the General, he said, "Don't worry about him. He's just a voice in the wilderness. He's nearly ninety, he's only got months to play with. Here, take a look at these other fine upstanding types. You"—he turned to the cameraman—"pan that camera around the room. See them, General? All those famous Jews? They don't want to die. They've got a lot to live for. But, by God, you don't play ball with me and I'll kill them one by one!''

"You said there were two conditions.''

"That's right. The second one is this. Out there in Arizona there's a Doctor Eugene Minter. Yes, Minter—M-i-n-t-e-r. He's not a part of this, in fact, he knows nothing about this hijack. You must have heard of him. He's a very rich man with important political views. I'm asking him now—on the air—to stand by at one of the TV stations he owns. The deal is that you give him fifteen minutes' network time to speak to the American people.''

"That's impossible!''

"Is it? Just think of the alternative. You turn me down and I start shooting the hostages. We've got plenty to eat and drink up here—that's the best of hijacking a big restaurant. Maybe I'll change my mind and shoot one hostage every hour on the hour. That way, we can spin it out over the next four days. Think about it carefully. You're going to give in sooner or later—tomorrow or the day after. But by then there'll be maybe twenty dead Zionists—or thirty or forty. They won't be on my conscience. You and the White House will be responsible. The ten million Jews of America will never forgive you.''

"But the networks are privately controlled. They don't belong to the government of the U.S.A. This is not a dictatorship, Captain Bell. We cannot order them to make time available for a coast-to-coast broadcast.''

"Well, you'll just have to try the art of persuasion, won't you, General? Appeal to their patriotism. And if that doesn't work, remember there're an awful lot of Jews in the TV top spots. Do they want to see their comrades gunned down one by one? Try that angle, General. Get the president off his ass and on to the telephone. You've no time to waste.'' Bell knew the American public would be glued to this dialogue.

"Assuming authority comes through for Doctor Minter's broadcast—and I have to take instructions on that—when would it take place?''

"At 2:00 P.M. Eastern time," Bell said.

"But that's hardly five hours away! It can't be done in that time. There are all the technical details to be arranged—*if* the White House agrees with your request.''

"Request, balls! I'm *telling* you, not *asking* you. I'll give you till three o'clock—no, make it four o'clock, Eastern time. That's seven clear hours. We're going off the air now but I'll be switching on the television set just this side of 4:00 P.M. If Doctor Minter doesn't come up on the screen on Channel Seven, you can kiss the first hostage goodbye. You hear me?''

"I hear you.''

Bell noted without surprise that Elliott was badly affected by his mate's wound. He had hung around as Bell was dressing the arm, trying to soothe Macrae with urgent whispers. His face was tense, the grooves in his thin cheeks even deeper with worry. Bell guessed he could be on the point of cracking up, so he took him off his other duties and told him to stick with the wounded man, to give him plenty of hot sweet tea, and to report back if his condition worsened. The morphine had taken effect; Macrae was drowsy, though he shivered from time to time as the shock of the wound intensified. With two of the team virtually out of action, the rest were pretty thin on the ground. Bell knew that he would have to reduce the rest periods to keep enough of them on duty at a time.

At ten o'clock, the two television sets showed a newsflash—a midtown store had suddenly gone on fire. Three minutes later, the announcer, almost shouting in his eagerness, reported that mysterious fires had broken out in another—and two minutes later, in yet a third. There were scenes of riot as panic-stricken shoppers fought their way out of the stores, the traffic was seizing up in jams half the length of Fifth Avenue, the Fire Department trucks could not get close to the stores for the traffic jams. All was chaos and pandemonium. The announcer cut to a TV reporter trying to interview a harassed fire chief at Tac HQ. The man could only suppose that it was not the work of an ordinary firebug but connected somehow with the World Trade Center hijack, a diversionary tactic perhaps.

Right on, thought Bell with an inward grin. Flamer, you beaut, he said to himself without irony. You hit it right on the button. Now for the Rockefeller Center. Flamer must have dumped the bomb there by now. Oh, it was going like a dream.

He told his men that this was all part of the big game plan. "They may have thought we were kidding, even with the snatch up here, but by Christ they won't think that now. We've got 'em right here"—and he held up his clenched right fist—"and let's keep 'em that way. On your toes, all the time. Let's show those sonsabitches down there in Washington!"

Just then, one of the Jewish hostages, a spectrally thin, white-faced man, had a massive heart attack. He had heard the news, and it seemed that he was connected with one of the midtown stores on fire. He stood up, made a bellowing sound that was part scream, part moan and ended in a throaty gurgle. Then he fell forward, his face smashing into an empty glass on the table in front of him. Bell asked with a shout if there was a doctor in the house. Two of the guests raised their hands, one of them the tireless Doctor Aranson. He told them to examine the man. Aranson felt his pulse, raised the man's head gently by the chin and looked searchingly into his face. Then he lowered the head and fastened his severe gaze on Bell.

"He's dead," he said. "You killed him."

"Cool it, Doc," Bell said. "He was a goner, anyway." He tore a page off his notepad and scribbled something on it. "Here," he went on, "you two—Six and Eight—carry the body over to the main elevator, leave it inside, press the button for the bottom floor, then step out fast! You with me?"

"Right, boss," one of them replied.

"Oh—and fix this note to the body—okay?"

They nodded, then grabbed the man's corpse by shoulders and legs and carried it out of the dining area.

As Bell had guessed, there was a small crowd of reporters and a couple of TV camera crews hanging round the lobby beneath. When they saw the elevator indicator light up, they milled around, unsure whether to run in case a squad of gun-toting hijackers emerged or crowd forward so that they wouldn't miss the first glimpse when the elevator doors opened. When they slid apart after what seemed an age the crowd surged forward and then halted in its tracks. There was a body half sitting against one side, eyes fixed open, mouth sagging open. Hand cameras flashed, the TV men fought their way to the front. The *New York Post* man, braver than the others, rushed into the elevator, as someone shouted, "Hey, don't touch it, it could be booby-trapped!" He plucked the note off the starched white shirt.

"Get this," he yelled. " 'Natural causes—this time.' What a cold-blooded s.o.b."

"Who is the stiff?" someone asked.

"Search me. Look in his wallet. He won't be needing it now."

Two hundred miles away in Washington, D.C., the National Security Council had had yet another emergency meeting. There were fourteen men and one woman ranged around the long table, representatives of the two Houses of Congress, the Armed Forces, the CIA, the FBI, the NSA, and the British embassy. The General was among them.

There was only one question to answer. Would they or would they not recommend to the president that he should accede—give in—to the hijack leader's demands? The argument bounced to and fro across the table. Some, a substantial minority, were in favor of toughing it out. The hijacker could be a con artist. Call his bluff and he might go down like a pack of cards. Why, he was an Englishman or something—not even a red-blooded American. And what an international embarrassment it would be to the president and the Congress to give way to some roughneck with a gun. And on television, too! They'd be the laughingstock of the world.

The counterargument was that, on humanitarian grounds, they could not risk the cold-blooded slaughter of American citizens—and in public, too, by means of television—let alone such distinguished citizens. At this point one of the opposition remarked that if the hostages had been a bunch of poor blacks from the Deep South, it would have been better all round, if you followed that argument through.

And the cynical view was that one didn't fool around with important Jews in an election year. "Look at those guys," said one representative, "look at their clout. Among them, they run most of Wall Street, the media, and Carnegie Hall. There's a bunch of Nobel Prize winners up there, world famous musicians, the lot. What did that leader say on the air just now? Something about the Jews of America will never forgive you. Damn right! They're still bleating on about their Holocaust and that was close on fifty years ago."

"That's enough," said the secretary of state, who was in the chair. "This is hardly the time to be making anti-Semitic remarks."

"Excuse me, sir, but I was merely stating a point, not giving my personal views."

"Point taken."

The same elderly senator persisted. "Let's spare a thought for the ones doing the kidnaping. Goddammit, Mr. Secretary, those are a bunch of American boys up there. Misguided, maybe, but Americans, all the same."

"I remind you, Senator, the hostages are American citizens. They're the ones we have to worry about."

"Well, gentlemen, and madam, we've been through all

this before. It really boils down to one question. Is that man up there serious or is he bluffing? If he's bluffing, then we just sit tight and call his bluff. If he's serious, there are graver consequences we have to discuss. General Bradford here is our expert on Special Forces and irregular warfare. He has the added advantage of having talked to this—this man, if only from a distance. I suggest we ask the General to give us his considered opinion.''

"Thank you, sir. Before I answer the question directly, there is one other issue to deal with. That is whether some form of military action should be attempted before we parley with him. I'm afraid the answer to that is a definite no. The NYPD explosives experts tested the elevator system and two of their men were blown up, killed outright. They also sent a team up the emergency stairs, and they took severe casualties from booby-traps. As the man said, short of saturation by suppressive fire from the opposite tower—and that has also been wired up with explosives—there's no way we can force the issue in a military sense.''

"Not even with a quick sortie with rocket-firing helicopters?'' someone asked.

"No, sir. You heard him on the television. He would merely line up the hostages at the windows and let them take the brunt of the rocket attack.'' The General wished himself to be spared from the ignorance that always seemed to surface on such occasions.

"But if he lost all the hostages that way—God forbid—he'd have nothing left to bargain with.''

"And doesn't he know it! He would always keep ten or twenty back out of harm's way. Whatever else he may be, that man is not a fool.''

"So we're left with one question then,'' said the secretary of state. "Is he or is he not bluffing? Reports say the leader is British. You, Sir Hector, as representing our British cousins here, what do you think?''

Everyone looked at the counselor from the British embassy. The whole of Washington knew that he was the chief spook in the embassy, the head of the local MI6 station—though why the Brits could not come out and say so no one knew. Must be part of all that stuffy protocol they still indulged in. And why for God's sake bring in a diplomat straight from central casting—Hollywood's idea of the upperclass stuffed-shirt Englishman? Sir Hector was tall and languid; his beautiful gray hair was worn slightly long with little horns brushed back and up over his ears. He had a clipped mustache and he wore his glasses on a black silk ribbon around the neck of his formal suit.

"First," said Sir Hector, "Her Majesty's Government wishes to extend the greatest possible sympathy for this most unfortunate happening. Her Majesty's Government further regrets deeply that a renegade Englishman should be involved."

"Thank you, Counselor, I'm sure that makes us feel considerably better. But you haven't answered my question."

"Details of his military records were faxed through from the Ministry of Defense in London a short time ago. Captain Bell was one of the most experienced, battle-hardened officers in the Special Air Service. He won a Military Cross in the Falklands. He was quietly discharged from the Regiment three months ago."

"Why?"

"His commanding officer considered he was becoming psychotic. And there was an incident in Northern Ireland."

"What kind of incident?"

"Two IRA suspects had been arrested. Bell was in charge of them. They were subsequently shot dead."

"You mean this Bell shot them?"

Sir Hector shrugged his elegant shoulders. "He never denied it."

The old senator broke in, "Why the man's nothing but an animal!"

"Through the chair," Sir Hector said icily, "I can only suggest you put your best animals up against him." He looked toward the secretary of state. "Sir, my government has authorized me to say that if you would like to have a contingent from the SAS to put an end to the siege for you, it would gladly fly them over at once by Concorde.''

There was an appalled silence. Sir Hector had to suck his cheeks in tight to stop his mouth breaking into a broad grin.

''Thank you, Counselor, but I don't think we shall need to take up that generous offer. On the strength of what you know, do you think the man is bluffing?''

''No, sir. But, for what it is worth, I would not recommend giving in to his demands.''

''Thank you, Counselor. Now, General, what's your view? Is he or is he not bluffing?''

''Mr. Secretary, there's dead security guards and a dead waiter up there. That poor little waiter just happened to be standing by when the guard grabbed him as a shield. Now they're both dead, along with at least three cops who were just doing their duty. Any man reckons that's a bluff I'll gladly play poker with!''

''So it's your view, General, we should recommend to the president that he authorize the broadcast?''

''I would hope, Mr. Secretary, you would get a unanimous—or at least a substantial majority—opinion from all of us here to put before the president.''

''In other words, you'd like a few more necks stuck out along with yours! Fair enough. Those in favor of authorizing the broadcast?'' Ten hands went up, including his own. ''Those against?'' There were four hands raised. ''That leaves you, madam,'' he said.

''I shall abstain,'' she said. ''One part of me wants to avoid further bloodshed, but not at all costs. Once we give way to this murderer, we open the door to any maniac who can grab a hostage and demand air time. It's a terrible precedent.''

''You're right, madam. It *is* a terrible precedent. But is there an alternative? General Bradford here doesn't think so, and he's our military expert.''

"There is an alternative," she said. "Issue an immediate order that no network, no independent station, is to broadcast the doings up there in the tower. And that includes the cable news company with the camera crew inside. Without the publicity, that Captain Bell has no case. Cut him off the air and he might as well surrender."

"That's not a bad idea," someone said. "I like it."

"May I speak, sir?" asked the General. "It is an ingenious idea but, with respect, I see no way to enforce it. First, it would mean the automatic execution of the camera crew. Bell would just blow them away if that TV channel was closed. And, in practice, does anyone seriously think the media is going to hand back their toys and go to bed without supper? Look at that case in Beirut where one of our camera crews got too inquisitive and refused to go away. Result?—an American hostage still captive who would otherwise be released. Look at that business where the Egyptian commandoes stormed that aircraft. Egged on by the media, which wanted some action. Result?—dozens of deaths that might have been avoided. I could go on and on. In Belfast, everything's nice and quiet until a truck comes down the street with a TV crew aboard. At once, the kids start flinging bricks and stones at the troops to give television a riot to film. Whatever the security situation, no matter how delicate, the TV and the press reckon it's their holy right to report it to the gawping public. They'd scream bloody blue murder—begging your pardon, ma'am—if the president tried to take away that right. I'm sure I don't have to remind anyone sitting around this table it's election year."

"But if the president were himself to go on the air and appeal to the media to lay off the World Trade Center?" said the secretary of state. "He's wonderful at putting that human touch over. Wouldn't a direct appeal from the president himself work?"

The General pushed his spectacles back up his nose and looked at the secretary of state. "For all of half an hour, I reckon," he said. "They'd all be wonderfully patriotic to start with. And then some smartass would figure out that the president had only put the stop on *future* filming. So he'd put together a retrospective, with some nice slow-motion shots of the waiter and the guard getting the chop. And another network would see this and go a bit further. And whoever's tied in with the cable news company would be pressing them to keep filming and save the lives of the camera team. Before you knew what the hell was happening, they'd all be back on the air and the press would be swarming around the WTC again like flies on meat! Pity that Bell didn't hijack a media convention."

"General, we'll consider that last remark unsaid. A democracy needs a vigilant press—they tell me," said the secretary of state. "What kind of speech do you reckon this Winter fellow would make?"

"Minter, Mr. Secretary, Eugene Minter. Oh, the usual kind of leftie rubbish—power to the workers, you have nothing to lose but your chains—that sort of stuff. Minter's been on our special watch list for a year or two now. Enormously rich, he must be one of the three or four richest men in the country, but a bit of a dreamer. Frankly, we don't see him as a major threat."

"But if he makes an inflammatory speech, incites blue-collar workers to riot, wouldn't the possible effects worry you?"

"The local authorities would have to crack down hard—and fast. We might have to call out the National Guard, though I doubt it. Let's not forget the attention span of the average viewer is very limited. They see something on TV this evening, they've forgotten it by tomorrow."

The secretary of state said, "Well, gentlemen and madam, you've heard General Bradford's views. I don't need to remind you of the General's distinguished career, both on the field of battle and behind the scenes in covert operations. As I hear his advice—and I mustn't put words in his mouth—it would be to accept that condition, that Eugene

Minter be allowed to broadcast. The point is, can all the arrangements be made in time?''

A voice down the table replied, ''A slip of paper has just been put in front of me. It seems that someone has already called in on Mr. Minter's behalf to say that he'll be standing by at his own station in Flagstaff, Arizona, from two o'clock this afternoon.''

''Not slow to seize the chance of instant stardom,'' the secretary of state observed. ''Now we mustn't delay too long in presenting our recommendations to the president. Those in favor of accepting the broadcasting condition? A show of hands, please. Ah, it's now thirteen to two. I know you always like to look ornery, Senator Kragmann, but I'm a little disappointed, ma'am, that you're still abstaining.''

''I still think it is wrong in principle,'' she said. ''The president has made speech after speech stressing that we in America do not give way to the hijacker or to threats of force. And what do we do when the first real example occurs on our own doorstep? We give in.''

''So you would sacrifice each and every one of those distinguished men up there in the tower?''

''If need be. I'm lucky. Not being Jewish, I don't have a relative up there, a brother or a cousin. To be honest, I don't know how I would feel in that situation. But it boils down to this. We either stick to our principles or we concede. We can't do both.''

''That is a splendidly idealistic view to take. But the vast majority here, ma'am, perhaps because we're all men, are against you. We think the practical course is the only one to follow. Agreed, fellas?''

There was a buzz of general assent. ''Right,'' he went on, ''that concludes the meeting. I'll report to the president at once. Please remain within easy call. We may have to convene again at short notice.''

''Hey, not so fast, Mr. Secretary,'' Senator Kragmann said. ''What about the second condition—his getaway arrangements? You going to put your own limo at that sonofabitch's disposal? Begging your pardon, ma'am.''

"I propose to ignore that remark. How long would it take, General, to have the helicopter and a long-range jet standing by?"

"One hour, sir, maybe two at the outside.''

"So we've time in hand to jolly him along, is what you're saying? Anyway, we would still need to negotiate further, fix the timing and other details. Let's leave that for the moment. All agreed? I really mustn't keep the president waiting any longer.''

It was one-forty-five Flagstaff time that same afternoon. Sayeed was sitting in an armchair in one of the dressing rooms behind the studio in the television station in Flagstaff, Arizona. Gene Minter was pacing up and down the room with his rangy stride.

Sayeed said, "Oh, Gene, do sit down. You're making me feel nervous, moving about like a caged tiger. I don't like being made to feel nervous.''

"No need for you to get on edge. *You're* not the one who has to make a speech to the nation.''

"True. But I know it'll go well. The speech is a fine one, you know most of it by heart, and there's always the autocue if you need it. What an opportunity! It may well be the biggest TV audience a single broadcast has ever had. *Think* of that, Gene. The timing couldn't be better. It'll be one o'clock on the Coast, midmorning in Hawaii, and nine o'clock at night in London, England. Ten o'clock in the rest of Europe. That'll catch the major news programs. They'll either run it in full or put out large extracts. Ever since it was announced, your switchboard here has been jammed with inquiries. The BBC's been on, RTF in Paris, Westdeutsche Rundfunk—the lot. Gene, you won't just be the man of the hour, you'll be the man of the decade!''

"And if you're right, we owe it all to Tim Bell. When I

think of the first time I saw him, sitting there so coolly in my library as though *he* were the owner and *I* the intruder. He kept his promise . . . unless at the last moment they cancel my broadcast. Do you think they might do that, Sayeed?''

"No way. That government spokesman on television this morning, he could see that Tim wasn't fooling. Remember how he grabbed that hostage by the collar and stuck the gun to his head? That wasn't play-acting. I've seen too much death not to know when things are for real.''

"Talking of death, I confess the bloodshed does worry me. That dead waiter who did nobody any harm. And all those security guards who were only doing their jobs. I had hoped it would be a bloodless coup.''

There was a knock on the dressing-room door. The studio manager put his head round it and said, "Seven minutes to go, Doctor Minter. I'll give you a final call at three minutes to the hour. We're all set to go.''

"Thank you, Cady. Sayeed, I'd better pay one last call to the bathroom. This tension certainly affects the bladder.''

On his return, Sayeed said, "Where were we? Oh yes, the bloodshed. Regrettable, I agree, but you can't make an omelette without breaking eggs. And don't forget, Gene, those security men were armed to the teeth. The guard Tim shot was only waiting for the chance to shoot Tim or one of his team. Those who live by the sword . . .''

"Perhaps you're right. I'm still not happy deep down.'' Minter rose to his feet and began to pace up and down the room again.

"Would you like a drink, Gene? A Scotch or something? There's a hospitality cabinet over here in the corner.''

"No, thank you. This is the most important thing that has happened in my whole life. I want to be stone cold sober for it.''

"Gene, I insist. A little brandy will only steady you. Believe me.'' Sayeed stood up and walked over to the drinks cabinet. He poured two fingers of brandy into a goblet, which he placed on the side table near Minter's chair. He stood looming over Minter, like a nursemaid with a naughty child, until the man picked up the goblet, took a sip, grimaced, and returned the glass to the table.

Sayeed felt restless, tense in spite of himself. There was a full-length mirror on the far wall. He went over to it and gazed at his reflection, coldly, objectively, as though he were staring at a stranger. He saw the shine of sweat on the broad sallow forehead, the dark shadows under the brown eyes. In a few moments, everything he had worked for over forty years, ever since as a small boy he had sworn to avenge his lost country, would come to fruition. Gene Minter, his mouthpiece, must not fail him now. He saw the lips of his image tighten, the teeth clench. Then, deliberately, he made his face relax, the mouth soften into a sly smile. He smoothed down the lapels of his expensive English tweed jacket. His chest seemed bulky with an unaccustomed weight. The moment of truth was at hand.

There was another knock on the door. This time, Cady, the studio manager, opened it wide and stood in the doorway. He was wearing earphones and carrying a clipboard. "All set, Doctor Minter, sir? I think we should make tracks. There'll be a very short announcement from the senior station announcer dead on the hour—thirty seconds at the most—and then you're on the air. By the way, I hope you don't mind, sir, but we've canceled the commercial slot coming up to the hour. Instead, we have a tape of organ music—sort of church music. It seemed more appropriate."

"Well done, Cady. I absolutely agree. One other point. There are to be no charges to outside stations, here or abroad, that carry my speech. You understand? If they want to run it, they can have it for free."

Cady's usual baritone voice became tenor briefly. "But there are literally hundreds of thousands of dollars involved, sir. Millions, maybe."

"I can't help it. Whatever sales you've made, unscramble them. That is an order, you understand."

"If you say so. You're the boss, sir."

He went ahead along the corridor. Sayeed said to Minter, "Gene, you look as pale as a ghost. Anyone would think you were going to your own execution, not a massive triumph. Can I come with you and sit in the studio off camera?"

"Of course. You're very welcome, old friend. You've been in this thing right from the start. Only proper you should be present at the climax. And don't worry about me. I'll be fine once the cameras begin to roll."

The hunter and the hunted, Bob Yardley and Tim Bell, four hundred yards apart, were watching their television screens. So, too, were the hundred hostages—avidly. They knew that their lives hung on what happened in the next fifteen minutes. The solemn music, Handel's Largo, died away and the screen was filled with the head and torso of the station announcer. He was clearly very nervous. He sipped from a glass of water, cleared his throat, and looking straight into the camera, began.

"Ladies and gentlemen, on this very special occasion, I have the honor to introduce to you Doctor Eugene Minter, the well-known educationalist and benefactor. As he will make abundantly clear in his talk, Doctor Minter is in no way responsible—has no connection at all—with the terrible events taking place at this moment in New York. He has never met or even seen the man, the hijackers' leader, who has made this strange request.

"I have to tell you that at first he was most reluctant to accept the opportunity. He believes with the utmost sincerity that democracy should not bow to the rule of the gun. He has only agreed to speak in the hope that it will help to save the lives of our unfortunate and distinguished fellow countrymen who now find themselves in such a terrible situation.

"I know he will speak from the heart and I ask you to listen carefully to his words. Ladies and gentlemen, I give you—Doctor Eugene Minter!"

The camera swung to Gene Minter. His face was tense and a muscle in his cheek twitched involuntarily. He held his hands in front of his chest. The fingers were lacing and unlacing, as though they held a red-hot penny that they must not release. Minter's Adam's apple bobbed convulsively. Then at last he started his speech.

"My friends, I never dreamed that I would have the opportunity to address the nation—indeed, the whole world—in this way. I only wish I could have spoken to you in far different circumstances. At peace and not because an evil man—for force wrongly used is always evil—has blackmailed our government into authorizing my speech. I do not know this man—I utterly condemn his acts—and, as you have just been told, I only agreed to speak in the hope that our heroic countrymen held hostage will be safely released.

"But perhaps this dreadful hijacking contains a moral for all of us to ponder. It is the symptom of a dreadful disease. For America, my friends, this great country of ours, is sick of a fever. The fever of materialism. Is it not significant that the hijacking should take place in the very heart of the Wall Street district? The cancer that grows unchecked in the very body of the United States.

"Consider the degradation and despair of our inner cities! The increasing ranks of unemployed, the hopeless men and women with idle hands, who desperately want work. We are the richest, the most bountiful country in the whole world, and yet one-quarter of all our men, women, and children live on or below the poverty line. Yet there in Wall Street the millionaires grow even richer just by manipulating pieces of paper! They do not plow, they do not sow, they do not reap. They just buy and sell money, parasites living off the sweat of the workers.

"And where does the basic fault lie? In the capitalist

system, my friends. For over a hundred years, it has grown unchecked. Only one man, the late President Roosevelt, tried to curb its excesses, and he was reviled and thwarted at every turn.

"But, you ask, how does one overturn such a powerful, such an established, system? There is an answer—and I will tell it to you."

He suddenly paused. His face had gone very red and there were beads of froth at the corners of his mouth. His eyes behind the horn-rimmed spectacles seemed unfocused, staring.

"There is an answer . . . an answer . . . I can tell you . . . I can . . ." his voice trailed away and then, gathering strength, it blurted out, "No, I can't! There is no answer—no answer based on lying and deceit and the gun. I am guilty, just as guilty as that wicked man, Captain Bell. I connived at the operation, I helped to fund . . ."

Sayeed came into camera view. "The speech, Gene," he said in a sibilant half-whisper, "get on with the speech!"

"I won't—I can't. Good never comes out of evil. I should have seen it from the start." Minter put his head in his hands.

And then Sayeed drew a pistol from an armpit holster, leveled it at the nape of the neck of Minter's bowed head and fired. The report reverberated out of millions of television sets worldwide. Blood and gristle and splinters of bone splashed on the broad table in front of Minter's body.

The camera wavered and then held on Sayeed. Before the studio staff could stop him, he held himself erect, stared coldly into the camera lens, and in a slow and measured tone said, "Palestine has always suffered from weak fools. Our cause will outlive the fools, the hypocrites, and the weaklings. My martyrdom will convince all of you of this. Let me be forever on your conscience." He put the gun to his own head and fired.

•   •   •

Doc Holliday blipped off the television set with his remote control. This was trouble—and trouble spreads fast. He called his office in Boise, Idaho, and told his private secretary to get on to the airport. The Lear jet with the long-range tanks was to be fueled up at once. Takeoff was to be at sixteen-thirty, just over two hours' time. The flight plan was Toronto, Gander, Reykjavik, and Stockholm, Sweden. He had a good friend or two among the Swedish timber men. A month's fishing on some remote lake there would be just the thing. His doctor had told him he ought to relax, take a break now and then.

"And make sure," he snarled on the phone, "that damn pilot is standing by with the engines warmed up when I get there—even if you have to tear him out of some woman's bed."

And, thinking of women, the three girls would have to go back to the whorehouse where he had found them. He would miss them, particularly Annie-Lou with the prehensile mouth. But he remembered his old dad quoting Kipling at him years ago: "He travels the fastest who travels alone."

It had been fun while it lasted. He hoped Tim Bell would come out all right. That guy had balls; he had stuck to his word and given those Jews a going over. Pity he couldn't be around to see what Bell did next. But when the shit hits the fan, the smart man shuts the door and stays outside until the fan stops spinning.

THIS NIGHT, THIS HOUR, THIS MINUTE, NOW.

▮14▮

THE NETWORK REACTED fast. Television screens were blacked out and soothing music, neither too sepulchral nor too jaunty, came over the air. Within a dozen seconds, the screens lit up again as the network cut to a different studio. There, an announcer said, somewhat breathlessly, "Owing to the unfortunate events just occurred, there will be a short break. Please stay tuned to this station. We hope to come back to you as quickly as possible." The screens went blank again and the music started up once more.

Up in the Windows on the World restaurant, Bell felt a void inside. He had been meaning to get out on his own in any case but the double deaths of his sponsors meant a quick rethink. The sooner the better now. He hoped to God that Harry Ginsberg, the poetic pilot, was locked into the TV station as he had ordered him to be. He also congratulated himself for holding out for the payment plan. Sayeed had organized that second payment to be made to the Swiss bank. If he was to avoid rotting in some dump like Paraguay for the rest of his life, he needed the

291

half million dollars to buy him time and a secure hideout and a skillful plastic surgeon.

His eyes ranged across the long room. The hostages were excited, talking animatedly to one another, instead of sitting in the sullen apathetic silence they had fallen into. He could sense a note of confidence rising in their voices. Conversely, his own men appeared confused and apprehensive. They would all have seen Sayeed when he visited their training quarters and they must be wondering why the hell he should shoot that guy with glasses and then himself.

"Quiet, you lot!" he shouted to the hostages. The buzz continued. He drew his Browning and fired a shot into the ceiling. The sudden crack of noise and the plaster flakes eddying down on the tables stunned the hostages into silence. "That's better. Now stay quiet, you hear me? That business on the box don't mean a thing up here. You're just as near a bullet as you ever were. So just shut your mouths and think about things."

He turned to his own men. "Four, stop draping yourself all over that pillar. On your feet, man! Your job's to watch those three tables for anything suspicious. So watch 'em, for Chrissake! And you, Seven, you go and relieve Six in the kitchens. I could use a hot cup of tea—so get on with it. The rest of you, on your toes!"

Just then the television screen to his half-right lit up again. The flickering lines settled into the face and shoulders of General Bradford, who said, "Are you there, Captain Bell?"

Bell signaled urgently to the cameraman to start filming again. He moved closer to the overhead pole microphone. As he did so, the General repeated, "Are you there, Captain Bell?"

"I am."

"I'm sorry you—your friends have come to such a violent end. So abruptly, too."

"No friends of mine, General. You heard the man— he'd never heard of me or seen me. He said so himself."

"I can hardly believe that. I suspect that when the government auditors put his private accounts under the microscope and scan all those interlocking company accounts, they'll find some hefty offshore payments to you."

"Let 'em search away. The point is—and don't you forget it—Minter may be dead but I'm very much alive up here. And I've still got your precious hostages."

"But you've lost your support outside, don't you see? Your rich sponsor. Look, Bell, we're both too adult to try to fool each other. Minter was your moneybags—why bother to argue? With him gone, you might as well give up. Even if you manage to get to South America, you still need money, lots of it, to keep you going. And you won't get another cent out of the Minter estate, I give you my word on that. Why not surrender with dignity?"

"Up your constipated ass, General! I'll give you a demonstration of my mindset. No, I'm not going to kill a hostage—I said I wouldn't if you put that broadcast on." Bell knew he needed impact and fast. "But, just to prove I'm serious, I'll show you what the IRA call 'kneecapping,' a popular game played by the terrorists of Ulster."

He whirled around, grabbed the same bald hostage he had singled out before by the collar and yanked him out of his chair. Before he had the chance to shout or protest, Bell had tripped him and sent him sprawling on the carpeted floor. The Browning slid into Bell's right hand. Stooping, he placed it to the back of the helpless man's leg and fired one shot, shattering the man's kneecap beyond repair. The man put his own hand in wonder on the knee, lifted it away and saw that blood was dripping off his fingers. The TV millions heard Bell's sarcastic tone replaced by the high-pitched wail of the shocked victim. Bell put the pistol away.

Decisively, he said, "Five and Seven, pick him up and take him away to the kitchens. Wash the wound and bind it tight. Tear up clean tablecloths or use napkins. And if he keeps on hollering, you have my permission to blow away the other kneecap!''

He turned back to the television screen. ''I could just as easily have put one in his head, General. Remember that. I still hold the cards. Now, have you fixed up the getaway transport?''

''Not yet, Captain Bell. Recent events have rather changed things.''

''Recent events have changed nothing!'' He slipped the Browning automatic out of its holster and held it up in front of the TV camera. ''This is still the ace of trumps— and I'm holding it. I'd've thought that last little demo would have convinced you. Do I have to shoot someone else?''

The answer came back hurriedly. ''No, I'm sure all of us here understand. But these things take time, Captain Bell. You demand a large helicopter in one place, and a jet aircraft with a range of up to three thousand miles in another. This can't be done by a snap of the fingers.''

''Don't give me that crap! Newark Airport is swarming with long-range aircraft. Fueling up takes no great time. If you don't have one of your own, for Chrissake, commandeer a big jet. You're supposed to be the government— well, bloody govern for a change! And the helicopter —borrow it from Andrews. Shake it up, General. Remember what the poet said—'The stars move still, time runs, the clock will strike.' Eight times, Harry.''

''What exactly are you demanding?''

''This. At first light tomorrow morning, I shall take all the hostages up to the roof. At oh-six-hundred. The helicopter will pick up my men and me plus a selected number of hostages—wired up, don't forget, General—and not for sound! The chopper flies us to Newark Airport. The rest of the hostages, if they have any sense, will stay quietly on the roof until you arrange to pick 'em off with other choppers. And then you can get a hotshot or two up from Redstone to disarm the elevators and neutralize the booby-traps on the stairs. You have one hour to come back on the air and tell me everything's been arranged. One hour—and then see what happens to the first hostage.''

In the annex to Tac HQ, Lister Hughes lit yet another cigarette. He inhaled deeply and then began to cough. ''These damn things'll kill me one day. Marlboro Country— you should see the ridges on my lungs! Bob, did something odd strike you about that last exchange?''

''You mean that bit about the clock will strike? And then I thought he said something about Harry. Who the hell's Harry when he's at home?''

''Exactly. Hey, they've been videotaping everything next door. Let's go and get a run-through, then we'll know exactly what he said.''

In under ten minutes, they had returned to their room. Yardley said, ''Here, I have it written down in his exact words. He said, 'Shake it up, General. Remember what the poet said—"The stars move still, time runs, the clock will strike." Eight times, Harry.'''

'' 'Shake it up, General.' That's straightforward enough —we can eliminate it. Then there's the quotation—tee tum, tee tum, 'Time runs, the clock will strike.' And then that bit about Harry. 'Eight times, Harry.' Do you reckon that's part of the poem?''

''Hardly. I'm a soldier, not a literary critic, but it doesn't sound to me as if it fits. The rest of the quotation has a kind of rhythm—dee dah, dee dah, dee dah, five times—but 'eight times, Harry' sounds different, slangy. In my book, it's a message to someone out there.''

''Yeah, but who? There must be a few million Harrys knocking around the U.S. of A.''

''Let alone the millions overseas. Don't forget most of the world's been watching all this—and Bell would be the first to know it.''

''So where do we go from here?''

"I suggest you take a break and a rest, Lister. If the White House accepts his terms, we'll still be on duty up to six tomorrow morning, and well after that, too. That's over thirteen hours away and it's going to be a long night. Why don't you have a hot shower and then get your head down for a few hours—you've been in those same clothes since yesterday—and when you've had a good rest, I'll take one."

"What'll you do till then?"

"Work on my plan."

"You and your plan!"

As soon as Lister Hughes had left the room wearily, Yardley put a call through to Angela back at Fort Bragg. When she answered, he said, "Hey, it's me. How's it going?"

"Oh, it's horrible, Bob! I can't bear to watch it—all that unnecessary shooting. What's come over Tim?"

"You tell me. You know him better than I do!" He heard her gasp in air and quickly added, "Sorry, I shouldn't have said that. I really am sorry."

"I suppose I asked for it."

"Look, Angie, this is very important. I must test your memory again. It could make all the difference between us winding this op up properly or giving in to that shit. Think for a moment—cast your mind back to that helicopter trip, coming back from Atlantic City."

"Oh, Bob, do you have to keep harping on about that? It's over, done with. I've now seen the other side of Tim—and it makes me sick. So please don't keep bringing *that* up again."

"You don't understand. I'm not getting at you, believe me. I think I can forestall Tim's getaway plan, but I need your help. Desperately."

"Okay," she said. "I'll try to remember. What is it you want to know?"

"When you flew back, you thought you recognized the pilot as the man you'd seen talking to Tim earlier—back in Atlantic City. Right?"

"Yes," she said, "that's right."

"And he was a chatty type, always spouting poetry on the intercom. Can you remember any of the bits he said?"

"Let me think for a minute. There was one bit I thought was rather unpleasant—sort of blasphemous. How did it go? Something about Christ's blood and the sky—no, I'm wrong—not the sky, the firmament."

"That's terrific. Good girl. Any more?"

"Oh, I'm glad it's helping you. Yes, there was something about riding in triumph through some foreign place. It sounded like 'Percy something.' "

"Percy something. Can't think of any place that begins with Percy. Anything else?"

"Yes, he quoted something that must be pretty well known. At least I'd heard of it before. I sort of vaguely connect it with Elizabeth Taylor and Richard Burton—some kind of play they were in. As we flew over the World Trade Center, he said a verse about the face that launched a thousand ships and burned some topless towers. I remember that bit specially, 'cause I thought at the time, if anything's got a real top, those towers have."

"This is great. Is that the lot?"

"No, there was one strange bit. Not the poetry, I mean. The pilot said something to Tim when he pointed out the towers. I mentioned it to Tim and he said there must be some other Tim on board. He got quite shirty about it."

"You reckoned the pilot *was* talking to him?"

"Yes, I do. Now I come to think of it, I'm sure he was the same man I saw talking to Tim earlier on."

"Angie, this is terrific! You've been an enormous help."

"Have I really?"

"Fantastic. Look, I must go—things are happening. I'll talk to you soon. Love."

As he rang off, he wondered fleetingly why he had used

that last word. Was it just a casual expression or did he mean it? There was no time for self-analysis but he still felt a strange little glow.

He went down the corridor and talked to a captain on the police commissioner's staff. When he asked to be put in touch urgently with a professor of English, he could see the man thought he had gone nuts but was too polite to say so. He gave a quick explanation, up to a point, and the captain made three phone calls on his behalf. Then he said to Yardley, "Professor Landis at Columbia. He's the guy for you. Here, I'll scribble down his home number. Good hunting."

"Is he likely to be there now?"

"Why not? Everyone with a TV set, which means everyone, is back home watching right now. Wish I was! I'm supposed to be a traffic expert, not a hijack heavy!"

Yardley thanked him for his help, then walked fast back along the corridor to his own room. He dialed the number; a woman answered. He explained who he was and that he needed Professor Landis' help as soon as possible. It turned out the cop had been a poor prophet; the professor was not at home, glued to the television set. He was in his rooms at the college, working on a literary paper. Yardley asked if she would be kind enough to let him have the professor's number there. After some fumbling and looking up her list of phone numbers, she did so.

He felt edgy, impatient. Time was sliding past. He sensed that Bell was going to make a break for it—on his own or with a hostage as insurance. But when and how? The "how" would have to be by chopper; Bell himself had closed all other exits. But the "when"? And was the poetry-loving pilot the accomplice? This next call would be the crucial one.

As he punched nine to get an outside line, he saw an open pack of cigarettes belonging to Hughes on the table alongside the telephone. He had given up smoking years ago on joining the Special Forces. All the same, he pulled a cigarette out of the pack and looked around for the matches. There were none on the table. Hughes must have taken them with him. Angry with himself, he plucked the cigarette from his mouth and crushed it in one big fist. He dialed the number.

A testy voice answered. "Landis. Who is that? This is most improper. I am not supposed to be interrupted during my private sessions. Who are you?"

Yardley explained quickly who he was and how vital it had become to discover what, if anything, lay behind the garbled quotations. He added that the safety of the hostages might depend on what help the professor could give him. The man sounded mollified, even beginning to get interested.

"Well, what is it you wish to know, Major Yardley?"

"It's this, sir. Can you tell me, please, if there's a poem with some lines in it about Christ's blood and the sky—or perhaps the firmament?"

"A sophomore could answer that one, Major. 'See, see where Christ's blood streams in the firmament.' It's from *The Tragical History of Doctor Faustus* by Christopher Marlowe. He was a contemporary of Shakespeare. It's a play."

"Doctor Faustus?"

"Yes, it's a perennial theme. Faustus sells his soul to the Devil and in return is given magical powers for a limited time. In the end, the Devil claims his soul."

Yardley said, "That's extremely helpful," though he was damned if he could see why. All the same, flattery usually got you somewhere. "The next quotation, sir, is something about riding in triumph through some place that starts with 'Percy,' or something like that."

"That's even easier. 'To ride in triumph through Persepolis.' Same author, different play. This one is *Tamburlaine the Great*. Tamburlaine, or Tamerlane, as he was more properly called, was a great conqueror. Marlowe always went in for bravura main characters. Anything else? I really do have a great deal of work to do.''

''I'm so sorry to have taken up your time, Professor Landis. But you've been invaluable so far. There's only one more quotation to locate. Something about launching a thousand ships and burning towers.''

''Really, Major. I know Shakespeare called soldiers brutal and licentious—but don't they teach you anything of literature at military schools? That is one of the most famous quotations in the whole of English literature! It's from the same play, *Doctor Faustus*. With his magical powers, Faustus conjures up the vision of Helen of Troy. As she passes by, he says—

'Was this the face that launch'd a thousand ships,
And burnt the topless towers of Ilium?'

And so on. Ilium was another name for Troy. When Troy fell, the Greeks sacked it, burned it to the ground. You said earlier that a helicopter pilot en route from Atlantic City to the West Side heliport made these quotations on the intercom to the passengers—or one particular passenger, perhaps?—and then diverted the flight path so that it went over the World Trade Center. All I can conclude is that he must have been a lover of Christopher Marlowe and that those two unsightly buildings must be part of the plot.''

''Professor, I can't thank you enough. I mean it. You've confirmed something I've half suspected. Thank you for your help, and for being so patient.''

As he put the phone down, he glanced at his watch. It was four-fifty. He suddenly thought of Bell's last broadcast. ''Eight times, Harry.'' Christ, that was it! ''The clock will strike''—eight times. Eight o'clock—twenty hundred hours—that was Bell's time for liftoff. And the chopper would be coming from Atlantic City with the setting sun behind it. Or was it tucked away in hiding somewhere nearer? He had to move fast.

Now did he play it safe, wake up Lister Hughes, explain everything including the conversation with the professor, and ask permission to go ahead? And what if Hughes felt it was too big for him and went higher up the ladder? An hour from now and it would be too late to move. They might just as well sit back and watch Bell getting away with it on television.

He remembered an odd phrase the General had used when he had last spoken on the phone. Something about Admiral Nelson and his blind eye. Of course, he put the telescope to his blind eye. He saw no signal for him to stand off, he pursued the attack—and won. No one argues with a victor. But if it had been a crushing defeat, what then? Nelson was probably reckoning he wouldn't be alive to face the consequences.

The Nelson touch. Should he go for it, or play it by the book? If the first way failed, that would be the end of his Army career, maybe even a spell in the stockade for deliberately disobeying orders in action. His orders were to stand by and await orders, not desert his post on a wild-goose chase.

But Bell was no goose. He was a killer who let nothing stand in his way, not friendship, decency or obligation. If he slipped out of this one, he could be another Carlos, a kind of folk-hero to those psychos and misfits who ended up in the terrorist camp. They needed a symbol. It was *his* job to smash it.

He strapped on his belt, adjusted the pouches and the holster, picked up his beret, and pulled it on his head. He would take a couple of men from the team standing by and leave Sandy Vaughan in charge. Okay, he thought, this is it—let's go.

Bell fingered the SAS cap badge in his breast pocket. It would soon be time to move on. Now that he had regained his coolness, he could admit to himself that he had first been shaken, then enraged, by the abrupt way Sayeed had killed Minter and then himself. It had taken all Bell's determination to make himself appear relaxed when the General had started taunting him. Kneecapping that hostage had not been smart, but that dusty-voiced old sod had pushed him into the gesture. He'd like to get General Bradford writhing on the ground one of these fine days. He'd have him howling for mercy before he got back on his feet.

With Sayeed alive, it might even have been worth sticking to the official plan and taking his men plus some hostages to Nicaragua. Once the dust had settled, he could have slipped quietly into the Palestinian net—the PLP or the PFLP or maybe Al Fatah. Any one of those groups could use an expert like him. Now it would be South America as a temporary base, a jumping-off place for South Africa. A renegade Englishman who had put two fingers up at the president and all the people of the U.S.A., and gotten away with it, a man who had lots of friends in the Selous Scouts and the ex-Rhodesian SAS—wouldn't the South Africans give him a welcome! It'd be a triumphal procession down Adderley Street, at the least.

He looked at his watch. Coming up to 7:00 P.M. He had not dared to repeat the message for Harry Ginsberg. Coming out with it once was a bit chancy. He just had to keep his fingers crossed that Harry had heard it. And now he had to pace this final hour to perfection. He needed to have himself and his two hostages on the roof a few minutes before eight o'clock but without rousing the suspicions of Clyde or his other men. He sensed that once he had gone Clyde would not long sustain the heavy pressure. He was a good number two under a strong leader. Left to himself and with the men getting jumpy at losing their boss, he would crumple within an hour or so. Bell could see him going on the air with a sense of relief and almost pleading to surrender. Well, half his luck. He and the rest were all expendable.

He sent for Clyde and told him that he was going to interrogate several of the hostages. It would be as well to know who they were and which were the most useful ones to take along as "insurance" when the choppers had been organized. "It'll be quiet in the observation area, I'll deal with them there in pairs, starting at that table over there. You relax, and see the guys off duty get their proper break. It could be a long night ahead of us. But we're winning, we've got 'em on the run!"

"You bet, boss."

The table of eight that Bell had spotted contained his two likely "rabbits." He left them to the end and saw the others first, two at a time. They looked rough, their once beautifully frilled and laundered shirts all crumpled and stained, their evening dress creased from all the sitting around, over a day's beard growth on their once-shining faces. But most of them were full of guts, he had to admit grudgingly to himself. Doctor, banker, publisher, or author, each knew he had the whiphand and hated him for it. They would do what he told them because he held the gun and they knew he would use it if he had to. But they had not lost their pride in what they were, in what they had achieved. There was none of that emotional transference between captive and captor. Time was running out. The two he had left to last had better be a softer touch.

They were. One was an overweight youngish man, a diamond merchant named Weinstock, whose belly strained against the cummerbund that acted as a corset. The other was small, pink-cheeked, with tousled hair, and looked more like a cheeky Aryan schoolboy than the Wall Street broker he turned out to be. His name was Lazarus. Pretty apt, Bell thought. The guy might get a real chance of rising from the almost dead.

"Listen to me," he said. "Listen carefully, I've no time to say it twice. I'm going ahead of the main body and I've got room to take two guys with me. This is your big chance. You could be home with your wife and kids by lunchtime tomorrow. Since that Minter got zapped on TV, your people are gonna have a tougher approach. If they don't provide the choppers, the whole op hits the fan. There are a few psychopaths in that team of mine. I've held 'em back so far but let me tell you those guys are hand-picked from the Anglo-Saxon Brethren! I thought that would make you sit up," he said to Weinstock. "Heard of the Brethren, have you? If there's anyone they hate it's a Jew. They'd cut your throat—or your balls off—as soon as look at you. *And* they wouldn't mind using a blunt knife.

"Do you want to come with me or stay and take your chances? Oh, there's a fee to join this club. It's gonna cost you each a million bucks for the ride. When we get to the other end, you'll have twenty-four hours to get your bank to telex the money to my bank in Switzerland. When I get the return telex to say the money's been credited, you're free. I give you my word. Did I say you might be home tomorrow night? I was wrong. But by Wednesday night, you could be safe at home with your families."

Lazarus said hesitantly, "What guarantee do we have that you'll play ball? Once the ransom's been paid, you could knock us off and walk away."

"That's a chance you've got to take. But look at it this way. I only kill when I have to. What's the point in knocking you two off after you've paid up? Besides, once we're in Nicaragua, I'd be a fool to commit a major crime and risk being arrested by the locals."

Weinstock said, "I just don't have that kind of dough lying idle."

"Well, you'd better bloody find it!"

Weinstock said, "With your permission?" He put a chubby paw inside his collar behind the black bow tie and yanked on a thin gold chain that was around his neck. The end came loose, to reveal a chamois leather wallet. He loosened the drawstring and tipped the contents into the palm of his left hand. There were five uncut diamonds, each as large as a man's fingernail. Half proudly, half fearfully, Weinstock held out his hand toward Bell.

"They're just bits of glass to me," he said.

"Those are diamonds of superb luster and quality," Weinstock protested. "Cut and polished, they would be worth well over half a million dollars altogether."

"Okay, I'll take 'em as a down payment." Bell scooped them off Weinstock's palm and slipped them into his top pocket, next to his SAS cap badge. "We'll get 'em valued in Nicaragua and write that off against the million. But come along, time's running out for you two. If you need to raise the money, I'll let you have two phone calls each once we get there. If you've got any friends or family, they'd better stump up. Are you coming with me or staying? You have just one minute to decide."

He pushed back the cuff on his left sleeve and put his hand on the table. The two men could see the second hand on his wristwatch jerking round the circle. They muttered quickly to each other, faces pale, eyes blinking. Bell watched them coldly.

"Time's up," he said.

"Okay," Lazarus said, "it's a deal. We'll go with you."

"You've got good sense," he said. The watch showed five minutes to eight. "Let's get cracking. You two go ahead. I'll be right behind you, so no funny games, you understand? One shout, one false move, and you both get it. Lead on—across in front of the elevators, then down that corridor. There's a door at the end leading to the emergency stairs and the roof. Stop when you get to the door. Come on, let's go."

They moved silently in file across the thick carpet and through the lobby, and had just reached the corridor when a voice behind him suddenly said, "What goes on, boss? You need a hand?"

He swung round. Christ, he thought, it's that bloody Geoghegan. I never did trust that creep. Is he a plant, for

God's sake? Aloud, he said, "Good thinking, Two. Yeah, I need somewhere quiet to give these guys a real grilling. Here, you follow 'em along the corridor, I'll bring up the rear. Watch 'em like a hawk."

The two prisoners, looking confused, stumbled ahead, with Geoghegan close behind. Bell slid his commando knife silently out of its sheath, stepped up behind Geoghegan and flung his left arm around the man's face and mouth. His right hand came slicing down and the knife point went in under the right ear and the angle of the jawbone. He plunged it deep and across, severing the windpipe and the vocal cords. Blood spurted, there was a dreadful gurgle from Geoghegan, and his body slumped on the floor as Bell pulled back. He leaned down, wiped the blade on the man's combat jacket, and sheathed the knife.

Weinstock was white-faced, trembling with shock. Bell slapped him across the face and said, "Move it! If you don't want the same, keep moving."

They went through the door and up the three flights of the emergency stairs. His two prisoners were panting with the unaccustomed exercise as Bell grimly drove them ahead. They stepped out onto the roof. It was a warm, balmy evening but thirteen hundred feet up in the air the wind surged and blew with some force. He shepherded them over toward the helicopter pad in one corner of the huge roof, well away from the towering mast. Would Harry make it with this high wind? he wondered. Christ, where was that damned helicopter? It was only a minute to eight o'clock. Jesus, Harry, come on—where the fuck are you?

And then he saw it, a gnat that would soon become a dragonfly, working its way up the New Jersey shore of the Hudson River. It was gaining height all the time as it crossed the broad expanse of water, aiming straight at the tower. There were two other helicopters on the ground at the West Side heliport. He wondered if they might be sent in pursuit. What could they do? They would hardly risk shooting down Harry's chopper in case it was on an official mission. And once they knew hostages were involved, they would give it a wide berth.

The helicopter clattered nearer, then was hovering directly overhead. Three long ropes hung down, each ending in a seat with straps. Bell pulled his prisoners together and shouted through the din and the buffeting of the downdraft, "I'm gonna strap you into those seats. I'll be in the middle. You see that dark ring around the two outside ropes, just out of reach? That's explosive, and I've got the remote control right here." He tapped a bulky pocket. "One silly move and I press the button. The explosive will cut the rope and you'll have a nice long drop before you hit the ground. So, no heroics, please."

He sat them into the improvised seats and strapped them in. Then he strapped himself into the middle seat. Great pilot, that Harry. He was holding the chopper almost rock steady in spite of the cross wind. He held out his arm toward the pilot's cabin above his head, with the thumb extended. In recognition, the pilot fed in the power, and the ungainly machine began to lumber skyward.

Fantastic, thought Bell. What a trick to pull off! To have the president and the whole fucking U.S. of A. under his thumb. And to get clean away with it. Who was the stupid sod who had said you can't win 'em all? Well, he had.

The helicopter had leveled out at around a thousand feet and was clattering diagonally across the Hudson in a southwesterly direction. Bell glanced at the hostages in turn. Their eyes were shut tight and there was a look of sheer anguish on their faces. They'd give no trouble for a while. He decided it was time to climb aloft and double check the plan with Harry Ginsberg. There should be a private jet, rented from one of Harry's drug-running friends, standing by on a remote airstrip in one of the countless wooded inlets of Chesapeake Bay. Five minutes to touch down and transfer the hostages and then it would be—Colombia here

I come! No Air Force fighter was going to shoot down that jet with two valuable hostages on board. The suckers have even bought the bullshit about going to Nicaragua. Christ, he thought, I've made it.

He gripped the strap above his head with his left hand and with the right released the catch on the sling that held his buttocks. Then, hand over hand, he swarmed up the twenty feet to the open side of the chopper. He swung his legs inboard and hauled himself inside. He saw at a glance that three rows of seats had been left—with a passageway up the middle—between the main doors and the cockpit. The other seats had been taken out to make a large baggage area. The cabin of the Sikorsky S61 was filled with the smell of stale perfume.

The chopper was rocking slightly in the cross breeze. The sun, low in the west, was shining straight into his eyes. He could just make out the back of Harry's head and his shoulders, as he sat in the pilot's seat. Bell moved toward the stepped up cockpit, steadying himself with a hand on either gangway seat and shouting as he went. "Hey, Harry, you're terrific! Right on the button and clean as a whistle. There's a bonus in it for you when we land. Steer well clear of Newark, there's bound to be a reception committee there. Is that private jet all set?"

Ginsberg seemed to hunch his shoulders. He said in a flat monotone, "Hi, Tim."

Bell was now only a few feet behind the cockpit. He started to say, "I'll come and sit beside—" Then he saw there was another man in the copilot's seat. He was wearing a baseball cap pulled down over his eyes and bulky earphones across his upper face. His arms were crossed in front of him. "Who the fuck's that?" Bell shouted. "I never said you could bring another guy."

Ginsberg said, again in that flat voice, "We need a winchman to get those hostages on board."

"Like hell we do! I'll be winchman. Once we've hauled

up the hostages, I want him out—fast. You'll go down, find an open space and hover over it. He can jump the last few feet, or I'll pitch him out. That's an order.''

The big man uncrossed his arms. Bell saw that he had a pistol in the hand that had been concealed. It was pointing at Ginsberg's guts. With his free hand, the man removed the earphones and pushed back the peak of his cap. ''Steady, Tim,'' he said. ''Don't lose your temper. The ballgame's changed.'' It was Bob Yardley.

Bell's stomach lurched. For a fleeting moment, he thought he was going to shit himself. Then, tightening his stomach muscles into rods, he said in the most casual tone he could find, ''Well, if it isn't Bob Yardley. We mustn't keep meeting like this. Folks'll talk.'' His hand strayed toward the transmitter around his neck.

''Hold it, Tim!'' Yardley swung the pistol toward Bell's face. ''Move that hand another inch and I'll blow you away.''

Bell had recovered. He appeared to relax but every nerve and muscle was taut. His mind raced over the possibilities. ''Well, it's a standoff, I reckon. You may get me but I'll still press the button. Won't look so good on your career sheet, Bob, to have knocked me off and lost those two hostages as well. That General friend of yours'll want me alive, wouldn't you say?''

''Cut the crap, Bell. It's all over. You've had it. Ginsberg here's going to fly us into Newark Airport, nice and steady. And that's the end of the line for you.''

''Who says so?''

''This says so.'' Yardley jerked the pistol an inch.

''You always were dumb, Bob. Oh, a real brave guy, but dumb. You and that fucking wife of yours—sweet bit of crumpet, by the way.''

Yardley looked at him, grim-faced. ''Nice try, Bell, but it won't work. You're not going to rile me that way. So, first off, you go and sit down in that third row, both hands on the seat in front of you. Move it!''

Bell seemed to obey, moving back half a pace, his eyes still fixed on Yardley. He said casually to Ginsberg, "Well, Harry, the power's in your hands now."

Ginsberg took the hint. He straightened his right arm on the collective lever and pressed it down hard, dumping all the power from the rotating blades. The helicopter dropped like a stone. Bell gripped the seat backs to counteract the negative-G but Yardley in the copilot's seat was flung upward by the sudden force. His right hand swung up and smashed into the roof panel above his head, and the pistol was knocked clear, bouncing into the footwell between his legs as Ginsberg raised the collective lever and put the power back on.

Bell went in fast, aiming a chopping backhander at Yardley's face. Yardley parried it with his elbow and grabbed for a screw grip on the front of Bell's smock, twisting the loose clothing tight. Bell battered him around the head but he clung on, forcing his way out of the seat and bulling his enemy back down the aisle toward the open baggage space. He knew that in the open with room to move, his superior size and weight would give him the advantage.

As the fight raged to and fro, it was all that Ginsberg could do, skilled pilot though he was, to keep the chopper steady. He was flying now in loose circles over the Hudson River, awaiting the outcome. If Yardley smashed Bell into submission, he knew he was a goner. Oh, Jesus Christ, let Tim win, he thought. He could hear the grunts of the two men as they fought and wrestled their way up and down the aisle, the thudding of fists on flesh and bone. He sensed rather than saw at the edge of his vision two large drops of blood splashing in a pear shape against a passenger window. At this rate, they'll kill each other, he thought. The fight seemed to be going on for ages.

Just then, he heard Bell shout, "Harry, I've got him! Tilt it hard to port!"

Ginsberg flung the Sikorsky S61 almost on its side as

though it were a paper dart. He held it there and glanced over his shoulder. Both men were on the floor by the open doors. Yardley was underneath, gripping Bell's wrists with either hand. The upper half of his body was out of the opening. Bell, on top, using his toes for leverage, was gradually forcing Yardley outward. With the chopper at a tilt, the sloping floor was giving him the advantage.

And then it happened. Yardley suddenly pulled away his left hand and swung it up and out until it hit the winch strap, half an arm's length out of the chopper. He grabbed it with his left hand, swung his body sideways and heaved at Bell with his right hand, all in one sudden act of violence. Bell, with nothing to grasp, plunged out through the opening and then began to cartwheel down, down through space toward the placid Hudson River. The last rays of the setting sun were staining its surface red—like blood.

Yardley flexed his legs, which were still inboard, and with one athletic move swung himself back into the chopper. He looked down and saw the black dot of Bell's body still falling through space. He knew it would take ten seconds to free fall a thousand feet and with the terminal velocity of 132 miles an hour, hitting water would be like hitting a brick wall. Ten seconds for a man, still conscious, to know they were his last ten seconds of life.

Half aloud, he said, "I'm not there to catch you this time, Tim." Then he walked up the aisle, slid into the copilot's seat, and snatched up the pistol from the footwell in front of him. "Harry," he said, "listen good. Bell's dead by now. You're on your own. Play ball with me and I put in the good word at your trial. You hear me?"

Ginsberg nodded.

"Right, we understand each other. Now first, you fly this crate nice and easy to Newark Airport. I'll tell 'em on the RT we're coming in, and they'd better start fishing for Tim. And when we get there, you put those hostages down as soft as a feather. Just think they're made of crystal. Understand me?''

Ginsberg nodded again.

''You don't say much, do you, Harry? I thought you were good with the words—poetry and that.''

Ginsberg said, ''What can I say? Like the man said, the rest is silence.''

Bestselling Thrillers — action-packed for a great read

___ $4.50	0-425-10477-X	**CAPER** Lawrence Sanders
___ $3.95	0-515-09475-7	**SINISTER FORCES** Patrick Anderson
___ $4.95	0-425-10107-X	**RED STORM RISING** Tom Clancy
___ $4.95	0-425-09138-4	**19 PURCHASE STREET** Gerald A. Browne
___ $4.95	0-425-08383-7	**THE HUNT FOR RED OCTOBER** Tom Clancy
___ $3.95	0-441-77812-7	**THE SPECIALIST** Gayle Rivers
___ $3.95	0-425-09582-7	**THE LAST TRUMP** John Gardner
___ $4.50	0-425-09884-2	**STONE 588** Gerald A. Browne
___ $3.95	0-425-10625-X	**MOSCOW CROSSING** Sean Flannery
___ $3.95	0-515-09178-2	**SKYFALL** Thomas H. Block
___ $4.95	0-425-10924-0	**THE TIMOTHY FILES** Lawrence Sanders
___ $4.95	0-425-10893-7	**FLIGHT OF THE OLD DOG** Dale Brown
___ $4.95	0-425-11042-7	**TEAM YANKEE** Harold Coyle

AMBUSH AT OSIRAK

A novel by
HERBERT CROWDER

Israeli forces are prepared to launch a devastating air strike on the Iraqi nuclear production facility at Osirak. Iraqi forces are fully aware of the oncoming attack. And the Soviets have supplied them with the ultimate super-weapon—the perfect means to wage nuclear war...